ROYAL LOVERS AND MISTRESSES

Christine

Reine de Suede

Published by The Navarre Society, London.

ROYAL LOVERS
AND MISTRESSES
THE ROMANCE OF CROWNED AND UNCROWNED KINGS AND QUEENS OF EUROPE

By
ANGELO S. RAPPOPORT, PH.D
Author of
"The Curse of the Romanoffs," etc

WITH SIX ILLUSTRATIONS IN PHOTOGRAVURE
AND THIRTEEN OTHER ENGRAVINGS

LONDON: MCMXXIV
PRIVATELY PRINTED FOR THE NAVARRE SOCIETY LIMITED

Table of Contents

v

CHAPTER IV

CHAPTER V

TABLE OF CONTENTS

TABLE OF CONTENTS

CHAPTER IX

Elizabeth Petrovna—Natalia Demyanovna—Colonel Vishnevsky—The Young Chorister—Gregory Razoum—The Shepherd and the Daughter of the Tsar—Elizabeth Ascends the Throne—Razoumikha's Visit to St. Petersburg—She is Received by the Empress—The Simplicity of the Favourite—Chancellor Bertyouzhev—Elizabeth's Love Affairs—Her Marriage to Razoumovsky—The Relations and Friends of the Favourite Count Cyril—His Genealogy—The Tarakanovs—Princess Voldomir, the Supposed Persian Heiress—The Duke of Limburg—Prince Radziwill—Princess Tarakanov goes to Rome—Sir William Hamilton—Alexis Orlov—The Fictitious Marriage—Princess Tarakanov made Prisoner—Her Incarceration in the Fortress of SS. Peter and Paul—Her Death in 1775—Razoumovsky Offered Title of Imperial Highness—His Dignified Attitude—His Death.

CHAPTER X

A Letter of Paul Petrovitsh—Mademoiselle Nelidov—Her Education—The Convent of Smolna—Death of the Grand Duchess Natalia—Paul's Sympathy for Mademoiselle Nelidov—A Platonic Affection—Paul's State of Mind—The Grand Duchess—Paul's Return from Finland—Court Intrigues—Mademoiselle Nelidov Retires to the Convent of Smolna—Friendship Between the Wife and the Mistress—A Change in Paul's Character—He Ascends the Throne—Reconciliation between the Empress and Mademoiselle Nelidov—Princess Gagarina—Mademoiselle Nelidov's Death.

CHAPTER XI

Two Courtiers—Gregory Potemkin—His Family—Education and Ambitious Designs—He Looks Round for a Rich Wife—His Love for the Empress—The External Appearance of Potemkin—A Bold Declaration—The Lucky Favourite—Honours and Wealth—Potemkin and Madame de Pompadour

List of Illustrations

xi

A DREAM BY WAY OF A PREFACE

Sleep hath its own world
And a wild realm of wild reality,
And dreams in their development have breath,
And tears and tortures, and the touch of joy.

BYRON.

S'il est vrai qu'au Jardin sacré des Écritures
Le Fils de l'Homme ait dit ce qu'on voit rapporté;
Muet, aveugle et sourd au cri des créatures,
Si le Ciel nous laissa comme un monde avorté,
Le juste opposera le dédain à l'absence
Et ne repondra plus que par un froid silence
Au silence éternel de la Divinité.

ALFRED DE VIGNY.

I DREAMED I was dead. It was not true, for had it been so I should have kept the secret to myself and never have published it. Yet it is only a question of time, and we all know that one day this prophetic dream of mine will be fulfilled. But that was not all: I dreamed I was in Paradise, i.e. at the gates of Paradise. Now this will probably never come to pass, not because I do not believe in Paradise, but because ill-luck has always been my lot in life. And just because I fear that I shall never be admitted among the happy favourites of fortune, even after death, it is pleasant to dwell on the possible heavenly delight, and enjoy it at least, in imagination.

Yes, I was dead and was standing before the gates of Paradise. I had been sauntering that day through Italian galleries in the city on the Tiber, and had spent some time in reverent admiration before the picture of Margarita, known as La Fornarina, the famous mistress of Raphael, the beautiful sinner, in whose arms the master was wont to forget in the evening the pure Madonna, at whose shrine he worshipped in the morning. Raphael Sanzio da Urbino saw this glorious creature for the first time when she was plunging her shapely feet into a cool fountain, and struck with her beauty he fell in love with her. Her picture, drawn by the hand of the enamoured master, now adorns the walls of the Barberini palace.

The contemplation of this *chef-d'œuvre* at first caused my thoughts to revert to other artists and their sweethearts, to Leonardo da Vinci and La Gioconda, to Titian and Violante, and then I gradually began to think of love in general, and of famous lovers in particular, of their joyous lives or their tragic fates, as the case may have been. I was musing during dinner and continued to do so when it was over. Leisurely seated in an easy chair I stretched out my hand and mechanically picked up a book from the table in front of me. It was a copy of Dante's *Divina Commedia*. I turned the pages and my eye was arrested by the story of Francesca di Rimini.[1] And I read :

> Amor, ch' a nullo amato amar perdona,
> Mi prese del costui piacer si forte,
> Che, come vedi, ancor non m'abbandona.
> Amor condusse noi ad una morte.

And so poor Francesca was in hell, because she had loved, but at least she was united to him who had been the cause of her misfortune. There was consolation in the thought. But Francesca was not alone there, many

[1] *Inferno*, canto v.

others whom the Florentine had seen in Inferno kept her company; Dido and Semiramis were there, and Thaïs of Athens, the famous courtesan. And yet many who had burned in life with the fire of love, and whom the splendour of Venus had overcome on earth, were in heaven. They had burned as long " as it became their locks," and even after; and they had not even repented, for they are represented as regretting nothing and repenting of nothing, but simply smiling, as well they might, at the power which " ordered and foresaw." They regretted nothing " of what might seem strange unto the vulgar spirits." [1]

Thus Cunizza, a gallant lady, " less famous for her repentance than for her follies," is reported to be in heaven, and Rahab, a *grande amoureuse* of the Old Testament, is supposed to have gone from Jericho straight to Paradise. Such are the immutable laws of fate !

I began to wonder where such ladies as Catherine II and Elizabeth, as Christine of Sweden and her friend Ninon de Lenclos were at present, and where the shades of Louis XV and the Marquise de Pompadour, of Henri de Navarre and his many mistresses, of Charles II and the affable beauties of his Court. I longed to know where all the *grands amoureux*, and especially the *grandes amoureuses*, from Laïs and Phryne to Lady Hamilton, and from Aspasia to Dubarry, had gone ;—all those whose names historians have recorded, all those who made mighty kings, great men and many fools of their time drink deep draughts from the cup of Circe. It is a pity, I thought, that Alighieri lived six centuries ago, had he lived now he might have revealed unto us some exceedingly interesting facts. Swedenborg, it is true, had also

[1] Dante, *Divina Commedia*, Paradiso, canto ix.

been permitted " to see what is in the heavens and what
is in the hells, and this for thirteen years," and he has
kindly consented " to describe them from things seen
and heard, in the hope that ignorance may be enlight-
ened, and unbelief dispelled." [1]   But Swedenborg lived
in the eighteenth century, and was evidently afraid of
libel actions, which involve heavy damages in modern
times.   The Swedish theosophist, therefore, unlike the
Florentine poet, speaks vaguely of the inmates of heaven
and hell, and mentions no names.

And thus " I pondered weak and weary," linking
fancy unto fancy until I fell asleep. Something similar to
what once befell Coleridge must have happened to me.
Coleridge was reading about Kubla Khan and his palace
and stately garden, when he fell asleep, and during that
sleep he composed not less than three hundred lines.
When he awoke his recollection was so vivid that he wrote
down the whole of the poem. If I but possessed Coleridge's genius I would fain write down all I heard and saw
in my sleep, but alas ! my recollection is not as good as
Coleridge's, neither am I able to give such a fine description of what I saw.   I shall relate my vision, but
in a very inadequate manner. Here it is.

At first I had a sensation as of falling. I had fallen
into the arms of Nature, the loving arms of mother Nature
as preachers and oily ethical philosophers would say ; but
they were only the cold arms of a tomb. I fell and fell
into a fathomless deep, and suddenly found myself before
a closed gate. I was blinded by a wide dazzling light,
and I knew that I was dead and that I was at the gates of
Paradise. There had been no " spiral slopes " and no

---

[1] Swedenborg, *Heaven and Hell*, London, 1899, p. 3.

" holy mountains " for me, no " sulphurous gusts of
malebolge " and no infernal hurricanes, and, what is
worse still, no wise Virgil and no sweet Beatrice to guide
me and to explain things. I shall have to fight my way
alone, in this world, without friends or love, as I have done
in the other, I grumbled,—and yet—I was glad I was dead.
I had often longed to be dead, not so much on account
of my cowardice and my wish to escape the struggle for
life—I had grown callous to suffering—but because
I always hoped that death would put an end to the tormenting doubts of my mind. During my stay on earth,
two things had constantly worried me : the thirst for
absolute knowledge and the feeling of flagrant injustice.
I could never understand why man should be made to
suffer. So that he might become better, the religious
teachers said. But why then did the innocent suffer ?
And besides, could not He who was All-Powerful make
us good without having to go through the ordeal of suffering ? Was not this arrangement a direct contradiction
of His Omnipotence ? What was the use of man's *infeli-
cità* and for whose pleasure had it been ordained ? And
did it not follow, I used to think, when I saw the innocent
suffer and the wicked triumph and prosper, that either
His conceptions of good and evil, of just and unjust, are
different from ours, and then religion, morality, goodness,
mercy and pity *in His Name* are an absurdity—or—
another horrible alternative—that His goodness and
benevolence are only a myth, an invention of lying priests.
The universe was ruled either by pure hazard or by a
spirit of malevolence. I could perceive in the world no
benevolent harmony and no sense of justice, no " soul
of good in things evil," but either chaos and " blind
fatality," or a pitiless ruler, giving unjust and severe

laws.—Oh, it was agony. And when I caught myself
so soliloquising, I grew melancholy and depressed and I
longed to know. Like Heine's youth on the shore of the
mighty sea I addressed my questions to the silent stars ;
like Leopardi's Frederick Ruysch I queried the mummies
in the ancient land of the Pharaohs, but all in vain. No
doubt what I thought men must have thought before me,
and what I suffered many must have suffered before me
in ages bygone. Many centuries ago, however, it seemed
as if this suffering was coming to an end, for one day the
world trembled and rejoiced, and a sigh of relief was
drawn : from Nazareth the Saviour had come. But
alas ! in His very name millions have again suffered and
still continue to suffer. The gods of antiquity and of the
modern Renaissance alike, of pagan polytheism and of
Judaeo-Christian monotheism, weighed heavily upon my
mind. Religion only claimed faith and belief and obedience, but never satisfied my yearning for absolute knowledge, clear and precise, and even science merely explained
but never justified.

There seemed to be a wall, high and unscalable, shut-
ting out the vision of my mortal eye and of my human
mind. I felt like a prisoner within his prison walls,
frantically pulling at the iron grating. Shall I ever be
permitted to scale this wall and to know and understand ?
I asked. I used to run my head against this wall ; I used
to wander, whilst others enjoyed life and its pleasures, in
the darkness of night. I fretted in the expectancy of en-
lightenment, even as a poor sufferer waits in the depth of
the night for the first rays of dawn. But the night seemed
to be interminable, dense and deep, and no ray of light
tinted with orient hues pierced its impenetrable darkness.
Everything appeared to be mystery except my suffering

and ignorance. The misery and horror of it! With
the feelings of a king to be only a beggar, with the
aspirations of a god to feel the nothingness of the feeble
creature, tossed about in the vast ocean of Being, to dream
of Titans, and lo! behold oneself as a mere pigmy, conscious of the knowledge of one's impotence and of the
impotence of one's knowledge; it was agony. Nature,
like a cruel stepmother, seemed to have taken eternity
and knowledge, the two trees in the garden of Eden, for
herself and to have left only ignorance and suffering for
man. What wonder, therefore, that I often felt tempted
to take a leap into the abyss of infinity and to make an end
of uncertainty! Like a man convulsively clinging to a
root at the edge of a precipice, I often strained my eyes to
look down into this abyss, and my lips were parched by an
indescribable thirst for the absolute, and my soul was
rent in twain by the torture of the Infinite. Oh, to
know! The very word sent a thrill of anxiety mingled
with joy through my veins. But my teachers of religion
and all good and pious men told me that I had no right
to take away the most precious gift given to me by Pro-
vidence, and to seek knowledge by courting death. They
consoled me with a *Beyond* and with a *Hereafter*, where
everything would become clear to me and where my sense
of justice would be satisfied. And I believed them, for
good and pious men and teachers would not lie, so I
thought, and they would surely not tell me stories and
assure me of things they did not know, and of a truth of
which they had no guarantee. I confess, however, that I
was worried at times that the truth had never been revealed unto me, as it had been revealed unto them. Why,
I asked, did not He who ordained all things deign to give
me a sign even as He had given to those pious and good

men ? Why should I be worse than they ? And if I am worse, it is no fault of mine. But I was told that I was not good enough to be deemed worthy of such grace and must be patient until I died. When I should have " shuffled off this mortal coil " my spirit would be shown truth eternal and would *know*. My blood pulsated faster in my veins and my heart was thrilled with ecstasy at such promises. In a next world I should know everything, and justice would reign supreme. What joy ! The mighty would be low and the downtrodden and oppressed would be blessed and dwell among the Cherubim and Seraphim. I rejoiced at the thought that mine, after all, was the better lot, for instead of a fleeting happiness extending over a few years I should enjoy bliss eternal in a world to come. Often, I confess, when I saw happy fools, happy through no merit of their own, but through a whim of fortune, spreading themselves out luxuriously in their gilded carriages on soft and silken cushions, whilst others and myself were walking in the mire, in constant danger of being crushed by the murderous vehicles of the rich, a pang of envy seized me, and a feeling of revolt swept through my frame like a hot wave, but I soon found solace in the thought that it was all for the best. And when I saw a stupid maiden leisurely reclining in her motor car and fondly caressing her lap-dog, disdainfully looking down upon the brave, clever, hard-working girl, working herself to death and supporting an aged mother and little brothers and sisters, I said : " Wait until we meet above—where justice will be meted out to us." And so I bore the cheerless burden of life in the hope of a hereafter.

And now I was really dead and would soon know and satisfy all the cravings of my spirit. I was at the gates of

Paradise, and I looked round for some one from whom to gather information as to the habits and customs of the place. I saw, however, neither griffon, centaur, monster, nor angel, but a melancholy gentleman, whose face seemed to be familiar to me.

" Tell me, sir," I asked, " are these the gates of Paradise ? "

He nodded assent.

" Thank you," I said, " I suppose I may walk in ? "

" No, it's full up."

" Full up ? " I queried. " But I thought I had suffered enough below and had a just claim to some compensation and reward. I am one of the downtrodden, the sufferers, the oppressed, and have always been told that my place was awaiting me here."

" I knew at once that you were one of the downtrodden," he replied. " I could see the majesty of suffering on your brow, and the pale cast of misery, which Destiny had placed upon it, and that is exactly why you cannot get into Paradise and why it is full when you arrive. It is very unlucky," he added, " but you always were unlucky."

I was puzzled.

" Pardon me, sir," I said, " but does my entrance into Paradise really depend upon sheer luck and blind hazard alone ? Is there no justice here ? "

" Justice," he smiled. " There is no justice. Nature knows no justice. Nature has something of the feminine in her and likes brutality and cruelty; they inspire her with respect. Did you ever find justice on earth ? " And without waiting for my reply, he pulled me by the sleeve and, bidding me look down through a kind of telescope, said : " Look at yon two human forms." I looked.

One was a crippled girl and the other a dazzling beauty, whose picture I had noticed in the daily press.

"Yon crippled girl," he said, "is yearning for love and life and joy, but she is condemned to suffering and sadness, because she is ill-shaped. Why did Nature fashion those two beings so differently?" he continued, in an almost fierce tone—"was it just? Why favour the one and ill-treat the other?"

"No, it was not just," I replied, "but I had hoped that here everything would be set right."

"You thought," he snapped—"the justice below ought to have given you an idea of the justice here. The poor cripple will always have her sad past to remember, while the happy favourite of Nature will revel in joyous remembrances. He was wrong, the poet, when he said:

> Nessun maggior dolore
> Che ricordarsi del tempo felice
> Nella miseria.

"He was wrong—there is as much suffering—ay, even more—in living again in memory through the sufferings of a cruel past. To make the balance of justice quite even all those who have suffered below ought to forget their past here and enjoy felicity, whilst those who had their share of bliss on earth should taste a life of suffering here."

"So I was told that it would be," I observed meekly; "so, at least, all religious teachers maintained."

"Then they deceived you," was his answer. "But if you are a philosopher you ought to be able to console yourself."

I thought I noticed a sarcastic smile playing round his mouth.

" You are committing a common error," I replied, glad to correct him for once, " in imagining that Philosophy is identical with a source of consolation and resignation. Philosophy neither consoles nor exasperates—it simply endeavours to instruct."

" Then your philosophers instructed you very badly, if they did not teach you not to expect anything when you have left the earth. Some are born lucky and others are destined to be unlucky—*voilà tout.*"

Fatality, as it would appear, moves the universe. And in earth or heaven, there lives no friend to the unhappy, none. " Nature disdains human grief and with servile homage she smiles upon the felicitous."

> " Nascemmo al pianto, e la ragione ingrembo
> De' celesti si posa," [1]

he murmured. And as he recited these lines I saw a look of despair in his eyes. I knew him at once. He was the melancholy poet of Recanati. But no—I was mistaken—his face suddenly changed and it was my own friend, Alfred de Vigny, who was standing before me. For

> Dreams are but interludes which fancy makes,
> When monarch reason sleeps, this mimic wakes.
> Compounds a medley of disjointed things,
> A Court of cobblers and a mob of kings.[2]

" What are you doing here, Alfred ? " I asked.

" I have been waiting here," he said, " for centuries —and I shall wait here for æons to come to see the Ruler of the universe. I must argue with Him even as

---

[1] And wherefore so
    Lies in the lap of the Celestials. (LEOPARDI.)

[2] John Dryden.

Job of old once argued with Him. I shall accuse Him of injustice before the tribunal of human justice."

"God before the tribunal of human justice. What a splendid paradox," I exclaimed.

He did not heed me and went on : "Who do you imagine are the inmates of Paradise ? "

I shrugged my shoulders in a dejected mood. " All those who were very lucky below, the rich, the mighty. Their good fortunes follow them everywhere."

"But is it not said : ' Blessed are the poor, for theirs is the kingdom of heaven ' ? " I ventured to observe.

"Swedenborg has explained that away long ago," he readily replied. "He had had conversations with angels, and it was ' given to him to know that the rich come into heaven as easily as the poor.' And in fact they do so much more easily even, because only clever people come into heaven, and are not the rich and the mighty ones on earth clever ? And are not the poor and the downtrodden fools ? And ' the fool shall not enter into heaven,' as a wise English dreamer said a while ago."

" I know, Blake said that. But Blake received messengers from heaven and wrote some of his poems under immediate dictation. He could ' touch the heaven with his finger.' No messenger from heaven ever came to me, and how should I have known who would be considered fool and who the wise man ? Alas ! it seems I have been labouring under a great misapprehension. I had hoped to see divine truth as soon as my spirit was free from the vegetable body. But my youth was consumed in useless endeavour, and wasted away, and heaven seems to have taken pleasure in my constant distress. My life was cheerless, and youth passed by me empty-handed. The sources of love suddenly dried up at the touch of my eager lips or left a bitter taste in my mouth. Destiny, cruel and pitiless, drove me onwards to unknown goals, and blind hazard seemed to have eyes for me alone, striking me in the most vulnerable spots. Oh ! what a fool I was."

" Yes, you were a fool," replied my friend, " but you are wise now. You were a fool to believe all that hypocrites told you in their own interest ; you were a fool to think them sincere simply because they pretended to be so. You were a fool to submit to laws and rules and regulations made by others, who either invented or upheld fables in their own interests. And because you and many like you were fools enough to submit to laws made by clever deceivers and did not think for yourselves, did not help yourselves and did not emancipate your bodies and your spirits from all sorts of fetters forged by clever egotists, you cannot enter the kingdom of heaven. You may linger here at the gates of Paradise and curse your own folly. You had the souls of slaves on earth, for you only knew how to obey and to tremble. You considered every institution sacred for no other reason but that of its existence, and you deserve punishment. But those who deceived you and exercised their rule over you physically or mentally, those who made you believe that their authority and their teaching were sacred, were clever. They enjoyed life and laughed at your asceticism and they are in heaven, because ' power is virtue ' ; instead of curbing and governing their passions they became ' better and wickeder.' "

" And so all the tyrants whom Dante saw in Inferno and Purgatorio are in Paradise ? "

" Yes, even so."

" Are Nero and Caligula and Djenghis Khan and many, many modern tyrants here ? "

" Yes—they are the lucky ones. They were lucky on earth to find so many fools willing to accept meekly their sacred superiority and to believe that they ruled by the grace of a superior power, and they are lucky to find on their arrival here ample room in the kingdom of heaven." And after a short pause : " But you can return to earth, if you like, and tell what you know to other men. You will thus not have lived in vain."

" Why should I ? " I asked. " I never cared to preach any Gospel. Everybody must find out the truth for himself. Besides, no one would believe me ; they would only call me a madman. If they did not crucify me, send me to prison or to a lunatic asylum, they would shrug their shoulders and sneer at me. Men never take into consideration what is said, but who says it.

" You are growing wise," he observed.

" But tell me," I continued, " is the lot of the rulers who reigned wisely and well on earth a better one here than the lot of those who spent their lives in enjoyment and pleasure and idle pursuits ? "

" Not at all," he replied. " I have told you already that there is as little justice in heaven as there is on earth, and if anything they are even better off here and enjoy greater opulence than the so-called good rulers. Thus there is a special Paradise for all kings and queens, who squandered millions, squeezed from hard-working sub- jects, upon their own pleasures and their lovers and mis- tresses. They are dwelling in company of their favourites in a most magnificent palace, known as the ' Paradise of the royal Lovers.' If you like I can show you a spot where you can climb up a tree and look through a window into one of the State apartments. There will be a great reception to-night in honour of the anniversary of the birthday of one Nell Gwyn. You will see them all, the kings and queens who sacrificed at the altar of Venus during their earthly existence."

" But when Dante was here," I observed—" all the tyrants who dealt in bloodshed and pillaging were in Inferno ; and such was the lot of all those who ' to sensual vices were abandoned,' and ' subjugated reason to appetite.' Was the Italian poet mistaken ? "

" No, but he lived six centuries ago, and could not tell the entire truth. He was afraid of the Church and of the Censor. Imagine the scandal that would have arisen had he said that Nero and Caligula were in heaven or that Cleopatra and Semiramis were in Paradise, and that their apartments were adjoining those of Rahab and Mary Magdalene. But they are all here and have been joined since by a host of other royal ladies and gentlemen, whose love affairs created a sensation in their time."

I was indignant after all. " All this is unjust," I cried. " I shall protest " ; and I made a move as if to force the gates of Paradise ; but he gave me a push, and I fell headlong down to earth—and awoke. " What a strange dream," I said, rubbing my eyes. " Truly ' a medley of disjointed things,' and yet what a wide realm of wild reality."

A letter, evidently just arrived, was lying on the table before me. I opened it ; it was from my publishers in London, who asked me whether I was willing to write for them a book on the lives of a few European sovereigns. I at once answered in the affirmative. But my respect for all rulers had greatly increased—were they not all in

Paradise ? And thinking of the passage in the *Divina Commedia* over which I had fallen asleep, and of my subsequent dream, and knowing now that all who had burned in life with the fire of love and all those whom " the splendour of Venus had overcome on earth " were enjoying such bliss in heaven, I decided to limit myself not to the history, but to the romantic episodes in the lives of these sovereigns. It is only just, I thought, that the records of those whose shades are so well treated in eternity should be known by mortal man. I shall write on royal lovers and mistresses. But here I was faced by a new and great difficulty. The number of royal lovers was so large that I required much more time than I actually had at my disposal. I decided, therefore, to choose the romantic episodes of a few sovereigns, preferably those with whose history I was entitled to assume my readers were not so familiar. Should my humble efforts find favour in their eyes, I will continue on a subsequent occasion to relate the love affairs of some of the many other royal lovers who have existed from the days of antiquity to modern times.

The present book is the result of my first effort. I should have liked to submit the proofs to the shades of my heroes and heroines themselves, but never since that day in Rome have they appeared to me even in my dreams. I have had therefore to content myself with more humble living friends, who have kindly consented to read the final proofs, Miss M. Edwardes and Mr. Channing Arnold, to whom I herewith beg to express my thanks.

A. S. R.

Rome, *February 2*, 1908,
Birthday of Nell Gwyn.

CHAPTER I

Uncrowned Kings and Queens

ROYAL lovers and mistresses! What a magic sound there is to bourgeois ears in these few words! Imagination is awakened by them and interest aroused. Our sympathies always go out to the lover, and more especially to the unhappy lover, whose path is beset with thorns; but if the lover happens to be a king, the mistress a queen, the episode becomes doubly fascinating. The touch of royalty seems to cast a glamour over earthly passions and to make Romance even more romantic. The love affairs of the world's celebrities, of poets, artists, philosophers, of heroes and great generals, men of thought and of action, are highly interesting. The world is keen to know of the women whom a Goethe or an Alfred de Musset, a Nelson or a Napoleon have loved; they must have been super-women who fascinated the hearts of those great men. For most of us are hero worshippers, after all; the private lives of great men, therefore, command our special attention. And are not kings and queens great men and women? They are so *ex officio*. A crown lends greatness to the most insignificant of mortals, and throws a halo over a head harbouring only a limited intelligence. Most of us are interested in the private lives of kings and queens, not because they made the history of their country—few sovereigns indeed have done so—but because the distance of the throne lends them enchantment. And we who throng the thoroughfares, eager for a glimpse of royalty and ready to applaud a living foreign sovereign whom future historians will perhaps style " a mere boy " or an " old rascal," we, in our enthusiasm, exclaim not *ecce homo*, but *ecce superhomo*. Every insignificant detail in the daily lives of royalty becomes an important fact, fraught with interest. No wonder, therefore, that their romances are so captivating. What are the love affairs of common humanity, with their idyllic happiness, their thrilling passions, exultant joy or poignant grief, compared to those of men and women of all ages who have ruled kingdoms and empires !

From Tiberius to King Leopold of the Belgians, from Cleopatra and Semiramis to Queen Christina of Sweden and Marie Antoinette of France—to come down only to the eighteenth century—the number of men and women who were the lovers or mistresses of their kings and queens has been legion. History has recounted their lives in detail, and contemporary chroniclers have woven a veil of romance over their lives ; poets have sung their praises and philosophers analysed their characters and examined their psychology.

Kings and queens are great men and women. So most of us believe, or profess to believe, and must it not follow that those, too, whom they honour with their love are not made of common clay ?

The world has long professed to judge things in accordance with a conventional code of morality. But the much vaunted social conscience is a mere myth. Society has no conscience, and no moral code, and if society often boasts of some semblance of a moral code, it is an exceedingly elastic one. Words and deeds are judged, not by their intrinsic value and on their own merit, but in exact proportion to the social position occupied and, one may add, social success enjoyed by the author of the words or the deeds. That which is a transgression in an individual treading in the modest walks of life, moving in the lower strata of society, is only an act of eccentricity if it is committed by one of the upper ten thousand. Words assume different meanings when uttered in the more refined atmosphere of a court, deeds assume other aspects when perpetrated in the shadow of a throne. A breath of malodorous air wafted from the street into royal precincts acquires at once an aromatic scent.

Almost in all European countries, as well as in the United States, the traveller will come across a certain class of women trafficking in their beauty and offering their favours to any bidder. Few of us can suppress a feeling of scorn at their approach, while only the most indulgent and unprejudiced among us allow a gentle pity for them to creep into our hearts. This female section of humanity has its counterpart in men, much more depraved and debased, who are selling favours instead of buying them. And yet the annals of history are full of the names of men and women who lived in the shadow of a throne, and who were not perhaps a whit better than their humbler brothers and sisters.

It would be wrong, however, to judge them *en bloc*. The psychology of these men and women has been as different as their history or their aims and ambitions, and their characters have been as varied as their fortunes.

Royal lovers and mistresses ! What ghosts of the past

these words can conjure up !   Away, away from squalid surroundings, from modest bourgeois life, from the hum-drum of daily toil and labour, from the noise and bustle of the streets, where crowds are hurrying in pursuit of food or idling in expectation of some commonplace pleasure.   Away to royal and imperial palaces, to gilded chambers, to silk and purple cushions, to soft couches and divans, to artistic furniture, beautiful paintings and exquisite tapestry.   Away from the scantily furnished bedchamber to the luxurious boudoirs, where an elderly royal debauchee is forgetting his suffering nation, his starving subjects, in the arms of a clever courtesan ; or where an aged empress is embracing her lover, a mere boy : squandering millions, squeezed from hard-pressed subjects, to pay the boy for his reluctant kisses.   Through mists of time the figures of these men and women loom up before our mental gaze—a motley crowd.   Here are Cleopatra and Semiramis and Catherine II, Christina of Sweden and Elizabeth of England.   Yonder emerges the gaunt, gigantic figure of Potemkin, by the side of the dainty Count Fersen, lover of Queen Marie Antoinette. Mazarin, ambitious, scheming and plotting, well be-loved by the Queen-mother, Anne of Austria, mother of Louis XIV, is followed by Razoumovsky, the modest, unassuming peasant-lover of Elizabeth, the clever but libertine daughter of Peter the Great.

To learn the varied histories of these shadows we shall have to follow them to many parts of the globe ; from sunny Italy and beautiful France to the cold north; from the Tuileries and the Louvre to the Hermitage.

What an interesting study their characters offer to the psychologist !   If some of them were low, vulgar volup-tuaries, coarse courtesans, others again were marked by

nature to rule and to command.   Nature has not always
placed the real kings and queens of men upon a throne.
Many born to govern have disappeared from the face of
the earth as unnoticed as they came.   It was their tragic
fate to walk in the humble ways of life.   But nature is
not always cruel.   To retrieve her injustice she often, as
if purposely, seems to place such men and women in the
vicinity of a throne.   They gain the affections of a
sovereign, and their soaring ambitions find ample scope.
Although uncrowned, they become the real kings or
queens, ruling the country through the feeble, infatuated sovereign, who is merely a puppet in their hands.

Was it Pascal who once said that the shape of Cleopatra's nose had changed the face of the world?   In
the beautiful arms of the siren of the Nile, Caesar almost
forgot Rome and his duty, his ambitions, his dangers
and his battles.   And it was in the arms of this same
Cleopatra that Antony lost his share in the dominion of
Rome, and the world.   For the pleasure of placing the
banners which he had captured in the battle of Coutras
at the feet of his mistress, the beautiful Corisande,
Henry IV imperilled the advantages accruing to him
from his victory.   The slaves became tyrants, the lovers
and mistresses whom their sovereigns lavishly paid for
their favours, dictated their will to the ruler, and were
obeyed.   They were the real kings and queens, those
Mesdames de Maintenon, those Pompadours, those
Mazarins, Potemkins and Struensees.   Whilst Marie
Leczinska, the wife of Louis XV, is occupying her time,
far from the bustle and noise of the Court of Versailles,
in prayers and moral readings, in works of charity and
benevolence, shunning the amusements and distractions
of a feverish and frivolous Court, whose motto had

become *après nous le Déluge*, the ambitious but graceful and gifted daughter of Madame Poisson, the Marquise de Pompadour, is wielding the sceptre of France. Whilst Marguerite of Navarre, Queen of France, *la soeur des dieux* as she was called, daughter of that most remarkable woman Catherine de Medicis, is leading a life of debauchery, the beautiful Gabrielle d'Estrées is the real Queen of France. Gabrielle's sons are baptized with the same pomp and ceremony as the " Sons of France." Her royal lover, Henry IV, could not resist the tears and supplications of his beautiful mistress. Poor Sully, faithful friend and mighty Minister, had a hard task to prevent his royal master from marrying her. Nearly all his life Sully had to stand between these sirens and the throne. Whilst Paul, Heir-Apparent to the throne of Russia, is sulking in Gatshina, leading a life of obscurity, suffering insults and humiliations and often reduced to penury—his mother provided him with only a scanty allowance—Catherine's lovers, the Orlovs and Potemkins, are ruling the Empire and squandering fabulous wealth. A strange spectacle that, to see ministers and generals, who had grown grey in the service of their country, dancing attendance in the antechambers of individuals whom they would have otherwise ignored, and whom they hated or despised whilst offering them to their face the most fulsome flattery. The walls of the Winter Palace, of the Louvre, and of the Court of St. James's have witnessed similar scenes.

These " king's and queen's morsels " had gained their power by the aid of Romance. But Romance to them was only a means to an end. Their ambitions were stronger than their sense of Romance ; the latter was only the royal road which led to the goal of power or

MADAME DE POMPADOUR.
By Belliard.

To face page 6.

wealth. How much did Mazarin care for the actual
love of the Queen-mother, Anne of Austria ; how much
Madame d'Etiolles, La Pompadour, for that of Louis XV ;
Orlov or Potemkin for that of Catherine, and Struensee
for the love of Caroline Matilda of Denmark ? Love in
itself was nothing to them ; what they cared for were
the riches and influence it represented. Poor deluded
kings and queens ! If they ever imagined that they had
been loved for themselves, they were sorely mistaken.
Those ambitious men and women were not only the lovers
and mistresses of their sovereigns, but of the entire
nation and the country. They had ensnared, not only
an old debauchee or an aged depraved woman, but
millions of subjects. Whilst pretending that they were
in love with the sovereign, slaves of their wills and caprices, submissive to their wishes, they in reality were
dictating their own laws. They lulled the sovereigns to
sleep in the arms of love and ruled the kingdom in their
stead. Whilst the royal wife was only the woman, the
mistress was in reality the queen.

Their ambition was stronger than their love, and when
they, at last, became aware that the passions they had
inspired had flickered out in the fickle hearts of their
sovereigns, they resigned themselves to their fate. They
left it to others to provide the fuel for that passion which
had been their stepping-stone to power, and kept the
power and influence for themselves. They were above
jealousy. But not only mistresses, even legally wedded
wives have often been above jealousy, as long as their
ambition was satisfied. When the Patriarchs grew old
their lawful wives sent unto them their maids to be
loved. At sixty the Empress Zoë married a soldier in
order to consolidate her power, and instead of asking for

his affection she herself introduced his mistresses into the palace. They were so sure of their own superior position, those ladies of the ancient Orient; they knew that the attraction of the senses has nothing whatever to do with genuine attachment and respect, that voluptuousness and affection are two entirely different feelings. The wives were the *matres familiae*, and the slave could never supplant and occupy the place of the legal wife. Livia, the wife of Augustus, picked out the favourites for her imperial husband; and Caroline, Queen of Naples, sent her husband, King Ferdinand, to Caserte, his Parc aux Cerfs, so that she might be free to rule with her favourites.

When David was advanced in age, his courtiers found him a Shunamite. Many were the Shunamites which clever Madame de Pompadour found for her royal lover, Louis XV. And when Catherine II wearied of Potemkin, the latter at once made himself the go-between of his royal mistress and her new lovers. There is a striking resemblance between these two favourites of sovereigns and favourites of fate, who both rose from a most modest origin to rule, the one over a king and a kingdom, and the other over an empress and an empire.

Let us go for a few instants to the Hermitage. In her private boudoir the Semiramis of the North is giving an audience to a young, well-built, vigorous and smart officer. He has been sent to the Empress by Prince Potemkin with a picture.

Did her Majesty like the picture, and would she buy it? Her Majesty, however, is examining the messenger with more careful attention than the picture itself. The officer pleases her, and she sends word through him to the Prince that she will buy the picture. Silently the young man withdraws from the august presence of his mistress, ignorant of the fortune awaiting him, to carry the reply to Potemkin. This officer was a candidate for the vacant post of favourite, whom Potemkin had thus recommended. Whilst the mighty minister had thus set the Empress's senses at liberty, he retained not only the control of her senses, but also the government of the Empire. He was not satisfied with the favours of the woman, but was courting the country, the nation and posterity ; he was yearning to inscribe his name in the annals of Russian history. His choice of a candidate for the position of favourite was always a very careful one, for had he not to protect himself from the dangerous ambition of a rival to whom the intimacy of the Empress gave such unique opportunities ?

As long as the young officer, therefore, contented himself with the wealth heaped upon him, and the honour of his office, he was allowed to enjoy it in peace. But woe unto him if he had ambitions and took it into his head to indulge in political ideas. His disgrace followed swiftly, and he was supplanted by another of Potemkin's creatures.

And now let us picture another scene taking place in the Parc aux Cerfs. The Hermitage and the Parc aux Cerfs tell the same tale. It is the same scene, only enacted in different surroundings and by different actors. In the place of Catherine II, Potemkin and a Russian officer, the parts are played by Louis XV, the Marquise de Pompadour and a French Court beauty. But both Potemkin and the Marquise de Pompadour were careful in the choice of the male and female Shunamites. They selected beauty, but were afraid of brains. Having gained an ascendency over their sovereigns, they apprehended nothing from physical grace; but an individual gifted with brains in the intimacy of the ruler was a constant menace to the position they held, and awakened the jealousy of their trembling ambitions. Both Potemkin, the son of an obscure Russian country squire, and the daughter of M. Poisson, in spite of the vast difference existing between them, belonged to the same race, the race of favourites, whose aim it is to be prime ministers, entering the Council by way of the boudoir and the bedchamber. They saw in their *liaison* with their respective sovereigns an audience on a royal pillow. Even in the relaxation of love they never for a moment forgot the sovereign and what the sovereign meant to them; their constant aim was to keep the ruler in their grasp, for the ruler impersonated the nation and the country, power, wealth and influence. The Pompadour and Potemkin were both admirable comedians, in feigning love for their sovereigns. Potemkin falling on his knees in the cabinet of his Empress and daring to declare his unhappy love, a burden too heavy for him to bear, vowing that he preferred death to silent suffering; Madame d'Etiolles pretending to be madly in love with Louis Bienaimé, but afraid of her jealous and suspicious husband, and deciding to die of despair, what a tragicomedy! But the comedy was well acted and the actors reigned. They had crept into the Winter Palace and Versailles respectively, and suddenly soared forth, meteor like, in all their radiant brilliancy and splendour, to the astonished gaze of courts and courtiers, of politicians and statesmen, of France and Russia, of entire Europe.

But Prince Potemkin and the Marquise de Pompadour are not the only ambitious favourites. The student traversing the historical catacombs of the past, examining as in another Pompeii the petrified relics of a former age, will come across many figures of men and women who held the reins of government in their hands by means of the love with which they inspired the respective rulers of the country.   Peace and war, revolutions and alliances were made at their command ; they made history and shaped the destinies of nations.   In that great comedy or tragedy which is called history they played the principal part.   The name of Potemkin calls forth in our mind another figure who, whilst the former was ruling Russia, was at the head of the government of Denmark.   This was Struensee, the lover of Queen Caroline Matilda of Denmark, wife of the imbecile King Christian VII.   Struensee, the son of a Lutheran preacher, and himself a medical man by profession, passed through the bedchamber of the Queen to the council room, to the office of Prime Minister and the dignity of Count.

But another figure looms large on the horizon of the student of history, a figure perhaps even more imposing than those of the three great favourites just mentioned.   It is that of the cardinal minister Mazarin, who gave his name to an entire epoch of French history. Giulio Mazzarini was of humble parentage ; his father was the son of a Sicilian artisan, and had risen in Rome to be Chamberlain to the Constable Colonna.   By dint of tact, adroitness and subtlety the grandson of the artisan succeeded in governing France during the minority of Louis XIV.   But he owed his future to the love which the Queen-regent, Anne of Austria, bore him.   It was the passion of a queen which raised him to his high office.   " With sovereigns, whoever possesses the heart, possesses everything," Mazarin is supposed to have said, and he possessed the heart of Anne of Austria. Little, however, did he care for her passion—anyhow the love with which he inspired the Queen was by far stronger than the one which he felt for her. He treated his royal mistress—as is evident from his Memoirs—with rudeness and almost brutality, and it is this treatment which has confirmed many historians in the opinion that Mazarin and Anne of Austria had been secretly married. A husband is allowed to be rude where the lover is expected to be polite.

They were not only consummate actors those favourites, but also subtle psychologists. They had made themselves acquainted with the respective characters, foibles, tastes, whims and fancies of the rulers. They flattered the weaknesses of the monarchs; and, whilst gratifying their tastes, acquired strength and power and wealth for themselves, and made their influence felt in home and foreign politics alike. They were fond of money and of all that money can give, and accumulated enormous wealth, but the keynote of their passions was ambition.

But three or four figures do not complete the gallery of these influential men and women, favourites, who often succeeded in clandestinely marrying their sovereigns and ruling the realm. The annals of history are full of these from Bathsheba, who made King David marry her and appoint her son King of Israel, to the late Draga, Queen of Servia; from Faustina, who picked out her lovers on the bank of the Tiber, to Catherine of Russia, who chose them among her soldiers; from Augustus to Louis XVIII, and from Aspasia to Diane de Poitiers and Madame de Maintenon. They have often been the governing principle, the universal cause

ANNE OF AUSTRIA.
After a painting by Simon Vouet.

To face page 12.

and the fatal origin of events in the government of peoples.

Aspasia, the brilliant courtesan of Miletus, came to Athens and made the acquaintance of Pericles. He was not a king, but he was the foremost statesman, and his power was paramount. Through her lover Aspasia ruled Athens, and exercised a wide-reaching and powerful influence over Athenian politics. Diane de Poitiers, the mistress of Henry II of France, Gabrielle d'Estrées, the sultana of Henry IV, Mademoiselle Nelidov, the favourite of Paul I, Countess Lichtenau, the beloved of Frederick William II of Prussia, Madame de Maintenon, and above all, the Marquise de Pompadour, all made their influence felt upon their countries.

But the student who carefully reads the pages of history is bound to admit that the number of female favourites who ruled as uncrowned queens is much larger than that of lovers of queens, who played the part of uncrowned kings. Woman is more ambitious than man, in spite of everything that has been said to the contrary. Not only the mistress and the favourite, but the wife and the queen has shown all through history an almost unbounded ambition. That woman is only made for love, and that the sentiment of ambition rarely enters her heart is as false as many other theories concerning woman, love and marriage expounded by men of all ages. She avails herself of love as one of the weapons nature has put at her disposal to enslave man and to make him subservient to her plans. Delilah lulling Samson to sleep in her beautiful arms is a scene which has been enacted many and many a time on the vast stage of the world's history. In palace revolutions women have always played a prominent part. In Rome

of the Caesars, in the harems of the Orient, in the gilded
apartments of Versailles, they exercised their influence.
Amurath beheading his sultana, and Paul I sending
away his favourite Mademoiselle Nelidov to prove that
they were not ruled by their women, are both endeavouring to prove what is not.   Amurath had another
sultana the next day, and Paul soon recalled his favourite
or fell into the nets of another.   Many were the rulers
who abdicated their power, whilst history only relates
of one woman who voluntarily abandoned a crown—
Christine of Sweden, but even she never gave up her
prerogative of meddling in European politics.   Semiramis and Catherine, Elizabeth of England and Elizabeth of Russia, and many others allowed their favourites
to do many things, but never did they let absolute
power slip from their hands.   And this predominance
of ambition is also to be noticed in the mistresses of
kings as compared with male favourites.   It was this
that made a wit once say that God refused woman an entry
into Paradise for fear that His omnipotence might be
infringed.   Kings have often married shepherdesses and
placed them on the throne; queens have never married
shepherds.   Justinian married Theodora, a woman he
loved, in spite of her antecedents, and made her Empress.
Peter the Great raised a Livonian servant to the dignity
of Tsaritsa and appointed her as his successor.   But even
if Elizabeth married Razoumovsky, the marriage remained a secret, which was denied by the noble Count
after the death of the Empress.   Would Madame de
Maintenon have been capable of such a sacrifice ?
Queens have never abdicated.   When ruling in their
own name they have often raised the men whom they
loved to high dignities.   They heaped honours and

wealth upon them, or on the other hand they threw them into the Euphrates or into the Nile, they sent them to the Tower or Schluesselburg; but they never allowed them to share their throne with them. Portia asserted that she was the wife of Brutus, not merely that she might share his couch and his table, but his secrets too; yet it is more than doubtful whether Portia would have given expression to similar sentiments had she been Brutus !

Woman is more ambitious than man; but in all times she has been compelled as wife, as queen, or as favourite, to avail herself of her womanly charm and of the allurements of love to gain power over him, for man must be made subservient in an underhand way. With love and charm as her weapons, woman has always succeeded in her ambitious designs, but she has always failed miserably when employing other tactics.

Woman has been striving for emancipation and equality with man ever since the days when the Lesbian poetess threw herself from the Leucadian rock, in her hopeless love for the handsome Phaon of Mitylene. But Sappho, the first suffragette of antiquity, failed in her aims at woman's emancipation; she offended Aphrodite, the goddess of love, so at least legend relates. Sappho had ideas the result of which would have been similar to that of the theories which the prophet of Yasnaya Polyana was to preach centuries later in his Kreutzer Sonata. In spite of the testimony of Plato, Sappho was not beautiful. Maximus of Tyre and Ovid say that she was black and insignificant, and Horace calls her Mascula, the masculine. She was masculine in her thoughts, her aspirations and her conduct, and, beloved by women, she never exercised any influence upon men. " When a woman is practising masculine virtues she is shunned by men," Nietzsche said twenty-five centuries later. For man is vain and resents the open attempt of woman to be his equal in mind. When Louis XV detected her ambitious designs behind the caresses of Madame d'Etiolles, he took umbrage and refused to see her again. Warned by the King's confidential valet Binet, Madame endeavoured to hide her ambitions for a while. The ambitious but feminine woman coaxes instead of arguing, and commands where she pretends to obey. Such has been the attitude of most of the mistresses and favourites of kings.

How much cleverer were the tactics of Aspasia and of the women of the eighteenth century. The Athenian citizen had no consideration for woman in general or for his own wife in particular. Socrates, on being asked how he could so patiently endure the insults of his wife Xantippe, replied : " Does one ever wax wroth with a goose ? " But woman took her revenge upon proud man. In the midst of Athens there appeared young and beautiful women who danced and sang and played, and playfully talked philosophy. They were charming, and man smiled and humoured them. They had come from Miletus and Asia Minor and opened salons in the city of the philosophers, and their salons were as much frequented as the *Hôtel Rambouillet* and the salon of Ninon de Lenclos in the eighteenth century. Socrates himself was a guest in those Athenian salons of the hetairas, and brought his friends and his friends' wives. They did not fear the ambition of those women, the citizens of Athens. They were only slaves and pretended to be such, intent upon giving pleasure to man. The Athenian despised them, and despising them did

Sappho
after a drawing by Staal

Published by The Navarre Society, London

not fear them. But the slaves soon became queens. They seduced the Athenians with their beauty and made them submissive and attentive pupils. They seduced first the senses, then the mind and the heart. They were artists in a land which breathed an atmosphere of art ; they were artists in ruling, whilst all the time they pretended to be ruled.

Greece, like the harem-ridden Orient, had condemned woman to a life of seclusion, to domestic inertia or drudgery, and whilst male Hellas was accumulating that civilization on the crumbs of which the Aryan world is still feeding, the Greek woman was not allowed to have any share in intellectual, social and aesthetic development. The Greeks, and in this respect the Aryan world, is still as Hellenic as Athens was twenty-five centuries ago, admired beauty and harmony of form even more than that of mind. For beauty of form was a religion in Greece, and physical beauty was a gift of the gods, personifying immortal beauty. The Greeks preferred sensations to sentiments. Whilst the Athenian woman lived and died in obscurity, writhing under injustice, Laïs and Phryne and Aspasia became the friends and equals of philosophers and politicians, of poets and senators, and of all those who were destined to be the immortals of the days to come.

It was first through beauty of form and feminine charm that they captivated the man ; for they had to be beautiful if they wished to reign, and they did their utmost to aid nature if the latter had not been too lavish in her gifts. And when once they had captivated man by their charm they enhanced their attractions by cultivating their minds, so that even when in later

c

years their physical attractions faded they still retained their sovereignty.

Those clever women of antiquity knew that it was idle to claim equality with man on the ground of equal capacities ; man is vain from the beginning and brutal withal. They hid their ambitions and appeared only as amiable women, and only when they had conquered by virtue of their feminine charm they made use of their brains. They played Delilah, and if Samson was obstinate, that was the only alternative open to them. Thus Aspasia—her name meant the " beloved one " in Greek—won Pericles by the brilliancy of her spirit, but above all by her charm, her amiability and refined coquetry. Xantippe, the wife of Socrates, was far from being a " goose " ; she, too, had ideas upon the emancipation of Athenian housewives; but she spoilt the effect of her words by the vehemence with which she uttered her sentiments and by the method of her persuasion.

Aspasia opened a salon and the aristocracy flocked to her reception. She was a queen and had her court. To her house strangers came from Sicily and Ionia to appreciate the charm and brilliancy of Athenian culture. It was there that they discussed politics with Pericles, art with Phidias, literature with Euripides, and philosophy with Anaxagoras. It was at her house that philosophers, statesmen, and poets met ; there that men could come into touch with Socrates and Sophocles amid brilliant gatherings of the great minds of Hellenic antiquity. Aspasia reigned supreme, and when she knew that she was queen of that intellectual court, she discussed with them philosophy and the state of her sex, and told her guests that women have

Aspasia

after a drawing by Staal

Published by The Navarre Society, London.

also higher aspirations, and ought to be more than mere wives and mothers.   Pericles, that same Pericles who is supposed to have said that the greatest glory belonged to those women whose vices and virtues are the least talked about by men, became a puppet in the hands of Aspasia, who ruled Athens through her lover. She became the Juno of the Olympian Pericles.   And Athens made war against Megara because Aspasia wished it.   But Aspasia was not the only one to exercise political influence through love.   She availed herself of the love of Pericles to satisfy her own ambitions, as the numerous favourites of occidental kings did after her. Tradition will even have it that when Aspasia grew old and feared that her physical charm no longer attracted Pericles, she adopted the same course as many favourites did adopt after her : she invited beautiful courtesans, slaves and even married women to her house, and in this manner debauched Pericles, and gained a further ascendency over him.   Her ambition was stronger than her love and her jealousy.   History repeats itself.   La Pompadour adopted the same attitude towards Louis XV, Madame de Parabère towards the Duc d'Orléans, Potemkin towards Catherine, and Countess Lichtenau towards Frederick William II.   That Aspasia loved the brilliant Pericles for himself—is very doubtful.   Even if she did, she consoled herself very soon for her loss ; for only eighteen months after the death of the most brilliant man of Greece, she became the mistress of Lysicles, a dealer in oxen or sheep.

Thargelia enjoyed the confidence of Xerxes, King of Persia.   And Cleopatra ! even Queen Cleopatra was only great through the love with which she inspired her mighty lovers, of whom she availed herself as of pawns on the chessboard of her ambitions. Gallantry, intrigues, grace and charm were her only weapons, and in order to remain on her throne she made Caesar and Marc Antony love her. And the example of the ladies of antiquity, of those Aspasias and Cleopatras, was destined to be followed by future European generations and especially by the women of the eighteenth century. Such have been and will be the tactics of nearly all the favourites of kings, who fill the pages of history. They availed themselves of their royal lovers, " as of a pack of cards, to play with them until the game was won."

The influence of Hellas—the admiration and worship of beauty of form—has been a far deeper one than is usually imagined, and this influence upon the Occidental world has not been eradicated even by the Galilean doctrine, although with the spread of Christianity the Aryan peoples began to speak, for a time at least, as if man were only spirit without a body. And to the sense of beauty and to the material pleasure of the senses the favourites appealed. Before penetrating into the council room, they employed the graces of the boudoir, before sitting down in the ministerial arm-chair, they spent some time at the toilet table. They governed their royal lover, and through him the nation ; but before ruling over the monarch they captured the man and the lover. Before becoming stern in command, like Empress Theodora or Pompadour, they knew how to be subtle in caresses. They knew man and his frailties, his vanities and his weaknesses, and they studied him between a caress and a kiss, with an apparent air of indifference for anything serious and a predilection for finery and frippery. Therein lay their secret, the secret

CLEOPATRA.
After a drawing by Staal.

To face page 20.

of success. Tact, perspicacity and dissimulation, aided by feminine charm, were their weapons. They analysed the man and detected his weak spots and calculated their mode of attack, an attack which they carried on cleverly and carefully. Beneath the folds of their exquisite gowns they carried their ambition and their power, and in a tender and soothing tone of voice they decided matters of grave importance. And what has been said of the women may be equally applied to the men. Mazarin, the lover of Anne of Austria, mother of Louis XIV, Mazarin with his sense of perspicacity, has noticed this fact and summed it up in the following words : " If you possess the heart you possess everything " ; and this heart he tried to keep until his death, although he cared very little for it. Before Anne appreciated the genius of Mazarin, before Catherine knew the work of Potemkin, before Caroline Matilda discovered the capacities of Struensee their passions were inflamed for the men. And the latter at first sought to capture the woman before gaining ascendency over the Queen.

But it would be doing an injustice to the memory of the many favourites who fill the pages of history if one were to make the sweeping statement that they were all swayed by ambition and love, that pure genuine love was excluded. By the side of a Biron and a Potemkin we find a Razoumovsky ; by the side of a Struensee and a Mazarin we find a Count Fersen ; by the side of a Pompadour, a Maintenon, we find Emilie, the gentle mistress of the Duc d'Orléans ; by the side of a Diane de Poitiers, a Gabrielle d'Estrées and a Henriette d'Entragues we find a Marie Touchet, the mistress of Charles IX, and Odette, mistress of Charles VI.

It would also be an injustice to imagine that the rule of these favourites, these uncrowned kings and queens, has always been fraught with disaster for the nation and the country. Sometimes it was quite the reverse, and favourites ruled instead of sovereigns for the benefit and welfare of nations. The reign of Mazarin, the grandson of the Sicilian artisan, was one of glory for France. The clever minister secured brilliant successes for her. On the ruins of the expiring federal monarchy he built the constitutional power of Royalty, and, gathering round this emancipated power all the classes of the nation, talents and interests, he led his adopted country into the path of glory. And although the revolt and disorders of the Fronde paralysed the interior policy of the Government, Mazarin was successful in his foreign policy. Turenne's and Condé's brilliant victories gained new provinces for France, and Mazarin signed the treaties of Westphalia and of the Pyrenees and thus ensured universal peace. And Struensee, the son of humble parents, was one of Denmark's greatest reformers. He ruled wisely and well, and whilst offending the nobility, whose privileges he crushed, he benefited the people who were smarting under the misgovernment. Justice, administration, the censorship of the press, the police, were all reformed, and suffering subjects drew a breath of relief under the rule of this grand vizier. And if little can be said in favour of the rule of the Marquise de Pompadour, one must at least admit that she contributed considerably to the development of art and industry, of taste and fashion.

And like the Marquise de Pompadour and Struensee, like Potemkin and Mazarin, many more have made the history of their country, and exercised an influence upon the nation, through the love of the sovereign.   It is the lives of some of these men and women that will be related in the following pages.

CHAPTER II

Diane d'Andouins, the Beautiful Corisande

I

HENRY, King of Navarre, afterwards King of France, had escaped the fate of the numerous victims of the Massacre of St. Bartholomew, thanks to the protection of Charles IX, who loved him well. But though Henry of Navarre, together with his companion, the Prince Condé, being forced to abjure the Catholic faith in order to save their lives, had yielded to the command of King Charles, they nevertheless were treated almost as criminals at the Court of the Valois and closely confined in the Louvre. Seventy thousand Protestants had been massacred throughout the kingdom in the name of a Religion of Love!

La Rochelle, where the Calvinists had concentrated their forces, held out against the besieging army of the Catholics and baffled the efforts of the Duc d'Anjou, until the latter, elected to the throne of Poland, was compelled to leave France. His departure aroused quite different feelings in the breasts of his mother, Catherine de Medicis, and of his brothers, King Charles and the Duc d'Alençon. Whilst the Queen-mother was greatly grieved, the brothers rejoiced. The Queen-mother had alienated the affections of both King

Charles and the Duc d'Alençon. A thousand suspicions had been raised in the mind of the King, who
was attacked by a mortal disease, against his mother,
who had brought from Italy the knowledge of subtle
poisons. Charles, partly out of resentment against
his mother, and partly in a feeling of remorse for
the barbarous action perpetrated on the night of
August 24, began to show marked favour to the
Protestants. The Queen-mother was enraged, but foreseeing the speedy death of the King, decided to await
this event. She had not long to wait. Charles IX
expired under great torments, and his brother Henry,
informed of the news, fled from Poland in the following
night to take possession of the throne of France.
Catherine de Medicis now endeavoured to cause
a rupture between her son, the Duc d'Anjou, and
the King of Navarre. Henry of Navarre's eyes were
at last opened, and he decided to escape from the Court
of the Valois and regain his liberty. He succeeded in
his design, and passing the Seine at Poissy, arrived
first at Alençon and then at Tours.

It was soon afterwards that Henry of Navarre went as a
matter of duty to visit the Comte de Gramont, whose
family had rendered him important services, and for
the first time met Diane de Gramont, known as " la
belle Corisande." The Comtes de Gramont were very
devoted followers of the princes of Navarre ; though
Catholics by tradition they had nevertheless faithfully
served Jeanne d'Albret, the mother of Henry of
Navarre. Philibert de Gramont, Comte de Guiche,
fought by the side of Henry in his battles, lost his arm
and soon afterwards his life in the service of his king.
On August 7, 1567, this same Philibert de Gramont

and Toulongeon, Comte de Gramont, known as
Comte de Guiche, Vicomte d'Aster, Mayor of Bordeaux,
Governor of Bayonne, and Seneschal of Béarn, married
Diane d'Andouins, Vicomtesse de Louvigny, the only
daughter of Paul, Viscount de Louvigny, and Lord of
Lescun. She was surnamed Corisande, after the fashion
of the time which made the grand ladies of the Court
of France adopt some name of a heroine, borrowed from
the novels of the chivalrous middle ages. Some thus
added to their Christian names those of Bradamante,
Marphise or Armide.[1]

Henry was sufficiently enamoured of Corisande to
make her a promise of marriage, signed in his blood; to
offer to recognize her son; and to weep bitterly when
the one she gave him died in infancy. His love for her
was augmented by the admiration and gratitude he felt
towards the woman whose heroic devotion to him,
during this war, went as far as to pledge lands and jewels
in order to procure him men and horses. She was the
soul of all his expeditions, a faithful friend in his days
of need, and Henry, in his turn, gave her strong proofs
of his attachment, and it was no fault of his that these
did not receive the seal of matrimony.[2]

The promise to marry his mistresses became almost a
habit with Henry de Navarre. Few ladies at the
Courts of Europe have been able to resist the amorous
advances of their kings and royal princes; and at
the Courts of the Valois and the Bourbons, the
royal lovers had an *embarras de choix*. Catherine de
Medicis made politics by means of beautiful women.

---

[1] Cf. Capefigue, *La Belle Corisande*, p. 64.
[2] Cf. *Amours du Grand Alcandre*.

HENRY IV., KING OF FRANCE.
After a drawing by Pierre du Monstier (?)

To face page 26.

She surrounded herself with a great number of such ladies, whom she employed to seduce the Protestant generals and make them harmless. She commissioned them to ensnare and lull to sleep the enemy whose activity she feared.

Bourdeille, Seigneur de Brantôme, in his famous work, *Vie des Dames Galantes*, recounts the names and exploits of numerous such Court beauties, who were only too ready to lend their ears to the whisperings of a princely or royal lover. But exceptions are to be met with everywhere, and some there were who would not have yielded to the promises of love, even if made by a king, not because they were troubled by any scruples, but because they set a high price upon their favours. The promise of a marriage, however, made by a king, was sufficient to seduce even the most exacting and ambitious Court beauty. And if Jupiter, the mighty Olympian, is supposed to have once made an ox of himself for love of a royal maid, one must not be astonished to hear of a King of France scattering his promises of marriage to his mistresses.

Henry de Navarre dipped a pen in the blood of his wounds and signed a paper in which he gave his royal word to marry the beautiful Corisande, once he had rid himself, by means of a divorce, of his wife, Marguerite de Valois, the famous Reine Margot, to whom he was only nominally married. We are told that Corisande refused to listen to the King's protestations of love, or to lend a willing ear to his assiduities until the contract had been signed with his blood. To do justice, however, to the Comtesse de Gramont, we must point out that she loved Henry for himself. Among the many mistresses of this king she was perhaps the only one who was disinterested.

She loved him in the days of his adversity. He knew it, and he appreciated it. He was grateful for her affection, and out of gratitude he gave her that contract signed with his blood.

In March 1586 Henry forced the Marshal de Matignon to raise the Siege of Castel, and, moreover, gained possession of several of the enemy's standards. The desire to bear these trophies of glory to the feet of his mistress and to rest with her on this triumphal couch, was irresistible. After the bloody battle of Coutras (October 29, 1587),[1] the King of Navarre, deaf to the murmurs of his army, which had been roused to enthusiasm by the victory, and heedless of the reproaches and prayers of the Prince Condé, who in a few days could have seized the passage of the Saumur, disbanded his nobles, neglected his opportunity, and indeed compromised the issue of the whole campaign, for the sake of conveying a fresh gift of banners to Corisande, who apparently preferred them to any other kind of offering.[2]

"The King," writes Sully, "was only too ready to give in to the prayers of the infatuated Comte de Soissons, whose impatience to resume his post of lover beside Henry IV's sister, Catherine, only equalled his own. The Comte found an accomplice of his passion in the King, who, in his eager vanity to present in person the standards and other spoils of war, which he had put aside for her, to the Comtesse de Guiche, left his army under pretext of the affection which he bore his sister, and the Comte de Soissons."[3]

Her devoted and disinterested affection produced

---

[1] Cf. d'Aubigny, *Mémoires*, éd. Lalanne, Paris, 1889, p. 84.
[2] Cf. *Journal d'Henri III*, tom. II, p. 411.
[3] Cf. Sully, *Mémoires*.

such an impression upon her royal lover that in 1586 the King, having reached a high pitch of amorous infatuation, was seriously thinking of carrying out his promise of marriage to the Comtesse de Guiche, and was only deterred from doing so by the silent disapprobation of Turenne and the drastic remarks of d'Aubigny. It was Henry's ambition to constitute a new kingdom, composed of the provinces of Aquitaine and Gascony, and to share it with Corisande, Comtesse de Guiche.

"On leaving the town the next morning," we are informed by d'Aubigny, "the King, who had forbidden any one to approach him, took his man to task, and held forth to him, for the space of two hours and a half, bringing forward at least thirty instances, ancient and modern, of princes who had been happily married to persons of lower rank, and others showing how the desire for a rich alliance had brought ruin, both on the person of the prince and on the State, ending with attacking the wickedness of those who sought to force a man of passionate temper into a loveless marriage. D'Aubigny, called upon to answer this harangue, began by inveighing against the wretched slaves who had furnished Henry with his arsenal of tales, doubly inexcusable, he added, since, themselves ignorant of passion, they only sought to foment the excusable passion of another.[1]

"All the tales you quote, Sire," he continued, "do not bear upon your case, for the princes you name were leading peaceable lives, and were not men driven about like yourself, who have only your own renown to uphold your character and estate. You must remember, Sire, that you represent four distinct persons, corresponding to an equal number of different claims upon you. You are Henry, the King of Navarre, the heir to the throne, and the Defender of the Church. Each of these persons has his own special attendants, to whom you have to pay various dues, according to their several demands. To those who serve Henry himself

---

[1] D'Aubigny, ibid. p. 87.

you owe your personal revenues ; to the servants of the King of Navarre, you owe the duties of sovereignty ; those who follow the presumptive heir to the throne must be paid with expectations, for it is this which attracts them, and you must allure them with hopes of fortune. The payment to be given to those who serve the Defender of the Church is a harder one for a prince to provide. It is zeal, good deeds, integrity, due reward to all who serve you in whatsoever capacity, or are your companions, with this condition, however, that they spare you as much of the danger as is possible, and leave the entire disposition of the honours and advantages of the war to you." [1]

D'Aubigny, however, was too much of a courtier to offend his king ; he knew that kings, even the best, wish to be flattered, and in order to strengthen his influence upon Henry he took care, whilst opposing the marriage of the King of Navarre with the Comtesse de Guiche, not to blame the love of Henry for Corisande. Returning, therefore, to the matter of Henry's love affair, he cautiously avoided blame, and endeavoured rather to excuse and encourage it, but on condition that the King should not allow it to enervate his powers, but would rather let it be to him a motive for more vigorous action, not indulging his passion with soft hours of repose, but using it as an incentive to courage and victory. And after that ? Well, after that he would not say no to it. D'Aubigny understood his king well, and knew that a question deferred for two years was as good as dead.

" A strong love has taken possession of you," were d'Aubigny's final words, " and it is no longer a question of trying to shake it

---

[1] D'Aubigny, l.c. pp. 88, 89.

off ; but in order to enjoy your love to the full, you must make yourself worthy of your mistress. You look astonished, but let me explain myself more fully : let your love spur you on to deal nobly and bravely with the business of life ; follow the advice of those whom you avoid ; do not neglect necessary duties ; endeavour to overcome those private defects of character which do you wrong, and having thus overcome your enemies and your weaknesses, and assimilating to theirs your character and circum-stances, you may then follow the example of those princes. Listen further to the advice of a faithful friend : do not let the future with its deceptive hopes lure you on to leave the duties of the moment only half fulfilled ; you will thereby lighten the burden of state for the one who, God helping, will be some day in power. But if you try to put your foot on the rung of the ladder while another is on it, the slightest shock will send you to the ground with your foot still poised in mid-air." [1]

The King thanked him, and promised solemnly that he would allow the affair between him and the Comtesse to remain at rest for two years.

Henry de Navarre was of an amorous disposition, and " had he been born on the throne of France," says Tallemant des Réaux, he would certainly not have become the great prince he was ; he would have been submerged in his love affairs ; for, in spite of the many vicissitudes and misfortunes that befel him, he would continually abandon important affairs of State to follow his pleasures and love of escapades.[2] Many were the ladies whom the King of France favoured with his royal love, as we shall have occasion to see in a subsequent chapter ; but the place these gallant dames occupied in the heart and mind of the King, and the influence they exercised upon him, were not the same.

[1] Ibid. pp. 89, 90.
[2] Tallemant des Réaux, *Historiettes*, Paris, 1862, vol. I, p. 3.

Madame de Guiche, Comtesse de Gramont, awakened in Henry a strong feeling of attachment, which had more in it of gratitude and esteem than of actual passion, and nothing in it to provoke his jealousy. His manner of speaking, when addressing her, is lively and easy, as that of a man who feels free even in his chains ; one detects nothing in it of that restless egoism which marks the deeper passions. He asks little, and is perfectly sure of Corisande's affection and loyalty : whether she is equally sure of his is a question which does not greatly disturb him. Moreover, he makes her the confidante of all his affairs and of all his impressions. He delights in describing to her, with the characteristic brevity and clearness of the soldier and the sportsman, the beauties of some surrounding landscape, which appears doubly beautiful when viewed by the rider, as he has seen it on some eve of, or some day after, a battle, when the soul is uplifted by the thought of the coming danger or the remembrance of past victory.

Henry's love for Corisande is best shown in his letters to her, which have become famous. These letters, full of natural careless gaiety and sincerity of expression, not only throw light on the different aspects of his political, moral and pleasure-loving nature, but reveal the degree of his attachment for her to whom they are addressed. In his communications to his other mistresses, Henry exercised a certain discretion, but he seemed to hide nothing from Corisande, whom he knew to be wholly and entirely devoted to him. To her he addressed the letter of June 17, 1586, full of affectionate gaiety not unmingled with melancholy. Henry was keenly alive to the influence of Nature ; only one who has been touched by it could give such charm to his descriptions.

He does not mind a trip on the sea in fine weather, but he much prefers the rivers, the islets, and the quieter pleasures of excursions among woods and dwelling-houses. It was on the return from an excursion of this kind that he wrote the following lines, which breathe an odour of spring—

"Yesterday evening," he writes, "I reached Marans. . . . How I longed to have you with me! I know of no place so suited to your taste. For this reason alone I am ready to exchange it. It is an island, surrounded by woody marshes, with canals at short intervals, along which the boats pass to fetch and carry wood. The water is clear and flows but slowly, the canals are of different widths, the boats of all sizes. A thousand gardens bloom amidst the desert land, but they can only be reached by water. The island is two leagues in circumference; a river runs below the castle, which stands in the middle of the town, where one may live as comfortably as at Pau. There are few houses where you cannot step into your boat from the door. The river opens out into two arms, deep and wide enough for the navigation, not only of larger boats, but of vessels of fifty tons. The sea is about two leagues away. More correctly speaking, this is not a river, but a canal. The vessels go upstream as far as Niort, a place twelve leagues off. The island is dotted about with in-numerable windmills and solitary farmhouses. Every kind of song-bird is here, as well as many species of aquatic birds. I send you a few of their feathers. As to fish, the number, size and price of them is quite ridiculous; a large carp for three sous, and a pike for five. There is plenty of business going on here, but all the traffic is done in boats.

"Here is wheat in abundance and of a fine quality. One could live agreeably here in time of peace, and in perfect security in time of war. One could be happy or sad here, according to whether the beloved object was present or absent. Ah! it does one good to sing here!"

The year of 1588 was one of rough experiences for

D

Henry.   The defeat of the German troops had counter-
acted any advantages that had been gained by the
victory at Coutras, and the death of the Prince Condé
left him to deal single-handed with the King and the
League.   " Alas ! " he exclaimed, " I am beset with such
great difficulties that I must needs soon become a madman or a genius." [1]

It is to Corisande also that he confided his agreeable
surprise at the more friendly attitude now adopted
towards him by Henry III, whom the fear of the Guises
had forced into more amicable relations with Henry of
Navarre. The latter congratulated himself on this
alliance with the King, as his party could not now be
looked upon as anything but entirely and irreproachably
national.   Henry, as the heir presumptive to the throne,
was anything but pleased at appearing to take up arms
against the King, when, in reality, his only enemies were
the Guises and Spain. " I think his Majesty will make
use of my services," he wrote a year later (March 8,
1589). " Otherwise he is in a bad way, and I foresee
his defeat."

His hopes, however, were again to be frustrated.   At
St. Cloud the forces of the two kings were ready to
march and besiege Paris, when suddenly the knife of the
assassin, James Clément, a Jacobin monk, mortally
wounded Henry III.   The King of France, it has been
observed, was murdered in the same house, and, as
appears, also in the same chamber, the same spot, and
the same month, where seventeen years ago he had
assisted, as Prince d'Anjou, at the Council in which the
massacre of St. Bartholomew was decided upon.   This
anecdote has, however, been discredited.

[1] Letter dated March 8, 1588.

The King of France being dead, Henry of Navarre found himself abandoned by both the Catholics and Protestants, the concessions which he made to the one party only serving to alienate the other. He was forced to abandon Paris, and there followed a season of disgust and disappointment. But the elastic nature of the King soon recovered itself, and as soon as he again found himself at the head of a few troops, he knew how to make the most of them, and how by word and example to swell their number. On the eve of the battle of Arques, while Mayenne was circulating the report that Henry was going to give himself up or else throw himself into the sea ; while the Spanish ambassador was already sending word of his death to Rome ; while Madame de Montpensier was telling everybody that they were going to bring him to Paris in chains, and the inhabitants of the Rue Saint-Antoine were letting their windows in anticipation of the coming spectacle of the passing captive, Henry had regained courage and hope, and it was to his *grande amie*, the Comtesse de Gramont, that he announced the state of his mind.

" My affairs are generally thought to be progressing favourably. I have taken Eu. The enemy, who at this moment have double the number of my troops, thought I was caught. Having accomplished this undertaking, I went on towards Dieppe, and am there awaiting them in a camp, which I am busy fortifying. To-morrow I expect to see them, and I trust, with God's help, should they attack me, that they will find it a bad bit of business for themselves." [1]

It says much for the character of Corisande that Henry had no secrets from her. He tells her not only of his

[1] Letter dated September 9, 1589.

expeditions and adventures, but also of his most secret plans in all their minutest details. She was not only his mistress, she was more : his confidante upon whose faith and loyalty he could safely rely. He came to her both with his joys and glad tidings, as well as with his troubles, sure to find in her a true friend, solicitous for the welfare of her king, even if she ran the risk of losing the lover. Corisande loved him, he knew it ; she loved the unhappy friend just as well as the successful king, and bestowed upon the former her pity, just as she gave her admiration to the latter. Many a legitimate wife could take a lesson from this mistress. And Henry loved her not only with his heart, but with his head too. It is not to a mistress, before whom one wishes to shine, but to a true friend, that one writes such pitiful letters is the following, which Henry addressed from Nerac to Corisande—

"I can hardly write. Believe me, I saw the heavens open, but I was not a good enough man to be allowed to enter. God has yet other work for me to do for Him. Twice in the course of the twenty-four hours I was bad enough to be almost ready for my shroud. You would have pitied me. If the crisis had lasted another two hours, I should now be making a feast for worms. . . . I must finish here, as I do not feel well. Bonjour, mon âme." [1]

"Heaven only knows what pain it causes me to leave here without kissing your hands. The Devil is unchained ; I am to be pitied, and it is a wonder that I do not succumb altogether. If I was not a Huguenot I should turn Turk. . . . All the torments that can assail a man, and that not one at a time, but all together, are let loose upon me. Pity me, my soul, and do not add your particular torture to the others. . . . My all, love

---

[1] Middle of January, 1589.

me. Your kindness alone supports me under this shock of afflic-
tion. Do not refuse me this help." [1]

But there is an end to everything, and the love of
kings and princes is not one of the most reliable and
stable things on earth. Until 1589 the correspondence
between Henry IV and Corisande continued without
intermission, but in 1590 it gradually ceased. His mistress already begins to suspect, to grow alarmed, to
threaten, to supplicate. Henry is obliged to reassure
her and to write : " I would rather die than fail in any
of my promises to you." [2] But at every fresh moment
there are angry silences, misunderstandings, ill-tempers,
which, although of short duration, leave behind a flavour
of bitterness and a dull sense of resentment which sooner
or later explodes in anger.

At last the moment came when Corisande finally lost
her power over Henry. The son she had borne him
was dead. Being no longer hampered with paternal
scruples, he found it easy to put aside those of a lover.
Death had unclasped the little arms that had kept such
an irresistible hold upon him with their weak embrace.
What power could now keep him beside the woman
who had grown from custom, even more than from
approaching age, faded and unromantic to his eyes.
How we feel the tragedy of it as we read the letter, in
which not a spark of the old passion is discernible ; where
Henry, in the sober and practical style of mere friendship, endeavours to interest Corisande in his plans,
while he shuts her out from his life, and asks her to use
her influence with his sister Catherine, that she may be
induced to separate from the Comte de Soissons and

[1] March 8, 1588.   [2] July 14, 1589.

listen to the solicitations of the King of Scotland. Poor
Corisande ! Here then is all the return for ten years of
devotion and loyalty.

Listen again to this cold unfeeling letter, dictated by
the insensibility of the man of ambition and business—

" Dear heart," he writes, " send me back Bryquesières, and
he shall bring you all you want, except myself. I am deeply
grieved to hear of the death of the little one yesterday. He was
just beginning to talk."

That is all. The funeral oration is soon over ; the
death of the child is a relief to him, and the promise
he made to d'Aubigny no longer weighs heavily on his
heart. Then follow a few particulars concerning military
affairs, and reference again to his request concerning his
sister and the King of the Scots.

" Please prepare my sister to receive him kindly, and remind
her of the state of our affairs just now, and of the high position
and character of this prince. I have not said anything to her on
the matter. Introduce the subject only in a general way, hinting
that it is time she married, and that there is no chance of another
partner for her."

We are now very far removed from the day when
Henry of Navarre was willing to sacrifice all the advantages accruing to him from the victory of Coutras, in
order to present her with the captured banners. It is
no longer the soldier seeking to escape from his honours,
and longing only to lay himself at her feet. But if
Henry transferred his love from Corisande to another
mistress, he nevertheless kept up his correspondence
with her to the close of 1590, and still favoured her with
his friendship. He writes her details of the whole of
this first glorious but fruitless campaign, and of his

victorious march to Paris and subsequent retreat owing to the unexpected death of Henry III, and even after she had been supplanted as mistress by Gabrielle d'Estrées, he still continued to write to her. One can hardly blame Corisande if, in consequence of a natural feeling of anger against the King, she sought to revenge herself by persuading Catherine, Henry's sister, to marry the Comte de Soissons against her brother's wishes.

But the fact of a promise of marriage still remained. Sully, whose lifelong task it was to battle with these unfortunate promissory documents, and who was forced to waste his diplomatic powers in searching out these " disgraceful papers " which Henry with irresponsible readiness signed for all his mistresses in turn, was now called upon to get rid of the compromising agreement as best he could. " I shuddered," says Sully, " when the King gave me the order." It was imperative, however, that he should carry through his task with success, for any miscarriage in a matter of this kind was not easily overlooked. Sully played his part with admirable duplicity. He got possession of the document, and what is more, also secured another one in which the lovers, in the sublime security of mutual attachment, undertook not to marry without his consent. Sully gave the former paper to the King, and kept the other himself, not saying a word about it. Thus he had it in his power to break the bonds of a love which he had pretended to encourage.

Although Henry IV's love for Corisande had evaporated, he retained to the end a sentiment of respect for her who had the good taste not to imitate his infidelity, and who, widowed of hope, devoted herself to the memory of what had once been. She had grown very stout and red in the face, and seemed ashamed, seeing herself as she was now, to think that it should be said that Henry IV had once been in love with her. Henry, on his part, endeavoured by every mark of confidence and by kindly treatment to ease the wound which he knew was incurable. Corisande nobly returned the infidelity of her royal lover by remaining faithful to him until her death, which occurred in 1620. Few virtuous women are capable of such dignity of revenge.

CHAPTER III

Dans le fond d'un château tranquille et solitaire,
Loin du bruit des combats, elle attendait son père,
Qui fidèle à ses rois, vieilli dans les hasards,
Avait du grand Henri suivi les étendards.
D'Estrée était son nom : la main de la nature
De ses aimables dons la combla sans mesure.
Telle ne brillait point, aux bords de l'Eurotas
La coupable beauté qui trahit Ménélas.

VOLTAIRE.

Gabrielle d'Estrées

IT was on November 8 or 9, 1590, during his campaigns, when he was fighting for a crown to which
his birth had entitled him, that Henry IV left his army
for a ride in the country to think out some military
operations in solitude. His way led him into the flower-
strewn valley of the Eure. On the decline of a hill he perceived a castle, beautifully situated ; it was the Château
de Coeuvres. The King of France was just preparing
to knock at the door of the manor when his astonished
gaze was suddenly met by a most beautiful apparition.
It was that of Gabrielle d'Estrées, the charming daughter
of the owner of the Château de Coeuvres, John Antony
d'Estrées. The first interview of Henry and Gabrielle

seems, however, according to contemporary historians, to have been a little less romantic. Henry simply paid a visit to the Château de Coeuvres, where he was received, in the absence of the mother, by the two daughters, Gabrielle and Diane. Gabrielle, the younger of the two, was just seventeen. She had a most graceful figure and a beautiful complexion; she was a dazzling blonde. Her whole bearing was full of natural grace and quiet dignity. Diane, the elder of the two, although lacking the graceful figure of her younger sister, was still possessed of the family beauty, and moreover had the advantage of that vivacity and liveliness which one missed in Gabrielle. The attitude of the two young girls was exceedingly correct. At the time when he first saw Gabrielle, Henry was thirty-seven, and in the full bloom of manhood.

According to Dreux du Radier's description of her, Gabrielle had a beautifully-shaped head, covered with an abundance of fair hair; blue eyes of a peculiar brilliancy; a lily-white complexion, only faintly tinged with rose, except at moments of strong emotion; the nose well formed, the lively, humorous curves of the mouth set off with fine teeth; the oval of the face such as painters love; the ear small and well set; the throat of a beauty which threw her other beauties into the shade; while the figure, arms, hands and feet, which corresponded with the head, composed a whole which no one could look upon unmoved. She was white of skin—we are told by Sainte-Beuve—with golden hair, which she gathered up into a knot, or left in waves round her face; the forehead was fine; the space between the eyes wide and generous; the nose straight and regular; the mouth small and smiling; and the whole

GABRIELLE D'ESTRÉES.
After a drawing by Daniel du Monstier.

To face page 42.

face, with its charming curves, gentle and attractive; the eyes blue, soft and clear, the glance quick and bright. She was a woman all over, in her tastes, her ambitions, even to her faults.

A certain fatality seems to hover over some families, and their members are predestined to follow a way in life which has been paved for them by their forbears. Gabrielle had inherited from her mother's family that wild dash of blood which naturally predisposed her for the irregular life she was to lead. This Madame d'Estrées, we are told by Tallemant des Réaux, belonged to the family of Bourdaisière, a race that gave more ladies of gay renown to France than any other. It is said that a Madame de la Bourdaisière was honoured in turn by the favours of Pope Clement VII, the Emperor Charles V, and Francis I. Twenty-five or twenty-six of the family, among them those who had taken the veil and those who were married, are stated to have carried on love affairs in high circles. Madame d'Estrées was the mother of six daughters and two sons. The eldest of these was killed at the siege of Laon; the younger, who was intended for the Church, and for the Bishopric of Lyon, and a cardinal's hat, became the Marshal d'Estrées. The hat was given to his cousin de Sourdis. The six daughters were : Madame de Beaufort, Madame de Villars, Madame de Nau, the Comtesse de Sauzay, the Abbess of Maubuisson, and Madame de Balagny. The last-named lady's figure was somewhat spoiled, but she was none the less unsurpassed in gallantry.[1] Her friendship with M. d'Epernon ended by her becoming the mother of the Abbess of Sainte-Glossine at Metz. These

---

[1] Tallemant des Réaux, *Historiettes*, Paris, 1862, vol. ii, pp. 5-7.

six daughters and the brother were known as the seven deadly sins.[1]

It was to this family that Gabrielle belonged, and amid such associations that she passed her childhood. How was it possible for Gabrielle to escape the contagion of such an atmosphere? Her freshness and innocence, as that of her sisters, were sullied at an early age. Even before she made the acquaintance of Henry IV, her reputation had run risks of being lightly handled. She inherited the fatal blood that lost none of its fire as long as it ran in the veins of the d'Estrées family.

It is therefore credible enough that Gabrielle was not quite innocent when Henry saw her at Coeuvres for the first time, and that, although it was by a lucky accident that she met her royal lover, the latter was not entirely ignorant, either of her existence or of her charms.

Her mother, Frances d'Estrées, so Bassompierre informs us, disposed of her daughters in the most unblushing way. Gabrielle, being only sixteen years old, beautiful in face and figure, was offered by her to Henry III. The Duc d'Epernon acted as go-between, he having for his own mistress Gabrielle's elder sister Diane, the mother of the Abbess of St. Glossine. King Henry III, hearing of her extreme beauty, and growing desirous of obtaining her, the matter was quickly settled by a sum of six thousand crowns being sent to Madame d'Estrées, two thousand of which, however, Montigny purloined on the way. When this came to the King's ears, he was so enraged that it was some time before

[1] Ibid.

he would allow the latter to approach him; a reconciliation, however, was at last effected by the Duc
de Joyeuse. Henry III soon grew tired of her, and
remarked that if he had " wanted a thin white thing like
that " he could have satisfied himself with the Queen,
and would have had no need to seek further. Whereupon the mother entered into business proposals with
others, but shortly after having brought her to the notice
of the Cardinal de Guise, the latter fell violently in
love with her. His infatuation lasted over a year, but
having discovered that Madame d'Estrées had also
shown off her daughter to M. de Longueville, he abandoned her, three or four days before the barricades.
M. le Grand (the Duc de Bellegarde), who was just
then in high favour, took a fancy to her. The King,
Henry III, who was quite willing to let him have what he
wanted, undertook to assist in the affair, and accordingly
made them go to balls dressed in the same colour, insisted
on their dancing together, and was quite delighted at
the admiration bestowed upon the handsome couple.
But all at once Madame d'Estrées carried off Gabrielle to
Coeuvres, together with her sisters Denan and Diane,
and shortly after, taking only her youngest daughter
Juliette with her, she left her husband, and went to
join d'Alègre, the Governor of Issoire, with whom she
was in love. Her daughters remained at Coeuvres with
their father, and the gentlemen in the surrounding
neighbourhood fell in love with them. Among these
was Brunet, brother of la Bussière, and Stanay, both of
whom were favourably entertained by Gabrielle, who
also received a visit from M. de Longueville, during his
stay at Coeuvres. Before meeting Henry of Navarre
Gabrielle thus seems to have been the mistress not only

of King Henry III, but also of several other gentlemen.

Bassompierre also informs us that Bellegarde had forsaken a certain Madame d'Humières, who had nursed him like an angel during a long illness of his while at Compiègne, for the sake of Gabrielle. The latter was just at that time occupied with Admiral de Villars, whom she left in order to join Bellegarde, who in his turn saw himself supplanted by the Duc de Longueville. While these two were striving which should win the prize, a third combatant, who was no other than Henry of Navarre himself, arrived on the scene of action, and profiting by their contention, himself carried off the desired object, the beautiful Gabrielle.

Kings do not like to be contradicted, they expect to see their slightest wishes, even in matters of love, promptly fulfilled. Henry, who was very tolerant in many things, suffered no contradiction in his love affairs. He, therefore, put an end to the conflict between Bellegarde and Longueville, who felt that it was ridiculous to quarrel over the possession of what was no longer theirs. Longueville, as a *pis-aller*, took Madame d'Humières, and Bellegarde in a little while found compensation in Mademoiselle de Guise, not abstaining from poaching later on occasionally on royal territory. For the present Henry was in love, and what was worse, in love enough to be jealous, and had told Bellegarde plainly that he would admit no sharer in his pleasure, adding that his passion was dearer to him than all the crowns in the world. The warning was repeated to Longueville, who, however, did not take the ultimatum so deeply to heart as Bellegarde. The former perhaps had no foundation for his hopes, while Bellegarde was forced to relinquish possession of a heart that had been given to him. He had no choice but to obey; at any rate he gave his promise to the King not to act contrary to the latter's command. How far the promise was kept will be seen later on. Bellegarde, however, allowed himself to complain bitterly to his mistress, who joined her lamentations to his; indeed, women being generally more demonstrative than men, where their passions are concerned, Gabrielle was not so careful as Bellegarde to hide her feelings. She even went so far as to declare angrily to the King that she was not going to be forced against her inclinations, that any violence would only awaken her contempt and hatred, if any attempt were made to prevent her marrying a man whose courtship had been encouraged by her parents. Her grief was such that she left Mantes without saying good-bye to the King, and returned to Picardy.

If one may believe the author of *Les Amours du Grand Alcandre*, this incident is supposed to have occurred in Compiègne, whither Henry had commanded Antony d'Estrées to bring his two daughters. Whether all these stories are history or romantic fiction cannot be stated with absolute certainty. There is no doubt a great amount of truth in them. Henry certainly saw Gabrielle again very soon after their first interview at Coeuvres. "The King's army," writes Sully in his *Memoirs*, "not only seized Chartres, but Corbie likewise. Parabèze had the conduct of the latter siege, in the absence of the King, who was kept at St. Quentin by his new passion for Mademoiselle d'Estrées." [1]

Resistance always excited Henry to action, and his

---

[1] Sully, *Memoirs*, vol. i.

first thought on recovering from the shock which
Gabrielle's departure had given him, was as to the best
means he could employ to triumph over it. He determined, cost what it might, to seek out his mistress, and
endeavour to appease her, and he carried out his intention with an alacrity and indifference to consequences
which, he flattered himself, could not fail to move her.
Seven leagues lay between Mantes and Coeuvres, and a
forest, infested with the enemy's troops, had to be
traversed before the house could be reached. But at
the risk of falling into an ambuscade, Henry set off,
accompanied with five only of his immediate friends.
When within three miles of Coeuvres he dismounted,
put on a peasant's dress, hoisted a bag of straw on to
his head, and started on foot for the house, whither he
had the day before sent notice of his arrival. But his
disguise produced a different effect to that which he
had intended. He had hoped that this double sacrifice of safety and of dignity would have rendered him
sublime in the eyes of his lady love. As it was, he only
appeared ridiculous to Gabrielle, who had been prepared to expect him. He found her in one of the
galleries alone with her sister Juliette Hippolyte, who
afterwards married the Duc de Villars. Gabrielle
received him with undisguised indifference, and coolly
ended by telling him that he was so ugly that she could
not bear to look at him. She haughtily added that such
a masquerade was unworthy of a King of France ; it
was so undignified. Gabrielle, say the gossips of the
period, would undoubtedly have adopted a different
tone had the Duc de Bellegarde been the one to employ
the same ruse in order to see her. She ordered the
King to change his attire, and withdrew, leaving him

alone with her sister. The latter was more indulgent, and took pity on the disappointed lover. Madame de Villars did her best to make excuses for her sister's incivility, and these excuses were all that Henry gained by risking his life and crown. Feeling somewhat disconcerted, he made haste to return to Mantes, where he listened meekly to the remonstrances of Marnay and Sully, to whom he had caused the greatest anxiety by his absence. He tried to banish the image of the ungrateful Gabrielle from his heart. In vain, all his efforts but seemed to render her more dear, and at last, not wishing to expose himself again to danger and ridicule, he determined that his kingly authority should be brought into service on behalf of his interests as a lover.

The Marquis d'Estrées was Governor of the Ile de France, and he received orders to repair at once to Mantes with his noble family, and in order to keep him on the spot he was given a seat in the Council. The *Vagabond* King, however, was forced to be constantly on the march in order to keep the scattered forces of the League from joining one another, and having but little leisure for love affairs in the midst of such constant warfare, it was some time yet before he was able to profit by the proximity of the fair Gabrielle. And thus whilst Henry was fighting his enemies and battling for a crown and a throne, Bellegarde and Longueville knew how to take advantage of his absence. Gabrielle wavered between the two, but on the whole showed greater favour towards Bellegarde. When at last the King returned to set his love affair in order, and again made it understood that he would suffer no rival in the field, Bellegarde retired into the background. Longue-

ville, on the contrary, who was more given to ambition
than love, and who was unwilling to pay with a life of
dishonour for the enjoyment of an hour's pleasure,
entered into a secret understanding with Mademoiselle
d'Estrées. He took back his letters and pretended to
return her all her answers, but with diplomatic fore-
sight, and in order to keep a hold over her, he took care
not to part with those in which she had most unmis-
takably declared her feelings. Gabrielle, justly indignant,
never forgave the man who had been capable of such
disloyalty.

In the meantime Henry had heaped favours upon the
father of his mistress, and had overwhelmed him with
honours. It was, therefore, quite natural that Antony
d'Estrées should take umbrage. His wife, Madame
d'Estrées, had left him and lived publicly in Issoire in
Auvergne with her lover, the Marquis d'Alègre, who
was much younger than herself. Several of his daughters
were leading a similar life, and the father could have
but little doubt as to the relations existing between
Gabrielle and the King. Antony d'Estrées was valiant
and honourable. He wished to avoid a scandal, and
decided to marry Gabrielle. Bellegarde was now out
of the question, and so the father cast his eyes upon
Nicolas d'Amerval de Liancourt, rich and well born,
but deformed and weakly. Such was the man whom
he picked out to be the guardian of his daughter's
virtue.

If the King had resented the rivalry of a lover, he
did not seem to be jealous of a husband. He preferred
rather to see Gabrielle under the authority of a husband
than of a father. He had less to fear from the weak and
deformed husband than from the stern father. But if

the King assented Gabrielle wept and protested. Henry consoled her; he promised her that on the day of her marriage he would himself appear to shelter her from any aggressions on the part of the authorized husband. M. de Liancourt did not accept his position without remonstrance, but he always found Gabrielle, according to her own account, in expectation of the King. This subterfuge remained such an unsurpassable barrier between them that the husband at last was forced to content himself with his wife's fortune as his share of the alliance. Soon after her marriage Gabrielle joined Henry's Court at Chartres, and never left it until her death in 1599. She enjoyed the privileges of a woman separated from her husband, and was accompanied by her aunt, the Marquise de Sourdis, who seems to have been a very intelligent woman, instructing her niece how to gain absolute sway over the King's mind. The aunt had her own profits in view, and thanks to the influence of the niece, the Marquis de Sourdis was made Governor of Chartres, when this town was taken. Henry, who had ardently wished to divorce his wife, Marguerite de Valois, and had even taken steps to gain the latter's consent, now abated in his zeal. He was afraid that once free, reasons of State would compel him to choose another wife, and that he would never be allowed to marry Gabrielle. But the course of true love, even that of a king, never does run smooth. Henry was still tortured by fits of jealousy. He was jealous of the Duc de Bellegarde.

In the letters which passed between Henry and Gabrielle there occur many passages revealing the state of the King's mind. One of these letters to Gabrielle was written in December, 1592. Henry was at St

Denis.   He had returned from his expedition against
the Duke of Parma.   After a scene between the King
and his mistress, the latter, accompanied by her uncle
and aunt, left for Chartres.   It seems that during the
absence of her royal lover Gabrielle had received a visit
from Bellegarde.

" There is nothing that could more increase my suspicions
than your conduct towards me," wrote Henry.   " You know
how annoyed I was at the visit of my rival during my absence.
The magic power of your eyes over me saved you half of my
complaints.   Had I, however, known about this journey as much
as I know now, since I arrived at St. Denis, I would have refused
to see you, and given you up entirely.   You tell me that you
will keep the promises which you made to me.   But just as the
Old Testament has been abolished by the appearance of our
Saviour, so all your promises have been made void by the letter
which you wrote from Compiègne.   You must no more say *I
shall act* thus, but *I am* acting.   Make up your mind, my dear
lady-love, to have only *one* servant.   It is in your power to change
me and oblige me.   You are wrong if you imagine that anybody
in the world will give you so much love as I can.   No one can
cope with me in faithfulness.   If I am guilty of some indiscretion
it is due to my jealousy.   What will jealousy not make one do ?
You must therefore blame yourself for it.   I am longing to see
you again, and this longing is so strong that I would gladly give
four years of my life for the power of seeing you as quickly as I
am finishing this letter.   I kiss your hands one million times."

What passion and what jealousy !   Poor Henry, poor
King !   Kings are, after all, only mortal, and not free
from the pangs of jealousy.

In 1593, Gabrielle became enceinte.   The King's
happiness would have been complete had it not been
for his jealous suspicions of Bellegarde.   The author of
Les Amours du Grand Alcandre asserts that Gabrielle

was still in love with the latter, but she had only to begin caressing the King to make the latter forthwith repent of his evil thoughts. An incident occurred which might have opened the King's eyes a little more, if good luck had not protected the lovers. The King being at Villers-Coterets, left one day to attend to some business a few leagues off. Gabrielle remained in bed complaining of illness, Bellegarde meanwhile having started off, as was supposed, to Compiègne. No sooner had the King left than a female confidante of Gabrielle's let Bellegarde into a small room of which she alone had the key, and she only waited for Gabrielle to dismiss her attendants to usher him into her mistress's room. Henry, who did not find what he went to seek, returned sooner than was expected. Bellegarde's only way of escape was to let himself into the closet, the door of which stood at the head of Gabrielle's bed. The King, immediately on entering, called for Gabrielle to bring him some sweetmeats, and if she could not come, some one else was to do so and break open the door. The alarm of the two culprits may be imagined.

When the King himself began to hammer at the door, Gabrielle complained that the noise disturbed her, but the King was deaf, or pretended to be so, and continued his exertions.

There was a window in the closet at some height from the ground, and Bellegarde, seeing no other way of escape, threw himself over and alighted on the ground, without doing himself much harm. The confidante, who had kept in hiding so as not to open the door, now appeared, hot and flustered, to ask what was wanted, and explaining that she had not understood that the

King was calling for her, went to fetch him his sweet-meats.   Then Gabrielle, seeing she was safe, heaped her reproaches on Henry for his suspicion.[1]

" I see," she said, " that you are going to treat me as you have treated the others, whom you have loved, and that with the usual fickleness of your nature you are now wishing to separate from me. You took me forcibly from my husband, and since the strong love I had for you led me to forget my duty and my honour, you have repaid me with nothing but suspicion, for which I have not even in thought given you the slightest cause."

" You do me an injustice, dear child," replied Henry. " Do you not understand that there is no greater mark of strong and genuine love than jealousy ? If I loved and valued you less, I should not be in such fear of losing you. However, as my conduct offends you, I promise you that I will be jealous no more. I deserve all your anger, but I am not unworthy of your forgiveness, since I make my confession here at your feet."

Sometimes, however, Henry took the infidelities of his mistress in good part, and proved himself above jealousy. He knew how to forgive.

Thus it appears that on one occasion Henry IV did not put himself so much out of humour about his mistress and Bellegarde, and dealt more leniently with the latter than he most likely would have done if he had chanced to come upon him in the sweetmeat closet. The King coming unexpectedly into Gabrielle's room, the Duc de Bellegarde, who was with her, tried to hide

---

[1] *Amours de Henri IV*, p. 78.

under the bed, but he was not quick enough about it to escape the King's eye. The latter said nothing, however, and the meal was served. Henry in the course of it threw a box of sweetmeats under the bed, exclaiming : " Il faut que tout le monde vive."

But even if the occasions on which Henry was still a prey to jealousy were still very frequent, Gabrielle had no difficulty in restoring his happiness and confidence with a few of her soft words.

" Ah ! how miserable I was last night," he writes, " away from the beloved one. I could think of nothing but the delight of her presence. Yet why should I praise your adorable beauty, since that and the trust in my unconquerable love has been the cause of your falseness to me. But may the truth of those sweet words you uttered to me the other night calm all my past unworthy thoughts ! "

Gabrielle declared that her love had been a thousand times greater than that of the King ; the King replied that she lied. Then followed delightful passages of arms between the two.

" Indeed, dearest love, you should rather fear that I should love you too much rather than too little. But this fault is pleasant both to you and me. See how I give in to all your wishes ; is it not to win your love ? And truly I believe I have it, and my heart is content."

On July 25, 1593, Henry made his solemn abjuration at Saint-Denis. Gabrielle's influence had been joined to that of Sully in persuading the King to this decisive act, and it was to her that he first gaily related the particulars *du saut périlleux*.

Gabrielle remained with Henry throughout the siege, and to the public eye appeared to have no thought but for him. Bellegarde was paying court to Mademoiselle de Guise, and Henry had no longer any cause for suspicion regarding him. He paid frequent visits to his mistress, either at the small pavilion on the summit of Montmartre, or at the one on the opposite side of the hill, which overlooked the plain of Saint-Denis, and which was known as Clignancourt. Gabrielle took up her residence in turn in these two houses.

On March 22, 1594, at seven o'clock in the morning, Henry entered Paris, which was " hungering to see a King." In June, 1594, at the Castle of Coucy, near Laon, Gabrielle gave birth to a son, who was named César, and the King's joy would have known no bounds had it not been for gossips and scandalmongers.

Gabrielle did not enjoy popularity among the women of the court. She occupied a position which more than one of these considered as her own. Her luxury and extravagance shocked the soberer-minded populace. The Huguenots found it difficult to pardon her for lulling the King's conscience to sleep and persuading him to abjure.

The birth of a child gave Gabrielle the claim of a mother, and the ever-increasing honours with which the King surrounded her led everybody to expect to see her shortly made Queen. Sully looked on with grief at Henry's unregal behaviour, which he feared was the preliminary to the culminating act of marriage. He maintained that Gabrielle's children had much more right to claim Bellegarde as their father than the King.

One day Beringhen, the King's chief valet de chambre,

showed the King a letter which he had found in Bellegarde's apartment, written by the latter to his mistress. The servant had been sent by the King to inquire after her health, she at that time feigning to be ill, so Henry ordered him to keep a watch upon them. This faithful servant, who was afraid his master was going to marry Gabrielle, spied upon them to such good purpose that he was able to inform the King one evening that he had seen Bellegarde going in to her. Whereupon Henry summoned Praslin, and ordered him to go and kill the gentleman who was in Gabrielle's room.

Praslin was taken aback at receiving such a command, and being, moreover, exceedingly fond of the two delinquents, though at the same time forced to obey orders, he gathered a body of archers, who made such a noise as they approached Gabrielle's quarters, that Praslin on entering found her alone, and he then confided to her the cause of his visit. Gabrielle, who appreciated his kindness in not taking her by surprise, promised never to forget his good offices, and fulfilled her promise by obtaining many favours for him later on.

The mistress, however, complained bitterly to the King, who admitted that he felt himself in the wrong, but at the same time reproached her concerning Bellegarde's letter. She swore that she had never seen it, and made her peace with the King, whom she could turn any way she liked. Bellegarde, however, did not come off so easily. He was forced to go away from Court, and bidden not to return until he could bring a wife back with him. He obeyed his King's command— went away, and returned married to Anne de Bueil, daughter of Honoré de Bueil, Sieur de Fontaines, who was killed at the siege of St. Malo, after this town had declared for the League.

The following story is told by l'Estoille : " News reached Paris of the death of M. d'Alibourt, chief physician to the King. It was hinted that an incautious word regarding the infant César had cost him his life. Not that the King was responsible for his death—what did he know of cruel and subtle poisons—but, as all the world believed, the mother, whom the matter most closely concerned, and to whom the King, contrary to promise, had repeated what was said, never dreaming he would thereby lose his good and faithful friend and physician." [1]

Henry, in response to these rumours, which did not fail to reach his ears, entered Paris in triumph on September 15, in company with his mistress, immediately legitimized César, and hastened forward the necessary measures for the dissolution of his marriage with Marguerite de Valois, so as to place Gabrielle on the throne.

On Thursday, September 15 (1594), relates the Chronicler, the King made his entry towards seven or eight o'clock in the evening, amid the flare of torches. He was mounted on a mottled grey horse, dressed in a suit of grey velvet laced with gold, and his grey hat with its white plume was on his head. The troops from Saint-Denis, with the city corps and the aldermen, marched in front. The gentlemen of the Court in their red robes awaited his arrival at Nôtre-Dame, where the Te Deum was chanted. It was eight o'clock when his Majesty rode over the bridge of Nôtre-Dame,

---

[1] L'Estoille, *Journal*.

accompanied by a large body of horsemen, and surrounded by the most splendid of his nobility. His face was radiant, and he responded with delight to the cries of " Vive le Roi " ; his hat was hardly out of his hand for a moment, his salutations being principally directed towards the ladies assembled at the windows. Madame de Liancourt was a little way in front of him, borne in a magnificent open litter, and so resplendent with pearls and precious stones that their brilliancy dimmed the light of the torches ; her dress was of black satin puffed all over with white.

On February 3, 1595, the parliament of Paris confirmed the legitimacy of César de Vendôme by letters patent, and Gabrielle thus assumed a high position in the eyes of the nation. Her influence henceforth increased, and no one dared to doubt her right to respect and consideration. Henry was at her feet, and France followed the example of her King.

The importance of the King's mistress was greatly augmented in the eyes of the Parisians by this triumphal entry, and she continued to be looked upon with ever-increasing reverence. In March, 1595, Gabrielle d'Estrées was created Marquise de Monceaux, and given possession of a castle, situated about two leagues beyond Meaux. Gabrielle knew how to captivate the King's heart and mind. Had it not been for her premature death, she might after all have become Queen of France when Henry had divorced his wife, Marguerite de Valois. She knew how to exercise her influence in a gentle manner. Always smiling, always courteous and kindly, Gabrielle played the part of comforter and peacemaker. Even those who could not love her found it impossible to hate her, recognising the charm of her modesty and the unobtrusiveness of her manners during this trying interval, when she held the place of queen as well as of mistress. And Henry recognized her as such. He valued her judgment in important State matters, and asked her advice. She was not a mere beautiful woman, but a dear companion. It was no longer merely for his pleasure that the King sought the company of Gabrielle; he made use of her at various times to help him out of the difficulties into which he was constantly plunged by the intrigues at Court. He hid nothing from her, and she never tired in her efforts to help and console him. The Court had reason to be grateful to her, for she used her powers generously, and none ever suffered loss or oppression through her means.

Sainte-Beuve rightly described her as a woman in whose presence one felt refreshed and reposed; she was far from wishing to engender dissension, he adds. Herein lay Gabrielle's whole art and charm: that she was able to invest the equivocal position in which she was placed with an air of dignity and decency.

Henry, though master of Paris, was as yet far from being King of France. He was still forced to be continually carrying on negotiations between the Catholics and the Protestants. Brittany, Picardy and Lorraine had to be conquered. He had to be on his guard against the visits of fanatic monks, and though Gabrielle was dead when Henry was really master of France in 1600, she had followed him in his days of struggle, and Henry was grateful for her devotion. She was faithful to the king, if she had not always been so to the lover. As a sign of mingled love and esteem, Henry presented her with the singular gift of the ring with which he had

" espoused France " at his consecration, and so they
were betrothed. All the presentation gifts made him
by the various towns ; all the keys, trophies of victory,
which had been solemnly handed to him by their citizens, became her property. He held nothing back
from the woman who had loved the nomad king, who
had followed him in his campaigns, and had been his
companion during the wild and adventurous days
of his early struggle. And so it was Gabrielle who
shared the triumph of his entry into Paris, who was
successively created Marquise de Monceaux and Duchesse
de Beaufort, and whom Henry fully intended to make
Queen of France. Most of the honours by right falling
to the Queen fell to her share while she was still only
his mistress. She was constantly with the King, was
present in Council and in the Assembly, and helped to
receive kings and ambassadors. It was her sorrowful
privilege also to be present at the attempt on the King's
life by the young student, Jean Châtel, which took
place in her own room on December 24, 1594. Nothing,
however, daunted her courage. The following episode
will show to what extent the King valued the judgment
of Gabrielle.

It was at the assembly of the chief inhabitants of
Rouen in 1596. Henry made a speech, an adroit and
soldierly speech, which would have had more lasting
effect if the hearers, who were charmed with his eloquence, had not also doubted his sincerity. Gabrielle,
who was more tactful than the King, and whose love
made her more keenly alive to his mistakes, was fully
aware that Henry had gone too far in his asseverations.
In the course of it he assured his audience that he had
come, not like his predecessor, to enforce his will upon

them, but to receive counsel from them . . . that he placed himself under their guardianship, etc.   In order to hear this speech Gabrielle had hidden herself behind the arras, and when the King asked her what she had thought of it, she replied that she had never heard a better speech, but that she had been rather astonished at hearing him say that he put himself under anybody's guardianship.   " I intended what I said," answered the King with an oath, " but I meant of course with my sword buckled to my side."

It was during their stay at Rouen that the Marquise gave birth to a daughter, Catherine Henriette, who was baptized with all the formalities which usually attended the baptism of the royal infants.   This daughter afterwards married Charles de Lorraine, Duc d'Elboeuf, and died in 1633.   The King did not hide his affection for Gabrielle, and kissed her in public.   It is interesting to quote here the following episode, related by L'Estoille—

" About this time a rumour spread that a famous magician in the Netherlands had predicted the assassination of the King, who, according to the details foretold of this coming event, was to be killed in his bed by a party of conspirators before the year was out.   Another tale also got wind of a great defeat of Christians by the Grand Turk, which victory was reported to have been granted to the infidel on account of his just behaviour in killing a girl he had been fond of, with his own hand, in order to satisfy his people, to whom the said unfortunate girl had not been acceptable.   Everything had prospered with him since.   The tale reached Henry's ears, who laughed both at that and the prediction, saying that it would take more than that to make him leave off kissing his mistress, and as a matter of fact, he kissed her openly before all the world, and she him, even in the Council Chamber." [1]

[1] L'Estoille, *Journal*.

In 1597 Henry purchased the Duchy of Beaufort for his mistress, and from henceforth Gabrielle d'Estrées, Marquise de Monceaux, was known as the Duchesse de Beaufort.

On March 23, 1597, this being the first Sunday in Lent, the King was still carrying on his festivities, running after all kinds of amusements with the Marquise ever at his side, while she continually took off his mask and kissed him. The whole night was spent in riotous excursions from place to place, and the King did not return to the Louvre till eight o'clock the next morning.

But on Wednesday the 26th, while everybody was laughing and dancing, came the disastrous news of the surprise of Amiens by the Spanish troops, whereupon Paris was suddenly plunged into grief, and the King, greatly troubled at this unexpected blow, turned his thoughts to God.

" It is His doing ! " he cried. " Those poor things who would not accept the garrison I offered them have been their own destruction." Then, after a moment's reflection : " I have acted as King of France long enough ; it is time for me to go and act as King of Navarre." Then embracing his mistress, who was weeping, he bade her good-bye, with the words : " We must mount and make ready for another war." Which he did forthwith, marching at the head of his troops, and letting them see that whatever his adversity, neither heart nor courage failed him, and that he was a stranger to fear.

Henry left, but shortly afterwards he wrote to Gabrielle as follows—

" My dear love, I must admit that we love each other very

well indeed.   There is no woman like you, and as for men, no
one can vie with me in passion.   I love you now just as at the
beginning of our acquaintance, and my longing to see you again
is more ardent than ever.   In ten days I hope my exile will be at
an end.   Make yourself ready, my love, my all, to leave on
Sunday next, and be at Compiègne on Monday.   Good night,
my heart, my all ; I kiss you a million times."

Henry's passion was as great and as ardent as in the
days when disguised as a peasant he stole away from his
army to join his lady love.   And yet Henry never forgot
that the lover was also king.   Gabrielle's influence was
great, but she never led him into follies.   She was as careful
of his interests and dignity as he himself.   Whether it
was solely devoted attachment or prudent calculation
is difficult to state.   Who can fathom the human heart ?
Were not Gabrielle's interests and future centred in the
King and in his successes ?

But the success of the Marquise provoked envy.
The p pulation and the Court reproached the mistress
with h r wealth and her luxury.   And yet it must be
admitted that if she received many marks of favour, she
was never grasping, and even Sully declares in his
Memoirs that she did not show great cupidity, a fault
which her position could have easily developed in her.
There was little sympathy between the minister and the
mistress, and although Gabrielle had favoured Sully's
nomination, Sully could not but fear this dangerous
rival.   He was in constant apprehension lest Henry
would marry the Duchesse de Beaufort.

Gabrielle had offended him by begging the post of
Grand-Master of Artillery, which Sully coveted, for her
father, who well deserved it in return for his military
services.   Sully finally bought the post from him, but

he did not forgive the preference that had been shown to d'Estrées.

It is true the favour Gabrielle enjoyed had been, at one time, to his advantage. But great politicians are very selfish :—this favour he now found in his way. The fear of her becoming one day queen haunted Sully perpetually. He felt that the King was slipping from his grasp, and was aware that there was a voice at his ear to which he listened more readily than to his ministers' counsel. He remembered the moments of awful fear he had gone through, and the cold sweat that had broken out all over him on the day when Gabrielle, whom by order of the King he was bringing back to the palace, had nearly met with a fatal accident. He saw again, as in a nightmare, the dangerous descent into Clermont, the four rearing horses, the carriage in which were the women and children of the Marquise tearing past, upsetting two mules with their burdens, the litter of the Marquise herself narrowly escaping the same fate, and finally brought to a standstill at the very edge of the precipice. With what vigour and willingness, at the express command of the Marquise, he had belaboured the cowardly coachman, who had leaped from his box at the first moment of fright ! But though his blows had been a relief to Sully's anger, they could not rid him of the superstitious fear that had beset him ever since, when he thought of all that depended on the preservation of that fair fragile being. He could not forgive her for being so loved by the King, that he, a Bethune, a Sully, was forced to tremble at the bare idea of an angry word from those beautiful lips, which might put a check for ever on his ambition, or of a tear from that beautiful eye, which might drown his fortune.

F

Already, in 1596, the King walking with him one day had opened his heart and told him what were his hopes of ideal happiness and glory. One was that he should get rid of his wife Marguerite and find another woman of suitable rank, of a gentle and pleasant disposition, who would love him, and whom he could love, and who would bear him children, in time for him to watch them growing up, and to instruct them as he thought fit, that they might become gallant and accomplished princes. Sully guessed that the King intended to marry Gabrielle.

In the meantime the negotiations for the dissolution of Henry's marriage continued. After many delays and obstacles Rome was ready to grant a divorce and to declare the marriage between Henry and Marguerite de Valois null and void. Henry was soon to be free, and Gabrielle, Duchesse de Beaufort, saw the crown of France within her reach. Although negotiations for a marriage between Henry and a foreign princess were being carried on, everything in the attitude of the King seemed to point to his decision to raise the Duchesse de Beaufort, the mother of his children, to the throne, in spite of public opinion and the advice of Sully.

Sully was working against it. Henry must not marry the Duchesse de Beaufort.

One day the powerful minister was discussing with his royal master, the qualities which the lady chosen to occupy the throne of France should possess.

" She must be a woman," replied Henry, " pleasant in appearance and character; for, above all, I wish to avoid that worst sort of wife, an ugly, ill-tempered, domineering wife." In short she must be beautiful in person, virtuous in conduct, amiable in disposition,

MARGUERITE OF FRANCE.
First Wife of Henri IV.

To face page 66.

clever, likely to be the mother of many children, of noble extraction and possessed of large estates. " But I fear," added the King, " that this desirable woman is either dead or not yet born."

However, he consulted the list of eligible princesses throughout Europe. Each was subjected to a critical examination and finally rejected ; not one escaped an ironical remark, not one was found who had not some scandal attached to her name. Sully, endeavouring to hide his disquietude, playfully proposed that Henry should repeat the Biblical experiment of bringing all the married and unmarried women of France together for his inspection, with the hope that he, like Ahasuerus, might find an Esther among them. The King took the joke in good part, but became impatient when he found that Sully would persist in ignoring the drift of his remarks. At last he broke out. " I can see why you go on like that, pretending not to understand me ; you want to force me to name the woman who is in my thoughts, and so I will. You are aware that my mistress is the only woman I know who fulfils the conditions I have enumerated. Not that I have decided to marry her ; but I should like to have your opinion on the matter in case I made up my mind to do so."

Sully seized the opportunity given him to represent to the King the disgrace that he would incur by so doing, and the shame he would himself feel about it later on ; how impossible it would be, he added, to prevent the endless intrigues concerning the succession which must inevitably arise from the irregularity connected with the birth of his children. Having expatiated on this matter, he advised the King to think well over all that he had said to him.

The King agreed that it was the best thing he could do, for the present. "You have said enough about it," he continued, "for this time, and I will not repeat any of your words to my mistress, as I do not wish to bring you into disfavour with her. She likes and esteems you, although she has a secret grudge against you, being aware that you are not a partisan of her or her children's cause. You put the State and my honour, as I have often heard her say, before my personal happiness."

Gabrielle, as has been pointed out, was doomed not to profit by Henry's freedom. Fate, at one with the wishes of her enemies in this, had decided on her death. Whether her death was the result of natural causes, or whether it was due to poison, as many historians are inclined to think, cannot be stated with any certainty. On the basis of the latest research, Gabrielle seems to have died a natural death. But it was a tragic end nevertheless, perhaps even more tragic because so natural and yet so sudden. Henry had had no foreboding of this disastrous termination of his doubts and difficulties. During the last days of her life, he was more in love than ever with Gabrielle, and she had never been nearer to the crown, which was destined only to adorn her tomb. She was expecting her fourth child. Henry wrote reassuring letters to her, and revived love and hope smiled gaily upon her. And suddenly from the tranquil blue of the sky the bolt fell. Henry's last letter to Gabrielle is dated October 29, 1598.

"I arrived here at four o'clock, after a good day's sport, and am now in my lodge, where the weather is splendid ; my children came to see me, or rather were brought to me. My girl is growing

strong and pretty, but I think the boy will be handsomer than
his elder brother. You implored me, dearest love, to carry as
much love away with me as I left behind with you. How happy
your words made me! for I have carried away such a load of
love that I feared to have left you without any. I am now going
to entertain Morpheus, but if he lets me dream of anybody but
you, I will have nothing more to do with him. Good-night, my
dear mistress, a thousand kisses on your beautiful eyes!"

No one had the slightest doubt as to his intention, as
soon as the divorce had been pronounced. The Pope
was in a difficult position. He was ready to annul
Henry's union with Marguerite, but he wanted to prevent the King of France from marrying the Duchesse
de Beaufort. Henry had the example of the King of
England before his eyes, and the Pope asked himself if
it were better to authorise an inexpedient union, or to run
the risk of depriving the Church of twenty-five million
faithful supporters? Clement VIII ordered a fast, and
kneeling beneath the crucifix implored the help and
guidance of God. Suddenly, after a long and painful
interval of meditation and prayer he rose, his eyes
streaming, his face alight with fervour, and dismissed
his followers with the prophetic words: "God has
intervened." A few days later, a messenger reached
Rome bearing the tidings of the death of the Duchesse
de Beaufort.

It was towards the end of Lent; the King and Gabrielle went together to Fontainebleau. As Easter was
drawing near they were obliged to separate, for it would
have caused too great a scandal had the King kept her
beside him during the holy season that was now approaching. At Henry's desire, Gabrielle consented to
keep her Easter in Paris, while he remained in the

country. It was not without many tears and much
distress of heart that the two agreed together on this
step. To soften the pangs of separation Henry went
some way with his mistress on her journey. Some evil
presentiment that this parting was their last made them
cling to each other, and at every fresh step of the
way they repeated their adieux with ever increasing
lamentation, till at last they reached Melun, whence
Gabrielle was to be taken by boat down the Seine.
Here there was a final heartbreaking farewell, and then
with a violent effort the two weeping ones tore themselves apart. La Varenne accompanied the Duchesse,
who, without passing through Paris, descended at
the hotel, belonging to the Italian Zamet, near the
Bastille.

Gabrielle alighted weak, tired, and tearful, sorrow-
fully conscious of the absence of all companionship and
protection ; her aunt and the King's sister both away,
and the Princesse d'Orange keeping her Easter at Rosny,
with Sully. Alone in the centre of a noisy city, of a
populace that was brooding angrily over some remonstrances of Parliament, and the violent discussion that
had arisen upon the execution of two fanatical monks,
who had tried to assassinate the King.

Gabrielle only received two visits, one from Sully,
who bore himself with his usual cold politeness. She did
her best to ingratiate herself with him, with smiles and
with assurances of friendship, which she begged him to
return. Sully received her advances with enforced
civility. The next visitor was the gay, artful, malicious
Princesse de Conti, who, having none of Sully's scruples,
was affable in the extreme, and charmed and soothed
the invalid with her merry laugh, her lively glances and

amusing chatter. This lady was quick to scent coming events, and possibly she had caught sight, somewhere, of certain crimson royal and nuptial robes.

Gabrielle confessed on Wednesday, April 8, in preparation for the following day's communion. On the Thursday she was taken in her litter to a chapel close at hand known as that of little Saint-Antoine, where a side-chapel had been set apart for her that she might not be annoyed by the crowd. Mademoiselle de Guise, the authoress of *Les Amours du Grand Alcandre*, relates that she was with her, and during the service Gabrielle showed her letters from Rome, stating that what she desired, the dissolution of Henry's union with Marguerite de Valois, and her own marriage to the King, would shortly be accomplished, and also two letters from the King. These were full of passionate expressions of devotion, and begging her to despatch Forget, the Secretary of State, the very next day to entreat the Pope to delay no further in giving his consent to that which, however, under any circumstances, he was resolved to do. As soon as the service was over she told Mademoiselle de Guise that she was going back to bed. She then entered her litter, and Mademoiselle de Guise followed in her carriage. Already during the ceremony the Duchesse de Beaufort had been overtaken by a fit of giddiness, which made her return home sooner than she intended. On alighting she walked about the garden, thinking the air would do her good, and according to some sucking a lemon, according to others eating a salad. Before she had taken many turns, however, she was taken so sick and giddy, that she fell as if in a swoon. They carried her to bed, where for a while she lay unconscious. When

Mademoiselle de Guise arrived she had somewhat recovered and was allowing herself to be undressed. Further fainting fits succeeded, each worse than the one before, during which her whole body was convulsed, and she kept putting her hand to her burning forehead. When coming to from one of these attacks, her sole cry was to be removed from her present lodging and to be carried to the house of Madame de Sourdis, her aunt, for she seemed to have a horror of remaining where she was. Her request was carried out, but only La Varenne accompanied her; the others, Zamet and Mademoiselle de Guise had remained behind. Her aunt, too, was absent. Gabrielle, however, thought herself safe under the roof of Madame de Sourdis. She wished perhaps to be carried from there to the Louvre, that she might die there where she was not to be allowed to live. She was so near the throne, but she was to die on the first step leading to it.

Gabrielle had hardly been placed on the bed in her aunt's house before the convulsions returned, and they now became so frequent that despite every effort made to relieve her, the lucid intervals came rarely and lasted but a few minutes. During one of these she expressed a wish to write to the King, and begged a gentleman, named Puypeyroux, to carry her letter to the King, and to let the latter know what had happened, and also to beseech him to give orders that she should be put in a boat and so carried to join him at Fontainebleau. She hoped, writes one who describes this scene, that the King, on hearing this, would come at once and marry her before she died, for the sake of her children. The messenger departed, and Gabrielle, to calm her impatience, tried to read one of the King's letters. But she was seized with another violent fit, the last and worst, from which she never recovered.

La Varenne, feeling the whole weight of the responsibility which rested on his shoulders, also sent messages to the King by Puypeyroux. He sent word that the doctors despaired of her life, as, owing to her condition, they were afraid to use the powerful remedies required in her case. As soon as Puypeyroux had seen the King, the latter ordered him back, and told him to wait for him at the ferry near the Tuileries, where he intended crossing, but was not to be seen. Henry then mounted his horse, and rode at such a pace that he soon overtook Puypeyroux, whom he reproached for his dilatoriness. Spurring on his way, he reached Villejuif, and here, or at Villeneuve-Saint-Georges, he found La Varenne's second letter. Gabrielle was dead, and all was over. Stunned, heartbroken, and in a fever of despair, he continued his journey, perhaps in a wild hope that the fatal tidings were premature. But other messengers met him confirming the news, and urging him to turn back. Finally a carriage was secured, and the King placed in it and driven back to Fontainebleau, where everything spoke to him of the one who had been there so lately with him to share his pleasures.

It was on Saturday, April 10, at about seven o'clock in the morning, that Gabrielle breathed her last in the arms of La Varenne. Thus without a relation or friend near her, without a priest or any consolation, she who was to be Queen of France died. Her suffering seems to have been so intense that even her face was disfigured by it; " her mouth was so drawn aside that it was hideous to behold," writes L'Estoille.

Madame de Sourdis, who arrived too late to be with

her when she died, covered her with a white satin cloak, and she lay in state on a bed of crimson and gold. But whilst Henry was mourning for his dead mistress, whom he seemed to have loved with a genuine love, Sully triumphed. A messenger despatched by La Varenne had informed the minister of the great event. Sully rushed to his wife, who was already in bed, and, kissing her, said : " My child, now you will no longer have to attend the levees of the Duchesse. She is gone. And now she is dead, may God grant her long life."

On Monday, April 12, the body of the Duchesse de Beaufort, with that of the dead child that had been taken from her after death, were buried in the Church of Saint-Germain l'Auxerrois, according to one authority; while according to another it was carried to Saint-Denis, where a service was held, and then on to Maubuisson, where the interment took place.

Thus died Gabrielle d'Estrées, Duchesse de Beaufort. The King of France put on black for the first week, and violet for three months, in sign of mourning. The Court had to follow the example of the King. But the time of kings is precious; they cannot afford to mourn long after those whom they love. Although Henry had written to his sister in reply to her expressions of condolence that " the root of his love was dead, and would never again bring forth blossoms," he seems to have consoled himself very soon. He married Marie de Medicis, niece of the Pope Clement VIII, soon afterwards, and presented her with the jewels that had belonged to Gabrielle.

Was the King in love with his newly-wedded wife ? In any case the Pope, France and the European courts had imposed her upon him. But the time of mourning was hardly over when the amorous Henry, before marrying Marie de Medicis, placed his heart at the feet of a new mistress, Henriette d'Entragues, to whom, too, as a means of breaking her stern resistance, he made a promise of marriage.

CHAPTER IV

Henriette d'Entragues

AFTER the death of Gabrielle, who was quickly forgotten—kings have not time to mourn long —Henry left Fontainebleau, where there were too many memories to keep his loneliness company. Having made up his mind to marry, in which resolution he was encouraged by all the wisest men about the Court and by the persuasions of his Parliament, and being in no doubt as to his wife's consent and almost as sure of the Pope's, there was nothing left to be done but to await the issue of such negotiations for an alliance as were being carried on in different quarters. During this period of waiting and leisure, when he was preparing to say farewell to the bachelor life which he had continued to lead, even with a wife by his side—but then he and the queen were hardly to be called married—the King thought he might as well amuse himself, and accompany the obsequies of his celibacy with a few gay rites.

Towards the close of the summer, the King returned to Paris, where those who were held in credit at Court simply because they pandered to their sovereign's licentious tastes, and knew how to tell him amusing tales, and to appear surprised and delighted at all he said and did, were so full of the beauty and cleverness and merry wit of Mademoiselle d'Entragues that the King would not be satisfied until he had seen her.   Having seen her once, he desired to see her again, and having seen her more than once he fell in love with her.   The report of this fresh love affair caused great distress to Sully, especially as he was told that the lady knew how to make herself so agreeable that the King found her good company.

Henriette d'Entragues would seem to have been pre-destined for the rôle she played.   The daughter of a king's mistress, she became herself a king's mistress. Her mother was Marie Touchet, the mistress of Charles IX ; her father François de Balzac, Seigneur d'Entragues, a Counciller of State, Governor of Orléans, and Lieu-tenant-General of Orléannais.   It was in 1578 that he, a former lover of Marie Touchet, succeeded Charles IX as her husband, his first wife Jacqueline de Rohan having died.   Their daughter Henriette was born in 1579.   Of Marie's two children by the King, Charles, known as the Bastard of Valois, alone survived ; he became finally Comte de Poitiers and Duc d'Angoulême ; a proud, ambitious and perfidious prince, destined to act the part of a conspirator.   Henriette was a woman of ardent tem-perament, bold, and keen of tongue ; she was ready with sallies and answers to put all the doctors to silence.   She did not care for history ; she was too acute and too dis-putatious.   Theology was what she liked ; she revelled in argument and in the subtle distinctions of the Fathers.   Moreover this dangerous creature was tall and lithe, a complete contrast to the late mistress with her simple style of beauty and somewhat ample figure.   Of Henriette's beauty there may be two opinions, but she was undoubtedly pretty and extremely lively.

The King, who only thought of his amusement, found himself captivated.   Her sharp wit and merry mischievous tongue spared nobody, not even the King himself, and the latter, sick and blasé at heart, revived under her sallies, and, content to laugh at first, ended by falling in love. Henriette had the soul of a real courtesan ; she was possessed of that voluptuous gaiety which exercised a strong fascination upon the elderly King, who laid his soul bare in his letters to his new mistress.

" My dearest love " (wrote Henry), " La Varenne and the foot-man arrived together. You tell me that if I love you, I must allow nothing to prevent our happiness. I think I gave sufficient proof of the strength of my love by the proposals I made, so that as regards those belonging to you, you need fear no difficulties. I shall not swerve from what I said in your presence and I shall not go beyond it. . . . I shall be delighted to see Monsieur d'Entragues, and shall not leave him in peace until our affair is settled one way or the other ? A man from Normandy has been here, who tells me that there will shortly be a terrible commotion, caused by your father, mother, or brother, set afoot in Paris ; that you and I must expect to see everything broken off, but that to-morrow he will tell me how to prevent it. Good-night, dear heart, I send you a million kisses."

A million kisses ; the elderly King of France is in love just like a schoolboy or a clerk. It seems, however, that if Henriette was destined by nature for the part she was going to play, her father and her family had done their best to put her up to it.

M. d'Entragues sold his daughter to the King for one hundred thousand crowns.

Notwithstanding the heavy expenses entailed by the renewal of the Swiss Alliance this year, the King insisted on a hundred thousand crowns being raised for him to give to Henriette But this was not all, for the King had to pay dearly for Henriette's kisses. Her father and mother kept such a close watch over her that, as she told her royal lover, it was not her will, but opportunity, which failed her to give him all he asked for in return. It appears that His Majesty had made Henriette a promise of marriage by word of mouth in the presence of her parents, but they insisted upon one in writing. Henriette endeavoured to persuade them that one was as good as the other with a king who could summon an army of artillery to carry out anything to which he had pledged his word; but, as she added to the King, since they stood out for a written document, if he loved her as much as he said, he ought not to make any difficulties about acceding to their wishes. And so well did she know how to cajole the King, and to make partisans of the courtiers about him, who encouraged him in his debaucheries, that at last he gave his consent, and put his signature to the following written agreement :——

" We, Henry IV, by the Grace of God, King of France and Navarre, do herewith promise and swear before God, on our faith and word as a King, to François de Balzac, Knight of our order, that in the case of his daughter, damoiselle Henriette-Catherine de Balzac, becoming enceinte in the course of six months from the first day of this present one, and giving birth to a son, we will then and on the instant take her to wife as our legitimate spouse, and the marriage shall be publicly solemnised by our Holy Church, with all customary pomp and ceremony. And to this said promise we promise to swear as above, to ratify the same afresh by our seals, immediately upon the receipt from our Holy Father the Pope of the dissolution of the marriage between ourselves and dame Marguerite de France, with the permission to us to remarry as we see fit. In witness whereof we hereto subjoin our signature. At the Bois de Malesherbes, this first day of October, 1599.

" HENRY."

But Sully had to be informed of this transaction,

and somewhat reluctantly the aged royal lover, blushing like a schoolboy, acquainted the old grumbler Sully of what had happened.

Being at Fontainebleau one day, Henry sent for Sully and, taking him by the hand, led him apart into one of the galleries. He then put the document into his hand, and turned away, either not to see his minister turn red or to hide his own blushes. Sully read it through deliberately, and then, the King asking him what he thought about it, Sully, with his usual prudence, said he should like time for consideration. This irritated the King, who insisted upon an answer at once. Sully, thus brought to bay, begged the King to promise him that he would not be angry nor owe him a grudge, whatever he said or did. The King having satisfied him on this point, Sully, not without considerable courage, in spite of the assurance just made him, tore the document in half. " As you wish to know my opinion of such a promise as this, Sire, there you have it." " *Morbleu!* " exclaimed the King, " I think you must be out of your mind ! " " You are right, Sire, I am a weak fool, and would willingly know myself even more of a fool if I might be the only one in France."

Sully went on to remind the King of what the latter himself used to say about this man and his daughter, when Madame la Duchesse (Gabrielle d'Estrées) was alive, and how he had once given him orders to clear Paris of *all this baggage*. Such weakness on the part of the King would afford the malicious food for laughter. He further pointed out that Henry would lose benefits for which he hoped by the dissolution of his marriage, the chief of which was to make a good alliance and have an heir ; the queen, Marguerite, would certainly not consent to resign

her title to a daughter of the Entragues family, nor was
it likely that the Pope would sanction such a step. The
King, feeling the force of his minister's arguments, and
yet unwilling to give in, left the gallery and retired to his
study, where he called for pen and ink, and, as Sully believed, there and then wrote out a fresh promise of marriage. Presently he came out, mounted his horse without
speaking a word to his faithful adviser, who was standing
by, and went off to Malesherbes to hunt, staying away
nearly two whole days.

It appears, according to l'Estoille, that about this time
Mademoiselle d'Entragues ceased to oppose any obstacles
to her union with the King. The matter cost Henry
dear. Presents also ran away with money, and Henry,
having on one occasion purchased a ring for Henriette,
asked to look at it again before paying for it, as he had,
he said, a short time previously given fifty thousand
crowns for one that was not worth half that sum. Sully
laughed up his sleeve at the way in which the King so
easily fell into the trap laid for him, at the pretended
honesty and inflexibility of the d'Entragues family, who
on the arrival of the King's first negotiator had with
assumed virtue bidden him leave the house that he had
come to dishonour, and had made a point of carrying
Henriette away out of the King's sight, and all this to end
in capitulating as soon as the gold bags reached them.

The climax took place in October, 1599. Henriette
probably did not wish the King's ardour to grow cold
under too severe treatment. By the beginning of
November, however, of this year, the act for annulling the
King's marriage with Marguerite de Valois had been drawn
up and signed, and the King then appointed Sully and
three others to treat with Joannini, the Duke of Tuscany's

G

envoy, concerning his marriage with Marie de Medicis. The alliance was concluded, and the contract signed by the end of the year 1599. When Sully entered his master's presence one day on business, the latter asked him what he had been doing. " We have been marrying you, Sire," he replied. Whereupon the King sat lost in thought, biting his nails and scratching his head, for a full quarter of an hour ; then, all of a sudden, striking his hands together, he exclaimed : " Well, if God orders it thus, so let it be ; there is no help for it ; since you say that it is necessary for the sake of my kingdom and my subjects, why marry I must. But I confess I am full of apprehension at the bare idea, remembering all the unpleasantness I went through with my first marriage, and besides that, I dread being allied to some woman of ill-temper who will drag me into domestic quarrels, which you, who know me, can well understand are more terrible to me than any political or military affairs, however grave their consequences may be." Reasons of State had forced Henry to this marriage ; but his heart now belonged to Henriette. The courtesan had captivated the elderly royal debauchee. Thus the year 1600 found the King a prey to a thousand conflicting feelings. The promise of marriage he had given to Henriette's parents was suspended over his head like a sword of Damocles. Honour and ambition were urging him to go and punish the Duke of Savoy for his breach of faith. Necessity was driving him into a distasteful marriage. He had to keep Sully in a good temper, to marry Marie, and to appease Henriette. By some means or other her parents had to be made to give up the written promise of marriage, which was a doubly dangerous document just now, since the conditions on Henriette's side had been fulfilled, and she was expecting a child. Henry, being a true Gascon, managed with his usual intrepidity and suppleness to get over his difficulties with as little inconvenience as possible. He dried the eyes of his mistress with the gift of the marquisate of Verneuil, and the added promise that if he could not escape from his political marriage, he would give her to the Duc de Nevers, who was a prince of the blood. As regards taking a wife, the dowry having been paid into his exchequer, he resigned himself to the inevitable, and sent gallant messages by Frontenac to the future Queen. On the 19th October, he received word that his marriage had been celebrated in Florence, and he sent orders to the different towns to make preparation for the reception of the Queen. The very same day, certain papers were handed over to a special messenger sent by the King to Rome, whereby the Tuscan marriage was rendered invalid, as it proved that the King could not, according to Canon law, ally himself with the Florentine, he being already engaged to the French lady. All this was no doubt done with the object of getting hold of the promise of marriage. He seems to have fathomed the ambition of his mistress, and this knowledge had somewhat sobered him.

On the 21st April 1600, we find him becoming imperative in his demands for its return, both to daughter and father. He is no longer the lover, but the King, who commands and threatens. Nevertheless, it was not until 1604, and then only by the payment of a ransom, that he recovered the disastrous document.

" Mademoiselle," he wrote from Fontainebleau on April 21, 1600, " the love, the benefits which I have bestowed on you would have moved the most unfeeling heart in the world, unless accompanied by so evil a disposition as yours. I will not reproach you further, although I could and ought to do so, as you know. I pray you to return me the promise you have by you, and not to oblige me to resort to other means in order to obtain it. Also send me back the ring which I gave you the other day. This is all I have to say in this letter, to which I should like a reply to-night.

"HENRY."

With this letter was also one dispatched to the father :—

" Monsieur d'Entragues, I am sending this messenger in order that he may bring back the promise which was delivered to you at Malesherbes. I beg you not to fail in sending it me, and if you prefer to bring it me yourself, I will let you know the reasons for this request of mine, which are of a domestic nature, and have nothing to do with the State ; these will convince you that I am right, and that you have been deceived, and that my natural disposition is rather inclined to over-kindness than the reverse. Assured that you will give obedience to my order, I will end with assurance of my good will towards you.

"HENRY."

The father did not return the document. But in July of this year an unexpected catastrophe put an end to all Henriette's ambitious hopes, and delivered her kingly lover from his worst anxiety. The promise of marriage was made on condition of the birth of the child. But a flash of lightning, entering her room and passing under the bed, so alarmed her, that she was prematurely confined and gave birth to a dead child. . . . She lay ill for a long time after this, and in spite of the attentions and promises of the King, who hastened to her bedside, she knew that now all was over. From this moment her face and character changed, and the desire for revenge entered her heart. Still clinging as a last hope to Henry's repeated assurances, which he continued unblushingly to reiterate up to the last moment before his marriage, she kept the King for a while in leash, going first to Lyon and then to Chambéry.   At Lyon, accustomed to triumphal entries, she met with the same reception as had been accorded to Diane de Poitiers.   The King, with the gallantry that was natural to him, and more anxious to flatter her than his army, sent her as a present the banners that had been captured at Charbonnières.   These trophies were at her desire carried with great ceremony to the Church of St. Just, for she had the sense and good taste to understand that flags of victory are more fitted to be near the altar than the boudoir.

The arrival of Marie de Medicis convinced Henriette that her hopes of sharing the throne of France with her royal lover were now gone.   She now wished to retain at least the place of titular mistress.

She ceased to threaten, she prayed and begged, and endeavoured to move the King by her grief and attitude of despair.   She was a consummate actress, and could adapt herself to every part which circumstances compelled her to play.

" Sire " (she wrote), " I am suffering the unhappiness which I always feared from our connexion.   I confess, however, that it was of myself that I was afraid, knowing how humble my position was in comparison with yours, and dreading from the beginning that the change would come which would precipitate me from the heaven to which you raised me to the earth where you found me.   My happiness depended on you, however, rather than on fate, since it has pleased you to pay with my sorrow for the gratification of your people's desire that you should marry.   Sorrow, not so much that you are bound to obey the wishes of your subjects as that your wedding festivities will be my funeral, that I shall be banished from your royal presence, and your heart, and subjected to the contemptuous glances of those who have seen

me in the enjoyment of your good graces ; rather therefore than
live and be treated with contumely in public, I prefer to suffer
in the freedom of solitude.   The generosity and courage that you
have inspired in me will not prevent me from humbling myself.
I speak in sighs to you, my King, my lover, my all.   You will
understand all the complaints that I do not utter, you will know
all my thoughts, for my soul is not hid from you.   There will
still remain to me in my exile the glorious remembrance of having
been loved by the greatest monarch upon earth, who was willing
to stoop and give the title of mistress to his servant and subject.
If kings preserve the memory of those they have loved, remember
the demoiselle who belonged to you, and who trusted in your
faith."

Henriette acted with discretion.   Had she remained
at Court she would have been degraded, possibly driven
away.   She went of her own accord, while the King possibly still cared for her and was capable of some regret
at her departure.   Not able to revenge herself on the
King for the forlorn position in which she was left, she
looked about for a victim, and, as we shall see, made choice
of Bellegarde.   And now Henry was free, and drew a sigh
of relief.   He was free to make love to his affianced
wife, Marie de Medicis.   But it was not in the character
of this King to remain faithful.   He soon began to write
love letters to his former mistress, and Henriette once
more appears upon the stage.

The Marquise de Verneuil, having found the Duchesse
de Nemours willing to undertake the delicate task of
introducing her, was presented to the Queen.   She
found that they were on an equal footing as regards the
prospect of motherhood, and thereupon began to chafe
at the difference of their position in public.   Henriette,
being a clever woman, saw the necessity of bringing her
wits into play, and she knew what she was about when

she picked out Léonora Galligai as her confidante. The
latter afterwards married Concini, Maréchal d'Ancre,
but at that time she was only a favourite among the
Queen's attendants. Thus the King hoped at last to have
found peace and tranquillity in this double *ménage*.

Henry was so sure of peace that, tired of the continual
moving from place to place caused by his divided affections, he took a step which may serve not only as a witness
to the unscrupulous manners of that time, but to the
entire subjection of every consideration to the King's
pleasure. He brought Henriette to Court and lodged
her at the Louvre, side by side, or more correctly, door to
door, with the Queen. The two women, the queen and
the mistress, were enceintes, and expecting their confinement within a month of each other. The King was
equally solicitous as to the welfare of both. On October
6, he wrote to his mistress—

" Dear heart,—My wife is going on well, and my son, God be
praised, is also flourishing. I am quite happy, except for the
grief of being away from you, which is, however, soothed by the
hope of being soon with you again. A million kisses. M.
d'Entragues has seen my son, and thinks him a fine child."

This promiscuous arrangement went on happily during
the remainder of the year 1601. Henriette had helped
forward the marriage between Léonora Galligai and Concini, and in return the queen's confidante had obtained
many unexpected favours for her. The birth of the
royal Prince and that of Henriette's child were celebrated together in all good friendship. Among other
festivities in honour of these events, the Queen arranged
a ballet, which was carried out under her orders by fifteen
of the most beautiful women of the Court. The re-

joicings were disturbed by an intrigue, of which the Marquise de Verneuil would have been the victim if her magnificent presence of mind had not come to the rescue.

Juliette-Hippolyte d'Estrées, Duchesse de Villars, had, even during her sister Gabrielle's lifetime, been favoured for a short interval with the King's attention. The latter being soon tired of her, her youth and her hair being her chief attractions, she had consoled herself by taking the Prince de Joinville for her lover. The neglected Queen and the discarded mistress saw their opportunity, and joined hands. Joinville gave up the letters written to him by the Marquise de Verneuil. The Duchess kindly undertook to place them where the King might see them. The latter was furious, and vowed never to set eyes on his faithful mistress again. He sent the Comte de Lude to her, laden with angry messages. Henriette was not a woman to allow herself to be taken by surprise. She would not even condescend to protest her innocence, but sent away the ambassador, who was taken aback by her calm behaviour. She declared that the letters had been forged by those interested in her downfall; and went so far as to accuse a secretary of the Duc de Guise, who was clever at copying handwriting, of the deed. Joinville, Bellegarde, in short the whole house of Guise, and the Marquise, acted their parts so well that they succeeded in convincing the King of the truth of their assurances. The end of the affair was not quite such as the Queen had hoped. The Duchesse de Villars was disgraced and expelled from Court; the Queen snubbed; Joinville went off to Holland or Hungary; and as someone had to be punished, the secretary was imprisoned. As to the Marquise, she condescended to forgive the King, who compensated her with a gift of six thousand pounds, which Sully, cursing and swearing, was forced to pay out.

And thus, side by side, wife and mistress shared the affections of royal husband and lover.

On November 22, 1602, Marie de Medicis gave birth to Elizabeth of France (who was married in 1615 to Philip IV, King of Spain). Two months later, on the 21st January, 1603, the Marquise de Verneuil gave birth to Gabrielle-Angélique, (who was married on the 12th December, 1622, to Bernard de Nogaret, Duc d'Épernon).

But if Henry had hoped to find complete peace, he soon found that he had been mistaken. He had reckoned without the temperament of Henriette and the jealousy of women. Maternity only rendered the Queen more jealous and susceptible to neglect. Fresh quarrels broke out every week which threatened at times to end in blows, and Henry was known to have been forced to take to flight to escape from the violence of his better half. Once, it is said, she lifted her arm to strike him, when Sully intervened, and knocked it down in none too gentle a manner. The King, driven to desperation, had serious thoughts of sending her back to Florence.

" As for his mistress, Henry's passion for Mademoiselle d'Entragues," writes Sully, " was one of those unhappy diseases of the mind which, like a slow poison, preyed upon the principles of life ; for the heart, attacked in its most sensitive part, feels, indeed, the whole force of its misfortune, but, by a cruel fatality, has neither the power nor the inclination to be freed from it."

Henry had to suffer the insolence and caprices, the inequalities of temper of a proud and ambitious woman.

Having discovered what power she possessed over the King—and Henriette was clever enough to find it out—she employed this power to torment him. One of her artifices consisted in talking continually to the King of her scruples : she regretted the facility with which she had yielded to his desires. But Henry knew that these scruples never troubled her with persons of inferior rank. This led to new quarrels. To complete his misfortune, his love for Henriette became a cause of unpleasant scenes between him and the Queen.

Marie de Medicis was not compliant by nature ; she was also given to jealousy, and being unable to make her rival feel her full hatred, she revenged herself upon her royal husband. Thus the unhappy King was exposed to the fury of two women, who, though rivals, seemed to work in harmony in tormenting the King. The Queen had learned that her husband had given a promise of marriage to Mademoiselle d'Entragues, and she tormented the King until at last he promised her to get the paper back from his mistress. Although he knew quite well that the promise was not in the least binding, to oblige the Queen he asked Henriette to restore the paper to him. The haughty mistress grew angry, and not only did she refuse to hand the paper over to her royal lover, but she insolently told him that it was quite impossible for her to live with him any longer. As he grew older, he grew jealous and suspicious, and she would only too gladly break off all connexion. Her sole reward for her sacrifices had been public hatred. A violent scene ensued and the King was on the point of striking the insolent Henriette. He quitted her abruptly, swearing that he would force her to restore the document. But the fumes of his wrath soon evaporated, and Henry

thought of the good qualities of his mistress, when not in
a capricious humour. He recalled the charm of her conversation, her sprightly wit, her poignant repartees, so
full of delicacy and spirit. He compared her temper with
that of the Queen, so different; and the contrast made
him still more sensible to the charms of the mistress. " I
find nothing of all this at home," he said to Sully. " I
receive neither companionship, amusement, nor pleasure
from my wife. Her conversation is very dull, and her
temper harsh; neither does she accommodate herself
to my humour, nor share my cares.   When I enter her
apartment and offer to approach her with tenderness,
or begin to talk familiarly with her, she receives me with
so cold and forbidding an air that I soon leave her in
disgust, and am compelled to seek consolation elsewhere."
And this consolation he went to seek in the company of
Henriette.

And Henriette was an accomplished courtesan, and
knew how to preserve her hold over the King. She knew
the right moment to retire on some pretence of devotion
or assumed scruple of honour, the moment when to throw
cold water on the King's ardour, and how to hold him in
abeyance. Henry was not altogether pleased at these
restrictions; he preferred *tout ou rien*.

Poor Henry ! If he had complaints to make against his
mistress, he had nothing to boast about as regards his
wife. The Queen found it insupportable that Madame
de Verneuil should speak disrespectfully of her, and that
this woman should talk about her children as if she wished
to compare them with hers, and that the King made no
attempt to punish her, although it was known that she
was in correspondence with her father and brother on
matters contrary to the King's interests,

Sully used his best endeavours, however, to bring about a reconciliation between the King, his master, and the Queen. And although he knew that he ran great risks in acting this part, he not only implored the King to banish his mistress, but also went to the Queen and tried to pacify her.

Henry assured his faithful friend and capable minister that he was quite ready to make so great a sacrifice, if he only knew that his wife would alter her conduct. But alas ! he feared the Queen would continue to torment him, even after his sacrifice. Sully was commissioned by the King to persuade the Queen to be more submissive to her royal husband. Without letting the Queen know that he was acting by order of his royal master, Sully did so. Marie de Medicis tried her best to follow Sully's instructions, but her natural disposition got the upper hand. Henry, tossed from one woman to the other, lost health and sleep, but seemed unable to make up his mind from which finally to separate.

It was at this time that the conspiracy, at the head of which were d'Entragues and the Comte d'Auvergne, the father and half-brother of the Marquise de Verneuil, was discovered. Father, brother and sister were arrested, the two Counts were condemned to lose their heads, and the Marquise to be shut up during the rest of her life in a cloister. The only advantage Henry obtained through this arrest was to have that famous document containing his promise of marriage restored, for Henry had not the heart after all to punish his mistress. He even extended his leniency to the other two criminals. Their sentence was commuted into that of confinement and banishment.

And thus the result of this proceeding was that the promise of marriage, the subject of so much intrigue and anxiety, was at last given back to the King on July 6, 1604. A written acknowledgment of its receipt was duly drawn up and signed by M. d'Entragues to prevent all future question as to its identity, or any fraudulent action in connexion with it.

The Comte d'Auvergne and the Marquise met the storm with unshaken intrepidity. The brother was indifferent and boastful, the sister insolent and ironical. His wife being allowed to visit the Comte, and asking what he wanted, his only reply was that if she would see that he was supplied with good cheese and mustard, she need not trouble herself about anything else. The Marquise declared that death had no terrors for her; that, on the contrary, she wished for it. " If the King takes my life, they will say, at least, that he killed his wife. I was Queen before the Italian woman. For the rest, I have only three requests to make to the King, a pardon for my father, a cord for my brother, and justice for myself."

Sentence was passed on the 1st February, 1605. M. d'Entragues and the Comte d'Auvergne were condemned to be beheaded; the Marquise was to be kept under strict surveillance at the Monastery of Beaumont-les-Tours. Henry, however, was still in love with her; he waited with impatience to grant her his pardon. In the renewed intercourse between them, it was he who seemed more like the suppliant and she the judge. He sought distraction in the arms of other women, but it was Henriette for whom he longed, whom he saw and embraced, in these, caring for them only in so far as they resembled her; and these inferior copies only made him the more anxious to regain the original. On the day when the verdict was made known, the Marquise and her mother went and threw themselves at the feet of the King,

who raised them, and mingled his tears with theirs.
Dinner was no sooner over than a council was summoned,
and the sentence of death was commuted to life-long
imprisonment.   Shortly after this, d'Entragues was set
at liberty; the Comte d'Auvergne, however, remained a
prisoner in the Bastille for twelve years.   The Marquise
was allowed to retire to her estates at Verneuil.   Seven
months later, the King granted her letters declaring her
innocence.

Henriette's power over the King survived all intrigues,
all revolt, and the loss of any real love for her on the part
of the latter.   To her influence was due the degeneration
of his character.   Perhaps therein lay the secret of her
power.   She was as irresistible as is the working of a slow
poison.   Hers was the love that sought to revenge itself,
and it was as implacable as hatred.   She could not kill, but
she could debase.   Henry loved her with his senses; she
knew it, and she held the King her captive, and from
henceforth he remained under the spell of this ruinous
fascination.   The quarrels with his wife broke out
afresh, and Henry was at last reduced to begging Sully to
find some way out of these continual brawls.   Sully
exhausted his efforts in the endeavour to carry out his
master's orders.   The only reasonable ways, either to
separate from the Queen, to send away all her
favourites, or to banish Henriette, were remedies too
dangerous or too painful to recommend.

In 1606, as in the two previous years, Sully was continually being charged by the King to carry his reproaches,
his threats or his propositions to Henriette, who as regularly sent Sully away, the bearer of reciprocal reproaches
and menaces, and with either a refusal of all propositions
offered her, or with demands of such a nature that it seemed

a lesser evil to allow matters to remain as they were. And so things went on. The Queen grew more and more discontented and reproachful. Henriette became more and more sulky. The King, more and more perplexed, was forced in turn to conciliate, and to appease her anger by the grant of fresh favours to the Concini, whom he hated. Henriette, to annoy him, would ask to be allowed to marry, sometimes a man whom she would not name, but who required a hundred thousand crowns as dowry; sometimes the Prince de Joinville, who was continually stepping in between the King and his mistresses; sometimes Condé's brother, the Duc de Guise. To these requests the King's only answer was an angry expostulation. Henry knew well in his heart of hearts that his mistress was worthier of his contempt than his love. He treated her to both. He could not hold her in high esteem, but the more he despised her, the more he seemed to adore her. He gave her affectionate particulars of his children—

" Dear heart,—I cannot bear to let a day pass without recalling myself to your memory, I, who love you perhaps more than I ought. Not that I repent of this, for I wish to continue loving you more than ever, but on the other hand, I wish you to love me entirely and without exception."

On the 22nd May, 1608, while out hunting, a hare led him on as far as the rocks near Malesherbes. The place brought back a flood of recollections, the result of which was the following letter to Henriette, the only one in which there is a trace of any real feeling. He recalled the first days of their love :—

" I longed to have you in my arms as then. As you read my letter, and the memory of the past comes back to you, I am sure you will feel that nothing in the present is worth anything in comparison ; at least that is how I felt as I walked along the roads that I so often traversed in old days on my way to you. When I sleep I dream of you ; when I wake I think of you."

But at last Henriette's subterfuges and aggravating behaviour awakened the King to the fact that the game was not worth the candle, and he felt he should like a quieter, more submissive mistress, who would not always be thrusting herself between him and the Queen. The latter was beginning to cause him some apprehension by her assumed resignation and melancholy, although he had been at some trouble to bring her to this state of mute endurance. Now she was willing to listen without a murmur while he read her letters from the Marquise, begging to be allowed to see her children. She spoke of her without anger, or tears, or scorn, and would not listen patiently to any ill words about her. And now, when this triumph of conjugal diplomacy gave promise of a little quiet enjoyment, and of undisturbed infidelity, Henriette upset the King's hopes with her capricious behaviour, her reproaches, and her sudden fits of devotion.

The King's cure, however, was not to be completed till he had seen the beautiful Charlotte de Montmorency. One flash from her eyes destroyed for ever Henry's ignoble love for Henriette d'Entragues. She seemed to him a partner worthy to adorn, and to be the companion of, his victorious old age. Ravaillac's dagger, however, put an end to this fascinating dream, for which the King was, as usual, ready to sacrifice glory and France. The King broke with Madame de Verneuil, who now began to indulge herself like a Sardanapalus, or a Vitellius ; she thought of nothing but the table, of ragoûts, and grew an enormous size. She still, however, retained her mental powers. Few people went to visit her. Her children were taken away from her, her daughter being brought up with the princesses.[1] The separation between the King and his mistress was not, however, absolute. The verve, the irony, which animated her declining beauty, still had attraction for the King. He would suddenly recall some cutting epigram, which forced back upon him the remembrance of one whom he had suffered, with impunity, to wound him with her biting tongue. Stout and coarse as she had grown, she still had power to draw him to her, with her remains of beauty and her inexhaustible store of *bons mots*. Added to her mental attraction, there were living ties between them in the persons of the children; and at any rate, she was good as a *pis aller*.

Henry's love affairs had come to an end. The knife of the assassin, Ravaillac, had brought them to a close. Many, and among them Henriette, were accused of having armed the hand of the assassin. But Parliament had no proofs. None of the accused were declared free of guilt, yet no one was condemned. Henriette, in spite of this acquittal, still remained suspect.

The last days of her life were solely occupied in trying to find a husband, but her ambition filled her most determined suitors with alarm. After the Prince de Joinville, it was the Duc de Guise's turn to flee from this unlucky woman, on whose hand they thought to detect the traces of blood. Henriette had, in a moment of weakness, obtained from the latter a promise of marriage, and had hastened to have the betrothal made public. But the Duc preferred lying to marriage, and absolutely denied his signature, and the genuineness of the marriage contract. Henriette tried in vain to prove her case. In

[1] Cf. Tallemant des Reaux.

H

vain she brought forward the original contract, and showed it to various witnesses assembled at the house of the Comte de Soissons. No one dared own the justice of her cause, no one even dared pity her. Seeing that she had to fight her battle single-handed, she resigned herself to her fate ; she could no longer bite, so with her habitual subtlety, she crawled and fawned. She submitted without a word to the Queen's *veto*, the latter having now no need to dissimulate her hatred; and she retired from public life, to hide her anger, and possibly her remorse, in solitude and obscurity. Repentance took a long time to kill her, for she survived for another twenty-three years, and died on the 9th February, 1633, aged fifty-four.

CHAPTER V

A Mary Magdalene of the Eighteenth Century

Madame de Parabère and the Duc d'Orléans

THE eighteenth century is the century of women. They reigned, not as modern suffragettes are dreaming of reigning, by right and law, but by grace and charm and love. In France, above all, it was the century of love, love sought after for love's sake, ennobled and beautified by refinement, splendour and *esprit*. It was the century of gallant adventures and sensational love-affairs. Love was admired and adored, and numberless were the altars consecrated to her who emerged from the foam-crested waves. It was the century of Manon Lescaut and of Paul and Virginie. For fifty years France, under the Grand Monarch, Louis XIV, privately married to pious Madame de Maintenon, had had to take its pleasures sadly. But Louis Dieudonné was now dead. His grandson, Louis XV, a boy of five, sat on the throne of France, and Philippe, Duc d'Orléans, reigned during the minority of the King. The Regency, as this period was called, was, according to Michelet, a revelation and a revolution : in the glare of broad daylight it suddenly revealed a society that had been accustomed to wear a mask for fifty years. As if by magic, the roofs were torn off and everything exposed to the public gaze. No restraint; *les dessous* became *le dessus*. The Duc d'Orléans was the first to give the example of a joyous life, and his famous supper parties in the Palais Royal, with their gaiety and splendours, remind one of the banquets of the Caesars in Rome on the eve of her decadence. But this licentiousness was far from being as gross and vulgar as that which reigned at the courts of St. Petersburg, Vienna and Warsaw.[1] France under the Regency enjoyed her carnival, but it was a graceful carnival. The participators drank no gin and no *vodka*. They grew tipsy, but they were intoxicated with champagne and wines of Spain, intoxicated above all with love. The Duc d'Orléans took Henry IV as his model. He devoted his days to work, and the evenings to pleasure. He found time for politics and leisure for love. Like Henry IV the number of his mistresses was legion. Pretty actresses and noble Duchesses, married martyrs unhappy in wedlock, and mad virgins in search of adventures, vied with each other for the favours of His Royal Highness. Although not ugly, the Regent was certainly not good-looking, but a certain charm emanated from his person. He was amiable and kind-hearted. Never did he avail himself of the power due to his rank and position to serve him in love. Philippe, Duc d'Orléans, was a soldier and a politician; he could play, he could paint, he knew a little of every science, but he was, above all, an artist. He loved liberty and he loved glory, but he also loved love. And as an artist, he loved the æsthetic element in love. He was never brutal. His famous suppers, although orgies of which Rome, in her days of depravity, would not have been ashamed, had an artistic touch about them.

[1] Cf. Michelet, *History of France*, vol. xvii., p. 72.

It was at one of these suppers that Madame de Parabère took up the place of honour.   She was the mistress
en titre of the Regent.

" My son," wrote the Princesse Palatine, mother of the Regent ;
Madame, as she was called, " my son is no longer a youth of
twenty ; he is forty-two, and Paris cannot pardon him his running
after women, just as an impetuous youth, with all the weighty
affairs of State on his hands.   When the late King took possession
of the kingdom, it was in a state of prosperity, and he could very
well afford to enjoy himself, but it is quite different to-day.   My
son must now work day and night, in order to repair what the late
King and his faithless ministers ruined.   It cannot be denied that
my son has a great weakness for women.   He has now a principal
favourite, a mistress *en titre*, named Madame de Parabère.   She
is a daughter of Madame de la Vieuville, who was lady of the bedchamber to the Duchesse de Berry.   It is there that my son made
her acquaintance.   Madame de Parabère is now a widow ; she
has a fine figure, is tall and well made ; her skin is dark and she does
not paint, she has a pretty mouth and beautiful eyes ; she is
rather stupid, but is a fine bit of flesh." [1]

Such is the portrait of Madame de Parabère, as drawn
by the mother of the Regent, who did not like her son's
mistresses.   But other contemporaries are more merci-
ful.   According to their testimony, the beautiful Parabère was vivacious and impetuous, but *spirituelle* withal
—a happy combination of character, which Court life
had greatly enhanced.   Her witty and original remarks
made her the soul of the gay supper-parties of the
Regent.   No vile interest, no ambitious idea prompted
her love.   She loved not the Regent, but the man, the

[1] *Lettres de Madame*, Mars 23, 1716.

jovial and amiable companion, and cared naught for his power and his jealous outbursts.[1]

Her grace, coupled with a certain malignity, seduced the Regent, who became very infatuated with her charms. The Regent was a busy man. Internal and external politics were very complicated at the beginning of the eighteenth century ; and in the whirl of his pleasures he never forgot his duties. But he sought to divert himself, to seek recreation and to escape the work and worries of his exalted position in the company of his gay friends. Such recreation he found in the company of Madame de Parabère. She offered him no serious talk, no sadness, no politics and no ambitions. Madame de Parabère was a true Magdalene : she loved much and repented afterwards, when she could love no more. Madame de Parabère was a child of her age, of the eighteenth century. The women of the eighteenth century were as unlike the women of pagan antiquity as the woman of a Turkish harem is unlike an English suffragette. They were no Aspasias talking of the immortality of the soul and of the liberty and emancipation of peoples, those ladies of the Regency. They were governed by their hearts, rather than by their heads ; their ideal was the ideal of beauty, and their virtue was the virtue of love. They were beautiful, and they knew how to love, these women of the France of the eighteenth century. It was the age of the Encyclopaedists and of Voltaire, but it was also the age of Coustou and of Watteau.

It was the age of Diderot, d'Alembert, but also of the Abbé Prevost.

Madame de Parabère was born in 1693, and baptized

---

[1] Barrière, *Tableaux de genre et d'histoire*, 1828, p. 5.

under the name of Mary Magdalene. There was pre-
destination in such a name. Her father was a de la Vieuville, descended from an ancient family in Brittany,
which had come over to France with Queen Anne of
Brittany in the reign of Louis XII. Her mother was a
niece of the Duc d'Argenson. The daughter had
inherited, not only the beauty, but also the temperament of her mother, and her inclination for gallantry.
Mademoiselle de Vieuville loved dazzling and gorgeous
attire, diamonds, dress, joy and laughter. She was
merry, overflowing, dissipated and charming. But she
seems, however, to have given no cause for criticism to
the gossips and the wits of the time until after her
marriage. Till then her conduct seems to have been
irreproachable. At eighteen Mlle. de la Vieuville was one
of the most admired and courted belles at the Court of
Louis XIV, which is to say not a little ; for Versailles,
at that time, could boast of many dazzling and radiant
court beauties. All-powerful Madame de Maintenon
took the girl into favour, and she was married to Jean
César de Beaudeant, Comte de Parabère. Some say that
she loved her husband, as she loved her lovers afterwards. This assertion is not without foundation, for it
could be said of her that love *c'était son métier*. But if
she really felt any affection for her husband, this affection was a very elastic one, for certain it is that her
flirtations began immediately after her marriage. Her
first lessons she took with that complete rake, as he has
been called, Lord Bolingbroke. The beautiful ladies at
the Court of Versailles had made the sojourn of the
brilliant English Ambassador in France a very pleasant
one, so that he hardly cared to return to his native land.
But among his many conquests, Bolingbroke seems to

have retained a deep and long-lasting impression of
Madame de Parabère. He kept up his friendship by
correspondence and with frequent presents. But Bolingbroke was away, and Madame de Parabère was thirsting
for love. She loved Martial de Montluzun, an officer of
the guards, but Montluzun was away, and Madame la
Marquise did not wait for his return. " Eternity," said
this sinner, " is only in heaven ; the earth is turning, and
we must turn with it." The Regent, who liked variety,
knew her ; he had made her acquaintance in her mother's
house. But the latter, who seems to have turned de-
vout in her old age, did not encourage any closer relationship, indeed she watched over her daughter, anxious
to prevent her from imitating the irregularities of her
own youth. Madame de la Vieuville, however, died, and
charming Madame de Parabère was free to take her
mother as a model and to sin in her youth, reserving
repentance for mature age. In 1715 Madame de
Parabère was already availing herself of her astuteness
and ingenuity in order to divert the suspicions of her
husband. Comte de Parabère was jealous, although
jealousy was not in fashion under the Regency. It was
no longer *bon ton* to love one's own wife, and reciprocity
of affection was good enough for the *bourgeois ménage*,
but not for people of quality. Marriage among the
nobles, such as it was practised at that period, had indeed become an indecency. The Comte de Parabère,
however, was not in fashion on this point, neither did
he wish to be ; indeed, he prided himself on not being in
the fashion—and he was jealous. A good story is told
of the manner in which Madame de Parabère knew how
completely to crush the rising suspicions of her jealous
husband. A beautiful lady, so the story runs, who

was no other than the Comtesse de Parabère, visited the
Regent. The gallant lover made her a present of a
diamond worth at least two thousand louis d'or (40,000
francs) and of a box worth two hundred louis d'or (4,000
francs). The lady liked the presents, but feared the
jealousy of her husband. But her effrontery helped her
out of embarrassment.

" My dear," she said to her jealous spouse, putting
on her most innocent and ingenuous air, " some friends
who are very much in need of ready money offered me
these jewels for sale ; they demand a ridiculous price.
It would be a pity to lose such an excellent opportunity."
The husband believed the story and gave the money.
The wife thanked him most effusively and kept the money
and the jewels.

When she appeared in society and people asked after
the generous giver who had made her such a magnificent present, she modestly answered—

" It is my husband."

" Yes," said the Comte de Parabère, proudly, " can
one do less for a charming wife, who loves no one but her
husband ! "

But society knew well enough whence Madame de
Parabère's presents came, and society laughed most
heartily, enjoying the joke. A moment, however,
arrived when the husband of lovely Mary Magdalene de
Parabère seems to have detected the intimacy existing
between his wife and the Regent. In his despair he
took to drink and drank himself to death, and his widow
celebrated the event at one of the gay supper-parties in
the Palais Royal. " Thus died M. de Parabère," writes
St. Simon, " but it would have been better if he had
left this world a little earlier." The merry widow de

Parabère, continuing to bear the name of her late
husband, who was now out of the way, distributed her
favours between her various lovers with equal ardour
and generosity. For she had many of them, and she
loved them all well. The three, however, whom she
loved most passionately were the Regent, Beninghen and
Montluzun. The others were cherished only at
intervals. For she was of a loving disposition, this
Mary Magdalene of the Regency. A characteristic trait
of her nature was the equality of her love. She often
changed the objects of her affections, but her heart
never remained vacant for a single instant. She abandoned her lovers and she was abandoned in her turn by
them, but the next morning, nay the very, same day, another had raised his shrine in the vacant heart of Madame
de Parabère. And she loved the successor with equal
ardour and equal vivacity; she was devoted to him
with the same submissive passion, for she saw everything only through the eyes of her lovers. She shared
the views, the friends and the tastes of her new lover, as
she had shared those of his predecessors. "This faithful devotion," writes a contemporary, "is as rare as a
constancy of many years devoted to one lover."[1]
Among the many mistresses of the Regent, this modern
Mary Magdalene was perhaps the most faithful and
the least ambitious. The Duc d'Orléans had profited
by the lessons given to him by his preceptor, Dubois.
Never did he allow his mistresses to gain ascendancy over
him or to exercise any influence over politics. They
ruled *him*, but they never ruled the nation. The Regent
loved his pleasures, he loved his favourites, but he loved
France even more.

[1] Cf. Count Caylus, *Mémoires*, 1874, pp. 17-18.

Philippe d'Orléans did even more. He did not entertain his mistresses at the expense of the country. He
opened the Palais Royal to his friends, his roués, and his
favourites, the companions of his orgies and his supper-
parties; but the Tuileries were practically closed to
them. With his mistresses he was only the Duc
d'Orléans; they were loved by him, but not by the
Regent of France. And when he had to choose between his friend Nocé and his minister Dubois, the
Regent did not hesitate. Nocé, whom he had forgiven
his rivalry in the favours of Madame de Parabère, was
exiled for having failed in respect to the Minister. The
roués were allowed to have every vice except one—ambition. When the ambitious Madame de Tencin spread
her nets to capture the Regent, he knew how to escape
her. " Serious words of business do not suit pretty
lips," he once said.

For this reason Madame de Parabère kept her place for
a considerable time in the intimacy of Philippe d'Orléans.
Madame de Parabère was the least avaricious and the least
ambitious of the Regent's mistresses; but it would be
wrong to imagine that she was entirely disinterested.
The estates which she acquired certainly prove that she
did not refuse the generous gifts of her royal lover. And
just because she was not ambitious, her influence over
the Regent lasted to the very end. When Dubois, the
Regent's preceptor and Minister of State, had obtained
the cardinal's hat; when the Regent had sacrificed his
friends to his capable minister, whom he despised,
Madame de Parabère was saved. Her lack of ambition
reconciled Dubois to this priestess of love. Among the
women Madame de Parabère was the only one to retain
her place; she was not sent away by the Regent.

Madame de Parabère had the satisfaction of leaving her royal lover of her own free will, with the consolation of having been one of the mistresses who came nearest to Philippe d'Orléans' heart. Because she knew how to be discreet, she often exercised an influence over the careful Regent, without alarming his prudence. Dubois was to be installed as Prince Archbishop of Cambrai. Saint Simon did his best to prevent the Duc d'Orléans from being present at the ceremony. The consecration of Dubois, we are informed by St. Simon in his memoirs, was fixed for Sunday, June 19. All Paris and the Court was invited to it, except St. Simon himself, who was on bad terms with the Archbishop. The consecration was to be magnificent, and the Duc d'Orléans expected to be present at it. But the indignation against the Duke was very great. The nomination and ordination of Dubois, and now the superb preparation, caused much scandal. St. Simon, therefore, decided to dissuade the Regent from attending the ceremony. With his usual frankness St. Simon told the Duc d'Orléans that people were greatly indignant about the whole matter, and if the Regent attended the ceremony people would say that he only came for the purpose of mocking God and insulting the Church. Hatred, disdain and shame would be the result. The Duke would, by his attendance, show the whole of France how dependent he was upon Dubois ; Europe would laugh at the Regent. St. Simon, having succeeded in extracting a promise from the Regent that he would not attend the ceremony, left happy and satisfied. But he had counted without la Parabère, as he calls her.

The reigning sultana, with whom the Regent had spent the night preceding the consecration, had made her lover promise, between two kisses, to attend the ceremony. The Marquise de Parabère admitted that St. Simon was right, but that the Regent would have to go after all. Here is the dialogue which is supposed to have taken place between the Duc d'Orléans and his favourite as related by St. Simon himself.[1]

The Duke told her she was mad.

" It may be," she replied, " but you will go."

" No, I will not go," he rejoined.

" I tell you, you will go," said she.

" But," observed the Duke, " this is very funny. You say that M. de St. Simon is right, then why should I go ? "

" Because I wish it," replied the Marquise

" And why do you wish me to go ? "

" Because——" said she.

" Because is no reason ; tell me why you wish it."

" If you very particularly wish to know it, then I will tell you. The Archbishop and I have quarrelled a few days ago, we have not yet made it up. He will undoubtedly know that you have been with me to-night. He will naturally conclude that it was I who prevented you from attending the ceremony ; nothing will make him give up this idea, and he will endeavour to harm me in a thousand ways. He will succeed in undermining my credit with you and ultimately part us. But I don't wish such a thing to happen, and therefore, although M. de St. Simon is right, you must go to the ceremony."

The Regent went, because Madame de Parabère wished him to go, and St. Simon was greatly vexed; Dubois never forgot this service rendered to him by the *maîtresse en titre*, and did what he could for her. He

---

[1] St. Simon, *Mémoires*, vol. xvii.

allowed her to keep her place until the Regent had had enough of her. Sooner or later this moment had to come. Philippe d'Orléans was not a man to remain faithful all his life to one favourite, and when Mary Magdalene de Parabère saw that she would have to vacate her place of sultana for another, she was clever enough to go of her free will before she was told to do so. She made her exit from St. Cloud with dignity. " In 1721," says Mathieu Marais, " she already refused to see the Regent because he was in the habit of frequenting the society of the opera dancers." [1] And although lover and mistress seem to have made it up, Madame de Parabère finally left the Duc d'Orléans when Madame d'Averne was on the point of supplanting her in the heart of her lover. She retired to a convent.

" Prince," she wrote to the Duke, " instead of waiting until you send me into exile, I shall exile myself. One must never drink together to the last drop, for the last drop often proves to be a tear of blood. Henceforth I shall only live for God. I am leaving your world and we shall only meet after death."

And so this Magdalene de Parabère had decided to repent. She left St. Cloud and, accompanied by her maid, returned to the Château de St. Heraye, which she had not visited since the death of her husband. But alas ! the repentance of the sinner was not yet complete. She thought she had found refuge in religion, but religion was still far from her thoughts and her heart. Love was much nearer to her. She was still thinking of the Regent, but above all of Martial de Montluzun. This young man had loved her passionately. He had fought a duel for her and, condemned

[1] Cf. *Journal de Mathieu Marais.*

to the Bastille, was supposed to have escaped to the
Indies; but in reality, de Montluzun had never left
Paris. Martial de Montluzun saw his mistress, the
repenting Magdalene, who had many other lovers, once
again. She believed in religion, but she also believed
in love, and she constantly wavered between the two
emotions, the amorous and the religious. She succeeded in reconciling the fear of God and the love of
man.

The Marquise de Parabère was altogether of a
generous nature and kind-hearted, and her conduct
towards a suffering and noble girl, a Circassian slave,
whose sad story made all Paris weep, testify to her loving
heart. The Circassian, Mademoiselle Aïssé, whose
letters have been published, speaks with the most touching affection of the Marquise. "She never leaves me,"
wrote the dying girl, "she is overwhelming me with her
presents, but above all with her affection and her love."
And thus Magdalene, although still too weak to resist
the sweet temptation of sin, was doing as much good as
she could. She died in her retirement away from the
Court and from the world where she had been the
centre of joy, love and laughter. Like another Mary
Magdalene, she, too, had loved much, and died with the
firm hope that much would be forgiven unto her.

CHAPTER VI

The Venetian Dancer and the Great Frederick

Barbarina Campanini

IT was in the year 1744. The Royal Opera in Berlin was crowded. La Barbarina, the famous, almost deified dancer, afterwards Countess Campanini, was performing before the King Frederick II and the Prussian Court. In one of the front rows were seated two of her most ardent admirers, Baron Coceji, son of the Chancellor, and another man, the son of a Berlin banker. Young Coceji was of gigantic stature and strength. He was very much in love with the signorina, and very jealous. Suddenly he imagined that his divinity was casting kinder glances at his rival than at himself. In a furious fit of jealousy he grasped his neighbour, a puny little creature, and to the amazement of the audience hurled him over the head of the orchestra upon the stage. Imagine the uproar and excitement.

As soon as the banker could pick himself up he came to the front of the stage and apologized to the house. " It is not my fault," he meekly observed, " if I so suddenly appear on the boards, but I have been flung here by Councillor Coceji."

The King remained quiet, the public followed his

example, and the performance continued in spite of this somewhat sensational interlude. The news of the incident came to the ears of young Coceji's father, and the next morning he solicited an audience of the King and requested the latter to punish the culprit for such a violation of respect for His Majesty. Frederick II did not punish young Coceji, but sent him to Glogau, in the capacity of Privy Councillor of Justice.[1]

Frederick II had no ill-feeling towards the young councillor of legation, but he exiled him from Court and from the presence of the fair dancer because he was in love with her himself. She had produced a very deep impression upon the heart of the woman-hater.

Frederick began his reign on May 31, 1740; he entered upon it with a good conscience, for his father's blessing was on his head. Heartfelt love and recognition had succeeded to anger; the dying King had understood that he was to have a glorious successor. The year after his accession, Frederick had already become the Man of the Century by his campaign in Silesia, which was the beginning of his renowned and victorious career.

In the intervals allowed him by his warlike plans and the cares of government, Frederick devoted himself enthusiastically to the arts of peace, founding universities and erecting theatres. He took a lively interest in the building of the Opera House, which was finished in 1743 concerning himself with all kinds of details, mixing himself up with the quarrels of the actors, and writing anonymous critiques for the Berlin newspapers.

The first opera performed in the new building was

[1] Cf. Campbell, *Life and Times of Frederick the Great*, vol. ii., p. 395.

Rodelinda, Queen of the Lombards, by Graun. The plays were at first performed by persons belonging to the Court, until a company of French actors arrived. It was, however, the Italian Opera that had the strongest interest for the King. In 1741 Fiorinella and Laura were engaged as singers for the royal opera, and in 1747 Joanna Astrua, a rival of Carestini's and Salimbeni's, was appointed with a salary of 6,000 dollars. Among the dancers the most prominent were Roland and Barbarina.

The King, who, in his capacity of impresario and manager, came unavoidably into somewhat close contact with the charms of the feminine portion of the theatrical company, seems to have fallen under the spell of the beautiful dancer, who rose into fame as the favourite of the woman-hating sovereign. She was a Venetian by birth. So much difficulty and strife had arisen before she could be secured for the Berlin stage, that Frederick looked upon it quite as a victory when he saw the beautiful Italian on the boards of his Court theatre.

Barbarina was the most talented, the most famous and honoured dancer then known. Her success had been great in London, Paris and Venice, and for some time it seemed as if her visit to Berlin was beyond hope. At last, however, by means of diplomatic negotiations, the Prussian resident minister at Venice, Count Cataneo, succeeded in carrying out Frederick's order, and in engaging the dancer, on conditions which would satisfy even the greatest stage celebrities of the present day. She was to receive seven thousand thalers yearly, and have five months' leave of absence ! As soon as she and her mother had put their signatures to this advantageous contract it was forwarded to Berlin for ratification in high quarters.

But the charms of her person and the accomplishments of her mind had already gained Barbarina many admirers. Among them was Lord Stuart Mackenzie, with whom she had entered into amorous relations. When she signed her contract she had just quarrelled with her lover, but in the time elapsing between her signing the engagement and her departure the lovers became reconciled. Lord Stuart promised more splendour and happiness than the Berlin engagement. Barbarina, therefore, refused to fulfil the contract when it was returned to her duly executed. She gave out that she was secretly married to the young Englishman, and intended returning with him to England as his lady.

This attitude annoyed the King, and the opposition to his wishes only made him more eager to get possession of her. He thereupon threatened the Venetian Republic with the consequence of his kingly anger if it did not exert itself to place Barbarina in his power. The Senate of the Republic considered it beneath its dignity to interfere in matters concerning a dancer, but Frederick ordered it to seize all the luggage of the Venetian Ambassador, Signor Campello, who was going to London. The Senate of the Republic was obliged to yield to the request of the Prussian King, and to assure Barbarina that Berlin was a beautiful town, that she would be entertained at a large court and be in the service of a most gracious King, and that she would have every reason to be satisfied and pleased. A strong escort of cavalry, however, accompanied the carriage sent for her, thus rendering all efforts at escape impossible. She was escorted to the Austrian frontier, and thence the Court of Vienna sent her under another escort to Peterswalde in Bohemia, on the Saxon frontier, the Court of Saxony further escorting her to the Prussian frontier. Thus the reluctant prima-donna was brought to Berlin. Her lover, Lord Stuart, and one of his friends, Count Calenberg, in vain exerted all their cunning and power to set Barbarina free. They followed her in disguise, tipped the innkeepers, and managed to convey love-letters to the lady. There was nothing wanting in the way of romantic details to this love intrigue, and it is not surprising that the rumour of it ran through the world.

Such a journey did not agree with the famous dancer. She fell ill upon the way from love and trouble ; her lover continued to follow her, and on their arrival at Vienna exerted himself to the utmost to secure her deliverance. Count Dohna was very much taken with this exceedingly amiable, noble and handsome young man ; indeed his person exercised such a fascination upon him, that he even dared to approach the King on his behalf. It was, he told his Majesty, Lord Stuart's firm resolve to marry the dancer ; in England such marriages were frequent, and Lord Stuart would have no difficulty in getting the consent of his family to the match. The latter could answer for the virtue of the woman he loved, and he was ready to go bail for 100,000 thalers, if he might be allowed to accompany her to Berlin, there to throw himself at the King's feet, and plead in person for that which meant life or death to him. Lord Stuart also addressed a very pathetic letter to the King, pleading his cause. Frederick replied in a letter written by his own hand. His only answer to the imploring prayers of the lovers was the order that Barbarina was to be ready to dance between the acts of a

French comedy that was to be performed on May 13, 1744. And thus the beautiful lady arrived in the Prussian capital, nearly dead with fatigue and grief, not quite five days before this date. It was somewhat strange that Barbarina's mother seems to have opposed the marriage with Lord Stuart, and had throughout been a party to the plot for separating her from her lover. Was there, perhaps, something apparent to the eye of the mother in the latter's character, which she deemed untrustworthy, or did her motherly instinct make her guess that greater honours were perhaps in store for her daughter than that of becoming the wife of an English Peer ?

The event, it must not be forgotten, was taking place in the eighteenth century, the century when beautiful women, crowned and uncrowned, ruled Europe. Frederick was a reputed woman-hater, but he had been amorously inclined in his youth. When Crown Prince, Frederick, as we are informed by the Margravine of Baireuth in her *Memoirs*, visited Dresden in the company of his father. " Augustus the Strong," says the Margravine, " loved the pleasures of this world, and had a complete harem. His excesses surpassed all description. The King of Prussia and the Crown Prince were drawn into a perfect whirl of pleasures and amusements." An endeavour was made to lead the austere King of Prussia astray by offering him temptations of the lowest description. Not only the King, but the Crown Prince also, was corrupted through the agency of the beautiful Formera and the Countess Orselska, the natural daughter of the King of Poland.

When Augustus the Strong visited Berlin in May, 1728, the Countess was in his suite, and the Crown

Prince renewed his intimacy with her.   Frederick the
Great had also a love affair with a certain Doris Ritter,
daughter of Rector Ritter in Potsdam.   The King grew
so furious when he heard of his son's new attachment
that he punished the girl and her father most severely.
Doris Ritter was condemned to be flogged, and to undergo
three years' hard labour in Spandau, for having allowed a
Crown Prince to make love to her.   She was set free in
July, 1733, and afterwards married a cab contractor
named Schomer.   She seems to have lived in very
straitened circumstances, and to have grown ugly.[1]

The Crown Prince also had a love affair with the wife
of Lieutenant-General Wreech.   But he turned a new
leaf when he married, and after he ascended the throne
Europe knew him as a woman-hater.   But a relapse
on the part of the King was not so impossible, and her
maternal instinct does not seem to have played the
mother of Barbarina false.

Barbarina's first appearance was a triumphant success : everybody had been on the tip-toe of expectation,
and the King looked upon her with the pride of a conqueror.   To have overcome so many difficulties, so
many love intrigues, and so much feminine obstinacy
was no slight achievement.   The fascination of this
beautiful dancer seems to have been even greater than
Frederick had expected.   The King was dazzled and
beside himself with excitement as he joined in the
general tumult of applause.   He made such a display of
his admiration for her that the whole Court came to the
conclusion that a turning-point had been reached, and
that the reign of a favourite was to begin.

[1] Cf. *Mémoires pour servir à la vie de Voltaire, écrites par lui-même,*
1784, vol. i., p. 216.

Frederick had shown, ever since he had ascended the throne, an absolute indifference for those hetairas and Court beauties who governed the Courts of Europe in the eighteenth century.   George Sand, in her novel, *The Countess of Rudolstadt*, makes the Princess Amelia of Prussia, sister of Frederick, say that the King had an incipient love for the Barbarina, that he often went to take tea with her, in her apartment, after the performance was over, and that more than once the prima-donna was present at the suppers of Sans-Souci, an occurrence which had never happened before her time in the life of Potsdam.   She was always present, according to a dispatch of the English Ambassador of January 22, 1746, at the parties of Sans-Souci, and her portrait, painted by Pesne, was hung in the library of the King.[1]   The great Fritz wrote verses praising the bewitching eyes of the charming Barbarina.

Barbarina became the object of universal homage. French, German, and even Latin songs of adulation appeared in the Berlin papers, and Frederick became more and more assiduous in his attentions.   He went so far as to demand that she might also be invited, whenever he himself was to be the guest of one or other of his generals.   It was reported that the dancer secretly accompanied him when he went to Pyrmont for the baths.   She is supposed to have occupied an apartment in the Palace for several months.   Need one be astonished at the speedy way in which Barbarina banished all thought of young Lord Stuart ?   The infatuated lover remained two months in Berlin, a witness of her triumphs and conquests, assailing her the whole time with

---

[1] Cf. Vehse, E., *Memoirs of the Court of Prussia*, 1854, p. 233.

letters and prayers, but to no purpose. At last he received a royal mandate ordering him to leave the capital. In a report of the superintendent of police at Kircheisen, dated July 4, 1744, which was forwarded to the King, we read : " The hired lacquey, whom Lord Stuart took from here, returned yesterday evening from Hamburg, and I demanded of him the letters for Barbarina, which had been entrusted to him with the command to give the one without an address into her own hands, the which I herewith forward to your Majesty. Lord Stuart has embarked for London."

From these letters, of which Frederick got possession in this underhand way, he could plainly see that young Lord Stuart was still anxiously endeavouring to protect his beloved one from all attempts on her virtue. In one he wrote :—

" I beseech you to be continually on your guard ! Make it a fixed rule for yourself, never to dine with anyone, whoever he may be, away from home, and never for one moment to be alone with any man. Do not approach too nearly to anyone or allow anyone to come too near you. On no account receive anyone when you are in bed ; you never consented to do it in the past, and I beg you, out of your love to me, to refuse firmly to allow it. Do not see the same man too often, so that you may avoid being made a subject of talk, which even when without foundation of truth, might still do you an injury, especially just now, when everybody has their eyes on you and exaggerates all you do. This evening I must go on board the vessel which is to carry me another hundred miles farther from you. Think of me when you hear the wind blowing, and think that it is perhaps bringing you my last blessing."

This good counsel never reached its destination.

That Barbarina exercised over the King a strong spell cannot be doubted. She was pretty, witty and accomplished, but there was something more—her own admiration for the King flattered Frederick. Barbarina foresaw in the youthful hero the man of the century. He was still in the bloom of youth, he had the refinement of intellect which lends grace to learning, he was a poet and an artist, crowned with the nimbus of the proudest kingly coronet, that of Prussia, which so well adorns the brows of men, since it is a symbol of their personal strength. And, moreover, Frederick's heart was a prize worth winning, since, kept in check by an iron hand, it so seldom gave itself away. She tried to please and to attract, and what wonder that the King, whose heart had once been not unsusceptible to feminine charm, should fall under the spell of the enchantress. Barbarina was not an ordinary woman, a stupid Court beauty, a coquette with a pretty face. She could not as such have attracted a man like Frederick. Barbarina possessed not only beauty and talent, but also superior mental qualities, which made her conversation attractive to the royal philosopher of Sans-Souci.

But Frederick soon wearied of his *inamorata*. As early as 1748 we find the King in an evidently perfectly cool frame of mind as regards Barbarina. He gave orders that she was to pay her own debts. The lady soon after departed for England in the company of her sister, and he saw her go with the greatest indifference. Whether, when she arrived in England she found that her former lover, Lord Stuart Mackenzie, had remained as faithful to her as his ardent devotion seemed to promise, is doubtful. Barbarina returned to Berlin after a few months' absence, and was privately married to the young son of the Lord High Chancellor Coceji. Her husband's family was naturally furious at this *mésalliance*. Every effort was made to prove the marriage invalid, and personal petition was made to the King to have the objectionable woman banished from the kingdom. Whatever the relations between Frederick II and the Barbarina had been, the King anyhow behaved very ungallantly. The beautiful dancer had the mortification of seeing her royal lover himself side against her. In writing to the Count of Haake, the King spoke of the object of his former love as a " seductive creature " who had enticed young Coceji into his mad love for her, and added that he would on no account suffer such an honourable family to be subjected " to such prostitution and annoyance " as a marriage of their son with a dancer. An order of arrest, a *cachet volant*, something in the nature of the French *lettres de cachet*, was issued against Coceji, who, at that time, had risen to the rank of Privy Councillor, and was therefore beyond his father's power. The orders were that he was to be conveyed under military escort to the Castle of Altlandsberg, such had been the father's request, so that he might be separated from Barbarina. At this critical moment the latter herself wrote to the King, beseeching him for his protection, especially as her marriage was to be blessed with offspring. In a well-written and animated letter she informed his Majesty that the breaking of the marriage-bond was the more inadmissible since she was about to give birth to " a Prussian subject," and with the intent of founding a family in Berlin had bought a house in the Behrenstrasse, and therefore claimed of his grace a right to remain as a citizen of his capital. In the course of her petition she makes a reference to her personal relations with the King. She writes:

" Your Majesty's high sense of honour, which abhors all treachery of the heart, gives me hope—but that which tells against me and of which my reverence forbids me to speak makes me fear everything ! May a gracious response to the supplications of your subject end the trouble of one, who has the honour to be, Sire, your Majesty's most obedient and dutiful servant, BARBARINA COCEJI."

It would appear from the above that she had refused the King's advances, and was afraid that he would now take this opportunity of revenging himself. Did Barbarina hesitate to yield to Frederick's advances because her ambition prompted her to put conditions on her favours which a Henry IV and a Louis XV would have accepted, but which the prudent Hohenzollern refused ? In any case Madame Coceji's letter accomplished its purpose. The King immediately countermanded all orders for a forcible arrest, and even endeavoured to bring about a reconciliation between the father and the newly married pair. In this, however, he appears not to have been successful. On the contrary, at the urgent request of the Lord High Chancellor the son was removed to Glogau, so that at least all communication with his family might cease. " This union," writes Vehse, " lasted forty years, but in 1789 Barbarina obtained a divorce. She possessed three estates in Silesia, the proceeds of which she used for founding an establishment for the benefit of young ladies of the nobility." [1]

In acknowledgment of the great service she had

[1] Vehse, ibid.

rendered Silesia, Frederick's successor conferred on Madame Coceji the title of Countess Campanini. She died June 7, 1799, in Silesia, greatly honoured by all the nobility of the province, who had entirely forgotten the dancer in the countess. *Tout comme chez nous.*

CHAPTER VII

The Story of Cinderella-Pompadour, or Countess of Lichtenau

" YOUR Majesty well knows that for myself I set
no value whatever on the foolish vanities of
Court etiquette, but I am placed in an awkward position
by my daughter being raised to the rank of a Countess,
whilst I myself am still in the humble station of a
bourgeoise."

Thus wrote from Italy Madame Rietz, the wife of
the Chamberlain Rietz, to Frederick William II in 1794.
Madame was then formally divorced from her husband
and created Countess Lichtenau, by letters patent, dated
April 28, 1794, which her own brother, the equerry,
brought to her at Venice. Her coat of arms bore the
Prussian eagle and the Royal crown. This incident
sufficiently proves that Madame Rietz had some influence over the King of Prussia, who hastened to gratify
her request.

Wilhelmine Rietz had been his favourite for a number
of years and she has been styled the Prussian Pompadour
of the Court of the profligate nephew of the great
Frederick.

Her name was Wilhelmine Encke, and her father was
a trumpeter in one of the regiments in garrison at
Berlin. After having obtained his discharge, he set

up a small public-house, but was afterwards appointed
French-horn player in the private band of Frederick
the Great.

The family moved from Dessau to Potsdam, and
Master Encke was appointed trumpeter to the King.
It was here that the Royal Prince made the acquaintance
of the three sisters. Charlotte, the eldest, was an imperious beauty, and fascinated the passionate and
amorous Frederick William. Wilhelmine was only ten
at that time, and it was her lot to act as waiting-maid
to her sister. She was treated by the latter as a real
Cinderella, and harsh words and harsh blows were often
her lot. But the good fairy was not far off, and Cinderella
was soon to find her Prince Charming. He was none
other than the Royal Prince Frederick William himself.
He had wearied of Charlotte and of her irascible temper, and one day, when his mistress had forgotten herself
so far in her wrath as to strike her little sister in the
presence of her royal lover, the latter interfered. The
Prince took Cinderella under his august protection, and
reproached Charlotte for her many faults, and especially
for her growing attachment to the Silesian Count
Matushka. According to a pamphlet published in 1799
and containing the purported confessions of Wilhelmine,
Countess of Lichtenau, the royal lover had surprised his
mistress in the company of the Count. Be it as it
may, Charlotte left Berlin and travelled in Germany,
Sweden and Paris, under the name of Countess
Matushka. Paris of the eighteenth century was less
rigorous than New York of the twentieth; and Parisian
society never inquired into the private lives of individuals before receiving them into its midst. Besides
Countess Matushka was a lady, and a very beautiful

lady too, and Parisian society, during the second half
of the eighteenth century, admired beauty. La belle
Polonaise, therefore, as the ex-favourite of the Royal
Prince was called, became a well-known figure in brilliant Parisian circles.

Whilst the eldest sister was thus enjoying her triumphs
abroad, little Cinderella had consoled Prince Charming.
Frederick William was attached to the family Encke, and
the eldest daughter away, he transferred his royal love
to the youngest, Wilhelmine. Master of her heart, the
Prince now took pains to form and cultivate the mind of
his favourite and to make up for a neglected education.
Madame Girard, a French lady, taught her the French
tongue, whilst the Prince himself instructed her in
geography and history.[1] Was it a labour of love or
simply a measure dictated by prudence ? It seems that
the Prince was afraid to confide the education of his
favourite to strangers, lest the story of his *liaison* might
reach the august ears of his royal uncle, Frederick the
Great.

The rapid progress made by the pupil increased the
attachment of the master, who, like a second Pygmalion,
began to worship the statue which his own hands had
embellished and which love had animated. Little
Wilhelmine's heart was throbbing with a sentiment of
gratitude for her royal benefactor, a sentiment which soon
changed into a tenderer feeling, whilst Prince Frederick
William united the tenderness of a father and the
constancy of a faithful friend with the passion of a lover.
Several children born of this union strengthened the
ties which united the two lovers, and their romance was
free from self-interest and calculation. Wilhelmine

---

[1] Cf. *Mémoires de la Comtesse de Lichtenau*, p. 14.

loved the Prince with her heart and soul. The annals of royal romances scarcely offer another example where the mistress of a royal Prince lived in such straitened circumstances as did the future Countess of Lichtenau.

The father Encke was dead, the eldest sister was in Paris, and Wilhelmine had the whole family on her hands. More than once she pawned her silver in order to provide a supper for her royal lover. But if the reason which had prompted the Royal Prince to take upon himself the task of schoolmaster of his mistress was to keep the matter a secret from his uncle, his labours were in vain.

The love affair of the Prince Royal had after all come to the knowledge of the King. Frederick the Great interfered and " loudly inveighed against his nephew's fathering several children of Wilhelmine."

" He thought," writes the Countess Lichtenau in her confessions, " that it did not become the destined ruler of a great and powerful nation to be governed and duped by women and a set of idle parasites. Such creatures were generally connected with a gang of adventurers who had no other aim but that of creeping into favour of the ruling prince, under the protection of a clever courtesan, and as soon as they had obtained that favour they would interfere with the most serious and momentous concerns of the State."

But the Royal Prince had done more than love Wilhelmine Encke. He had made debts, and this was even a more unpardonable sin in the eyes of the great Frederick than that of love. Violent scenes took place between uncle and nephew. The former threatened to exile the whole family of Encke and to hand over the Prince to his creditors. The lovers had to yield ; Wilhelmine Encke left Berlin under the escort of a French lady, and joined her sister, the Countess Matushka, in Paris. She remained in the French capital over six months. Out of respect for his uncle, her lover did not recommend her to the Prussian Ambassador, but handed her over to the good care of Mlle. de Launay, who introduced her to the Count de Lubersac. Through her sister, the Countess Matushka, Wilhelmine made the acquaintance of several great Russian nobles, among others the Princess Baratinsky and Bella Sinsky, the Counts Boutourline and Shouvalov. Whilst endeavouring to benefit by her stay in Paris, acquiring not only the language but also the tastes and ideas of the country, she kept up a continual correspondence with the Prince, whose thoughts were constantly with her.

But Frederick William was not of a faithful nature, and though Wilhelmine Encke was still dear to him, he was unfaithful to her during her absence. Many were the gallant intrigues in which he indulged in the meantime, and many were the beautiful ladies who made him forget, for a while at least, the absent Wilhelmine. His debts increased; the princesses of the opera and the French dancers were not so disinterested, and not so economical either, as the daughter of the trumpeter Encke. Frederick the Great almost regretted having compelled his nephew to send the latter away, and with the promptitude characteristic of this great King, he decided to choose of two evils the lesser. He therefore commissioned the Italian Councillor Philipini to negotiate with Wilhelmine Encke the question of her return to Berlin. The lady left Paris, and on her return to the Prussian capital was informed by Philipini that the King was well pleased with his nephew's love for her, and would in no way prevent the Prince Royal from seeing her as often

K

as he wished. His majesty, however, granted his consent to this *liaison* on one condition only. The couple should meet not in the capital but in the country, and if Wilhelmine acceded to this request she would rest assured of His Majesty's favour. The King thus wished to keep the Heir-Apparent away from the evil influence of the capital, and from the snares of more dangerous and more expensive *liaisons*. The Prince Royal received a large sum from his uncle for the necessary expenses, and his mistress found a beautiful country house which has since become the splendid Charlottenburg. Here it was that Wilhelmine Encke gave birth to a son who immediately received the title of Count de la Marke, a title which the infant was not destined to enjoy, for he died in his cradle. A sure sign of the affection which the Prince bore the mother is proved by his almost inconsolable grief for the death of this child of love, and by the splendid mausoleum erected to his memory in the Protestant temple of Berlin by the sculptor Schadov.

To satisfy, however, Prussian public morality, or, as the Countess writes in her Confessions, " to make the old King quite easy," Prince Frederick decided to marry his mistress to his favourite chamberlain, son of his chief gardener, named Rietz. Wilhelmine Encke became now Madame Rietz. Her royal lover was present at the ceremony, and afterwards stood sponsor to the son born of this new union. Thus public opinion was satisfied, but the intimacy existing between the Prince and Madame Rietz was in no way disturbed. Her beauty and charm, but above all her intelligence, refinement and conversation fascinated the Royal Prince, and his attachment for her grew stronger and stronger. But a change was soon to take place in the life of Wilhelmine. The iron King was dying, and on the night between the 16th and the 17th August, Rietz, the chamberlain, entered the bedroom of Frederick William and woke up his master, addressing him as " your Majesty."

An event of European importance had occurred. Frederick the Great was dead, and his nephew Frederick William II was now King of Prussia.

At the time the King mounted the throne Madame Rietz was not living with her husband and only saw him at rare intervals. The affection of the King for Madame Rietz remained the same as that which he felt for her when Prince Royal. Her education had greatly enhanced the charm of the favourite, and made her even more attractive than before, captivating the somewhat fickle heart of her royal lover. Wilhelmine Rietz was a perfect musician, and could talk with ease of Greek and Italian art and literature. Her splendid *salon* in her residence, Charlottenburg, became the centre of brilliant assemblies. Neither was the daughter of the modest trumpeter lacking in tact and knowledge of human character. She knew her royal lover and his weaknesses, she knew that it was impossible for him to remain faithful to her, and that his delinquencies were many, but she had the tact never to show any jealousy. Like Madame de Pompadour, she was content with her royal lover's friendship. Madame Rietz has been accused of having also resembled Madame de Pompadour, in the fact that she recommended new favourites to the King. From these accusations raised against her it appears that whilst she allowed the king to have other mistresses she played the part of Pompadour and retained a preponderant influence over political affairs. But the Countess Lichtenau protests most emphatically in her *Mémoires* against such insinuations. The most influential counsellors of the King were the Count Haugwitz, the Marquis de Lucchesini, a Florentine, and Johann Wilhelm Lombard; all these gentlemen owed their credit and influence to the protection of Madame Rietz.

A change had also taken place in Wilhelmine's mode of living and household. It was natural that the King, being now his own master, should compensate Madame Rietz for her disinterestedness shown when she was Mademoiselle Encke.

Wilhelmine was not avaricious. For a considerable time, during the lifetime of Frederick the Great, she had often been in very straitened circumstances, with only the very small pension granted to her by the Prince Royal. She managed to make both ends meet, to keep up her house in Charlottenburg, educate her children and support her mother. When her royal lover ascended the throne he granted her a pension of 500 louis d'or (10,000 francs) per month, and furnished her residence in Charlottenburg in a very elegant style, and with great taste. Never, however, writes the Countess Lichtenau in her *Mémoires*,[1] " was there ever found in her apartments any trace of that Oriental luxury of which she was afterwards accused." The next King, Frederick William III, visited these apartments and found them very agreeable, but by far less magnificent than he had been led to believe.

Her son, Alexander de la Marke, had died and the mother naturally inherited the house which the King had bought for the young Count, " Unter den Linden." In this house the King had a theatre constructed, and

[1] Cf. p. 43.

it was afterwards asserted that on this stage plays of a questionable decency had been produced, and that the access to this theatre was limited to a very restricted circle of friends. One day a young girl clad in nothing but a *tricot* impersonated Venus. Madame Rietz protests most vehemently against these accusations— " Owing to the various circumstances of war and the illness of the King," she writes in her *Mémoires,* " only three performances were given on the stage, Unter den Linden." One of the performances was a concert at which Madame Rietz sang a duet with Conciliani, the second was a French play called " The Savages," in which the actors playing the parts of the savages had to appear *en tricot ;* the third play was the opera *Cleopatra,* played by the artists of the Royal Opera in the presence of the entire Court. " The King was anxious to be present at the performance of this famous opera," she writes, " but was afraid of exposing himself to the draughts in the Royal Opera, and the performance was therefore given on the small stage of the house Unter den Linden.

Madame Rietz was destined to play a prominent part in the political affairs of that period, and although she herself denies that she had ever taken any interest in politics, she deserves in some degree the epithet of a German Pompadour. The French Revolution had broken out, a throne had been abolished and a King beheaded. The Sovereigns of Europe formed a coalition, and England, anxious to destroy the French army, was at the head of it. Spain, Portugal, Italy, Austria and Prussia took up arms against France.

The Prussian army, under the Duke of Brunswick, was camping on the Rhine, and Frederick William joined it.   Madame Rietz did not wish to leave the King, and established her headquarters at Spa.   Here she was at the head of the partisans of peace.   Her influence was well known in Paris and in London, and at Spa a number of French diplomatic agents were working very hard and utilising the credit and influence of the favourite to bring about an understanding between Prussia and France.   Lord Arthur Paget, too, had done his best to gain the influence of Madame Rietz in the service of England.   But Madame Rietz was in favour of peace. Why should the King care, she asked her royal lover, what form of government existed in France ?

The King passed his evenings in the company of the favourite, who availed herself of her opportunities to gain the King's ear for her ideas.   England was alarmed ; Pitt sent Lord Henry Spencer as a special Envoy to Berlin.   Here the English Ambassador soon learned that the only person who had sufficient influence to make the King return to the coalition was Madame Rietz.

Although both Prussia and Austria were tired of the burden of the French war, Frederick William would as yet not listen to any proposed negotiations with the regicides, and England, knowing what an influence Madame Rietz had over her royal lover, endeavoured to gain her adherence for a continuance of war.   Lord Henry Spencer, English Ambassador, wrote, therefore, to Madame Rietz shortly before the treaty of Bâle, asking for an interview.   He was anxious to talk to her on a very important matter.   The favourite made an appointment with the English Ambassador between seven and eight in the evening.   The latter was exact to time, and, after talking for a while on some indifferent topics,

he explained that having heard of the King's intention
to conclude peace with France he wished to call Madame
Rietz's attention to the great harm which such a step
would bring to Prussia.   England was ready to offer a
subsidy of several millions to Prussia.   Lord Henry
Spencer then requested Madame Rietz to obtain for him a
secret audience of the King, and to dissuade the latter
from concluding any treaty with France.   He offered her
for her trouble the sum of 100,000 guineas.   Madame Rietz
had an interview with her royal lover, in which, so at
least she maintains, the favourite informed the King
of her conversation with the English Ambassador.
Whether Madame Rietz's influence had been overrated,
or whether she herself was in favour of a treaty, is uncertain, but at any rate Lord Henry Spencer did not
succeed.

Shortly after this incident the Treaty of Bâle was
concluded.   In a confidential report to his government
the French Minister, the Abbé Lebrun Tondu, says
that the conclusion of the treaty was due entirely to the
influence of Count Haugwitz, of Lombard, and of Madame
Rietz.   For Frederick William was still decided to protect the Monarchists.   Billaud Varennes, a polished and
cultivated gentleman who wrote poetry, and knew how
to talk to ladies; Fabre d'Églantine, the poet; Tallien, a
man of letters, had several interviews with the favourite.
Fabre d'Eglantine had known her in Paris, and renewed
his acquaintance at Spa.   Through Madame Rietz, the
French agents influenced Frederick William; and thus
the Treaty of Bâle was concluded in 1795.

Madame Rietz, evidently pleased with her success in
the political sphere, thought the moment propitious to
gratify one of her most cherished wishes—a visit to Italy.

She was a splendid musician and an ardent admirer of art and of Italy, the classical cradle and home of art, and she expected great pleasure from the realisation of her dream. In a spirit of self-sacrifice, as wonderful as that of Madame de Maintenon, she had charged herself with the education of the King's sons by his other favourites, the Countesses Ingenheim and Danhof. Madame Rietz now asked her royal lover's permission to take his children to Italy, and thus, accompanied by a numerous suite, she left Germany.

In her *Mémoires* Madame Rietz maintains that she went to Italy to recruit her health. She was advised to take the waters at Pisa. The King insisted on her departure, and thus to Pisa Madame Rietz went, to return as Countess Lichtenau. On her way, however, she stayed at Vienna, where a disappointment awaited the favourite of Frederick William. The attitude of Prussia, in concluding the Treaty of Bâle, was still fresh in the memory of the Austrian Court, and Madame Rietz, who was generally known as having furthered the peace negotiations with France, was sure to meet with scant courtesy in the Austrian capital. Court etiquette in Vienna was very strict, and the rules very rigorous. In spite, therefore, of the endeavours of the Prussian Ambassador, the Marquis de Lucchesini, Madame Rietz was not received at Court. The result of this incident was that, at the instigation of the Marquis de Lucchesini, the King of Prussia, following the example of Louis XV, conferred upon his mistress the title of Countess Lichtenau. If one is to believe the rather doubtful memoirs of the Countess herself (for they are supposed to be spurious), the letters patent reached Madame Rietz only at Venice. She never solicited this honour, declares the Countess ; she knew that her new dignity would only tend to make her unpopular with the German lower classes and hated by the nobility. The King had often insisted upon her accepting a titled name, and ever since he had ascended the throne Madame Rietz had had many arguments with him on this matter. It was somewhat strange, Frederick William had pointed out, that a mother should not enjoy the titles conferred upon her children. Whilst in Italy however there was a question of marrying her daughter, the young Countess de la Marke, to Lord Hervey, son of Lord Bristol, and Madame Rietz at last yielded to the insistence of the King. But, maintains Madame Rietz, the letters patent creating her Countess had been made out long before she started for Italy. It was only left for her to avail herself of the title. On her return to Berlin the new Countess had to encounter hatred and jealousy on all sides.

It was at Florence that Madame Rietz appeared for the first time under her new name. Under the blue Florentine sky, surrounded by the beauty of Nature and Art, she drew in deep draughts of the joy of life. Never did the new Countess dream that whilst she was enjoying herself her royal lover was swiftly approaching his grave, that his son and successor would have her arrested and imprisoned, and that grave accusations would be raised against her, who had been a loyal friend to the King.

She went to Naples to the Court of Queen Caroline. It was here, at the brilliant Neapolitan Court, the centre of voluptuousness and dazzling fêtes, that the daughter of the trumpeter Encke, now Countess Lichtenau, made the acquaintance of Emma, Lady Hamilton. While a monarchy was tottering to its ruin, Countess Lichtenau, received enthusiastically by the Queen and her inseparable friend, rose to be one of the brilliant stars in that joyous society which was passing its life in fêtes and masquerades.

The roaring thunder of war was soon to be heard, Nelson was to appear on the scene, but in the meantime joy and laughter, life and love, reigned at the Court of Naples.

Countess Lichtenau, like Lady Hamilton, made the conquest of an Englishman during her stay in Italy. Lord Bristol, Bishop of Londonderry, became passionately enamoured of the beautiful and accomplished favourite of the King. He was immensely rich, this prelate, and he loved Wilhelmine. The latter accepted his homage and his presents, and seems to have been proud of her new conquest. And thus whilst the Vesuvius of war was preparing to send forth its fiery lava, whilst the Corsican Corporal was ready to swoop down, eagle-like, from the heights of the Alps upon Tuscany, the trio of beautiful ladies were enjoying themselves at balls and feasts in the ancient ruins of Pompeii and Herculaneum.

" With much pleasure," wrote Lord Bristol, " I learned this morning that your charming personality is now in Pisa, but that you intend to break your word and to bury yourself in marshy Venice, instead of enjoying with me the delights of that terrestrial Paradise which is called Naples. Here you are expected with the greatest impatience, and I shall follow you with the greatest assiduity ; we shall enjoy a perpetual spring and the most beautiful sky which Nature ever made ; we shall pass delightful days in listening to the divine *Paesiello*, the inimitable *Cimarosa* and the more than human Hamilton. If you dare commit this infidelity towards me, I shall call down every malediction upon your head for this treachery, and Apollo and the Muses will support me.

"Do you know that this morning I passed two hours of real delight in simply contemplating your elegant bed, where only the elegant sleeper was missing."

A few weeks later Lord Bristol writes from Naples :—

"For heaven's sake, dear Countess and adorable friend, do not vegetate in that malodorous atmosphere of Rome, the city without citizens, of senators without a Senate, under a sky half water and half air, but come to the terrestrial paradise and enhance its delights by the charm of your presence.

"Yesterday I took your apartment. It is in *Crocelle* that you will make people happy by your presence, and where you will recuperate your health, regain your gaiety and forget an Irishman, and a holy bishop (Lord Bristol), more worthy of your affection, on account of the deep attachment he has for you, will take his place."

Three months later Lord Bristol seems to have been on still more intimate terms with the Countess :—

"You may rest assured, my dear Wilhelmine," he wrote, "that the first use I shall make of the resurrection of my strength will be to join you in Rome. When the mountain refused to come to Mohammed, the good prophet went to the mountain."

In June, 1796, the infatuated lover indulged in another amorous epistle, which contained the following passage :—

"In an hour I depart for Germany, and as the wind is north, with every step I make I shall say : This breeze comes, perhaps, from her, it has touched her rosy lips and mingled its scent with the perfume of her breath, which I shall inhale, the perfume of the breath of my dear Wilhelmine."

For an English Bishop of eighty the letter is fairly passionate.

Passing through Rome, Lord Bristol happened to occupy in Civita Castellana the very room where Countess Lichtenau had dined a few weeks previously. He saw her name written in her own handwriting on the mantelpiece, and the amorous Bishop went into ecstasies over this discovery.

"Allow me to tell you," he writes to her, "what a pleasure it is to be in the same room which you have occupied and which, in my imagination, still retains the imprint of your dear footsteps."

The Countess accepted not only the homage of this Falstaff, but also his princely presents, jewels, carriages and horses. But she is growing old, the beautiful Countess, and she is trying to hold Eros fast by his wings, and while she is enjoying herself in Italy, in company of the aged lover who was already a grandfather, she is writing charming letters to Frederick William, full of her impressions and of analyses of her sensations. She talks of art and artists, of her conversations with Canova, Winckelmann and Angélica Kauffmann. The Countess's letters are full of passion, enthusiasm, anecdotes, life and vivacity.

But the horizon of her happiness was suddenly darkened. In the midst of her enjoyments, of art, fêtes and love, Countess Lichtenau received grave news from Berlin. Frederick William was very ill, and a serious issue was feared. The royal family was at the bedside of the King, "but only the presence of Countess Lichtenau," wrote the Court-Marshal Bischoffswerder, "could perhaps save the King, who was anxious to see her." Countess Lichtenau was in Venice when she received the fatal news and the urgent request of Bishoffswerder for her to return. Accompanied by her friends, the Comte Saint-Ygnon, the Comte de Dampmartin, and especially by that amorous *polichinelle* Lord Bristol, she started for Prussia. She arrived at Charlottenburg, where she found the King greatly changed. But the presence of the favourite seemed to produce a beneficial influence upon the health of the dying sovereign. For eighteen months Countess Lichtenau never left his side. The King, ill and irritated, felt only at his ease in her company. Like Louis XV in the case of Pompadour, Frederick William ordered his ministers Haugwitz and Bischoffswerder to work in the apartments of the Countess, where he constantly passed his time, and like the Pompadour, the Countess Lichtenau thought of nothing else but of how to procure enjoyment and distraction for the King. She arranged plays and *tableaux vivants* with exquisite taste. The Court and the diplomatic corps were present at the performance of a lyrical play under the title of *Antony and Cleopatra*, an allusion to the love of Frederick William and the Countess Lichtenau.

The King's physicians had advised the waters of Pyrmont as an efficacious cure, and here also the favourite endeavoured to amuse and interest the King, and to make the last moments of his life happy and joyous.

Either by error or to please, the doctors pronounced the King completely restored to health. The news caused universal rejoicing. Everyone was persuaded, or pretended to be, that the danger had completely passed. Preparations for a general holiday were set on foot.

Games, music, plays, dances, a supper for 500 guests, fireworks and illuminations filled the day, which terminated with a ball continued till dawn. In the morning, as the rejoicings were beginning, the King felt ill, and persons intimate with him begged him not to expose himself to the fatigues of the day. " One of the greatest trials of a King's life," he replied, " is to be responsible to the public for all his actions. If I do not appear to-day I shall offend a number of people, whose imaginations have been eagerly looking forward to this day. To some, I hope, it is a matter of feeling, but the greater number seek only to gratify their love of pleasure, their vanity or their curiosity. If I shut myself up I shall offend them ; praise, flattery and affection will be followed by complaints, murmurings, and perhaps even insulting speeches."

The King therefore dressed himself with care. The struggle to look pleased in spite of his sufferings was a great effort. His extreme courtesy and kindly look lent an almost celestial charm to his face. The spectators were touched by his look of gentle and compassionate melancholy. He went from one end of the town to the other, sometimes on foot, sometimes in his carriage and stood for hours at a time. Not a sign of impatience or weariness betrayed his illness.

While Frederick William was able to enjoy music and take exercise the days seemed to him short, but when the least sound of a musical instrument, and the shortest walk caused him fatigue then time hung heavily on him. The sick man's commissions frequently sent the Countess to Berlin ; sometimes her personal affairs detained her there some hours. Free access to the marble palace was not always accorded to all courtiers, and the petu- lance of Saint Ygnon was singularly out of place, where weakness was daily increasing. Frederick William was dying. Everybody knew it, and her friends, foreseeing a

catastrophe, advised the Countess to leave Charlottenburg, to take away her jewels, her diamonds, worth
about 50,000 crowns, and her drafts upon the Bank of
England, amounting to 120,000 pounds sterling. But
the Countess Lichtenau refused to leave the King.
She had gathered a merry company about him,
and continued her endeavours to amuse the dying
monarch. Saint Ygnon said that she was like the
servant of an old curate keeping away the relations and
heirs so that she might be able to govern undisturbed.
When the long October evenings set in a party assembled
every day towards seven o'clock in Frederick William's
room, the French emigrants being the soul of the circle.
Play was prohibited, and the breathlessness of the invalid
forbade any long conversation. Reading was resorted to,
the book chosen being *Le Voyageur Français*. A talented
artist would have found here an interesting and melancholy subject for a painting.

At the end of the room, lit by the soft sad light of
candles in alabaster vases, the King could be seen, pale
and emaciated, a coverlet drawn over his knees to hide
his swollen legs. His heart-breaking glance, in which
could be read suffering, resignation and kindness, travelled
slowly over the assembly. The Countess Lichtenau
would be on his right, the Marquise de Nadaillac, whose
distinguished intelligence charmed him, on his left; then
Saint Patern, Prince Maurice de Broglie, l'Abbé d'Andé-
lard, and another Frenchman. Saint Ygnon would take
the rôle of reader, while the children playing in a corner
of the room occasionally interrupted. A spectator
suddenly introduced, and not previously informed, would
certainly never have guessed that he was witnessing the
last days of a monarch whose doings interested the whole

of Europe.   Nevertheless there was something majestic in the scene.   The Queen, the Prince Royal, the Princess his wife, and Princess Louise, could obtain permission to pay one visit only.   The Marquis de Saint Mexent, a man of the world well versed in the ways of Courts, frequently said, " The King of Prussia ends his days as though he were a rich benefactor ; all the relations are excluded by the housekeeper.   I do full justice to the purity of our intentions, but in this select circle the important consequences which result from the manner in which the last moments of a King are employed are not sufficiently taken into account."

A man devoted to the Countess of Lichtenau, both by feelings and duty, considered it incumbent on him to remonstrate with her.   He assured her in the most pressing fashion that " Berlin, the provinces, the whole of Prussia, and the different European countries had their eyes fixed on her, that every day reproaches accumulated on her head, which would be a source of imminent danger to her ; that the French members called by her to form this small select circle, though honoured, were no doubt exceedingly uneasy, that in France, if a King were to die surrounded by foreigners, the scaffold would claim the men guilty of such imprudence."   The Countess listened with indifference, continued her usual line of conduct, and said to her intimate friend Mdlle. Chappui a few moments later : " That man always thinks that he is writing history."

On Saturday, November 12, Frederick William gave a last supper, at which a touching incident, showing his exceeding courtesy, occurred.   The footmen, on account of his illness, had prepared an arm-chair for him, but he would not be seated until two similar chairs had been brought for the Marquise de Nadaillac and the Countess Lichtenau, and even then he apologized to the men before he sat down. No repast could be more sorrowful or painful. None of the guests uttered a word or ate a mouthful of anything; the plates were cleared at the hasty ringing of a bell. A convulsive movement made by the sick man showed that he was suffering agonies. Before half-past nine every guest had left, greatly troubled; the majority of those who had assisted at the supper never saw the unfortunate monarch again. They all shared the same presentiment of disaster, and wept.

From that night the marble palace was closed to any one not living within its grounds. Needless to say that the doors were always open to Bischoffswerder and Rietz.

The rapid approach of the fatal calamity plunged the Countess into profound grief, but unfortunately she did not acquire discretion. On the Monday the sick man told her to open an enormous red morocco portfolio on his desk; it contained innumerable letters which the Countess had written during twenty-seven years to her benefactor, her lover, and her friend. A big fire warmed the room, no embarrassing or suspicious witness was present to hinder a decisive step; it was easy, wise and even necessary to consign the voluminous correspondence to the flames, and to restore the portfolio to its accustomed place. Deaf to prudence, the Countess, moved by a curiosity which will not surprise men who know women, was seized by a sudden wish to re-read the letters. She called instantly for horses, and with the portfolio under her arm, crossed the ante-chambers and entered her carriage before the eyes of several people.

L

Driving quickly to Berlin she shut herself up in a boudoir with her eldest sister, and spent several hours in reading. Every scrap of paper was read before being burnt.

It was a rash, imprudent act. Whilst she descended the palace steps, bearing her dangerous burden, malignant eyes watched her. Couriers instantly informed the Crown Prince of the supposed theft of papers of the highest importance to the State. Ministers devoted to the Prince, and honoured with his confidence, were instantly convoked. The Countess Lichtenau, frequently accused before by this secret tribunal, had never yet been charged with so serious an offence. All the members were unanimous in looking on her as guilty of *lèse patrie*. The rigorous fate threatening her was no longer veiled in mystery. The last scruples and the filial tenderness which had up to that moment pleaded for the Countess in the Prince's heart were vanquished on behalf of the public weal.

On the Wednesday morning decency and sentiment moved the sick monarch to send for his wife and eldest son. Towards eleven o'clock the Queen and the Prince Royal reached Potsdam. Brought into the King's room, an infinitely touching scene took place, tears were shed and caresses exchanged. The dignity of the sovereign, however, replaced the tenderness of the father. " I appreciate too well, my son," said the King to the Prince Royal, " your rare qualities to doubt that you will cause the happiness of our faithful subjects, and that you will maintain the lustre and honour of the Brandenburgs. Your grief touches me, but this is not the time to give vent to it. Last winter you were more dangerously ill than I am to-day, and heaven restored you to my love ; we are all in God's hands. I still cherish the hope that this is not my last farewell or my last embrace. Nevertheless, surrounded by danger, it would be inexcusable to postpone my paternal benediction. As to you, Madame, I am grieved, believe me, to have caused you sorrow, but I pray you to remember and be assured that I have never for a moment ceased to cherish and esteem a wife so virtuous."

The Queen and the Prince were choked by tears and sobs. The King, fatigued by his emotions and exertions, begged them to withdraw, and made a sign to the Countess to accompany them. During the visit he leant on his friend's arm, and under the pretext of speaking with difficulty he, on several occasions, asked her to act as his interpreter. The Prince was comforted by this extraordinary reticence, and congratulated himself on escaping from a difficulty which had caused him great anxiety. He would have refused nothing at that moment ; sensitive by nature, upright and faithful to his word, he would have scrupulously complied with any promise given to his dying father.

When the Queen, the Prince Royal, and the Countess Lichtenau had gone into the ante-chamber, the Queen, either from innate good-nature or from deceitfulness, said a few kind words to the Countess, and even thanked her for her assiduous and tender care of the dying monarch. The Prince Royal never uttered a word, and his glance betrayed a menacing and sinister indignation.

For the first time the Countess was alarmed, but had the courage to hide her feelings, and returned to the room with a calm look. Frederick William awaited her with impatience.

" What did my son say to you ? " he inquired with

anxious tenderness, as soon as she appeared. Silence on
the part of the Countess. " Did you not hear me ?
What did my son say ? "

" Nothing, Sire."

" What ! not a word ? "

" No, Sire ; no doubt his sorrow at the sufferings of
a beloved father left no room for other thoughts."

" It is amazing, I did not expect it, I cannot understand it."

During the rest of the day, although his sufferings
increased, he repeated at intervals : " Countess, did not
my son say anything to you ? " Then raising his heavy
eyes to Heaven, he sighed deeply. To all appearances
his heart, soon to cease beating, felt in anticipation the
trouble which was speedily to fall on the woman for
whom he had cherished an unalterable tenderness for
years. He pressed her hands with sorrow and affection.

Various questions were hazarded to obtain from him
permission for his two younger sons, his daughter, the
Princess of Orange, and the other personages of the
royal family to visit him, but he refused with an obstinacy quite out of keeping with the gentleness of his
character. Several persons were convinced that in his
great affection for the Princess Louise he could not bear
to bid her an eternal farewell, and that he could not
exclude her from the general .permission without committing an injustice, violating the rules of decency, and
causing himself infinite pain. He was loving to the last
breath of a life which terminated so cruelly.

Towards four o'clock rumours of an extraordinary
nature were circulated in the castle. The pupils of a
military school were playing in some shrubberies close

to the new gardens, when two children digging in the ground discovered close to the surface a sack, containing 30,000 francs, which bore no sign of dampness. The money was all in gold pieces stamped with the marks of different parts of France, Saxony and Prussia. The heads of the school took the money and went to give information. Rietz in great amazement sent two confidential chasseurs to the place. They returned with the news that the gardens from whence the money had been taken were already surrounded by non-commissioned officers, who guarded the avenues. A sergeant had confided to them that this watch had been strictly kept night and day for a week. Rietz's surprise changed to sorrow. He realised with a sigh that the elect of the marble palace, at one time so powerful, were at this critical moment nothing but prisoners in a gilded cage. His sorrow and mortification, however, did not blind him to the necessity of instantly sending a horseman to the Prince, with information of an incident which none could, or would, explain. The most detailed report of the adventure had been already received at the palace in Berlin.

That night, at the first sign of the death agony, the enemies of the Countess prepared a trap into which her usual rashness caused her to fall. Her sorrow, bordering on despair, brought on violent convulsions. The doctors with one accord begged her to withdraw and to lie on her bed for a few minutes. They persuaded her to leave by solemnly assuring her that the King was not near his end, and promising that if a crisis occurred she should be summoned to perform the heart-breaking but sacred duty of receiving the last breath of her august friend. If the King's life was prolonged, they added, she would be better able, after taking a little rest, to attend to his needs, her services being precious to him.

Rietz, a French gentleman in waiting, and three chasseurs remained in the room. Bischoffswerder and two officers of superior rank waited in the ante-chamber. The Countess, choked with sobs and overcome with anguish, sent some one every quarter of an hour to make inquiries as to the sick man's condition. It had been resolved to keep her out of the room, and the reply was always reassuring, the dying man being reported to be calm and even sleeping. This deception, cruel in appearance, perhaps saved the unfortunate woman from the deepest insults. It is doubtful if she would have been allowed to re-enter the castle ; by her injudicious retreat she had lost the field.

At midnight the King, still conscious, prayed God to release him from his terrible sufferings ; his prayer was not answered until seven o'clock in the morning. Continual and painful fits of suffocation preceded the end, which occurred on November 17, 1797.

Bischoffswerder immediately dispatched one of the two officers he had in readiness to take the news to the Commandant of Potsdam, temporarily placed the second in command of the Marble Palace, and mounting a horse rode in hot haste to Berlin. This speed, which was perhaps scarcely decent, was occasioned by the fear that some messenger more active even than himself would forestall him in bearing the sad but important news. He was beset with anxiety. Although sure of his conduct during the whole course of his life, although in receipt of kindly assurances from the Prince Royal himself, he well knew the crowd of enemies he must necessarily have made during the long period he had been in favour. His reserve towards

Rietz, his aloofness from the Countess, were not sufficient to allay his fears. After the first outburst of filial sorrow the new monarch offered his father's old friend the decoration of the Black Eagle; and the latter disguised his feeling of satisfaction with words of gratitude. Not that Bischoffswerder, since he had obtained it for others, would have been unable to procure this distinction earlier, but he had not considered it worthy of his notice. The reality of the favour he enjoyed seemed preferable to an outward sign of it. He felt, now, that this distinction, conferred on him after the death of his benefactor, would be a safeguard against any vague rumour which might gain credence.

Upon Bischoffswerder's arrival Count Haugwitz was dispatched to the Marble Palace with the new monarch's orders. The King received the oath of the garrison of Berlin and took horse for Potsdam.

The enemies of the Countess had, to the ruin of the unfortunate woman, cut off all resource. Count Haugwitz's note assured the King that he would not be troubled by her importunate prayers, and declared that the career of this once famous woman was terminated. He was right, a victim of fortune's fickleness, she lay on her bed a prey to suffering and sorrow, abandoned by those who on the previous day crouched at her feet offering the incense of flattery. A number of notable persons did not blush to go out of their way rather than pass before the house, though they had once cringed to obtain an entrance. Speeches, gestures and looks proclaimed her exile; her pretended partisans and her ungrateful protégés fled at the approach of such messengers as she hazarded to send to them. The orders of Count Haugwitz were followed at the Marble

Palace. Seeing that Saint Ygnon wished to speak with him, he ordered two sergeants of the guard to arrest him. It was a simple way of avoiding a painful explanation. " Here is a Frenchman with an anxious face, approaching, in his despair he may cause us some trouble ; arrest him gently, and keep him in custody until further orders." The more excited Saint Ygnon became the more zealous were his two guardians in securing him. The small procession passed under the windows of the Countess. Anxiety and fear were for the first time added to her grief ; she read, with alarm, on several faces, signs of that "infernal joy which is engendered by jealousy and ingratitude."

Abandoned to despair and tormented by nervous convulsions, the Countess Lichtenau was slightly comforted after the King's death by the message, which it was thought advisable to send her, that Count Haugwitz had been entrusted with the new King's orders. She rose from her bed and lay on a sofa, surrounded by the three illegitimate children of Frederick William II, her own son, her friend Mademoiselle Chappui, and two other individuals who had remained faithful. This group, composed of innocent and desolate persons, would have moved the hardest heart to pity. Nevertheless Count Haugwitz did not put in an appearance, and servants dispatched by the Countess returned with the news that it was impossible to approach him. Count Zastro suddenly entered the room and announced to the Countess that he had received orders to search her papers, and to demand the keys of her desk and cupboards at her Berlin house. Although he was courteous and gentle, yet his tone was necessarily severe, and the King's children, terror-stricken, threw themselves into the Countess's arms. They were dragged away. Their tears and sorrow did credit to their character, the more so that their governesses had employed every ruse to embitter them against a woman whose fortune had made her the object of envy and hatred.

The papers confiscated at Potsdam proved to be nothing but verses, songs and love letters, calculated more to amuse a boudoir than to occupy the attention of a serious council. Towards ten o'clock at night the Countess's friend, Mademoiselle Shulsky, received permission to return to Berlin. She was presented with the carriage and four horses, of which up to then she had only enjoyed the use. At first she was paralysed by fright, but afterwards, being reassured, she abandoned herself to her grief. As soon as she had left Count Saint Ygnon was released ; he had so completely lost his head at the unexpected outrage upon him that it was long before he could be calmed. His fears for the future were so exaggerated that, in spite of their grief and cruel anxiety, the Countess and those around her could not help smiling. Once inflamed, a vivid imagination creates gigantic phantoms which reason cannot vanquish.

For three days the Countess was consoled by the false hope that she was only detained while her innocence was being established. The Grand Marshal sent a message to the effect that it would be sad for her to witness the search of her house, and unpleasant to be exposed to the first outbreak of hatred which her numerous and powerful enemies had no further reason to conceal. Various councils decided that it would be advisable for her to return to Berlin by night. Overcome with grief, her whole thoughts being occupied with regret for her august friend, it was easy to deceive her. On the Sunday her horses stood harnessed from dawn till midnight, but the garden gates remained closed. On Monday at seven o'clock in the morning, her illusions were abruptly dispelled by a major of the guards, accompanied by a lieutenant, a secretary and four non-commissioned officers, who demanded an interview. She then heard the order for her arrest, which she had refused to believe would be possible. She was deprived of the portrait of the queen-mother; her mother, old and ill, was taken from her; and the society of Mademoiselle Chappui was denied her. The Count Saint Ygnon was arrested formally. In fact the vestibule of the house was converted into a prison, small and isolated; each side of it being guarded by a sentinel. Under the weight of misfortune, the soul of the Countess rose to a higher degree of elevation, her tears, murmurs and sighs being all devoted to the memory of Frederick William II. She scorned to give heed to the whispered and vile insults which subordinates know so well how to pile upon those whom the great have sacrificed to their anger and caprice. To their shame, the most distinguished personages did not blush to be allied with cooks, servants and lackeys in abusing a woman weighed down by disgrace. In all countries, at all times, courtiers given to flattery are addicted to the same vices as their valets.

Six weeks passed, during which time the Countess was allowed no communication with the outer world. So strict a watch was kept that she and her companions were ignorant of the events which were succeeding each other with rapidity. This death-like silence was broken by order of a commission composed of members enjoying public esteem and confidence. They brought wisdom and justice to their task, which no doubt was a painful one. Their first order was that the captive was to be allowed a two-hours' walk. This exercise, taken in a picturesque and beautiful place, restored the Countess's health, which was much impaired by her courageous but fruitless efforts. The sight of the Marble Palace frequently gave rise to a violent outbreak of grief.

The tribunal informed the Countess that general surprise had been caused, both to the public and to the King, by the discovery of the notes for 500,000 crowns of the Dutch loan lying untouched in a desk. These were so easy to negotiate that the general idea had been that they had long since been sent out of Prussia. " If I had had millions in my power," replied the Countess, " I should have hastened to place them under the care of my Sovereign ; besides, I never asked for this sum. The late King thought that having honoured me with the title of his oldest and most constant friend, his generosity should provide me with a more than decent position. I received his gifts with submission, respect and gratitude."

The trial began on the morrow. The accused was naturally perplexed by a cross-examination in which questions, often delicate, followed swiftly one upon the other. The commissioners, therefore, graciously allowed the Countess to reply to the questions on the day after they were put to her.

M. de Beaunoir's ' Travels ' furnishes interesting material on this subject ; no one can doubt that this impartial writer drew his information from authentic sources. The following is a verbatim extract from his book :—

The charges against her were seven in number.[1]

1. To have betrayed State secrets.

She replied, and brought proof, that she had always been the King's friend, and had never interfered with the Cabinet.   In Countess Lichtenau's hour of misfortune, when she was betrayed and abandoned by all, Bischoffswerder had the nobility to publicly declare, and to assure the King privately, that she had never interfered in any political question ; that she had never brought private pressure to bear upon any minister ; that she had never put in an appearance in the Council chamber ; nor had any voice in the Cabinet ; but had been satisfied with being all-powerful in the boudoir.

2. To have taken advantage of the King's weakness of intellect to encourage the *superstitious chimeras of the Illuminati.*

She proved that for a whole year she had been the declared enemy of the mystic sect and its apostles, but seeing that her incredulity afflicted the King, and even impaired his health, she had withdrawn her opposition. She had feigned to believe that the sensitive and loving soul of her august friend could be brought into contact with that of the Comte de la Marke, whose memory was always precious to the most affectionate of fathers.

3. To have drawn on the royal coffers, especially on the building fund.

She replied that it was true that the King had caused a house to be built for her at Charlottenburg, whither he loved to retire, and a small theatre in her house at Berlin, where he wished to see French comedies presented ; that as the King never gave her any money from his private

---

[1] Cf. Dampmartin, A. H., *Quelques traits de la vie privée de Frédéric Guillaume II.*   Paris, 1811, p. 368.

coffer, nor any in hard cash, he paid the expenses of her establishment by bonds on his treasury, and that in auditing the accounts it would be seen that it was not these bonds that had exhausted the treasury.

4. To have procured for herself a gift of lands at Pyrmont which belonged to the royal domain.

She replied that the lands of Pyrmont went with the title of Countess Lichtenau; that up to that time she had enjoyed the title only, and supposed that the King had the right to join the lands to the title.

5. To have taken from the crown the beautiful diamond known as the " Solitaire," and to have torn rings from the fingers of the dying king.

She replied by indicating the drawer of the cabinet in the King's room in which the diamond would be found, and where it afterwards was found. As to the ring, this was the story. The King wore two rings, one a ring with a stone engraved with cabalistic signs, known as a talisman; the other a simple ring holding a lock of hair belonging to the Count de la Marke. Ten or twelve days before his death the King wanted to take off these rings to wash his hands; he was unable to do so himself, and the Countess had great difficulty in removing them. She saw that the fingers were swollen with dropsy, a general swelling of the whole body having set in. Not to frighten the sick man she did not replace the rings, but put them in a small coffer belonging to the King, and here they were found.

6. To have taken away the King's portfolio three days before his death.

She proved that the portfolio only contained her letters to the King, from the first day of their intimacy, and that they dealt with their intrigue only. She stated that she had openly taken away the portfolio, and had given it to a footman named Müller to carry through the ante-chambers and gardens, which were full of people. She pointed out that if the portfolio had contained secret papers nothing would have been easier than for her to steal them without being detected.

7, and last charge, to have kept his family from the dying King.

She defended herself against this charge by showing that the King had always seen his family when he wished to do so; that she herself had pressed him to summon the Prince Royal and the Princess to Pyrmont; that in the last interview with the Queen and her son she had been compelled by the King's wish to act as interpreter.

In spite of the kindliness of her judges, men of feeling as well as of talent, the Countess languished until February 17, 1798, uncertain of her fate. These gentlemen had promised on their departure that a decision should soon be arrived at. Three months to a day after the death of Frederick William the black clouds of uncertainty were suddenly dispelled. About eight o'clock in the evening an officer came to her, and read the King's order as to her future. By this order she was deprived of her house both at Berlin and at Charlottenburg, and of her lands and property connected with the Dutch loan. Her furniture and jewels were left her to clear her debts, a pension of four thousand thalers was her only income. She was further condemned to live in the fortress of Glogau in Silesia. She listened with a serious but calm countenance, offered no complaint and shed no tear. She left at ten o'clock, having with great difficulty obtained permission to stay three hours in Berlin. Her request was only granted on the express condition that, content with

arranging her private affairs, she would receive no one
but her mother and sister—a superfluous precaution, as
few persons now troubled themselves about her.

Through all her many trials the Countess preserved
her calm bearing. Pursued by misfortune, unjust hatred,
treachery, ingratitude, a generous feeling for her fell as
balm on her wounded heart. M. Filistri, an Italian poet,
espoused her cause with energy and courage. He brought
. to the King's remembrance the great Frederick's letter, in
which the latter censured those who had temporarily
arrested Madame du Barry. The old and able politician
pointed out that this insult, offered by a young inexperienced King to the memory of his grandfather, would strike
a dangerous blow at royal power. Filistri was not satisfied
with one attempt ; with respectful but firm courage he
approached the two Queens, the new favourites, the
Princes, and the Ministers, pleading his friend's cause.
The former favourite of a King passed two months in the
fortress of Glogau. She bore her punishment with
resignation, and employed her leisure in writing her
memoirs. She was then set free and allowed to reside in
the town of Breslau, and to receive the visits of her old
friends. Thanks to the intervention of the French
Minister, part of her fortune was afterwards returned
to the Countess.

After her liberation, the Countess, although advanced
in years, still made men fall in love with her, nor
does she seem to have remained faithful to the memory
of her royal lover. Fontano, a young artist, who
assumed the name of Francis Holbein, an enthusi-
astic admirer of the music of Mozart, Haydn and Beet-
hoven, and who charmed the society of Berlin by his
songs, fell madly in love with the old mistress of

Frederick William. Wilhelmine, the daughter of the trumpeter, loved music, and was not insensible to the love of a musician. At the age of fifty she married, with the royal consent, this admirer. Holbein, however, left her in 1806, and Wilhelmine went to Vienna, where, as she relates in her *Memoirs*, she was, in the most unseemly manner, attacked in the public street by a foreigner, who had been enraged by some virulent pamphlets directed against her.[1]

Great events had in the meantime revolutionized Europe, and the Prussian Court was too busy struggling against the Corsican Giant to think of this Cinderella-Pompadour. In 1811 she went to Paris to see her daughter Frederica. The Countess Lichtenau's services to France were not forgotten, and she was very well received in the *salons* of the French capital and at the Tuileries. The former favourite of the King of Prussia was also presented to Napoleon at St. Cloud. In Prussia the old Countess was by degrees forgotten, and she died, in complete obscurity in 1822, at the age of sixty-eight, in that Berlin where she had once played such an influential and brilliant part. *Sic transit gloria mundi.*

[1] Cf. Dr Vehse, ibid.

CHAPTER VIII

Countess Maria Aurora of Koenigsmark and Augustus the Strong of Saxony

Il a affecté d'être un autre Alcibiade, en se rendant illustre dans les vertus et dans les vices également.

COUNT J. H. FLEMING on Augustus II.

ON October 28, 1696, at Goslar, between seven and eight in the evening, a noble lady gave birth to a boy. The event was kept strictly secret, and remained so for years. The child was christened on the 30th under the name of Maurice. This was the future famous Maurice of Saxony. His parents were Frederick Augustus I, Elector of Saxony and King of Poland, known as Augustus II, the Strong, and Countess Maria Aurora of Koenigsmark.

Augustus was renowned for his extraordinary strength, his life of debaucheries and pleasure, and his many love affairs. " Quand Auguste buvait," people said, " la Pologne était ivre." Augustus, as Elector of Saxony and King of Poland, had, like Louis XV, very many favourites. He is supposed to have been the father of three hundred and fifty-four children. Among his favourites the best known are the Countess of Koenigsmark; the Countess Esterle ; Fatime, a Turkish beauty ; the Princess Lubomirska, afterwards Princess of Teschen ; and the Countess Cosel. It is the story of the Countess of Koenigsmark, mother of Maurice of Saxony, which will be briefly related in the following pages.

Aurora, Countess of Koenigsmark, possessed a fine intelligence and every possible charm, added to distinguished birth. She was of medium height and elegant figure; her features were of an unequalled delicacy and regularity. Her teeth were even and as white as pearls; her bright black eyes full of fire and tenderness. Her dark hair contrasted admirably with her brilliant complexion, which required no assistance from art. Her throat, arms, and hands were of a dazzling whiteness, which put those of others in the shade. In a word, it seemed as though nature had exhausted herself in her favour. Added to these bodily perfections, she was exceedingly talented, had caressing manners, and was a fine and witty conversationalist. Her original ideas were originally expressed, characters and eccentricities were described with a never-failing brilliance and animation, but withal she was ever courteous. Her disinterested generosity was unparalleled, and her kindness of heart was such that she was ever ready to render a service and never injured another. She was devoid of bitterness and rancour, forgetful and contemptuous of offences, humble, modest, and not in the least aware of her extraordinary qualities. She spoke French, Italian, and Swedish, and even understood Latin, and wrote the prettiest verses in the world. She liked music, the play, luxury and pleasure; she drew to perfection; was well versed in history and geography; and ignored nothing of what is known as *Belles Lettres*. Such is the portrait of this famous beauty drawn by the author of *La Saxe Galante*. It is not extraordinary that with all these charms she should have captivated the susceptible heart of Frederick

Augustus. He loved her at first passionately, and when his fickleness caused him to leave her, he still continued to have the greatest consideration for her. Of all his mistresses—and he had many—she was the only one for whom he seems to have retained any esteem.

Maria Aurora, Countess of Koenigsmark, was the daughter of Curt, or Conrad, Christoph of Koenigsmark, who had married Maria Christina, a daughter of the famous Field-Marshal Wrangel. She was born in 1668 or 1670, and at the death of her father was still in her teens. She received a very careful education from her mother, who seems to have been a most excellent woman. Soon after the death of her husband (1673) the dowager Countess left Stade and went to Hamburg. An elder daughter married Count Axel Löwenhaupt, and when her mother died in 1691 Maria Aurora went to live with this sister.

Curt of Koenigsmark had also a son, Philip Christoph, who was a thorough Koenigsmark, dashing, daring, gallant and beloved by the ladies. In Venice he had made the acquaintance of Augustus, and followed the latter to Dresden. He then entered the service of the Elector of Hanover, where he became the lover of the Princess Sophia Dorothea of Celle, wife of the heir-apparent. But in 1694 Philip Christoph of Koenigsmark suddenly disappeared. He had probably been assassinated.

The young Countess of Koenigsmark, with her sister the Countess of Löwenhaupt, had come to Germany to recover the property of this only brother, who had left a considerable fortune in the hands of the Lastrops, merchants of Hamburg. As the Count's cash-box had been removed after his death, his sisters had no proof of this fortune other than that their brother had often written and spoken to them of it. After his death they claimed the money, but the Lastrops hearing that they had not got the receipt given to their brother, denied having any property of his beyond some diamonds worth about 40,000 crowns. They offered to deliver these up to the sisters provided they could prove the Count's death, and his dying without a will. One of their clerks betrayed them, and told the Countesses that the Lastrops had property to the value of 400,000 crowns belonging to the Count of Koenigsmark. The sisters appealed to the Hamburg Regency, but the influence of the Lastrops, who were related to all the members of the Senate, prevailed over justice.

Nothing remained for the sisters to do but to proceed to Dresden and implore the protection of the young Elector, Frederick Augustus I, or Augustus II. They were furnished with good letters of recommendation from the King and Queen of Denmark to the Dowager Electress. This Princess received them with the greatest cordiality, recognizing instantly the worth of the sisters. She conceived for Maria Aurora a friendship which almost amounted to tenderness, as did also the young Electress. The Elector was at the Leipzig Fair when the sisters reached Dresden, and on his way back he stayed to hunt in the neighbourhood of Meissen ; so that nearly a month passed before they could lay their grievances before him. On his return to Dresden the Dowager Electress presented the Countesses to him with the words : " These ladies, my son, are daughters of the House of Koenigsmark, and have come to implore your protection. They are worthy to receive it, both by their birth and by their own merits. I join my prayers to theirs, and I beg you to use every means in

AUGUSTUS THE STRONG OF SAXONY.
By P. Drevet.

To face page 164.

your power to satisfy their claims." The Elector was so amazed at the beauty of Maria Aurora that he could hardly take his eyes off her face.

"Your Highness sees here," she said, "sisters of the Count of Koenigsmark, whom you honoured by your favour, and who had the honour to accompany you upon some of your travels. We have come, Monseigneur, to implore you to obtain justice for us from some merchants of Hamburg, who have dared to defraud us of property confided to them by our unfortunate brother. You bestow your favours on all who approach you, you ignore the meaning of the word refuse. What may we not hope from you, therefore, we who have come from the other side of the world to implore your protection ? "

"You may rest assured, dear lady," replied the gallant Augustus, "that I shall see that you receive justice, and that if I am unfortunate enough to fail, I will make reparation for the wrong done you by the Hamburg Senate. Meanwhile I beg you to remain at my Court, I will give orders that you receive the attention you merit, and my courtiers will learn from my example how great should be their respect for you."

The young Electress entered the room at this moment, and so put an end to the private interview ; the Elector addressed a few polite remarks to Countess Löwenhaupt, and the conversation became general. The intelligence shown by the beautiful Aurora was admired by every one ; on all sides she heard nothing but praise. She accepted this adulation with such noble modesty that she seemed to be scarcely aware of it. Augustus himself was so touched by her beauty and simplicity that he there and then conceived for her a quite extraordinary passion and esteem.

His impatience to declare his love was extreme. He visited Maria Aurora the next day, but as the Countess Löwenhaupt remained present at the interview he was unable to speak privately to the object of his passion. His eyes, however, spoke for him, and Aurora was woman enough to notice the impression she had made upon the heart of Frederick Augustus. Her sister remarked it also, and teased her upon the point when the Elector had retired. "We have not come here to compete for the prize of beauty," said her sister, "and the Paris who comes to judge might at least wait until he is asked to do so."

Aurora blushed at her sister's remark, but cast down her eyes without replying.

"I beg of you," pleaded the Countess of Koenigsmark, "to let the allegory drop. What have I done that you should make war upon me ? What Paris do you speak of, and what conquest have I made ? "

"But surely," replied the elder sister, "you cannot compel me to believe that you did not notice the Elector's admiration for you."

"I do not see how you can have remarked it ; it seems to me that the Prince simply treated us with ordinary politeness."

"That is true," said Countess Löwenhaupt, "but he did not look at me in the same way."

"You are quicker than I am to notice such things," replied the sister, her serious tone showing that the conversation displeased her, "and as you are married, and your husband was your lover, you are learned in the language of the eyes. As for me, I have never loved ; and I do not know when a man loves me, until he tells me so."

Some callers being announced, the conversation

ceased, and in the evening they went to a reception at the residence of the Dowager-Electress. The Elector was there, and after the usual greetings he approached the Countess of Koenigsmark. " I cannot restrain myself from telling you, he said, overcome by his passion, " that your charms inspire me with the desire to live for you alone. I hope I do not offend you, for if my respect, my attentions, and my homage were offensive to you, I should be the most unhappy of men."

Aurora knew that resistance stimulates—if not love, at least passion, the passion of many men at any rate, and she decided not to yield too quickly.

" I believed," she replied, " that in coming here I should have nothing but praise for your Highness's generosity ; I did not expect that your kindness would put me to shame. I humbly beg you, therefore, to desist from a course which can only diminish my gratitude, and the great esteem I have for you."

Upon this she beckoned her sister, the Countess Löwenhaupt, who was standing near. " The Elector is questioning me upon the Court of Sweden ; you will be better able to answer than I can."

That was a rebuff and a revenge. She had given a lesson to both the Prince and her elder sister.

The Elector was pained and embarrassed beyond measure, but put several questions to Countess Löwenhaupt before retiring, in the hope of hiding his discomfiture.

" If ever there was a man to be pitied, I am he," he said to his favourite Beuchling. " I adore an ungrateful woman who hates me, who despises me perhaps, and I feel that I must love her still."

Beuchling realised the seriousness of his master's

passion, but knew that the noble lady would in the end yield. He was a courtier, a man of the world, and what was more, he was not in love, and consequently more clairvoyant.

" Does your Highness," he said, with the freedom he enjoyed in speaking to the Prince, " despair because a lady of high birth does not succumb at the first word ? No, Countess Koenigsmark is not to blame. She replied as a girl of distinguished birth should reply ; it was the only means of ensuring your respect as well as your love. What would you have thought had she surrendered as soon as you spoke ? You would have despised her, and perhaps ceased to love her." He under-stood human psychology, this courtier ; and he knew women too. Whether Augustus was only swayed by his passion, or whether he was really a superior man hating woman's hypocrisy and pretence, preferring frank-ness and sincerity, one cannot say. In any case, he assured his friend that had the Countess at once admitted that she loved him, such an attitude would have only tended if possible, to increase his love.

" But do not try," he continued, " to justify a cruel woman ; tell me the means of subduing her."

And then master and favourite consulted together, and as a result of their conference the Elector wrote a letter to the noble lady, and M. Beuchling under-took to deliver the letter. This he did the next morning, choosing the hour when he knew that the most distinguished personages of the Court would be present. As the favour he enjoyed gave him the advantage over others, he had no difficulty in approaching the Countess of Koenigsmark. He talked on different subjects, and gradually led the conversation to poetry. The Countess

was fond of poetry, indeed she wrote verses herself.
Beuchling being also a poet, recited to her one of his
odes, and as he saw that she was interested, he said that
he was eager to show her some verses he had written
upon the amours of the Elector and Mademoiselle de
Kessell, but that he could not show them to her in
public. She rose instantly and led the way to a recess,
where, having recited the words in question, he seized
the opportunity of speaking of the Elector's passion,
and drew such a vivid and pathetic picture of it
that Countess Koenigsmark was quite touched.
Seeing this, Beuchling lost no time in presenting the
note, which she took, and slipping it into her pocket,
told him that he was not to wait for an answer. She
then rejoined the company, but her impatience was great
and a few moments later she retired to her room and
read the Elector's note, which ran as follows :—

" If my despair was known to you, dear lady, I am convinced that however you may hate me, your kindness of heart
would induce you to pity me. Yes, Countess, you cannot
be more grieved than myself that I dared to declare my passion.
Suffer me to expiate my fault prostrated at your feet, and since
you wish for my death, do not refuse me the consolation of
receiving my sentence from your own lips. The state I am in
will not permit me to proceed further. Have confidence in
Beuchling, he is my other self, he will tell you that my life or
death is in your hands."

Could Aurora resist such passionate words ? Few
women can.

The Countess of Koenigsmark was quite overcome
in reading the letter. Still she hesitated for some time,
and knew not whether to be kind or severe ; but finally
the fatal attraction which, in spite of herself, was over-

powering her, compelled her to write the following answer :—

" So little does it become a private individual to sit in judgment on sovereigns, that I am at a loss how to address your Highness. One does not easily condemn those whom one esteems, much less desire their death. Judge then, Monseigneur, whether I desire yours, I, who join gratitude to my esteem and respect."

Having finished the note, she returned to the room and gave it to Beuchling, saying, " These are the verses you asked to see, but pray do not show them to any one." No sooner had she taken this step than she was beset by anxious thoughts; the company became irksome to her, and she pretended to be indisposed. Retiring to her room, she went to bed, where, reflecting upon the matter, she reproached herself for the crime she thought she had committed. " I have been conquered by an attraction which in spite of myself draws me onward ; all my resolutions are vain. Alas, I could not avoid accepting the note or answering it," she cried, " shall I be strong enough to hide my affection ? I must leave this place and return to Sweden, and if my sister attempts to prevent me or to know the reason, I must inform her." Aurora determined to adopt this course. She decided to fight her passion, of which she was no longer mistress.

While she was thus distressed the Elector was equally so ; her note did not in the least satisfy him ; the word "respect " with which it ended jarred him. " It is only the respect that she considers she owes to my rank that has caused her to receive and to answer my letter in this cold fashion," he said, but he immediately kissed the note repeatedly because it came from Countess

Koenigsmark's hands. Beuchling, however, was there to console his master. He succeeded in pacifying the Elector, inducing him to promise to be patient until the following day, when he could put his fate to the test.

On the morrow, Countess Koenigsmark, hearing that her sister was up, sent word asking her to come. She told the latter that the air of Dresden disagreed with her, and begged that they might leave immediately, especially as their presence was useless, since the only thing the Elector could do would be to intercede with the Emperor to induce him to compel the Senate of Hamburg to give them justice against the Lastrops.

Well might the Countess Löwenhaupt look amazed at her sister's request. She flatly told her that she could not believe it was a question of health, as she seemed to be quite well; she begged her therefore to confide to her the real motive of this sudden decision. "Is it not rather, my dear sister," she said, "that I guessed right a little while ago, and that you are afraid of the Elector?"

The young Countess Koenigsmark attempted to answer; she wished to make a full avowal, but she was too overcome, and a storm of tears spoke for her. "Don't compel me," she cried, "to tell you a thing of which I have not the strength to speak, though I have the wish to avow it. Think only that prudence does not require an independent girl of my age to remain exposed to the dangers of this Court."

Countess Löwenhaupt understood. She knew the Court and the Elector, and perceiving to what dangers her sister was exposed, she consented to leave Dresden immediately. In reality, however, she did not like the idea of leaving Saxony. She was on intimate relations with the Prince of Furstenberg, who, after the Elector, was the most amiable man at the Court. He was tall and well made, his manners were distinguished, and no one surpassed him in gallantry and politeness. He had a fine intelligence, a happy gift of expression, and was successful in obtaining anything he desired. Had he been more sincere and less unscrupulous in his amorous intrigues, he would have been a perfect man. When he first saw the two beautiful sisters he was attracted by the Countess Koenigsmark, but his keen sight detected that the Elector was in love with her. He was too fine a courtier to become a rival of his master; propriety forced him to retreat, and as there was no woman at the Court to whom he felt attracted, he attached himself to Countess Löwenhaupt. She appreciated his charm, and they were soon on very intimate terms. Countess Löwenhaupt, therefore, was careful not to fall in with the plan, and though she promised to leave Dresden, she had no intention of doing so, but intended, on the contrary, to make her sister remain. Countess Koenigsmark was comforted by her sister's promise to take her back to Sweden. For the rest of the day she looked pale, " and her melancholy eyes," writes a chronicler, " gave her a languid look, which by no means diminished her charm." When towards evening the Elector called, the object of his passion had just retired to write a letter, and he, thinking that she avoided him, was so perturbed that he hardly addressed a word to the other ladies. Countess Löwenhaupt, knowing what was troubling him, approached, and said in a low voice, " She avoids you, but she would not do so if she hated you."

"What," cried the lover, "are you aware of my sufferings ? "

"Do not invent unnecessary ones," the Countess replied. "She loves you, trust to me, I will do all in my power to serve you."

Her speech was interrupted by the appearance of Aurora. The latter was unaware of the presence of the Elector, and finding herself suddenly face to face with him she was abashed. She blushed, lowered her eyes, and greeted him without daring to look up.

"You look so beautiful, dear lady," said the Elector, " that I can scarcely believe that the alarming news given me of your indisposition was well founded. I think you must have wished to try your friends, in which case am I happy enough to be counted among the number ? I deserve to be, on account of my anxiety at the rumour of your illness."

" I know too well, your Highness," she replied, " what is due to you, to count you among my friends ; I must respect and revere you as a great sovereign and the protector of my family. Nevertheless I am deeply grateful that your Highness should have shown an interest in my health."

It was well known at the Court of Dresden that Augustus preferred speaking privately to ladies, even to those he did not love. The other guests therefore retreated, and the two lovers seized the opportunity to speak openly to each other. Augustus pleaded his love with such passion that Countess Koenigsmark's resolution was soon overruled. She had neither the strength to keep it nor to hide her love. Aurora confessed to the enraptured Prince that she loved, and both vowed to love each other for ever. The Countess

of Koenigsmark imposed one condition upon the
Elector—that their understanding should be kept secret,
but the Elector having related what had passed between
her elder sister and himself, they resolved to take
her into their confidence, and parted at last, happy
to have made known their love. Before leaving, the
Elector spoke to Countess Löwenhaupt, and told her
how the matter stood, begging her to induce Aurora
of Koenigsmark to allow him to announce to the world
that he adored her. She promised to do her utmost
for him, and he left the happiest of men.

Countess Löwenhaupt rendered the Elector such
efficacious service, that she succeeded in removing all
her sister's scruples and fears. She informed the Elector
of the success of her intercession, and impressed upon
him that his triumph was assured.

Maria Aurora of Koenigsmark promised Augustus to
follow him to Mauritzburg.

The Elector had never been happier than when he
obtained his lady's consent to the journey to Mauritzburg. They swore to love each other eternally, and
he was so enamoured that he was continually renew-
ing his protestations of devotion. Aurora of Koenigsmark, having bidden her lover a tender farewell,
left him delighted. The Elector's joy knew no
bounds.

Before the departure for Mauritzburg the happy
lover sent a gown of extraordinary richness to the young
Countess Koenigsmark, with a superb set of diamonds.
Her sister, Countess Löwenhaupt, was not forgotten,
and received magnificent presents, though considerably
inferior in value to those intended for Aurora.

Augustus left for Mauritzburg to prepare everything

for the reception of Maria Aurora, who left Dresden accompanied by the Countess Löwenhaupt, and the most beautiful ladies of the Court, wearing riding habits. She started soon after the Elector, who had ordered the most extraordinary entertainments for them. Entering the Forest of Mauritzburg they perceived a superb palace. Their carriage having stopped to allow of their admiring the magnificent edifice, the door suddenly opened, and Diana came out surrounded by her nymphs. It was Madame Beuchling who impersonated the goddess. The chaste goddess made a pretty speech, and addressing herself to The Countess of Koenigsmark, referred to her name Aurora, and begged her, as though she were the goddess of that name, to enter the palace and receive the homage of the sylvan gods. The beautiful Countess accepted the invitation.

The ladies having alighted, Diana conducted them to a drawing-room ornamented with paintings representing the principal events connected with Diana. The death of Endymion, the punishment of the rash Acteon, were depicted with exquisite art. Diana ordered her nymphs to attend to the needs of Aurora and her suite, and immediately the floor of the room opened, and a table covered with delicacies appeared. The ladies being seated, the sound of hautboys, fifes, and pipes was heard. The god Pan then entered, followed by fauns and other forest gods. Pan was the Elector himself, and the fauns were chosen from the finest built men of the Court. Diana, that is, Madame Beuchling, invited Pan to be seated near Aurora, an invitation which the happy god eagerly accepted. What compliments the god paid her, what eagerness he displayed to serve and please her, and to persuade her of his passion. " How charming you are, how

I love you, I shall love you eternally," they repeated to one another.

The meal ended, and now there came the sound of horns and dogs. The ladies ran to the window in amazement, and saw a stag dash by, pursued by hunters. They expressed a wish to follow the hunt, and immediately there were horses ready for them, and open carriages waiting to convey those who did not wish to ride. Caught in the toils, the stag rushed into a pond close to the Castle of Mauritzburg. The dogs followed, and on reaching the edge of the water the ladies found gondolas waiting, which conveyed them to an island in the middle of the pond, whence they witnessed the death.

At one end of the island was a magnificent Turkish tent, furnished also in Turkish style. While they were admiring it twenty-four young Turks came in, superbly dressed and bearing great silver baskets of delicacies. A few moments later the high officials of the harem entered, followed by the Grand Khan, shining with jewels. This was the Elector, who joined the ladies, and having thrown a richly embroidered handkerchief to Maria Aurora of Koenigsmark, placed himself on the sofa beside her. Cushions were presented to the other ladies, and as soon as they were seated, several dancing girls appeared, who entertained them with their leaps, postures and Turkish dances. At the close of the performance the Elector arose, and giving his hand to Countess Koenigsmark, escorted her to her gondola. Augustus, Countess Löwenhaupt and the Prince of Furstenberg stepped into it with her. The other ladies offered seats in their gondolas to such cavaliers as pleased them. They remained some time on the

water, listening to melodious music. Returning to
shore they re-entered their carriages, the Elector driving
in an open one by the side of the Countess of Koenigsmark. They were escorted by janissaries and grand
officers mounted on horseback, and followed by the ladies
in other carriages. In this way they reached the Castle
of Mauritzburg.

The Elector conducted Maria Aurora of Koenigsmark to her apartment, which was furnished with great
luxury. The damask coverings in the bedroom were
embroidered in silver, representing the loves of Aurora ;
and Cupid held up the curtains in festoons, and appeared to be throwing poppies, roses and anemones on
to the sumptuous bed. " Here, Countess," said the
Elector gallantly, " you are the sovereign, and from
being a great lord I become a slave."

"Ah ! " answered the Countess of Koenigsmark,
" whatever your position, you would always be dear
to me."

Kissing her hand, the Elector left her to change her
gown, and to put on other clothes himself. Countess
Koenigsmark arrayed herself in the dress the Elector had
given her, and looked more beautiful than ever. The
Elector, eager to please, dressed himself with great care, his
suit being embroidered with diamonds and pearls. When
the Countess had finished her toilette, he came to her,
and was greatly charmed to see her wearing the dress he
had given her. He escorted her to a room where a
comedy representing the fascinations of Psyche was
given. The play, entitled *Psyche avec ses Agréments*,
was followed by a supper. Countess Maria Aurora
found a bouquet of diamonds, rubies, emeralds and
pearls on her plate, which informed her that she was the

N

queen of the ball, that was to take place later. The
ball was opened by her and the Elector, and looks of
admiration and perhaps of envy followed them from the
assembled company. A round of pleasure and amusements went on for a fortnight, including balls, at which
the Countess Koenigsmark shone brilliantly above all
others ; and thus Augustus lived in a happy Eden
with his beloved.

Augustus was so much in love that having made a
journey to Dresden, he forgot to call on the Electresses,
and returned instantly to Mauritzburg. Hearing that
he had been to Dresden, the Princesses were exceedingly
hurt at his neglect. The young Electress wept bitterly,
and the Dowager protested that she would remain no
longer to suffer such insults, but would retire to the
Château de Lichtenberg, which had been assigned to
her. She gave orders for the carriages to be got ready.
The Countess Koenigsmark was greatly grieved to hear
of what the Elector had done. She reproached him
with it, saying that the greatest proof of his love would
be that he should continue to show the Electress all the
consideration that she deserved, and insisted on his
return to Dresden, protesting that she would not be the
cause of the Electress being deprived of the pleasure of
seeing him. Upon being informed of this, Augustus,
perceiving that his mistress did not intend to cause
trouble and domestic quarrels, was charmed, and his
esteem for the beautiful Maria Aurora was re-
doubled. The Countess Koenigsmark always showed
the most respectful consideration for the lawful wife of
her royal lover, and so far from preventing the Elector
from visiting her, always urged him to be as kind and
considerate to her as possible, to repair the great loss

she had sustained in losing his affections. The Electress, seeing the Countess of Koenigsmark's kindness to her, showed no jealousy of the Elector's favour. " I am consoled," she would sometimes say, " for having a rival, by her being a person of worth " ; and even the Dowager-Electress, whose strict virtue made her an enemy of all gallantry, could not condemn her son for loving such a lovable person. The two princely ladies received the titular mistress, and were even intimate with her. It was quite natural, therefore, that the courtiers should treat her with equal consideration and respect. But in justice to this favourite it must be said that she never lost her modesty, gentleness and courtesy, and that availing herself of her favoured position, she took the initiative in succouring the unfortunate. It was not the Prince but the handsome man whom Aurora loved in Augustus.

On their return from Mauritzburg to Dresden the Elector put a sumptuously furnished house at his mistress's disposal. But Aurora knew the fickle character of her royal lover. She was quite prepared, it seems. to see herself sooner or later supplanted in his affections, Consequently she made up her mind to avail herself of her influence to obtain a sure, independent and honourable position. She therefore expressed a wish to become Abbess of the famous Convent of Quedlinburg. This convent had been founded in the tenth century, and the Abbesses enjoyed the rank of princesses of the Empire. The ladies of the chapter were mostly princesses or members of the nobility. The Abbess of the convent was at that moment the Princess Anna Dorothea of Saxe-Weimar. But Aurora could hope to survive her, and if she was only elected coadjutress, that is, appointed successor, she would be satisfied. And thus, in spite of many intrigues to prevent it, the mistress of a King was nominated to the position of abbess of an ancient convent for unmarried ladies. The Elector prevailed upon the *chanoinesses* of Quedlinburg to elect his mistress as head of the chapter, which gave her a right to the title of Madame.

Augustus supped each night with her, and gave magnificent parties in her honour, at which the whole Court was present. Foreigners from all parts came to Dresden, and returned home full of admiration for both lover and mistress. Madame Koenigsmark's happiness, however, was somewhat marred by the departure of Countess Löwenhaupt, who could no longer resist her husband's orders to return.

" Now I am alone," said Madame Koenigsmark to the Elector, " I renounce all that is dear to me for you; what misery if you abandon me."

" No, Madame," cried the Elector, " you have nothing to fear; I am yours for all my life. Rest assured that the perfect charms which have enthralled me, and which I find in you alone, shall be the guarantee of my fidelity. I shall find in no other the charming and admirable intelligence which makes me feel the happiest of men when I am by you. Put aside these fears, which grieve me, and are an insult to me. In you, dear Countess, I adore not only perfect beauty, but a beautiful soul, intelligence and kindness of heart; these so raise you above all other women, that I know I shall never find your equal."

" How good you are, dear Prince, and how well you know how to reassure a heart which fears, because it loves too well. May you ever think the same; you are my happiness and joy. Yea, dear one, as I can no longer refrain from addressing you, for love banishes all restraint, I value your tenderness above greatness and power. You are a thousand times more powerful in my eyes by your feelings than by your rank. You are my master, master of my heart, and of my life."

But in spite of such tender passages between the two lovers, the day came when Aurora was abandoned by her royal lover. In 1696 she gave birth to a son, who was afterwards the famous Maurice of Saxony; he was a faithful portrait of his father, from whom he inherited the same expression, strength, manners, and even the same turn of mind. The birth of the child filled the Elector with joy. He named it Mauritz (Maurice), in memory of his conquest over the child's mother at Mauritzburg. Later on he gave him the title of Count of Saxony.

The Countess Koenigsmark's son was born in October, and in November Countess Esterle appeared at the Court of Dresden as the new titular mistress of Augustus. Aurora, on her return to Court, behaved with the utmost dignity. She showed no jealousy and made no scenes, and by her conduct kept the friendship of the Elector, when his passion for her had flickered out.

She remained to the very end the friend of her unfaithful lover who was the father of her child.

In 1702 the position of Augustus, who in the meantime had been elected King of Poland, was such that he ardently desired to gain the friendship of Charles XII, King of Sweden. His former mistress understood how to act as messenger. She left Warsaw in 1702, and visited Charles—who, by the way, was known as a woman-hater—in his camp at Wuerzau, not far from Mitau.

Aurora Koenigsmark, with all her modesty, loved luxury and fêtes, and preferred the life at the Court of Dresden, where her beauty still brought many admirers to her feet, to the life in the Convent of Quedlinburg.

Many of the biographers maintain that she did not always remain faithful to her attachment for her royal lover, and that if Augustus loved many women after Aurora, the latter, too, favoured many men with her love. After she had passed the age of forty she still kept up a correspondence with many admirers. Gradually, however, the King grew very cold in his attitude towards the mother of his famous son. Her presence in Dresden became very unwelcome, and as, moreover, her stoutness made travelling uncomfortable, she was obliged to pass her time in Quedlinburg, and it was at Quedlinburg that she died and was buried in 1728, her body finding rest in the famous crypt of the Convent.

CHAPTER IX

The Romance of a Handsome Shepherd

SHE was a Princess, he was a young shepherd. Her father was a mighty emperor; his was a poor Cossack. The only thing which their fathers had in common was the love of drink; both used to drink, and both, when drunk, beat either their wives or their children and servants. But her father, when sober, did great things and performed mighty deeds; he built ships and organised a great army; he won battles and conquered many lands, and he amassed great wealth. She lived in a luxurious court, surrounded by fabulous wealth, and was waited upon by a retinue of servants; he lived in a hut and tended his father's flocks. But the shepherd was very handsome, and moreover he could sing divinely, and when the Princess heard his melodious voice and saw his handsome figure, she fell in love with him. She took him to her court, and when afterwards she ascended the throne she heaped honours and riches upon him and secretly married him.

It is the story of Elizabeth Petrovna, the daughter of Peter the Great, and of Alexis Razoumovsky, the shepherd of the Ukraine, which I am telling.

"I dreamt last night," said the Cossack woman, Natalia Demyanovna, "that I saw the sun, the moon and the stars peeping into my hut, so that the light dazzled me."

Her cronies laughed at this strange dream. But three days afterwards, Colonel Fedor Stepanovitsh Vishnevsky was returning from Hungary to the Russian capital. He had been buying Hungarian wines for the Empress Anna Ivanovna. His way from Koselets to Tshernigov led him through the village of Lemesh, where he stopped. Mass was just being said, and the Colonel entered the village church. He was surprised to hear a melodious voice among the choristers. It was that of the young Alexis Razoum. He was the second son of Gregory Razoum, a poor Cossack, who used to drink, and when tipsy beat his children. Alexis was born in 1709. He was a handsome lad, possessed of a very pleasant voice. These qualities, coupled with his desire for learning, made him a favourite with the clergy of the village. One day Gregory Razoum came home very much in liquor. He surprised little Alexis over a book. But although his name was Razoum—meaning intelligence in Russian—old Gregory had a deeply rooted aversion, bordering on contempt, for book learning. More than once he had belaboured his son with his fists when catching him in the act of reading. Now on seeing his son disregarding the paternal commands, the old Cossack, in a paroxysm of rage, snatched a hatchet and hurled it at the head of the studious boy. The hatchet missed its aim, the poor lad having escaped through the window. Little Alexis found refuge with his teacher, the priest of Tshamer, who taught him to read, to write and to sing hymns. It was his singing that led to his fortune. Colonel Fedor Stepanovitsh Vishnevsky was a connoisseur, and being struck, not only with the voice but with the extraordinary beauty of the lad, he persuaded the village priest to let Alexis go with him to Moscow. Thus the little Cossack shepherd left his native village, to return after years as Count and Field-Marshal, the favourite and even husband of the Empress of all the Russias.

Vishnevsky introduced his young protégé to Count Lowenwolde, then Grand-Marshal of the Court of Anna Leopoldovna, who placed the Ukrainian singer in the Majesty's choir. It was here that the young Princess Elizabeth, daughter of Peter the Great, saw him. If the Princess was enchanted with the voice of Alexis, his beauty struck her even more. In the veins of Elizabeth ran the blood of her impetuous father Peter and of her licentious mother, Martha, the Livonian scullery maid who had ruled over Russia as Catherine I. Elizabeth had an ardent nature, and had grown up in the atmosphere of a corrupt and libertine Court. She had had many love affairs before she made the acquaintance of the Ukrainian singer. She had been accustomed to the loose morals of a court where licentiousness reigned supreme, scarcely hidden by the veneer of a semi-civilisation. She saw the handsome Cossack and loved him. A word to Count Lowenwolde, and the fortunate chorister was transferred to the small court of the daughter of the Romanovs. Alexis Razoum soon lost his voice, but Princess Elizabeth, appointed him her own musician, and he played the *bandoura* ; she changed his name to that of Razoumovsky, and entrusted him with the management of her properties. All these marks of confidence were to safeguard appearances, for the son of the Cossack Razoum had in reality become the lover of the daughter of Peter the Great.

Alexis Razoumovsky, as he was now called, did not forget his mother in his days of fortune. After the old Cossack Gregory had drunk himself to death, the family fell into great distress. The widow, Razoumikha, was at a loss where to find bread for the famished children, and whilst the son was in the capital, enjoying the favours of the future Empress of Russia, the mother was begging from door to door in Koselets. But fortune soon smiled upon this simple-minded *mater dolorosa*. News arrived from Alexis. He sent his mother some money which enabled her, not only to set up an inn, but also to marry her daughters. There were three of them. Agafia married a weaver, Anne a tailor, and Vera wedded a Cossack. Such were the brothers-in-law of Alexis Razoumovsky, who was soon to become the husband of an Empress.

In the meantime quick changes had taken place on the Russian throne. Anna Ivanovna died. Before her death she nominated Ivan Antonovitsh, an infant two months old and the son of her niece Anna Leopoldovna, Duchess of Brunswick, as her successor. The Russian people were growing tired of the rule of the foreigners, and Elizabeth, whom the Regent Anna Leopoldovna had begun to suspect and to treat with the utmost severity, became the idol of the admirers of Peter the Great. A conspiracy was formed, which resulted in the arrest of the infant Emperor, and the accession of Elizabeth. Alexis Razoumovsky was promoted lieutenant-general and made Gentleman of the Chamber. In April, 1742, Elizabeth was crowned in the Uspensky Cathedral in Moscow. On this occasion she overwhelmed her favourite with her bounties and presents. During the ceremony Alexis Razoumovsky acted as train bearer to the Empress. He was subsequently made Grand-master of the Hounds, and lord of vast tracts of land and estates, which had hitherto belonged to Count Munich.

The fortune of the son was soon reflected in the mother and the whole family. One fine morning the whole village of Lemesh was astir. The inhabitants had assembled before the house of Razoumikha, and were staring with open-mouthed amazement at a gorgeous carriage stationed in front of the inn kept by the widow. Messengers had come from the capital to fetch the relict of the Cossack Gregory Razoum. Her cronies assembled to congratulate her on her unexpected fortune and to wish her luck on her journey. They emptied a glass for the sake of good old times, and old Razoumikha entered the carriage, accompanied by her daughter and her son Cyril. A gorgeously bedizened gentleman came to meet the old peasant woman before she reached the old capital. It was her boy, Alexis. But the astonished mother would scarcely believe her own eyes. How could she recognise in this fine and brilliant gentleman her ragged boy, who used to guard the flock? Alexis Razoum had a birth mark on his body, and not until he had shown it to the bewildered mother did she recognise him as her son. The carriage proceeded to the capital. The old Razoumikha was to be presented to the Empress, and the Cossack woman was powdered and dressed in Court fashion for the great occasion. She was given minute instructions how to behave when in presence of the sovereign of Russia. She was to fall on her knees and prostrate herself. Attired in her gorgeous garment, Natalia Razoumikha was being conducted into the presence of Elizabeth, when traversing one of the

rooms of the palace, her own image reflected in a mirror
astonished the eyes of the simple-minded peasant.
Who could that splendid apparition be, thought the
bewildered Razoumikha, but the Empress, and she
promptly prostrated herself in great awe. She had
failed to recognise her own transfigured self in the large
mirror. The daughter of Peter the Great graciously
received the mother of her lover, who was now lodged
in the palace. But the widow of Gregory Razoum, the
modest Ukrainian peasant and innkeeper, could hardly
grow accustomed to the atmosphere of a brilliant Court.
She felt out of place in these vast and luxurious apartments ; the dazzling attire made her feel uncomfortable. She was sighing for her own former life, for the
fleshpots of her native Ukraine, for the gossip of her
village friends, and for the society in which she could feel
thoroughly at home. And when the Court prepared to
leave Moscow for St. Petersburg, Madame Razoumovsky
obtained her son's permission to return home. Her son
Cyril, however, and her daughter remained behind.
One can imagine the sensation caused by her return to her
native village, where she had now become a very important personage. There is a story told that before she left
Moscow she was present at the private marriage of her
son to the Empress.

Alexis Razoumovsky was a simple-minded man, and
honours and wealth never turned his head. Unlike
Potemkin and Orlov after him, unlike Biron, Duke of
Courland, and many others, he never had the ambition
of ruling the Empire through his Imperial mistress. He
was genuinely attached to Elizabeth, and seems to have
loved her for herself. He loved the woman in the
Empress, and was grateful for the honours she heaped

RAZOUMIKHA.
Mother of Alexis Razoumovsky.

To face page 188.

upon him and for the love she bore him. When in liquor Alexis Gregorevitsh could be brutal, as those who came in contact with him experienced to their regret; but when sober he was kind-hearted and modest. One day Elizabeth was on a visit to her ex-Court-Marshal Lowenwolde; her lover accompanied her. To the Empress's great surprise, she suddenly saw Alexis Razoum-ovsky fall on the neck of one of the butlers and embrace him effusively.

" Have you taken leave of your senses, Alexis Gregor-evitsh ? " asked the astonished Empress.

" He is an old friend of mine," modestly replied the favourite.

Alexis Razoumovsky rarely sought for honours, and even when he was created a Count of the Holy Roman Empire by the Emperor Charles VII, an honour which Potemkin afterwards eagerly solicited, he put little value on it. His Imperial mistress raised him to the dignity of Field-Marshal, and he thanked her for the gracious kindness thus bestowed upon him. " But you know, Elizabeth," he added, " you may raise me to the dignity of Field-Marshal, but you will never succeed in making a good soldier of me."

It was this lack of ambition which made the favourite liked in Court circles and gained him many friends. It was also due, to a certain extent, to his unassuming modesty, that a still greater honour was in store for the former shepherd. Among his friends was the Chancellor Bestyouzhev, considered one of the cleverest and most distinguished politicians at the Court of Elizabeth. He had been sent into exile at the beginning of the reign of Ivan Antonovitsh, but was recalled by the regent Anna Leopoldovna, and even took part in politics. Bestyouzhev-Ryoumin knew French and German, and thus possessed a great advantage over many other courtiers, and though Elizabeth did not like him, she could not do without him. The clever politician, however, knew that without a mighty friend at court he would sooner or later fall a victim to court intrigues. He was astute enough to guess the influence of Alexis Razoumovsky, and from the very first made friends with the former shepherd. But what Bestyouzhev most dreaded was to see the Empress fall in love with and marry one of the princely adventurers who visited the Court of Russia, in the hope of mending their broken fortunes by means of a good marriage.

When Elizabeth was young, her father, Peter the Great, conceived the plan of marrying her to the King of France, Louis XV. The idea was very dear, too, to Catherine I, when the latter ascended the throne of Russia after the death of her husband. The former Livonian servant was anxious to see her daughter married to a Bourbon, and reigning at Versailles. Catherine, very illiterate herself, certainly knew nothing of education, and that of Elizabeth had been sadly neglected. But the Empress insisted upon her daughter's acquiring a good knowledge of French. It was more important, she said, than anything else. When Peter II ascended the throne, there was a talk of his marrying his aunt, Elizabeth Petrovna. And, indeed, there are plenty of reasons to believe that the young Tsar was not only in love with his aunt, but that a close intimacy existed between them.

And now, although Elizabeth had refused many offers of marriage, there was still the danger of her accepting a foreign Prince. Bestyouzhev was a diplomatist, and as such he was very prudent, foreseeing all possible eventualities. True, for the present the ex-shepherd of the Ukraine sat at the Winter Palace as the mightiest personage in Russia, and his friendship guaranteed the Chancellor against court intrigues and cabals. But who could rely upon the favour of princes and sovereigns ? Might not Elizabeth choose another favourite ? Elizabeth was not exactly a model of faithfulness in matters of love. Bestyouzhev therefore made up his mind that the best thing to do was to make securer the bond already existing between the Empress and her paramour. The ex-shepherd, the son of the Razoumikha, should marry the daughter of the Romanovs. The vice-Chancellor went carefully to work. Elizabeth was leading a life of debauchery, but the daughter of Martha Skavronskaya was very superstitious, and in order to silence the voice of her religious conscience she observed the minutest details of the orthodox religion. The clergy, and especially her confessor, Doubyanski, possessed unrivalled influence over the Empress. Bestyouzhev won over to his plans, this priest, who under his modest clerical garb hid a tactful and clever diplomatist, and the two succeeded in persuading Elizabeth to marry her favourite.

In the little village church of Perovo, near Moscow, the nuptial benediction was given to the couple. And thus the handsome shepherd had acquired the highest honour to which a Russian subject in his wildest dreams could aspire. He was married to the beautiful Princess, his Empress, and Alexis Razoumovsky, who had passed his youth in a miserable hut in the Ukraine, now sat at St. Petersburg in his gorgeous apartments adjacent to those of the Empress. His influence was now paramount. Although the marriage had been kept secret, all the world looked upon Alexis Gregorevitsh as the husband of the Empress, and paid him homage accordingly. He accompanied his Imperial wife everywhere, and she dined in his apartments when he was indisposed. He occupied the same position as that of Madame de Maintenon by the side of Louis XIV. When he had an attack of gout the Empress tenderly nursed him in his apartments, and all the festivities of the Court were suspended. When leaving the theatre or the opera, the Empress might often be seen buttoning up the fur coat of the Count and adjusting his fur cap. The courtiers, descendants of the most ancient houses of the Russian nobility, vied in their submission to the former shepherd. When not drunk, Count Razoumovsky was one of the best hearted men in Russia, and the dazzling height he had reached, the wealth and honours heaped upon him, never turned his head. He had none of the contemptible pride usual to *parvenus*. Although born a peasant, he was, as far as character was concerned, a gentleman by nature, incapable of ingratitude and meanness.

One day, recounts Prince Dolgoroukov in his *Memoirs*, certain goods from the estates of the Count had been bought by a Russian merchant for the sum of 70,000 roubles, but before the cargo had been delivered it was burned down. In great excitement, the superintendent of the estate came to inform the Count of the mishap. "Oh, how unlucky," he exclaimed, "that this should have happened before the buyer had taken possession of his goods." "Not at all," replied the Count; "on the contrary, it is very lucky that it so happened; it would have meant ruin to the poor merchant, whilst, thanks to the grace of God, it will not affect me in the least."

COUNT ALEXIS RAZOUMOVSKY.

To face page 192.

The favourite forgot neither his family, nor his former friends and benefactors. When in 1744 Elizabeth visited Koselets, the native village of Razoumovsky, not far from Lemesh, the latter availed himself of the opportunity to see his relatives. He received the humble Cossacks, their wives and children, in a house which he had had constructed, and there, in the bosom of his family, the husband of the mighty Empress, knowing neither pride nor arrogance, spent many pleasant hours. The friends, who had been instrumental in paving his way to fortune were also handsomely rewarded by Razoumovsky. Vishnevsky, who had taken the poor chorister to the capital and thus laid the foundation-stone of his fortunes, was made a general. His old master, the clergyman of his native village, was called to the capital, and Alexis Gregorevitsh asked him to choose some lucrative position for himself. The old man hesitated for some time, but suddenly discovered the position that just suited his tastes and abilities. One evening he visited the opera, and his taste for music induced him to ask his protector to appoint him conductor of the orchestra. The naïve request of the old man made the favourite smile. He appointed him inspector of some Imperial garden with considerable emoluments. Many of Alexis Razoumovsky's relatives, simple illiterate Cossacks, were appointed superior officers in the Ukrainian army. Such were his brother-in-law, Dragan, who henceforth changed his name into that of Daragan, and his uncle, Demeshky. His niece Avdotja (Eudoxia) Danilovna was married to the Count Bestyouzhev-Ryoumin, son of the Chancellor, and when visiting Vienna, soon after her marriage, she was received with the utmost amiability by Maria Theresa. The Empress, the descendant of the House of Hapsburg, was seeking the alli-

o

ance of Russia against France and therefore flattered this daughter of simple Cossacks, who was now a great lady and enjoying considerable influence at the Russian Court. But it was especially the younger brother Cyril who benefited by the fortune which had smiled upon the lucky elder brother.

Count Cyril was much younger than the favourite. Born in 1728, he was only fourteen when Elizabeth ascended the throne. Cyril was sent abroad, under the guidance of the young academician, Gregory Teplov, a natural son of the archbishop Theophan Procopovitsh, to study, and to acquire the polish of a gentleman. The young Cossack studied at the Universities of Göttingen and Berlin, and visited France and Italy. At the age of fifteen, the boy was made Gentleman of the Bedchamber, at sixteen created a Count ; and at eighteen he was appointed President of the Academy of Sciences. In the same year he married Catherine Ivanovna Naryshkin, a grand niece of the sovereign. Cyril Razoumovsky was only twenty-two when the dignity of Hetman of the Ukraine, vacant since 1750, was re-instituted, and the son of the Razoumikha was appointed Hetman, or Viceroy of the Ukraine, and led the life of a petty sovereign in the capital Batourin. He prevailed upon his mother to take up her abode in his princely residence. Simple-minded Màdame Razoumovsky, however, preferred a modest dwelling to the luxurious apartments in her son's palace, and the national *borshtsh* [1] and *kasha* [2] to the dainties of the French cook.

Like his brother Alexis, Cyril never forgot his modest origin. In 1744 Count Keyserlingk obtained for Alexis the title of Count of the Holy Roman Empire. In the patent the Count Razoumovsky was said to be descended

---

[1] Cabbage-soup.   [2] Gruel.

from the princely family of Bogdan Rojinsky, whose father, Prince Eustace, had been Hetman of the Ukraine from 1514 to 1534. The Princes Rojinsky were moreover descended from the grand dukes of Lithuania, of the race of the Yagellos, which became extinct in the seventeenth century. Cyril Razoumovsky, when Hetman of the Ukraine, one day visited Kiev. On this occasion he was presented by the monk Michael Kosatshinsky, professor at the ecclesiastical seminary, with a beautiful volume, bound in gold.

" This book contains the genealogy of your excellency," said the monk.

" My genealogy," asked the Hetman, in astonishment, " but surely, your reverence, my genealogy cannot be so voluminous as this."

" The family of your excellency is descended from the illustrious house of the Princes Rojinsky," explained the professor.

" What stories are these which your reverence is telling me," laughed the Count, " my genealogy is a very short one. My father was a simple honest Cossack ; my respectable mother, to whom may God grant a long life, is a good and honest woman, and the daughter of a simple peasant— an honest man, too. I am Count and Hetman of the Ukraine on the two banks of the Dnieper, with the rank of Field-Marshal, thanks only to the kindness of Her Majesty, our gracious benefactress. That is all my genealogy, your reverence. It is a short one, but I do not wish for any other. Adieu, your reverence."

Truly, they were gentlemen by nature, these two noble shepherds, raised by the amorous caprice of a sovereign to the highest dignities in the Empire, and transformed from guardians of the village flock into rulers over vast provinces.

Elizabeth was not exactly a model of constancy in matters of love. She had the temperament of her parents. When her fiancé, Charles August of Holstein, died, she refused the offers of many suitors who aspired to her hand. She either preferred her liberty, or, as has been mentioned, had secret hopes of marrying her nephew, Peter II. But even while she was so intimate with the Tsar, she entertained a *liaison* with Boutourlin and afterwards with Simon Naryshkin. Prince Ivan Dolgoroukov, however, wishing to see his sister married to Peter II, revealed Elizabeth's conduct to his sovereign. The nephew was furious against his aunt, and the latter henceforth decided to choose her lovers from among young men less known in Court circles than Boutourlin. She looked for them even among her domestic servants. One of these, who enjoyed great favour in her eyes, and for whom, when he was exiled to Siberia by Anna Ivanovna, the daughter of Peter the Great shed bitter tears, was Shoubin, a simple sergeant in the Semeonovsk regiment. And even when already legally married to Razoumovsky, Elizabeth not infrequently had other lovers. Such were Peter Shouvalov, Roman and Michael Vorontsov, and her servants Charles Sievers, the sailor Lialin, and the coachman Voytshinsky. In 1749 Ivan Shouvalov became the principal favourite. With the exception perhaps of the last-named, Elizabeth's heart, in spite of her many infidelities and aberrations of affection, belonged to Razoumovsky. In any case he retained his influential position until the death of the Empress. And even after the accession of Catherine, he was treated by the latter with every mark of respect.

Elizabeth's marriage with the handsome Ukrainian shepherd was not without issue. She had a son and a daughter, named Tarakanov, after a village Tarakanovka, in Little Russia, which belonged to their father. The episode of the Tarakanovs is too full of romance in itself to be omitted.

It was the year 1772, and Catherine sat on the throne of Russia, which seemed suddenly to be tottering. Peter III had been strangled at Ropsha, and Ivan Antonovitsh, the infant Emperor dethroned by Elizabeth and kept prisoner in the casemates of Schluesselburg, had been dead since 1764, but the Northern Semiramis again trembled on her throne. Emelyan Pougatshev, the famous Cossack of the Don, an outlaw and a brigand, had raised the banner of revolt against Catherine and her government. At the head of a vast army of Bashkirs, Tartars, and Calmucks, he was burning castles and massacring the nobles. The population was expecting him in feverish impatience. It was about this time that a woman, who at first called herself Princess Voldomir and afterwards Tarakanov, but who was supposed to be none other than a daughter of the late Empress Elizabeth and Alexis Razoumovsky, made her appearance. It is in Paris that we first meet this beautiful and elegant young lady, whose good looks, coupled with a majestic dignity, charmed all those who came within the circle of her acquaintance. She was accompanied by two friends, a Baron von Schenk and a Baron Embs. She kept open house, and among those who paid homage to the mysterious and beautiful stranger was Count Oginsky, Hetman of Lithuania, an illustrious patriot and one of the leaders of the Polish nation. He had come to Paris to plead at the Court of Versailles the cause of Poland, which Catherine was dismembering.

Princess Voldomir was said to be a Circassian, and heiress to fabulous wealth in Persia. French financiers gladly advanced her money in her temporary pecuniary embarrassment. But money which she was always expecting from Persia never came. Baron Embs (who was no baron at all, but the son of a rich merchant of Gand, who had been expelled by his father) was arrested for debts and forgery, and the Princess suddenly left Paris. She proceeded to Frankfort, where she succeeded in finding a protector in the person of Philip Ferdinand, reigning Duke of Limburg, who, though in debt himself, offered hospitality to the princess in distress at his castle of Oberstein. Philip Ferdinand, who liked to play the petty sovereign in his lilliputian dukedom, fell in love with his guest. He wished to imitate Louis XV, but the clever Circassian was no la Vallière. The Duke promised her marriage, and the fair lady gave in to his assiduities. But, in the meantime, the duke's pecuniary position was growing more embarrassing every day, whilst his affianced wife—owing to strange rumours about her conduct—seems to have given him cause for suspicion. The Princess Voldomir, however, had already grown indifferent to the affections and faith of the Duke of Limburg. She had found a new protector, who was no less a personage than the famous Prince Radziwill. Catherine had crushed the independence of Poland, and many illustrious Polish patriots had left their native land. Among these exiles was Prince Radziwill, who was now residing in Mannheim, not far from the castle of Oberstein. Among Radziwill's confidants was a young Polish patriot named Domansky. This impetuous youth fell desperately in love with the Princess, and remained faithful to her until her death. A story was now circulated that the Princess Voldomir was the daughter of the late Empress Elizabeth, and the rightful heiress to the throne of Russia. She had in her possession a precious document, the testament of her mother in which she was appointed her successor. Whether Radziwill believed this story or not is very doubtful. He was astute enough, however, to see in this pretender to the Russian throne a useful ally. It was decided that the Princess should follow him to Venice, and thence to Constantinople, there to solicit the assistance of the Ottoman government to regain the throne of Russia for the granddaughter of Peter the Great, and her former independence for Poland. A letter from a relative of Radziwill in Paris, the Countess Sangusko, stated that Louis XV had approved of this plan. And so to Venice, and thence to Ragusa, the Princess went. Here she was treated with all the honours due to the future Empress of Russia, and the Consul of France, Descrivaux, offered her his own delightful villa. But her fortune was on the wane.

The treaty of Koutshouk-Kainardji put an end to Radziwill's hopes, and the journey to Constantinople was consequently abandoned. The pretended granddaughter of the Tsars did not lose heart, however. She decided to go to Rome and to gain the interest of the Vatican. In Naples she made the acquaintance of Sir William Hamilton, the future husband of Emma Lyon, who quite fell in love with her, enchanted by her fascinating beauty. But while in Rome her resources became exhausted and she decided to appeal to the generosity of Hamilton. It was a large sum she asked, and Hamilton addressed himself to his colleague, John Dick, banker and Consul for Great Britain in Leghorn. John Dick happened to be on intimate terms with Alexis Orlov, who was commanding the Russian fleet in the harbour of Leghorn. Orlov had already received orders from Catherine to make the adventuress a prisoner, by fair means or foul. The victor of Tsheshme

decided to avail himself of the opportunity. The Princess
was given unlimited credit at a bank in Rome, whilst Orlov
sent word that, having convinced himself of the authenti-
city of her claims, he was ready to put his services at her
disposal, and by helping her to the throne of Russia,
wreak his revenge on Catherine and her new favourite.
He implored her to go to Pisa, where the winter was less
rigorous than in Rome. She should take care of her life,
which was so precious to Russia. Clever woman though
she was, she was caught in the snare, in spite of the en-
treaties of Domansky, whom love and genuine attachment
had rendered clairvoyant. In Pisa she was received with
the honours due to an empress. Orlov paid her marked
homage. But it was more than respect to his sovereign
that he endeavoured to show. He loved the woman, but
not daring to give utterance to his feelings, he commissioned his friend, John Dick, to act as go-between. John
Dick made love in the name of his friend, who implored
her to consent to share with him the throne of Russia,
which he was going to conquer for her. The comedy was
played to perfection, and the woman, flattered and dazzled, believed. She accepted the offer, and a fictitious
marriage ceremony was celebrated. In perfect confidence
she accepted her husband's invitation to witness from
the flagship a naval fight, given in honour of the occasion.
In vain did Domansky implore her not to go. She refused to listen to him, and, accompanied by this faithful
friend and another attendant, she embarked with Orlov
for the flag-ship. But, alas ! here a sad surprise awaited
her. Scarcely had she reached the deck, when Orlov
disappeared, her two companions were disarmed, and she
made prisoner. She wrote a few lines to Orlov, but he
played his part to the very end, and an officer brought her

an orange wrapped in a piece of paper upon which Orlov had scribbled his reply. He was a prisoner himself, but implored her not to lose heart. Fortune would still smile on them. She dried her tears and hoped. Orlov had immediately dispatched a courier to St. Petersburg, to inform Catherine of the success of the ruse, and the next morning Admiral Greigh set sail for Cronstadt, whilst Orlov remained at Leghorn in command of the fleet.

The Princess was taken to St. Petersburg and imprisoned in the fortress of SS. Peter and Paul. Prince Galitzin questioned her, but she never admitted that she intended to give herself out as the daughter of Elizabeth. The illness with which she was afflicted made rapid strides. The fortress of SS. Peter and Paul is not exactly an ideal retreat for consumptives. Many a robust political criminal imprisoned in this Russian Bastille became a shadow in the short span of a few months. Her condition being very grave, a priest was sent for, but the man of God also endeavoured to question her on her adventures.

" Read the service for the dead, that is all you have to do here," she curtly observed.

The Princess died in 1775. Another story, however, was circulated at the time asserting that the prisoner perished in one of the subterranean cells, during an inundation of the fortress. The officials had neglected to take the necessary precautions. This is only a legend ; but a picture by Constantine Flavitsky, representing the agony of this girl, standing in her cell and facing death, as the waters of the Neva rush suddenly into her prison, was exhibited in Paris in 1867. It created a great sensation and evoked deep-felt sympathy with the fate of this unhappy woman, supposed to have been the issue of the romantic union of an empress and a former shepherd.

Elizabeth was dead. Catherine II was on the throne. Peter III was strangled at Ropsha by Catherine's friends. The Empress was contemplating her marriage with Gregory Orlov, and the supporters of this plan, especially Chancellor Vorontsov, quoted as a precedent the marriage of Elizabeth and Razoumovsky.

One day Vorontsov called on the venerable Count. The former favourite of Elizabeth was reading the Bible at his fireside. Vorontsov informed him that her gracious Majesty had decided, in case of her marriage with Orlov, to confer upon Razoumovsky, as the husband of the late Empress, the title of Imperial Highness. He would only be required to produce the necessary documents. The ex-shepherd looked astonished.

" Such conduct would be an indignity, and I will not accept the honour," he exclaimed. " Is it not enough that I, a simple Cossack, am now a Count, a Field-Marshal and a millionaire ? "

" But you were legally married to the late Empress, and have the documents in your possession."

" Will you excuse me for a moment," said the Count, and he disappeared into the adjoining cabinet. In a few minutes he returned, carrying a large envelope tied up with a pink ribbon. He carefully opened the envelope, took out several documents, faded with age, silently looked through the contents, and then with a solemn air, threw them into the fire. And whilst the flames were rapidly consuming these precious documents, the son of Natalia Demyanova Razoumikha turned to Vorontsov with a sigh of relief. " Tell those who sent you that I have never been anything but the humble slave of my august benefactress, Elizabeth. Never did the late Empress so far forget herself as to marry one of her subjects. I kiss the hands of the present Empress, and hope that she will allow me to enjoy in peace the favours which have been heaped upon me."

Vorontsov understood. He faithfully reported the incident to the sovereign. Catherine, too, understood. She took the hint. Was she grateful to Razoumovsky? In any case Orlov never became the husband of the Northern Semiramis. Count Razoumovsky died peacefully in his Anitshkov Palace at St. Petersburg in July, 1771.

CHAPTER X

The Platonic Affection of a Tsar

Mademoiselle Nelidov

"AT this solemn moment of my life I have a sacred duty to perform which I owe to God and to my conscience. I desire to justify one who is entirely innocent of the accusations brought against her on my account. I am aware that the evil world has falsely interpreted the spiritual union that exists between her and me. Before that divine tribunal, that awaits to judge us all, I solemnly swear that she and I will be able to appear before it as free of reproach as regards each other as we are towards any one else. Would that I could seal this vow with my blood ! But I swear to its truth as I bid farewell to the world. I declare that our connexion has been pure, holy, and without sin. I take God to my witness."

Thus wrote in 1790 Paul Petrovitsh, the son of Catherine II, to his mother. The Prince was endeavouring to assure his mother that the rumour that Mademoiselle Catherine was his mistress was false, and that the relation existing between him and this maid of honour was purely platonic. My intention is neither to contradict nor to confirm this rumour (contemporary biographers differ on the point), but simply to give a brief sketch of this somewhat remarkable woman, who exercised an

PAUL I.
After a portrait in the possession of the Academy of Science in
Petrograd.

To face page 204.

enormous influence over the irascible Russian Caligula of the eighteenth century.

According to contemporaries, Mademoiselle Nelidov was not pretty. Her hair and complexion were dark ; but she was slender and graceful, with bright intelligent eyes ; her face, although plain, was full of expression. Moreover, she danced with incomparable grace and spirit. She could sing, and her conversation, though never over-stepping the bounds of decency, was amusing and extremely witty.

Mlle. Nelidov was born on December 12, 1758, in the village of Klimiatino, in Smolensk ; her father was lieutenant Ivan Dmitrievitsh Nelidov, her mother Anna Alexandrovna Simonov. Her parents were in easy circumstances, and owned about five hundred serfs in the districts of Smolensk and Tver. Catherine Nelidov had a sister named Natalia, and six brothers. Like most of the daughters of Russian landowners at that time, she was brought up in the country among nurses and servants, surrounded by the simple scenes of rustic life, which left an enduring impression on the sensitive soul of the little girl. But the future favourite of a Tsar was destined to receive a better education than most girls of her class. News reached their distant corner of the province that a school for the daughters of the nobles had been established at the Convent of Smolna, under the immediate patronage of the Empress Catherine. Anna Alexandrovna, the mother of Mlle. Nelidov, at once decided to start forthwith for St. Petersburg with her daughter Catherine, who was then just six years old. She was anxious to make arrangements at once for placing Catherine in this educational establishment, but had yet to ascertain under what conditions she might be admitted. The Empress's idea was to create an altogether new race by means of education, and for this purpose she endeavoured to isolate the children who were chosen from all outside influence. The first condition imposed on those who wished their daughters admitted to the school was that the parents must sign an agreement not to withdraw their children before their education was completed, the course of instruction lasting for twelve years.

Mlle. Nelidov gained many a distinction while at school. Her personal appearance and superior qualities of disposition raised her above the level of her companions.

By the time she was twelve years old she had already shown signs of her mental abilities. At this tender age she was a perfect little prodigy, thanks to her remarkable talent for dancing and acting, in which she exhibited incomparable grace of action and a genuinely artistic feeling.[1] Mlle. Nelidov was not exactly pretty, but her eyes were full of expression, and the remarkable animation and mobility of the face compensated for the lack of beauty.

She had with truly feminine intuition found out while still sitting on her bench at school how to make the most of such gifts as she possessed, so as to outshine her companions. Every one who visited Smolna spoke with enthusiasm of her intelligence, her grace of manner, her extraordinary talent for dancing.

It was during her life at the convent that Catherine Nelidov was chosen to act a painful and prominent part, which brought her neither pleasure nor happiness. The attention of the Empress was drawn to her, and she

---

[1] Cf. Shumigorsky, *Yekaterina Nelidova*, St. Petersburg, 1902, p. 12.

MADEMOISELLE CATHERINE IVANOVNA NÉLIDOVA.
After a portrait at the Court of Peterhof.

To face page 206.

was finally appointed one of the maids of honour to
the Grand-Duchess Natalia Alexeevna, the wife of the
heir to the throne.

From the first moment of her introduction, Mlle.
Nelidov found herself plunged in all the intricacies of
court intrigue.

The sudden death of the Grand Duke's first wife was a
great loss to Mlle. Nelidov; she had known the Grand
Duchess Natalia while a girl at school, and had received
many kindnesses at her hand. The Grand Duke did
not delay in making preparations for a second marriage,
and finally chose the Princess Sophia Dorothea of Wur-
temburg, who was admitted into the Greek Church
and received the name of Maria Feodorovna. The young
maid of honour was presented when her new mistress
entered the capital, and was afterwards removed to the
Grand Duke's Court, in the company of the Countess
Roumyanzev, who had been nominated by the Empress
to the post of grand mistress. It was a difficult position
for a young girl of seventeen, inexperienced in the ways
of life and separated from all her friends and relations.
It was deprived during the first two years of much of
its danger by the presence of the Countess Roumyanzev,
to whom she was able to turn for advice. But the
young girl quickly accustomed herself to court life, and
with her perspicacity soon saw, observed and judged
for herself.

Thus the relations between the Empress and her son
soon became known to her, and her sympathy was at
once enlisted on the side of the Grand Duke.

Fresh from the convent and full of enthusiasm, the
character of the young Prince of twenty-four was calculated to inspire her with admiration. His courtliness

and benevolence, his aspirations after truth and justice, his anxiety to make his people happy, all these qualities appealed to her, and she could not help contrasting the quiet and pious life led by him in the midst of his household with that of the Empress's Court.

The sympathy existing between Mlle. Nelidov and Paul was no secret to the Court, and about 1782 it began to be whispered that the maid of honour was the favourite, or rather the mistress, of the Grand Duke. And indeed Mlle. Nelidov had become an important personage. During the six or seven years that had elapsed since she left the convent she had grown more serious and more a woman of the world. Meanwhile the position of the Grand Duke had during this period become even more equivocal, for Catherine systematically excluded him from all public affairs. She, moreover, deprived him of the friends to whom he was attached, among them Prince Alexander Kourakin. It was natural, therefore, that having none of his old acquaintances about him with whom he had been accustomed to exchange ideas and sentiments, he should seek the society of Mlle. Nelidov, whose vivacity and conversational powers, combined with her nobility of character and soundness of judgment, suited the taste and corresponded to the aspirations of the Grand Duke. "The natural amiability and chivalry of his manner lent an air of intrigue to his relations with the maid of honour, but," says Shumigorsky, "the plainness of the girl prevented any idea of there being any serious connexion between them." [1] Moreover the Grand Duchess, Maria Feodorovna, made use of her maid of honour to

[1] Shumigorsky, l.c. p. 18.

accomplish her own ends, and for this purpose was anxious not to part with her.

It is generally asserted that Mlle. Nelidov's feelings for the Grand Duke were of the purest. The position he held during his mother's reign, apart from any personal qualities, was alone sufficient to awaken sympathy. Those around him could not fail to notice how the treatment he received gradually embittered a nature naturally cheerful and impulsive. The liveliness of his disposition degenerated into an irritability which in later days vented itself in violent fits of rage, while his prudence became suspicion. Angry at the position assigned to him, he grew gloomy and surly, always ready to imagine that people were wanting in respect to him, and, in his fear of being surrounded by the Empress's spies, giving ear to self-seeking tale-bearers. His mental powers began to show signs of failing. His brain and nerves were always on the stretch, and though as regards thought and morals he remained on the same high level as formerly, his acts, the fruits of a deranged imagination and soured disposition, began to trouble his household by their inconsistency and violence. All his friends agreed to treat him as a beloved invalid, over whom it was necessary to keep a certain watch, their one wish being to make his life as happy as possible. Soon, however, it became necessary to exert a more direct influence upon him, and then it was that the invalid became aware of the guardianship in which he was held, and he determined to get rid of his overseers and to exercise his independence. Now was the moment for intriguers, who urged him to all kinds of adventurous undertakings to serve their own purposes, and it was about this time that Koutaïssov, Paul's valet and barber, gradually acquired such a powerful ascendancy over his master.

And how did Paul's wife, the Grand Duchess, look upon this intimacy of her husband with another woman ? Was she content at heart to see her exercising so strong an influence over the Grand Duke ? Mlle. Nelidov often called the latter " her little Paul." She allowed herself to be led away with the idea that she was acting the part of a guardian angel ; her pride was gratified in seeing the Grand Duke subject to her in mind and heart, and she forgot what gall it must be to the Grand Duchess to look on. The situation, at all times painful, became doubly trying when the court was being held at the country residences of Pavlovsk and Gatshina, and if Maria Feodorovna, as has been often stated, availed herself of the influence of the favourite, she must nevertheless at moments have felt the sting of jealousy. Mlle. Moukhanov asserted that the good understanding between Paul and his wife was never interrupted during the whole time that the Prince was paying court to Mlle. Nelidov. In another memoir, however, we read that the wife, in her anger against the favourite, complained to the Empress. For reply Catherine is reported to have led her daughter-in-law to a mirror, and to have said : " See how beautiful you are ; your rival is an ugly little thing ; leave off fretting, and rest assured of your charms." [1] In one of her letters Maria Feodorovna accused the favourite of wishing to play the part of Madame de Maintenon as soon as she, the Duchess, was dead, and she always feared that her death might occur while giving birth to a child.[2]

[1] Cf. *Russian Archives*, 1878, vol. i., p. 308.
[2] Cf. Rappoport, *The Curse of the Romanovs*, p. 216.

Empress Maria Féodorovna
after a portrait by Lampy

Published by The Navarre Society. London

Before starting for Finland, where he hoped to take part in the military operations, the Grand Duke sent a note to Mlle. Nelidov written on a scrap of paper : " Know," he wrote, " that when dying I shall think of you." The attentions of the Grand Duke, who made no attempt to conceal his feelings, did not fail to bring discredit on Mlle. Nelidov, and from 1785 onward she was generally regarded as his mistress.[1]

The Grand Duchess became daily more at variance with her husband, owing to the natural bent of her mind and her moral sentiments ; while the Grand Duke continued to find increasing pleasure in the companionship of Mlle. Nelidov. Nevertheless, he never forgot that he was the future autocrat of Russia, and his detailed supervision of military affairs was preparatory to his taking the reins of government. The Grand Duchess, finding herself unable to direct her husband's thoughts, and unsuccessful in her efforts to check his fits of passion, was forced to submit to her fate with gentle resignation. She could not but compare Paul's administrative occupations with the continual claims upon her of her own family, for whom she was always soliciting the Empress, and his aspirations after all that was great and beautiful with the prosaic and monotonous life she was forced to lead.

Mlle. Nelidov's relations with the Grand Duke were no longer a secret after the campaign in Finland. Her character suited that of the Grand Duke to perfection, while in his wife's society he found the sedater qualities which were less to his taste. He felt a confidence in the sincerity of the maid of honour, who never feared to express her opinions, nor hesitated to act accordingly, while in

[1] Shumigorsky, l.c. p. 20.

the quiet submission of his wife he had a sense of opposition, and of a silent censure of his conduct. Paul had something of the mystic in him, and was attracted by the lively faith of Mlle. Nelidov, and by her inclination towards the more mysterious side of religion. Shumigorsky endeavours to prove that his attachment was purely platonic. " The disinterested attachment of the young girl flattered the Grand Duke. To idealise the object of his affection, and to lavish a platonic adoration upon her, was quite in keeping with Paul's chivalric nature.[1]

Mlle. Nelidov on her side had a truly feminine gift of insight and, with a full understanding of Paul's disposition, knew how to humour him, and how to control his temper, in which endeavours Maria Feodorovna had never been successful.

Paul himself on several occasions attested to the essentially honourable, and one might almost say religious, connexion between him and Mlle. Nelidov. There was even a touch of mysticism in it. Paul, always pious and sincere, wrote the following letter to her, on the occasion of his forwarding her a book of a religious character :—

" The bond which unites us, the history of our relations with each other, and their development; the circumstances amid which you and I have passed our existence, in a word, everything connected with us, has in it something so peculiar that I must ever retain the memory of it. I send you, as I think, a present of value, for I therewith oblige you to think of God so that you may grow closer to Him. At the same time I make myself also the best of presents. That is my way of loving those who are dear to me. Who can say that there is anything criminal in this ? Read my book, dear friend; open it where you will and make no rule for yourself at what hour or for how long you are to peruse it; be guided only by your impulse. Forgive me all I

[1] Ibid. p. 23.

write to you ; be indulgent towards the one who loves you more than he loves himself; it is in this spirit that I beseech you to accept what I send. God alone knows how greatly I love you ; may God shower all his blessings upon you, while I remain for ever your servant and friend."

On his return from Finland, he had a serious illness, and anxious to prevent any unkind attacks on Mlle. Nelidov, when he was no longer able to protect her, he wrote to his mother the letter quoted above, begging her not to forsake his friend if he died.

Notwithstanding his assertions, however, rumour still maintained that Mlle. Nelidov was the mistress of Paul. The court of the Northern Semiramis and St. Petersburg of the eighteenth century smiled cynically at the theory of platonic affection.

Paul was naturally aware of the accusations, but remained as imprudent as ever, and even seemed to take pleasure in redoubling his attentions to Mlle. Nelidov, when they were together in public. This necessarily placed the latter in a humiliating position, and she openly expressed her wish to retire from court, where she began to find the life unbearable. Maria Feodorovna, convinced of the platonic character of the relations between her husband and her maid of honour, was naturally not the less offended by their intimacy. She therefore began to make efforts towards the removal of Mlle. Nelidov from court, and enlisted against the latter all those about her, who were certain of Mlle. Nelidov's evil intentions. The latter, however, remained on the spot, and the position of the Grand Duchess grew daily more difficult and painful. " We preserve a correct attitude towards the little one (the name with which the Grand Duchess had contemptuously christened Mlle. Nelidov), but I must confess that since matters have been placed on this footing, someone's behaviour has been less scrupulous; caresses are lavished upon her in public. She is a false young woman; every word she utters betrays her duplicity; however, I shall continue to walk in the way that I have marked out for myself, convinced that it is God who sends me this trial."

At the beginning of 1792, the Grand Duchess was expecting her confinement. In a letter to Plestsheev she wrote: " You will laugh at me, but each time I am confined, I feel that Mlle. Nelidov, knowing how I suffer, and that my life is possibly in danger, begins to picture herself a second Maintenon. Be ready, therefore, to kiss her hand with all due respect; and practise to keep an unmoved face, that she may not detect upon it any signs of sarcasm or mischief. You will laugh at my prophecies, but they are not so foolish after all."

Mlle. Nelidov, tired of the accusations of the court, as to her being the mistress of the Tsarevitsh and the cause of quarrel between the latter and his wife, decided to retire to the Convent of Smolna where the early days of her youth had been passed.

The Grand Duke begged her, however, to remain, and she gave way for the time, but carried out her decision in 1794.

Yet her attachment to the unhappy Grand Duke was such that she again returned to Pavlovsk, the residence of her Imperial lover. It was then that the Grand Duchess Maria Feodorovna was at last convinced that the maid of honour was a genuine *friend* to her husband. She sought her assistance and advice. The efforts of Mlle. Nelidov to reconcile Paul with his mother proved, however, futile; they, moreover, irritated the Tsarevitsh against her, and a breach was the result. And, strange to say, the wife who had not considered it beneath her dignity to avail herself of the friendship of the favourite for her own purposes, was not slow in abetting the rupture between Paul and Mlle. Nelidov. Consequently the favourite again left the Court and retired to her convent. In a letter addressed to Prince Kourakin she accused her imperial lover or friend of baseness and treachery. His protestations merely disgusted her ; only for a noble heart could she feel sympathy, and even his remorse could not excuse the baseness of which he had been capable.[1]

Paul's character had undergone a change for the worse ; he was becoming more and more suspicious and irritable on the least occasion. Excited by the events which had occurred in France since 1789, he saw revolution and Jacobins at every turn. He kept away from his mother, and scarcely ever went to St. Petersburg. The Grand Duchess was rightly afraid that Catherine would declare Alexander her heir and exclude Paul from the succession. And it was perhaps ambition that made the Grand Duchess forget her jealousy. She availed herself of Mlle. Nelidov's influence over Paul to save her husband and herself from a catastrophe. A throne was at stake, and the natural jealousy of the wife was lulled to sleep.

Both these women loved Paul, each in her way, but if truth is to be admitted, the wife seems to have been less unselfish than the favourite in her love for the Tsarevitsh. When Paul had at last ascended the throne, in 1796, he begged his favourite to return to Court. She yielded, and a reconciliation between Mlle. Nelidov and Maria Feodorovna, now Empress, took place. This time

[1] Shumigorsky, p. 62.

the friendship lasted all their lives, as is attested by the correspondence exchanged between the two ladies. Mlle. Nelidov regained her former influence over Paul, and had it continued she might have perhaps saved Paul from the catastrophe which awaited the Emperor. But her place was suddenly taken by another woman, who had the advantage of being exceedingly beautiful. The enemies of Mlle. Nelidov, fearing her enormous influence over the Emperor, introduced to him a certain Princess Gagarina, with whom the Tsar fell desperately in love. The lady, although even in this case it was maintained that her relation to Paul was purely platonic, became the mistress of the Emperor, and all her friends came into power. Her father, M. Lapoukhin, who seems to have been as complacent as M. d'Entragues, the father of Henriette d'Entragues, mistress of Henry IV of France, was created a Prince, in recognition of his services to the Crown.

Mlle. Nelidov again returned to the Convent of Smolna, where she lived to the age of eighty-two. She died in the arms of her niece, the Princess Troubetzkaya, in January, 1839.

Princess Anna Petrovna Gagarina
after a portrait in possession of Prince P.A.Golytzin

Published by The Navarre Society, London.

CHAPTER XI

The Cyclops and the Northern Semiramis

" There is something barbarously romantic in his character."— THE
PRINCE DE LIGNE.

ONE day in 1774 two courtiers met on the staircase
of the Winter Palace in St. Petersburg. " Any
news at Court ? " asked the one who was mounting.
" Nothing," replied the other, "except that I am descend-
ing, and you are ascending."

The two courtiers were Alexis Orlov and Gregory
Potemkin. The latter, who was mounting the staircase
of the Winter Palace, was on the point of supplanting his
rival Orlov in the affections of Catherine II.

Gregory Alexandrovitsh Potemkin was the youngest
son of a Russian nobleman, who lived on his very modest
means, one of a small official circle in a little village of
White Russia.

Gregory had several brothers and sisters, and from
information received from the latter it seems that he was
born in the year 1748. He himself declared that he did
not know the actual day of his birth—but his ignorance
may possibly have been assumed ; anyhow, he never seems
to have mentioned it.

There had always been a leaning towards a monastic
life in his family. Many of his relations were monks ; an
uncle, who had risen to high rank in the army, threw up

his commission and retired to the cloisters at Kiev.   It is
even said that Gregory himself had thought of taking the
vows when he was young, and that he would probably
have followed the example of so many of his family, if
good fortune had not smiled upon him in time.

When about thirteen years of age Gregory entered the
Preobrashensky Guards as a sub-officer, and in due time
rose to the full rank of officer.   On becoming first lieutenant, he gave up his profession, receiving upon his
leaving, as was customary, the title of lieutenant-colonel.
For some time after this he was without occupation,
chiefly spending his days in travelling to various districts of
the Russian Empire, in order to visit those of his relations
who were in holy orders.   It is uncertain whether these
journeys were undertaken for the sake of collecting information which would be of service to him in his designs.
It is sufficient to know that during this period he gained
the greater part of that knowledge of which he knew how
to make an exceptional use.   What wonder that he did
not care to apply himself to other learning of more real
value ?

His lack of education was probably due to his parents'
lack of means ; it was such that he remained in obscurity
during his youth, and no one knew anything of his existence until his star arose.   As a proof of his unpolished
manners and his want of a due sense of honour his biographer quotes the following anecdote.   His travels being
over, and being in the possession of the knowledge he
required to further his ends, Potemkin was anxious to
put his plan at once into action.   He chose St. Petersburg
as his scene of operations.   On his way thither in 1767,
he passed through Riga.   Being at dinner there one day
in company with some Russian officers, he fell into dispute

with a certain Major von Loys, a Livlander by birth. Potemkin, as was not unusual among Russians, made use of offensive language, applying opprobrious terms to his adversary. Major von Loys, who had not been brought up in Russia, was so incensed at Potemkin's behaviour that he threw a key at the latter's head. Any man of honour in any civilised country, continues Potemkin's biographer, would have demanded the usual redress insisted upon by those of Potemkin's rank, but the latter was far too prudent to risk his life in a duel. Potemkin's head was so full just then of all his plans and projects for the future that he could not think of staking his life for such a trivial matter. He preferred discretion to honour, and so, on receiving the key on his head, he pretended that he considered the quarrel now at an end, and hastened on his way to Petersburg to carry out his plans.

And how did this—in many ways—remarkable man proceed in carrying out his ambitious designs ?

If we are to believe some of the writers of the period, the first thing Potemkin set about was to find a rich wife, whose family was to be of position in the country. His means just then were not in a very satisfactory condition ; he had more debts than income, and the one thing necessary for the part he intended to play was money.

Convinced of the indispensability of this talisman, and equally persuaded that there was no shorter way of getting possession of it than by marrying a well endowed wife, he turned his eyes to the daughter of Field-Marshal Razoumovsky who was looked upon as one of the richest men in Russia.

Potemkin approached him on the subject, but Count Razoumovsky, who either forgot that he had once been a choir boy himself, or who remembered too vividly that his brother had once been the favourite of the Empress Elizabeth, proudly and contemptuously refused to listen to his suit.

The rejected Potemkin received his rough dismissal with corresponding bitterness of heart, and like the fox in the fable, told the Field-Marshal that he would one day repent of what he had done; that the time would come when he would wish for nothing so much as to be able to give him his daughter, but that he (Potemkin) would then have no further need of her.

And, strangely enough, this day predicted by Potemkin did arrive. He had self-confidence, this officer, and believed in his good luck.

Potemkin's star was in the ascendant, and fortune soon favoured him. He had again joined the Army and distinguished himself in the war, and Field-Marshal Roumyanzev chose the young and ambitious officer to carry important dispatches to the capital.

Potemkin, full of his bold projects and expectations, rushed off to St. Petersburg to hand Field-Marshal Roumyanzev's dispatch to the Empress Catherine II. Everything fell out according to his wishes, and his interview with the Empress, as was customary, took place without witnesses. Here was exactly the opportunity he sought, and upon which he had reckoned.

Having fulfilled his commission, Potemkin threw himself at Catherine's feet, and in this position, the subject made a formal declaration of love to his sovereign. He assured her " that it was impossible for him any longer to hide the ardent passion he felt for her—that he was perhaps laying himself open to punishment for the steps he had taken, but that he would rather die than bear any longer the torment of his unspoken love."

The Empress heard him with patience, and was not at all angry. Catherine, after all, was a woman, and consequently flattered. It was sweet to be wooed after having constantly been in the habit of wooing. Smiling kindly upon the bold lover, she told him that she would think over what he had said; that he was to wait quietly until she let him know her decision.

Potemkin was tall and well built. His face, however, was not prepossessing; he was pale, with black hair, and squinted, some even affirmed that he could not see at all with one eye. Nevertheless there was that *je ne sais quoi* about him, which often makes repulsive men attractive to the opposite sex. Potemkin himself must have been a fine psychologist and well able to judge woman rightly. Moreover, he must have had a high sense of the full weight of this *je ne sais quoi* in himself, since, lacking any other recommendation, he ventured to make this sudden declaration of love to a woman like Catherine, his Empress.

There was a certain ungraciousness and laziness in Potemkin's disposition, mingled with an unbearable haughtiness, which often degenerated into rudeness, and which led him generally to ignore the greetings of those he met. He appeared to take little notice of what was being said, and he himself seldom spoke. Added to this he had certain habits which were not calculated to give others a good impression of him; such were, a frequent contortion of the face, biting of the nails, and a shifty wandering glance of the eye. Potemkin afterwards lost one eye in a quarrel with the Empress's former favourite, Alexis Orlov, and the latter thenceforth spoke of his rival as the Cyclops.

On the third day after his bold declaration, the Empress

sent for him, and had a tête-à-tête with her new lover.
The result of it was that she first of all bade him not to
return to the army. He was to await further preliminary
arrangements, namely, those which the Empress found
necessary for the honourable dismissal of the one who
had hitherto filled the post now to devolve on Potemkin.

This matter being put in order, Potemkin had not to
wait long before he was raised to the rank of Brigadier-
General, and at the same time to that of the Empress's
favourite, his appointment being accompanied with the
usual formalities and the public announcement of the fact.
From this time forward, Potemkin, who now enjoyed
the unlimited favour of his sovereign, rose with unpre-
cedented rapidity from one honour to another. He
became a Major-General, and was then given the important post of Adjutant-General to the Empress, a
promotion hitherto unheard of, and which gave unequi-
vocal indication of the future exalted position which
awaited him. Honours were heaped upon him by foreign
rulers. The King of Poland bestowed the order of the
White Eagle upon Potemkin, and this was the first of the
unusually large number of foreign and native orders with
which his breast was adorned. For as the increasingly
high favour in which he stood with the Empress became
known abroad, all the foreign courts grew anxious to show
marks of respect to the new favourite of the great Empress,
and each thought it necessary to send its particular order
as a preliminary tribute. These orders were showered
upon him in such abundance, that it would have been
impossible to support their combined weight had he
been of twice his stature and strength. It being, therefore, beyond his power to wear them all at the same

time, he was in the habit of making use of them as a sign to certain Ministers that he had a special favour towards their court. These, therefore, could safely reckon on Potemkin's support if he appeared in their respective orders. So infallible did they consider this indication of Potemkin's political attitude, that any Minister from a foreign court, noticing that he had not worn his particular order for some time, took it as an alarming proof of inimical feeling on the part of the court favourite. Whereupon it was the usual custom to endeavour by presents and other means to win back the latter's good-will.

Catherine II was not content with having raised her favourite to such high honours and to such a pitch of dignity. Riches also she desired to heap upon him, and she was ready, it seemed, to drain the wealth of her realm in order to gratify this longing, and Potemkin, although extravagantly inclined, and fond of show and luxury, found it impossible to spend the enormous sums which he received from her. He indulged in all kinds of wild projects, whereby he might let the world know of his surplus of fortune. At last the idea occurred to him of founding a library, unlike anything of the kind known before. In short, the books were to be composed of bank-notes, of from four to ten thousand roubles, bound in different styles. Each leaf was to be a note of five-and-twenty, fifty, or a hundred roubles. There were few private libraries of which the whole stock amounted to the worth of one of even the medium-sized volumes of this extraordinary collection. When, however, the novelty of this method of gratifying his vanity had worn off, he converted this huge pile of dead capital into cash. No previous favourite had held such unlimited sway over the Empress Catherine II as Potemkin. Her passionate attachment to him was not sufficient to account for this. Other causes were at work, and Potemkin, in truth, was cunning enough to turn the Empress's lust for renown to good use, and by heaping gifts before the altar of this god, to make it serve him as a talisman.

Potemkin, as can well be imagined, had been subjected to a bitter persecution from those who were jealous of his good fortune. But he knew how to fight his enemies, both those who gnashed their teeth at him in impotent fury from a distance and those who came to close quarters with him in their efforts to overthrow him and lay him low. He met them with their own weapons : cunning with cunning, deceit with deceit, and thereby made it plain to them that they were mere tyros in comparison with their adversary and that their attacks only served as opportunities to him to show his strength. His unshaken intrepidity and unbroken success were so much the more to be wondered at that his assurance could not have arisen from the sense of a blameless life, or have had the support of a quiet conscience. His moral qualities might with success have been handled by his enemies as weapons against him, but the good luck which continued to serve him as armour turned their arrows aside, even those which hit where he was most vulnerable. The majestic tide of his high fortune bore him bravely and proudly along on its bosom, and he was clever enough to steer clear of the rocks that threatened to wreck him, and to sail valiantly amid the threatening billows. He seemed to gather renewed lustre, and to become doubly formidable, after every fresh overthrow of his enemies. Here is an instance. Potemkin's expenditure was so considerable, that notwithstanding the large revenues he owed to the generosity of the Empress, of which the above-mentioned extraordinary library is sufficient proof—he ran into debt. The prayers and complaints of his creditors made no more impression upon him than their threats. He went so far on one occasion as to order a foreign merchant, who was suing him for a large sum, to be set upon and beaten. Vehement expostulations concerning this and similar misdeeds were addressed to the Empress, the result being that Catherine paid the creditors and told her lover not to run into debt again. But so well did this man understand the manner of dealing with her that even when he was found guilty of such misdemeanour as a woman is very rarely ready to forgive, he knew how to get himself out of the difficulty. The Empress had presented him with a palace adjoining her own, with which communication was had by a secret passage, and Potemkin spent his nights here in unbridled licentiousness among other women, even admitting his own nieces to these orgies. His criminal behaviour becoming known to his enemies, they wasted no time in bringing the delinquents, and what condemnatory proofs they could find, before the Empress, not doubting for a moment that her jealousy would be aroused and the hated favourite now be ignominiously degraded. Catherine, it is true, was at first highly indignant, and heaped reproaches on Potemkin, which augured danger for him. But his enemies were again to be disappointed, for Potemkin merely answered: "I watch over your safety while others are asleep," thus glossing over his shameless misconduct with a few ostentatious words, which were sufficient, however, to disarm the Empress. By some sort of enchantment the figure of the unfaithful lover was metamorphosed into that of a watchful guardian. The Empress embraced him with fervent gratitude—and everything was forgotten.

It is seldom that men who rise so rapidly from one high

Q

station to another know when they ought to stop. And Potemkin was no exception to the rule. His ambition and love of money drove him to extravagant extremes, and one unbridled longing after another kept his head busy with intrigues.

When Potemkin noticed that Catherine was wearying of his physical love, he gallantly submitted to her wishes. He did not insist, but, like Madame de Pompadour, he kept the control of the Empress's love affairs, and so retained his power, and thus when the bonds of love had been dissolved he tried to gratify his ambition. He knew the weak side of Catherine's character; he knew that it was impossible for her to exist without a lover, and that his own downfall was certain if he left her to choose her own favourite. So he undertook to choose one for her, Catherine promising him that she would abide by his choice alone, and would dismiss anyone who did not please him. " This understanding between them," writes Potemkin's private secretary, " placed him on the same footing towards the Empress as that of Madame de Pompadour, when her own charms were failing, towards Louis XV. She kept her title of mistress, and provided other women for him, and in this manner continued to hold a position of respect at Court and to retain the favour of the King until the end of her life."

Potemkin went and did likewise—thereby giving indubitable proof of the kind of passion he felt for the Empress. He continued to hold the post of favourite-in-chief and supplied the Empress with under-favourites, from whom he had nothing to fear. For this purpose Prince Potemkin employed several agents, whose duty it was to make acquaintance with the Russian lieutenants—foreigners were excluded from the business. As soon as one was found

Catherine II

after a drawing by Staal

Published by The Navarre Society, London

with such physical qualities as rendered him—according to prescription—suitable as a favourite for the Empress, particulars concerning him were immediately sent to Potemkin. The latter then put his name down in a private list he kept by him, and when the post became vacant, or was likely soon to become so, he sent for the lieutenant whom he thought most likely to obtain favour, and giving him a portrait, ordered him to take it to the Empress, and to ask her if she liked it and wished to buy it. If the Empress, who looked more at the bearer than at the portrait, answered that he might take it back to Potemkin and tell him that she did not care about it, the latter understood what that meant. The officer, who was quite unconscious of the purport of his commission, was forthwith struck off the list, and another candidate was fetched and sent off in like manner. When Catherine II at last sent word that the portrait pleased her, and that she would like to keep it, it was left behind with her, and the young officer returning to Potemkin was informed by the latter of the good fortune that had befallen him.

The chosen one was at once given the title of Adjutant-General to Potemkin, which raised him to the rank of Lieutenant-Colonel, and he usually remained for six weeks at the Prince's castle, during which time he was fully instructed in all such things as would be required of him as the Empress's lover. He was drilled in matters of etiquette, so as to make a good appearance at Court, and fitted with a wardrobe according to the latest fashions, so that he might be ready whenever sent for to enter upon his new duties. When the day arrived, it was made publicly known that he was the chosen favourite, and that he had been raised to the dignity of Aide-de-Camp and Brigadier-General. He himself wore the Empress's cockade in his hat, to show that her favour had been bestowed upon him.   He was next conducted to the rooms in the Imperial Palace which he was to occupy in his new position, and the following day he received the usual presents, which consisted of personal ornaments and a considerable sum of money.   This, in a few words, is the outline of the ceremonies gone through on the occasion of a fresh lover being introduced to the Empress.

History offers many examples of female rulers of the earth who succumbed to the imperious demands of passion.   Posterity may not approve of such excesses, but, knowing the weakness of the female heart when subject to like temptations, it can at least excuse and even forgive these anointed of the Lord, when—like so many of their poorer sisters—they fall a victim to love.   But it turns with disgust from the contemplation of the crowned sinners, who, unmoved at heart by any emotion, merely make choice of a man for the gratification of their lowest desires—and among these not one enjoys such odious reputation as Catherine II.

She had apparently so destroyed all her higher feelings by her constant self-indulgence that she no longer felt shame at her disgraceful career, and unblushingly made a public parade of her lovers, whom she changed with as much indifference as her clothes.   Only a man of such degenerate character as Potemkin could have stooped to the degrading office of serving his Empress in this fashion. It raised him, however, high in her favour, so that he was allowed to take any kind of liberty with her, without calling forth more than a passing displeasure on her part, as may be exemplified by the following anecdote :

" The Empress had invited a select party to dine in the Hermitage—this being the division of the Imperial Palace which

was connected by a private passage with Potemkin's rooms. When
the hour came to sit down to table Potemkin was missing. The
Empress sent a page of honour to inquire after him, who returned
with the message that the prince was still in bed. ' We will have
our meal without him then,' said the Empress. But the guests
had hardly got through their soup, when Potemkin appeared in
a dressing-gown and a nightcap, and in this costume sat down in
the seat left vacant for him. The Empress, taken aback at this
unheard of effrontery, threw down her table napkin, and exclaiming angrily, ' This is too much,' rose from the table and went
back to her own room, whither the rest of the company followed
her. Potemkin alone remained unruffled, and continued to sit
placidly at table until he had finished his meal; he then went
back to his rooms to dress himself. Everybody expressed astonishment at the Prince's behaviour, which had not even the excuse
of being amusing, and quite expected that such an insult to the
Empress would bring about his dismissal. The affair was soon
known throughout the town. But the anticipated pleasure in
Potemkin's downfall did not last long, for as soon as the latter
had dressed himself, he went straight to the Empress, and managed so successfully to exonerate himself from any blameworthy
intention in his conduct that, if anything, he was more in her
good graces than ever."

After this, it was generally thought that Potemkin's
position was an assured one. All hope of displacing him
being over, the efforts of his enemies were now turned to
winning his favour and protection. Only a few of the
higher-minded about the Court preserved their attitude of
contempt towards him, the greater number of courtiers
wooed and flattered him. In this way he gathered a
strong party about him, and his influence on affairs of
state exceeded any that had been hitherto exercised by an
ordinary subject. Thus equipped with royal favours,
riches, dignity and power, he stood at the head of the
Russian realm—only the title was wanting to make him

Emperor. In 1775, on the occasion of the conclusion
of peace with Turkey, Potemkin was nominated Count,
and the following year Frederick II sent him the
order of the Black Eagle. Joseph II, too, flattered the
powerful favourite, and when the Empress asked him to
confer upon Potemkin the title of Prince of the Holy
Roman Empire, Joseph II not only readily consented, but
even determined to be himself the bearer of the patent of
nobility. He paid the Empress a visit under the assumed
name of the Count of Falkenstein ; Potemkin went some
distance to meet him, and received his diploma of rank
from, the Emperor's own hands.

But Potemkin's ambition was boundless. His aim was
to become the husband of his Imperial mistress. He
still maintained relations with the monks, and soon
found an opportunity of availing himself of their services.
In 1776 he accompanied the Empress on a pilgrimage to
the Troitza Convent near Moscow. Here the favourite
was suddenly seized with a fit of remorse. His conscience
smote him, and he flatly refused to continue his scandalous *liaison* with the Empress. The monks supported
him, and in order to impress the Imperial sinner a
dramatic scene was enacted. Potemkin appeared in the
monk's cowl, and told her that henceforth he would devote
his life to God. Catherine, however, clever comedian as
she was, acted her part well. She understood the scruples
of her favourite and appreciated his resolution. The
Empress appeared moved but did not yield. She left
Potemkin the choice to follow her to Court or to remain
in the monastery—and he followed the Empress.

The overwhelming pride of Potemkin attracted such
displeasure and hatred towards him that at last he did
not always manage to escape the darts of his enemies.

Against him were formed various parties, whose secret machinations were not entirely without success. Indeed at one moment he stood in such danger that the Empress thought it necessary to send him away from Court for some time.

She ordered him to retire to his province in the Crimea ; but he coolly answered her : " I have nothing to do there just now ; I am more needed for the present at Court."

" But I insist upon it," repeated the Empress ; " be off without delay."

" I will go to Petersburg then," replied Potemkin, " I have more to do there than in my province." (The Court at that time was at Tsarskoê-Sélo.)

However, he finally repaired to one of his estates, situated at about thirty versts from the capital. There he had time to think well over his affairs, and he decided that it was necessary to win over certain leaders and members of the hostile parties to his cause. These were all in high positions of trust, but not firmly established in the Empress's favour. This circumstance Potemkin turned to good account in pursuance of his arranged plot, and he succeeded in making a compact with them, which led to successful results.

He had scarcely been absent a fortnight before the Empress sent for him to return to Court, and a very short time after it became known that the above-mentioned individuals had gone over to his side.

This was a fresh blow to his adversaries' hopes, for at the head of his newly composed party were two men of importance, Prince Vyazemsky, the Procurator-General of the Russian realm, and Count Bezborodko, a Minister of State and Postmaster-General, who was also a favourite of the Empress.

Potemkin, Bezborodko and Vyazemsky formed a triumvirate, and became the virtual rulers of Russia both as regards her internal and external affairs ; and as certainly as Catherine II believed she was the sole sovereign, as certainly did she only follow out the commands of these three. Potemkin was the leading spirit, whose idea of governing the Russian nation, as he plainly declared, was to hold a brandy flask in one hand and the knout in the other.

"In order to govern a State"—such were his own words—"no great knowledge is required ; it is a machine which runs of itself when it is once started ; it only wants now and again to be set in motion."

If Potemkin had come out victor from the many attacks made upon him, he found it an easier matter to extricate himself from another affair, which, owing to the Empress's jealousy, might have ended badly for him.

It was the custom for the chief lady-in-waiting and the Adjutant-General for the day to keep watch all night in the Empress's ante-chamber. On one occasion this duty fell to Potemkin and the daughter of Admiral Tshermitshev. Possibly in order to keep himself awake and on guard, he entered into pleasant conversation with the lady, which gradually became of such an intimate character that she took offence. She endeavoured her best to ward off his advances, but he, forgetful of what was due to a woman of her position, grew so violent, that the Countess, finding her threats of no avail, fled screaming from the room. The noise awakened the Empress, who got up to ask the meaning of this unseemly behaviour. Potemkin related what had happened in his usual jocular manner, and Catherine, instead of venting her anger on him for his indecent conduct, turned upon the Countess, expressing her displeasure at this lady having, for such a trifling matter, disturbed her mistress's rest.

The Countess went at once and complained to her father of what had happened. The Admiral, naturally incensed at Potemkin's conduct, appealed to the Empress, who made answer to his complaint in words unfit to repeat, so hideous a proof are they of the incredible depravity of the Empress.

Count Tshermitshev himself was so shocked that he immediately made arrangements for taking his daughter away from court. He asked for leave of absence that he might travel abroad for two years, and was answered that he might remain away " as long as he liked." This is how it came about that the Admiral and his daughter were frequently met at foreign courts.

Seeing what kind of woman Catherine was, it is no matter of surprise that a lady-in-waiting was not safe even when by her side from the persecutions of an old *roué*. Potemkin himself came off scot free from the affair, while his innocent victim and her father were forced to leave the country.

Intoxicated with the success of the Turkish war, Potemkin quite expected to re-enter St. Petersburg in triumph like one of the conquering leaders of old Rome. But he waited in vain for the proposal that such a demonstration should be made, and wishing to spare his people disappointment at such inexplicable ingratitude, he sent in a request that this acknowledgment of his military services should be awarded him. Who could have believed that the Court would have so far ignored its obligations to him, as to consider his demand extravagant ? Catherine had to refuse his request and leave the hero to such gratification as he could find in the consciousness of his own merits ?

Anxious, however, to present him with some personal recognition in acknowledgement of her heart-felt gratitude, she sent him a gold crown, richly studded with precious stones, mounted on a Spanish velvet hat.

This remarkable present, which was generally looked upon as more fitted for a hero of romance, and by some considered a somewhat ambiguous gift, was highly acceptable to the modest recipient, and being thereby consoled for the refusal of his demand, he finally returned to St. Petersburg—not in a triumphal chariot—and was received by the Empress with such open demonstration of her regard that she forgot for the while what was due to her personal dignity.

Potemkin's idea of a triumphal entry had emanated from his desire to emulate Field-Marshal Roumyanzev, who had been met with such demonstrations of honour on his return from the Turkish campaign. The latter, having defeated the Turks in several sanguinary engagements, had been led into Moscow in triumph, a crown of laurels on his head and a palm branch in his hand.

And Potemkin ? He had lost forty thousand men while besieging an ill-defended place, had wasted immense sums of money for no purpose, had always remained himself at a safe distance from the scene of action, and now wished to be looked upon as a conquering hero. What is more, the crown he received in place of the laurel wreath nearly turned his head, and with more shameless audacity still he begged the Empress to decline to make peace with the Turks unless they would declare Wallachia and Moldavia independent ; this province was then to be united under a reigning duke, which of course was to be himself.

He was re-possessed with the passion of becoming a

sovereign. He had failed in his efforts to become successively Duke of Courland, King of Poland, Duke of Livonia, and finally King of the Morea ; now he wished a dukedom to be created for him. And the crown he had received from the Empress had much to do with this revived ambition.

I will pass over the festivities which Potemkin at this time organised for the entertainment of the Empress and his own special friends, to make mention of two other requests which this insatiable man made to the Empress.

Not satisfied with the unlimited power he already possessed, he desired Catherine, as a further gratification to his ambition, to give him a written document empowering him to make full and unquestioned exercise of his will in all matters, and at the same time he demanded the dismissal of the favourite Mamonov, of whom he had suspicions, and the permission to find some one else to take his place. Both these requests met with a formal refusal.

Potemkin's pride had never received so severe a rebuff as this, and the spoilt favourite felt that his dignity would be disgraced if he humbled himself to make further petitions to his benefactress. He therefore pretended that he was suffering from violent toothache, and shut himself up for a fortnight in his own house. The Empress guessed the reason of his indisposition, and finally decided to let him have the written authorisation which he required ; Mamonov, however, was not sent away. Potemkin now abandoned his seclusion and shortly after joined the army, not as happy at heart as he appeared, for Mamonov was a thorn in his side.

Potemkin observed the same precautions as regarded his personal safety in the ensuing campaign as on the occasion of his first military undertaking. The generals under him were allowed to carry on operations as they liked, while he took up his headquarters at Jassy, the Moldavian capital.   His presence shed abroad an unheard-of magnificence, intended to dazzle the eyes of the inhabitants, whom he looked upon as his future subjects. Potemkin hoped to ingratiate himself into their favour by the many brilliant festivities which he organised in their honour.

The campaign was of shorter duration than the former one, and at its close, Potemkin, crowned with further honour and victory, returned to Petersburg to recover from the great fatigues he had endured during the campaign—namely, in feasting and dancing at Jassy—and he spent the greater part of the following winter in recuperating his expended strength, for which purpose he found no place so suitable as Petersburg.

The grateful Empress made him a present of another palace, in front of which it was her intention to erect a pyramid on which were to be inscribed his heroic deeds. Nothing, however, came of this proposed monument. The sculptor, unless gifted with exceptional imagination, would certainly have found some difficulty in inscribing deeds worthy of renown under Potemkin's name.   With the gift of the palace, however, Catherine's recognition of his services by no means came to an end.   She followed the example set by the Emperor Joseph II in his manner of rewarding Field-Marshal Laudon : she presented Potemkin with the Yekaterinoslav regiment, which in future was to be known under his name.   On the 27th of December, 1789, the regiment gave a handsome feast in honour of its transfer to the new commander.

Having now invested him with unlimited power, the Empress began to stand in some awe of her favourite.

Those about them had many anecdotes to tell in proof of this, and the contentions which arose owing to his exorbitant demands were not hidden from the public.

Full of well concocted plans for the future, and angry at heart at not having been able to oust the favourite Plato Zoubov, Potemkin left Petersburg for Jassy at the close of the winter. He undertook this journey in the hope of winning over the Turkish Ambassador at the Czistov Congress to a favourable consideration of his demands; and could he also, he thought, obtain a promise of the Polish crown for the Empress, there would be no further obstacle to the carrying out of what he continued to call his great plan. A plan founded, however, on the destruction of the well-being of so many of his fellow-creatures was not likely to be so easily accomplished. On the other hand, his fellow-countrymen would have been willing to see him Governor of Moldavia and Wallachia, and indeed, master of the whole Turkish race, if only they might never see him on the Russian throne—a consummation of glory which was by no means far from his own thoughts. Death alone could put a limit to his ambitious intrigues.

Potemkin had hardly reached Jassy before he was taken ill. Nobody, however, believed in his illness or took any notice of it, since he was known to pretend indisposition either from sloth or for the purpose of hatching some plan in secret. His malady, however, assumed a somewhat serious aspect, and apparently the seeds of it had been carried away by him from St. Petersburg. Notwithstanding this Potemkin gave the Turkish Ambassador plenty to do, until he suddenly awakened to the fact of his growing suffering. Then he was seized with an alarming attack of conscience; recollections of heinous crimes drove the sleep from his couch ; nowhere could he find rest or ease from his torment. His own house became unbearable to him, and he determined to take a journey to Bender.

In company with his niece, wife of the State Crown Commander-in-Chief, Branitsky, who had been his faithful companion on all his journeys and campaigns, he started from Jassy on the 15th October, 1791.

On the 16th of this month death overtook him unexpectedly. Suddenly, while driving, his pains became doubly violent ; so great was his agony that he could not remain in his carriage, but got out and threw himself on the grass beside the road. It was evident poison was raging within him, and bellowing like a half-slaughtered ox, he rolled on the ground, buried his face in the grass, and so for more than an hour lay struggling with death, until he breathed his last.

His character and power being known, the achievement of his ambitious purpose of one day mounting the Russian throne was far too likely a probability for many of the better men not to think of it with fear and trembling, and the manner of his death leaves little doubt as to its cause. A man whose ambition is equalled by his cruelty does not hesitate to make a path for himself with a dagger in his hand. Such a man was bound to awaken fear in Catherine's heart, and that the Empress knew how to rid herself of those of whom she wished to be quit is proved by the murder of her husband. It was no use hoping that he would meet his death on the field of battle, or in the ordinary course of life ; there was, therefore, only one remedy left, a remedy readily resorted to in Russia, that of poison.

It was forbidden to speak of his being poisoned in Petersburg, or anywhere in the realm ; but whispers escape the arm of the law, and so the manner of his death did not remain a secret—while the prohibition only added certainty to surmise. Thus died a man, in many ways most remarkable, one who was a match for the Northern Semiramis. He had risen from obscurity and poverty to fame and wealth, and to be the lover and friend of an Empress.

Greed, pride, ambition, sensuality—these chiefly composed his character. He was also addicted in a high degree to the pleasures of the table, particularly to delicacies, among which the confectionery from Savoy he found especially delectable. It was not unusual to see many more carriages drawn up in front of his palace than before that of the Empress—crowds of civil and military persons of distinction thronged his ante-chambers, but only few were honoured with an audience. He seldom rose before noon, and it was considered a mark of exceptional favour to be admitted to visit him in bed, or during his toilet This finished, he repaired along the private passage to the Imperial Palace, never condescending to any of the usual courtesies if he met those whom he considered beneath him, still less entering into conversation with them. An adjutant then went into the assembled guests and said, " The Prince has gone to visit the Empress." Whereupon they all hastened to the Imperial Palace in the hope of getting sight of the dreaded Prince.

He behaved in exactly the same manner when he visited his province : all the generals, governors and other distinguished persons, the exact day of his arrival never being known beforehand, waited for days at their nearest post station to see him pass, and the Empress could not have had a more magnificent reception prepared for her than Potemkin met with in the various towns of his dominion. But all these proofs of respect were wasted, for at whatever place he arrived, he remained sitting in his carriage, and slept, or pretended to do so, and his people feared to arouse his anger by waking him. The fresh horses were brought out and harnessed with all possible haste, and the journey was continued, Potemkin not having glanced at a single person, much less spoken to anyone.

Potemkin's death was the signal for universal rejoicing throughout Russia. Even his own adherents showed no sign of mourning—they knew too well that their welfare had only depended on his mood for the moment—and any show of loyalty on their part had been mere flattery to advance their own ends.

Among those best pleased at his departure was the favourite Plato Zoubov, for Potemkin had been as much dreaded by him as he by Potemkin.

Potemkin never married, and as he therefore left no legitimate children, his enormous property was, not quite justly, divided among his heirs. Besides what he owned in Petersburg and the surrounding provinces, he had estates elsewhere, among them many in Poland and White Russia.

Added to these there was an enormous amount of capital lodged in English and Dutch banks, and a large sum of ready money amassed from the gifts of the Empress and from those of various Courts, his own expenditure never having been very extravagant, since the Empress's cellars, kitchen, and carriages had always been at his disposal.

The most valuable of the possessions he left behind, however, were his countless ornaments and jewels, and the furniture of his palace, which was of a costliness beyond belief.

When Catherine received the news of her former favourite's death, she is said to have fainted several times.

But she was too busy to mourn long, and other men were soon enjoying the affections and friendship with which she had for so many years favoured the mighty Cyclops.

CHAPTER XII

The Story of Columbula, the Daughter of the Apple-Vendor, and King Christian the Terrible of Denmark

ONE hot summer morning, Eric Valkendorf, Chancellor and principal adviser of Christian II, was walking through the streets of Bergen.

A riot in which all classes took part had arisen in Bergen on account of the taxes, and Prince Christian, the son of King John and grandson of the late King Christian I of Denmark, who, as Viceroy of Norway, was then residing at Upsala, had sent his Chancellor to Bergen to put matters right, which task he had quickly accomplished. The bad state of the roads had made the journey a great fatigue for a man of Valkendorf's age, and he therefore remained on in Bergen in order to rest himself. Having recovered from his fatigue, he was tempted by the beautiful weather to take a stroll through the streets. Among other places of interest, he paid a visit to the market, where the Hansa merchants carried on business in great numbers. As his eye wandered scrutinisingly over the crowd, he suddenly caught sight of a woman, stout and of more than usual height, who was apparently engaged in selling fruit, sweetmeats and similar commodities. She had immense pen-

dulous red cheeks, the like of which he had never before
beheld ; there was a dark, almost mysterious glow, in the
eyes, and a cruel haughtiness about the protruding lips.
Her whole person reminded him of the fabulous and
Titanic women of northern sagas, and he shuddered as he
met her gaze.[1]

His feeling of horror was mitigated as he turned his eyes
to a second figure who was neighbour to the giantess ; a
young woman of sweet and beautiful countenance, fitted
to disarm the sternest onlooker. A certain fulness of
form did not detract from the soft lines of the figure,
which was clad in a plain neat dress ; a profusion of fair
hair fell in plaits over the dazzlingly white throat and
bosom ; while a row of pearly teeth shone between the
lips of the rosy mouth. A silver cross, which rose and fell
continually with her frequent and suppressed sighs, was
the only ornament the woman wore. Beneath it was a
small bunch of roses, which served to set off the whiteness
of her skin. The woman was leaning forward, her head
on her hand, tears and smiles meeting in the dark eyes,
wrapt in melancholy thought, as if in contemplation of
some great impending unhappiness at which the heart
trembled in advance. The Chancellor, after he had
recovered from the shock of the sight of the saga-like
woman, approached the baskets as if to purchase something, and asked from what country she and her neighbour came.

The giantess replied : " We come from Amsterdam,
sir ; my name is Sigbrit Wylms ; this is my daughter,

[1] Cf. Francisci, E., Trauersaal III ; Altmeyer, J. J., *Isabelle d'Autriche
et Christiern II*, Bruxelles, 1842 ; Allen, C. E., *Histoire de Danemark*,
1878, vol. i, p. 272.

who is called Dyveke. We are poor, but upright people, and earn our living in an honest way. Many noble earls and knights, and many lively priests and monks, have cast their eyes on this tender young flower, but I have trained and protected, and watched over her strictly to save her from their wild pranks and mischievous approaches. Is it not so, my sweet puppet ? " she said, raising her voice. " Mother Sigbrit holds fast to good manners and behaviour. Such a sweet flower will meet one day with the right gardener, who, to the happiness and honour of her and himself, will set her in the right place and surround her with the beauty and comfort which befit her. A dream has forewarned me that another lot awaits her than that which ordinarily befalls one of her station. But even if she never becomes a queen, you have only to look at her to see that she is a queen among her fellows. Envy dies in her presence, which commands unhesitating homage. Her young friends and others call her the little dove. I would gladly have spared her the fatigue of the journey ; but in our country, notwithstanding the mild government of the gracious lady Margarita, things are growing dearer every day. In Norway, on the contrary, matters are better for those who are poor, and we have to earn our food and our clothes and shelter by the industry of our own hands, and we do it in a becoming and honest manner. Is it not so, my little Dyveke, my sweet little dove ? "

Columbula had blushed more than once, and lowered her eyes in a shame-faced manner, during her mother's curious speech. The Chancellor did not concern himself much more with the mother, but having said good-bye to the two women and promised to come again, he began to make assiduous inquiries concerning the condition and character of the little dove. Everyone, high and low, spoke well of her, nor was there a shadow of scandal in connexion with her name. Her modesty, her elegant manners, her dignified and amiable behaviour, were the theme of everybody's praises. Her speech was like the song of the nightingale, her beauty equal to Helen of Troy's, with the added charm of innocence, and nothing too much could be said as regarded her rare disposition and mental qualities, for a noble spirit glowed through the beautiful living statue, notwithstanding the poverty of its visible surroundings.

Primed with this information, Valkendorf returned to Upsala, and after the discharge of business matters, began relating to the Prince how he had found this flower of beauty at Bergen. Christian's hot blood took fire at once, and day and night he saw only the image of Columbula, as she had been described to him by the Chancellor. He spoke of nothing but the Dutch maiden, and expressed an ardent desire to see her with his own eyes as soon as possible.

On mature reflection Valkendorf began to repent of his imprudence, and foresaw trouble ahead. He regretted having held a torch to the Prince's inflammable desires, especially when the latter's passion for the unseen object grew almost to a madness. He felt, moreover, ashamed at the thought of acting the part of go-between, and began, in his hopes of lessening the Prince's excitement, to modify the picture he had drawn of Columbula's charms. But it was too late. Christian was not to be turned from his desire, and only laughed when the difficulties and fatigues of a journey to Bergen were pointed out to him as obstacles to his fulfilling his purpose. Everything had to be prepared in haste, and within a short space of time the Prince found himself inside the walls of the

town that held the precious treasure he was seeking.   He
entered it at the head of a splendid retinue, and was
received with all pomp and ceremony.

A contemporary gives the following description of
Christian's entry into Bergen :—

" Being little over the middle height, his broad shoulders and
muscular development lent something of a gigantic appearance
to Christian's figure.   He was dressed in a velvet mantle and a
wide hat, also of velvet, from which hung long drooping white
feathers, that in vain strove to lighten the shadows of that dark
face, made darker by its frame of encircling black hair.

" The violent passions for ever surging at his heart had driven
all look of youth from the face ; at certain moments, indeed, it
assumed an almost savage appearance, but as a rule, he kept his
feelings sufficiently under control not to betray them to the
general eye.   On this occasion he looked almost amiable, and
showed no impatience at the way being barred by the thronging
crowds, which only allowed him and his followers to move forward
at a foot's pace.   With a commanding wave of his hand he
motioned the feudal lord, who wished to speak to him, to take
his place among those behind him, whereas he called forward
the Burgomaster and several of the Councillors, and conversed
with them for some time.   He returned the huzzas of even the
most insignificant citizen with a friendly greeting ; but when
any of the merchants of Lubeck, or of other German towns,
whom he recognised by their foreign dress, approached him, he,
on the contrary, gave such evident signs of impatience that his
attendants immediately forced them to retire.   He went so far
as to say in a loud voice to Frau Sigbrit, who was pushing forward,
not content to witness the procession from a distance, that she
was to get out of the way.   Frau Sigbrit replied in an equally
loud voice, that, as a respectable citizen's wife she had as good a
right to be there as anyone else ; she refused to move, and
made a struggle for it with the servants of the feudal lord, keeping
her stand in defiance of the Duke's orders.   This was the first
meeting, so far from amicable, between Christian and Sigbrit,
the two who were to become such confidants in after days.

When the Duke at last reached the square in front of the Council House, all the young girls of the town advanced to meet him. Among them was the sixteen-year-old Dyveke, who outshone them all in beauty, and a close observer might have fancied that at this first sight of her the Duke's glance became suddenly alight with unusual fire. Dyveke, at least, seemed to notice this, for she lowered her eyes, the colour on her cheeks deepened, and perhaps for the first time in her life she was put out of countenance, her embarrassment only adding to the attractiveness of her appearance, for her beauty needed only the final touch of modesty to render it perfect. This perceptible embarrassment on her part was later put down by her detractors as only artfully assumed, but it was not so, for anyone, at such a moment as this, could easily distinguish between art and nature." [1]

Christian, after he had been some time in the town, and had got through all his more serious business, thought he would like a little pleasure, and he gave orders for a ball to which all the chief burgesses and their wives and daughters were to be invited. To make sure, however, that Frau Sigbrit and her daughter would not be missing, he gave a trusty messenger commission to bring them with him on the feast day, and they made no difficulties about accepting the invitation. The looked-for day arrived and the guests assembled in goodly numbers. All the most important inhabitants were present. Every man had done his best to clothe the women of his party in as festive garments as he could afford, and the married and unmarried ladies of beauty and elegance, vying with each other in the magnificence of their dress, presented a feast to the eyes. Each was anxious to attract the eye of Prince Christian to her particular person, but no one succeeded in so doing. If one is to

[1] K. Hauch, *Wilhelm Zabern*, Leipzig, 1836, pp. 106–8.

believe a contemporary chronicler, " the Danish gentleman found more than one among those noble, proud faces
worthy of his admiration, or of even more, but Columbula
shone supreme above them all." Her mother had not
failed to do her part in adorning her daughter suitably
for the occasion. Her dress was not only resplendent,
but as far as decency allowed, of a style to show off to
great advantage Dyveke's personal charms, and indeed
some thought that neck and shoulders were rather too
fully displayed for good taste. But dress in her case
seemed an unnecessary adjunct, for there was that in the
charm of her person which made poverty of array of no
consequence. The Prince had but to look at her to
acknowledge the truthfulness of the Chancellor's description. He gazed upon Columbula, dazzled and infatuated by her beauty, unable to take his eyes from her face.

Young and old whispered together as her slim figure
swept past them in the dance, and many a pretty woman
was guilty of a contemptuous smile. The men, who at
first had flocked around her, drew back when they saw
themselves likely to be in the Prince's way.

All this did not escape Mother Sigbrit, and she began
to nurse high hopes. These were not diminished when
she saw the Prince lead her daughter to the dance ; the
two seemed to fly through the ball-room rather than
dance. Instead of following the usual custom, and open-
ing the ball with one of the principal ladies, he first led
out a girl who was standing next to Dyveke, and then,
the first dance being over, he offered his hand to
Dyveke, and danced with no one else for the remainder of
the night. The Chancellor Valkendorf, who was in the
full confidence of the Prince, told the latter that some of
the principal guests were offended at being passed over in

this way, whereupon the Prince answered in a loud voice that he was sure the lady of the feudal lord would wish him to choose what partner pleased him best.   And again seizing Dyveke's hand he hastened back to join the dancers.   Dyveke herself seemed carried away by some higher and irresistible power, against which she found it impossible even to attempt to struggle.   " As the load-stone attracts the iron, as a skilled sorcerer exercises his magic over subordinate spirits, so did the duke attract and overpower the girl so that she seemed to lose all power of volition."

Columbula's movements were so natural and graceful that it seemed impossible this could be her first introduc-tion into high life.   Her speech, her behaviour, every-thing added to Christian's delight, and he could not gaze long enough at her fascinating face and person.

The festivity was carried on late into the night, but the guests at last dispersed.   Columbula, with the rest, was preparing to depart, but was detained, not without re-sistance, and finally conducted by the Prince to the royal castle ; no common dwelling, he said, should ever again house so noble a guest.   The girl had not remained un-moved by the attention and caresses of so renowned a lover, and the personal attraction of the Prince finished the conquest.   Ambition and love fought against her virtue and helped to make her indifferent to the verdict of the world.   Christian enjoyed his happiness to the full ; he swore to remain faithful to Dyveke for life, and she, on her part, had no difficulty in swearing likewise.   Mother Sigbrit, with a keen eye for the future, had abstained from all interference, and as the Prince could not remain in Bergen, it was arranged that she and her daughter should, for a short while, keep quietly at home until a suitable residence had been prepared for them at Upsala. The Prince, amid many kisses, tore himself away from Columbula, and so overpowering was his longing after her that, on arriving at the capital, he hastened on the building of a stone house on the borders of the Fyris near the town, sparing neither labour nor cost. Hither came Sigbrit and Dyveke, and there they remained until the old King's death.

Time did not diminish the Prince's passion; Dyveke ruled over his heart and feelings, Sigbrit over his mind. The latter had a remarkably acute intelligence, and an exceptional knowledge of men and their passions, and moreover she delighted in intrigue, and was of a cruel, cunning and revengeful disposition. She knew how to make all her knowledge of use to Christian, and so wormed herself into his confidence, that at last he did nothing without first consulting her and was entirely under her guidance. He did not keep his connexion with her daughter a secret long, and soon openly went about with her as his mistress.

But his father's health grew so rapidly worse that he sent a pressing letter to his son, begging him to return to Denmark. Christian obeyed, but not without unwillingness. He left directions with the two women to follow him as quickly as possible.

He was received in Copenhagen with all the honours due to him for having brought the civil war in Norway to an end, and as the conqueror of Sweden. Singularly enough, not the slightest rumour of his love for Dyveke got wind in Copenhagen; dread of their future ruler kept everybody's lips shut in Upsala, where the matter was an open secret. If it had become known, however, Christian would certainly not have given up what he cared for so much.   He now shared the cares of government with his ailing father, and entered upon his new duties with zeal and earnestness.   Many of his decrees give sign of good understanding and keen-sightedness, and of a just and tactful appreciation of affairs.   He won a reputation for love of justice, and people looked forward to a brilliant future for the three kingdoms.   He continued in the same intimate relationship as before with Sigbrit and her daughter, only bringing a little more caution to bear upon it ; they were in many ways helpful to him, proving themselves infallible sibyls even in political matters. After a while he allowed his love intrigue with Dyveke to become known, and in consideration of his other admirable qualities, the public overlooked this weakness, or possibly were too much in dread to notice it.   It was hoped that in time some wife of his own rank in life would exercise her influence over him, still more that the Prince's passion, as is usual in such cases, would not be a lasting one.

King John died, and was succeeded by his son Christian, the second king of that name, on February 26, 1513.   He was now urged to make a suitable marriage, and the choice fell, for political reasons, on a Princess of the House of Austria, namely on Isabella the daughter of Philippe le Bel, sister of the Emperor Charles V, who was reputed to be one of the most pious, virtuous and well brought up of ladies, and to belong to the school of her niece Margarita, the unforgettable Governor of the Netherlands.   Beauty of person, and a dower, which in those days was thought a considerable one, added to her attractions.   A few difficulties had to be overcome before the betrothal took place, the chief of these being Christian's connexion with Dyveke, a rumour of which had reached the court at Brussels. The ambassadors of the King had to pledge their word that the affair should be put a stop to entirely. Christian willingly assented to all demands ; he was determined above all things to attain the end he had in view. The young Queen was brought in state to Copenhagen ; Sigbrit and her daughter remained for a while out of sight.

But the union of Christian with the sister of Charles V did not loosen, after all, the bonds of love which existed between the King and his beautiful mistress, and Dyveke's mother, Sigbrit, soon became Christian's principal adviser and Prime Minister.

The lawful love beside an amiable and gifted wife became tedious to Christian, and he was not long in returning to the feet of the woman whose possession was to him sweeter than life. The King made a present to his mistress of the Castle of Hvideur, and a fine stone house was erected right in the middle of the Amager market-place, and there Christian might be seen the daily companion of the two women.[1] No business of the State remained a secret to Sigbrit ; it was she who examined, revised, and occasionally annulled the decrees of the Council of State ; the well-being or otherwise of the subjects of the King depended almost entirely on her advice and decisions.

In spite of the remonstrances of Charles V, and of Valkendorf, who was now Archbishop of Drontheim ; in spite even of the laws against adultery which he had himself promulgated, Christian did not break off his relations with Dyveke. According to a letter addressed

---

[1] Cf. Altmeyer, l.c., p. 13.

to Christian by Valkendorf, the young Queen broke down when she learned the story of her royal husband's love affair, and in a letter to her sister Eleanor, she complained of her sad and bitter lot.[1]

A cruel and sad event, however, suddenly put an end to the King's happiness. Columbula suddenly fell ill, and no doctor's skill had power to save her ; she had partaken of some cherries from the royal gardens which, as it was afterwards maintained, were poisoned. The beautiful mistress passed away in agony in the arms of her royal lover in 1517. But the King's agony was perhaps even greater than that of Dyveke ; it was some time before he recovered his senses, and the effect of his beloved one's death was so singular, that those who had wished her out of the way began to fear that something worse was now threatening them than anything that had gone before. The King's heart seemed to have died with her, and hatred, suspicion, pride, cruelty, all his worse passions, that had been kept in check by his love, now took violent possession of him. Nor was one of the chief objects of Columbula's death attained, for Sigbrit obtained a greater hold over the King than ever, their mutual determination to wreak vengeance on those who had done away with the one they loved drawing them closer together. Both became more and more convinced that Columbula had not died a natural death—the chief thing now was to find out who was the arch culprit.

Suspicion fell chiefly on the steward of the royal household, Torbern Oxe, since he had shown himself attracted by Dyveke's beauty, and had been accused by one whom he had injured of poaching on the King's private territory. The following are some details of this affair.

[1] Ibid. p. 16.

Hans Faaborg, the native of a little sea-coast place on the island of Rügen, had succeeded by his many engaging qualities and talents in rising to the position of chief treasurer. Not content with this, he began to spread slanderous reports concerning those who stood in his way of yet higher promotion, and by his haughtiness and self-conceit had made himself universally detested. No one stood more in his way than Torbern Oxe, and to make sure of getting rid of him he took care that his report concerning the amatory relation between his enemy and the King's mistress, of which he declared himself to have been an eye-witness, should not fail to reach the King's ear. What made his accusation the more probable was that the unfortunate Torbern had once been a suitor for Dyveke's hand. Sigbrit and Christian had looked upon this as an unjustifiable act on the part of one in the service of the Court, and had been incensed at the audacity of the request.

The King stifled his wrath at Faaborg's tale, but inwardly harboured an inextinguishable hatred, both towards the denunciator and his victim. The former, overgrown with pride, had set his heart on a canonry at Rothschild, and finally obtained it, whereupon the King, disgusted with his insatiable avarice, and anything but sure of his fidelity, determined to get rid of him. He therefore gave orders to Faaborg to follow him to the residence, and there on the spot to receive the necessary documents for his installation. At the same time, Torbern Oxe was commanded, as soon as the treasurer arrived, to order the latter to deliver up his treasury accounts, and to go through them carefully and inform the King exactly how they stood.

The steward of the royal household found his enemy's

books and papers in as chaotic a state as he could have
wished ; many sums were unaccounted for, and leaves had
been torn out of some of the books.   This was sufficient
ground for a criminal suit.   The tribunal which sat on
his case, found Faaborg guilty of embezzlement and of
abuse of the King's trust, and condemned him to be
hanged.   Christian did not hesitate to confirm the sentence, and Faaborg was executed on the 10th October.
Public opinion was divided as to the extent of his guilt ;
few cared for him sufficiently to bewail his fate, but there
were those who thought his crime had not been fully
proved, that there had been irregularity in the proceed-
ings of the Court, and that his death had been hastened
all too much.   The matter, however, was allowed to
drop, and was not again revived until 1517.   Meanwhile
Dyveke, who had been the indirect cause of Faaborg's
death, and had had no difficulty in lulling the King's
suspicions, had herself breathed her last, and the King
was wholly absorbed in his grief for her.   An unexpected
incident suddenly brought the affair of Faaborg and
Torbern to life again.

As the sentry was one night going his rounds along the
castle walls, he noticed as he passed the gallows, where the
treasurer's body was still hanging, that there was a light
above its head.   The news of this soon spread through
the town, and finally reached the King's ears.   The guard
was called and closely questioned, and repeated what he
had seen.   Christian was very uneasy, and ordered him,
should he notice the light again, to let him have word of it
at once, that he might see it with his own eyes, and make
sure of the truth of the story.   He had not long to wait,
and receiving the summons, the King went to a small
tower in the wall, and thence had a good view of the light

burning on the gallows. The figure of the executed man seemed to have grown larger, and produced an indescribable impression on the imaginative mind of the King. " It was undoubtedly either a northern light, or a meteor," writes a contemporary, which so often surprises the traveller in the north unacquainted with physical laws and natural phenomena. The King, however, being superstitious by nature, was immediately convinced that this was a sign from heaven to testify to Faaborg's innocence ; he had the body taken down, and buried with ceremony. It was now Torbern Oxe's turn to become the object of general suspicion ; the guilt of Faaborg's death, and the murder of the beautiful Columbula, were both laid at his door. It was reported that she had been poisoned with some preserved cherries. Faaborg, as her adorer, had been previously looked upon as the perpetrator of the deed, but double suspicion now fell on his persecutor. Christian sought the first opportunity to make Oxe feel the weight of his revenge, but he went cautiously to work, not wishing to make a mistake a second time.

The unhappy steward hastened his fall by his own folly. Not long after these events, on the occasion of a court banquet, Torbern Oxe being present in his capacity of master of the ceremonies, the King, who had drunk somewhat freely, turned to him, and said in an apparently friendly and innocent manner : " Tell us, dear Torbern, without reserve, is what our deceased treasurer told us privately true, that you yourself had a great longing after the beautiful little dove. Do not hesitate to speak frankly, no harm shall come to you for it, but there are important reasons which make us wish to be clear on this matter."

Torbern Oxe's friends who were present were alarmed at this sudden question, and made signs to him to try and evade it.   But Torbern Oxe, led on by his evil fate, and stupidly believing that the King no longer cherished his great affection for Columbula, and further convinced that her removal had been for the King a service, replied jestingly : " It is indeed true that I coveted Columbula, but I was never intimate with her."

On hearing these words the King suddenly ceased speaking ; his face visibly changed colour, and his eyes blazed with wrath.   One of the nobles present whispered to Torbern : " Some demon, who longs for your destruction, must have prompted your ill-advised words, you could not yourself have uttered anything so indescribably imprudent."

The King, however, left Torbern undisturbed for a while, but not for long.   The Chief Marshal, Magnus Götze, one day appeared and ordered him to deliver up his sword and to follow him to prison.   He was brought up for trial before the Imperial Diet.   His confession concerning Dyveke was the chief charge, but the King also expressed his opinion that Torbern had been probably her murderer.   The Diet, however, declared that they did not punish on grounds of suspicion only.

When this verdict was brought to Christian, he was thrown into a tumult of anger, and exclaimed : " If we had as many friends as Torbern has relations in the Diet, the verdict would have been different.   If, however, the business cannot be carried through in this way, we must set to work to find some other means."

He accordingly sent for a number of peasants from a neighbouring district, four spears were stuck into the ground in front of the palace gates, in the form of a square,

S

and within these, which served as judicial barriers, Torbern's sentence was pronounced. This improvised jury no sooner heard the royal herald proclaim the charge against the royal steward, than they gave way to their feelings with a shout : " We do not judge Torbern ; it is his own deeds that do so." Torbern Oxe being thus summarily condemned, it was only a question as to what sort of death he should die. The numerous relatives of the prisoner hastened to endeavour to mitigate the King's anger. They finally decided to get up a petition, signed by both sexes in all parts of the kingdom, and then to choose some distinguished man and a woman in high position to present it together to the King. The Papal legate, Angelo Arcimbaldo, and Queen Isabella herself, offered their services for this office. The petition was signed and handed to the King ; the legate exercised his utmost powers of eloquence ; the Queen, at the head of the wives and maidens, who together with her knelt weeping before him, endeavoured to soften Christian's heart.

But Christian saw only Columbula's suffering face, and turned away in angry scorn. Torbern's fate was not to be averted.

Sigbrit was prudent enough to remain out of sight ; she knew caution was necessary to preserve her position with the King. Torbern Oxe only begged for the life of his friend Knut Petersen, whom a like fate was threatening, and then with resignation, and many prayers, he mounted the scaffold, October 29, 1517. His friend obtained his reprieve, after taking an oath never to come into his Majesty's presence again as long as he lived.

A herald went through the streets to announce the execution of the criminal, and to warn all others against similar misdeeds.

This tragic tale was spread abroad, and alienated many hearts from the King, especially among those of rank and position in the country.   They saw in it a signal of future dangers, and a painful proof of the King's inclination to cruelty.   Sigbrit continued to exercise her influence over him, indeed it grew daily stronger, and so great is the power of custom, so blinding to the understanding, that even the good Queen Isabella was in friendly relations with her, and many of the most distinguished at Court no longer blushed to make use of her to attain their ends.[1]

The story of Sigbrit's last years is soon told.   Christian's reforms, but above all his cruelties towards the Danish nobility, at last brought about a revolution.   Frederick Duke of Schleswig-Holstein, was elected king, and Christian, defeated by his uncle, was compelled to leave the country as an exile in 1523.   But before leaving Copenhagen he helped Mother Sigbrit to escape from a land where her life was in immediate danger.   She was put on board a ship and escaped to Holland, where she died.

[1] Cf. E. Francisci, loc. cit.

CHAPTER XIII

Christina of Sweden and the Marquis de Monaldeschi

ON November 10, 1657—a tragic event, which at the time caused a stir in Europe, took place at Fontainebleau. The Marquis de Monaldeschi, courtier and favourite of the famous Queen Christina of Sweden, was executed by order of his royal mistress. The latter, without questioning her rights, infringed the hospitality offered her by the Court of Versailles by condemning to death and executing her former lover. Many historians have attributed this action on the part of the Queen to the sentiment of revenge of an outraged woman—who thus punished the faithless lover who had betrayed her. Modern research, however, has endeavoured to whitewash Christina, and to prove that not only did love count for nothing in the tragic death of the Italian, but that the life of Christina had throughout been one of chastity and purity.

Christina was the daughter of the famous King Gustavus Adolphus, and on the premature death of her father she ascended the throne of Sweden. The young Queen was profoundly sensible of the high importance she derived from her birth, and impressed with the necessity of governing with her own hand. She was of an imperious character, and the idea of resigning the rights over

her person to a man was appalling to her.   It is to this
trait of her character that her refusal to marry has been
attributed by her admirers.

" My temperament," wrote Christina in her autobiography,
" is an ardent and impetuous one, and my inclination for love
was not less than my ambition.   This temperament of mine
would have precipitated me into terrible misfortune had I not,
by the grace of God, been saved by my very faults.   My ambition and pride, and the horror I had of submitting to anybody,
saved me from the precipice at the edge of which I often stood.
Had I been a man this temperament of mine would have made
me lead a life of licentiousness—and had I not felt in me the power
of resisting the ardour of my nature I should have married.
But, by the grace of God, I had the strength of depriving myself
of the most legitimate pleasures, and influenced by my natural
aversion to marriage I remained single." [1]

Modern historians have believed Christina's assertions,
and it is not for us to doubt the word of a Queen.   It will,
however, be permitted to us to point out that when
Christina wrote the above lines she was in Rome, where
rumour accused her of carrying on a love affair with
Cardinal Azzolino, a Prince of the Church, and under
these circumstances, the Queen could not confess the
truth.   How could she reasonably be expected to admit
what kind of life she was leading ?   What woman would
have done so ? [2]   And if one is to believe contemporary
memoirs, the French doctor Pierre Bourdelot, the Count
Magnus de la Gardie, Monaldeschi, Cardinal Azzolino
and many others had also enjoyed Christina's favours.

Although Christina had decided not to marry, her single

---

[1] Arckenholtz, *Mémoires concernant Christine de Suède*, Amsterdam,
1759, vol. iii., p. 5 f.
[2] Cf. Bildt, Baron de, *Christine de Suède*, Paris, 1899, p. 18.

condition did not prevent her from enjoying a life of gaiety at her Court. She divided her time between books and pleasure. She studied astronomy and ancient languages, and invited scholars and philosophers to Sweden from all parts of the globe, conversing freely in their company, and when absent exchanging letters with them. She rewarded them for the sacrifice of their time with large sums of money, and displayed a truly regal munificence towards them. The renowned Descartes was overcome with delight at her knowledge and intelligence. " There is nothing nobler, finer, more god-like and divine, than this young woman," he writes to a friend, " who carries the wisdom of Plato on her lips, and gifts of gold in her hands."

The French litterati, Ménage, Benserade, Pascal, Labruyère, who were the stars of the Hôtel Rambouillet, rendered equal homage to the " Northern Muse," as Christina was named. Hugo Grotius, Salvius Meibom, were her devoted servants, and many men of learning sought her acquaintance.

But men younger and more gallant than these worthies were among her followers, and plays and tournaments enlivened the Court, the Queen herself, as was the fashion among the crowned heads at that time, taking part in the masques. Her intellectual tastes, however, always found their chief satisfaction in the world of antiquity, and at her command Meibom arranged a Greek musical play in which the instruments were copied from old models, and Naudi, a learned French doctor, arranged an antique dance to accompany its performance. Christina's conduct, in more than one way, points to a life not quite free from reproach. The several descriptions of the Queen, given by those who knew her intimately, so entirely agree with one another that one may take it for granted that there was some truth at the bottom of them.

One tells us that she dressed like a man, had a masculine voice, and behaved in all ways like a man. When in Hamburg, she walked about in a long overcoat, and with a wig, hat, and sword. Another tells us that she had plenty of wit, but at times swore like a trooper, and forgot the decencies of society. A third declares that she only combed her hair once a fortnight, and that her clothes were often torn and spotted with ink. She insisted on her companion Mademoiselle Sparre reading aloud improper passages to her from *Moyens de Parvenir*, and chose Petronius as her favourite among classical authors.[1]

Madame Christina, writes the Duchesse d'Orléans, in her frank style, was a lady fond of gallantry, and that to no moderate degree. La Grande Mademoiselle had told the Duchesse that she had known Christina lay herself stark naked on the black satin coverlet of her bed, and then invite her lovers in. She was very vindictive, and extremely licentious, and talked of things of which only the worst debauchees make mention.

"We find," writes Raumer, "the harshest censure passed upon her in a contemporary letter preserved in the Harleian MS. No. 3,493, and partly given in Grimoard's *Lettres de Gustave Adolphe*, p. 291. Among other things we are told : Her figure is without symmetry ; she is round-shouldered, and her hips out of line with the rest of her body ; she limps ; her nose is longer than her foot, the eyes rather fine, but her sight is bad ; her laugh is ugly, her face, when she is amused, wrinkling up like a piece of parchment when thrown on the fire ; one breast is half a foot lower than the other, so that the neck on one side seems quite flat ; her mouth is not ugly as long as she is careful not to laugh ; she neglects her teeth, and it is not pleasant to

[1] Cf. Raumer, Fr. v., *Geschichte Europas*, Leipzig, 1835, vol. v., p. 371.

approach too near her. She is said to have had beautiful hair, but since she had it cut off to enable her to play the vagabond, she wears a black wig. Her style of dress is not less extraordinary than her person, for, in her wish to make herself conspicuous from the rest of her sex, she wears very short petticoats and a tight-fitting jacket, a man's hat and collar, or else a handkerchief round her throat like a horseman starting on an expedition; when she puts on a woman's necktie, she is careful to have her vest buttoned up to the chin, and to put on a little collar and cuffs such as we wear; in short, to see her going along, buttoned up to the chin, in her black wig, her short skirt, and her humped shoulders, you would take her for a monkey dressed up. . . ."

One may conclude therefore that Christina, who hated women, and all that was womanly and tender in youth, did not stop at anything, but deliberately consented to the most outrageous offences against decency, erroneously imagining that she was thereby giving proof of a manly independence of spirit.[1]

On the other hand, she was not above certain feminine weaknesses; and the manner in which she brought about Monaldeschi's death cannot be justified by any excuse nor from any point of view, however guilty he may have been of gossiping about her secrets, or of having unwisely boasted of her favour.

For a long time it was Bourdelot, without doubt, who held the highest place in the Queen's favour. For this very reason he was the object of inveterate hatred.

[1] Christine acknowledged that she felt an invincible antipathy for everything done or said by women; and she gives a true description of herself when she says further that she was choleric, contemptuous and mocking. "I never gave quarter, I was sceptical and little inclined to devotion, and the ardour and impetuosity of my character made me as much a slave to love as to ambition." And yet she could resist (?) out of the pride that would not let her be subject to any one. Cf. Arckenh., iii, 53–6.

The nobles were embittered against him, because the Queen withdrew herself from their company, seldom showed herself in public, and nearly always dined in private ; the doctors because they had been thrown into the shade by Bourdelot's lucky cure of the Queen, the clergy because he encouraged Christina in unbelief. His most persistent enemy was Count Magnus de la Gardie, who unremittingly pestered Christina with his complaints. Everybody was ready to do anything to get him sent away, or better still, put away, and Bourdelot only escaped by good luck, and, as it was, never ventured out of doors without a strong escort. His calumniators pursued him even to the French Court. Christina, partly out of gratitude for the restoration of her health, and anxious to secure his help in future should she require it ; partly because she attributed the enmity against him to envy, which only confirmed her in her determination to please her own fancy, protected him from his opponents and gainsayers. She had a just view of his character ; she knew his faults, she told Chanut, and was aware of his excessive pride ; but he had many good qualities, was a philosopher without being a pedant, was an agreeable and well-informed conversationalist, and well up in the knowledge of medicine. Without his help she would now have been dead ; she therefore owed him a large debt of gratitude ; it was a disgraceful thing, that as soon as Count Magnus had declared himself his enemy, so many of her servants should have taken part against him. This conviction may have been founded on an error, but it at least condones the Queen's conduct. Many at court, as was the case with Count Magnus, brought disaster on themselves by reason of their ill-will towards Bourdelot ; even the Queen-mother did not escape. The latter, as wife and mother, felt herself called upon to make certain representations to Christina regarding religion. She therefore told Christina that the noise and bustle of the Court obliged her to retire to Nykoping, but before leaving she considered it her duty to inform her of the complaints made by the people and the clergy against Bourdelot, who, it was reported, was endeavouring to turn her away from the faith of her fathers, although she could not believe that the daughter of Gustavus Adolphus, who had shown such zeal in supporting this religion, would listen to anything said against it. Christina listened at first in patience, but seeing that the Queen-mother was growing less restrained in her eloquence, she stopped her, thanking her for her advice, and adding that these matters were beyond either of them to decide, and must be left entirely to the clergy. However, they continued to argue, growing more and more excited, until Christina cried out angrily that she knew who had put her mother up to saying all this, but that she would make her repent of her imprudence. Thereupon she left the room, and the Queen-mother burst into tears. When the subject was mentioned to Christina, she answered that the Queen-mother had brought the trouble on her own head ; hearing, however, that the latter was inconsolable, her kindness got the better of her anger, and she went to the older woman, and without touching again on the sore subject, brought about a reconciliation. The Queen-mother, however, stuck to her resolution of returning to Nykoping.

Christina was just then seriously occupied with the change in her religious views : Bourdelot's enemies accused him of being the cause of this, and so annoyed him by their attacks that he grew ill. Continual complaints, especially from de la Gardie, and the general enmity against her favourite at last brought Christina to the resolution of sending Bourdelot away. Her reluctance to carry out this determination made the business of getting him from Court rather a long one, and meanwhile the Queen fell ill, and she hoped for recovery only at his hands. She finally sent him off with, it is said, 10,000 thalers of ready money, and 20,000 in reserve; and a royal coach carried him to Denmark.

His proud and overbearing character, his power of satire, by which he used to punish his enemies, made him hated by the Swedes, who at all times objected strongly to the foreigner. Judging by the change in Christina's conduct after his departure, it seems that he exercised some kind of magic power over her. Count Magnus and the remainder of his enemies were not, however, satisfied with absence only. The Count had vowed his destruction. Word was brought the Queen, that Bourdelot, after he had left, had been heard to speak disparagingly of her and her ministers, and that he had boasted of their submission to him; Magnus begged the Queen not to bestow the benefice upon him for which she had solicited the King of France, but rather to take revenge on his haughtiness. Christina answered that she had no wish to be his protector; on the contrary, she considered him merely as a man eaten up with pride, and had always been aware of his faults; she had only waited to see how far his pretensions would carry him. She assured the French resident Minister that she would certainly not grant him the prebendary unless agreeable to the King of France; a prebendary of 5,000–6,000 pounds rent was too good for him. Others declare that she said she would have nothing more to do with Bourdelot, and that she spoke of him

with contempt and dislike.   It is related that one day the
Queen finding a letter from him in a pocket, she put it to
her nose and exclaimed, " How it smells of medicine,"
whereupon one of her attendants answered, " It reeks of
pestilence," and she immediately threw it away unopened.
Whether there be truth in these stories or not, one thing is
certain, that Bourdelot was made prebend ; that he continued to enjoy the Queen's favour ; and in later days
carried on an unbroken and friendly correspondence with
her.

After Bourdelot's departure, his ally Pimentel rose
considerably in favour. The State suffered no disadvantage from him, rather the reverse, for he hardly ever interfered in public affairs, confining his attention mostly to
personal matters. Nevertheless he aroused as much
enmity among the nobles as Bourdelot, and as a Catholic
he was hated by the people.

Everyone tried, through the agency of the foreign
ambassadors, to get rid of him, and complained against
him that he had done great harm to Sweden.   De la
Gardie was among the chief of these grumblers, and he
expressed his opinions to the French resident Minister,
for he was a firm adherent of the French, while Oxenstiern
and others were the allies of Spain.   The Queen justified
her friendly attitude towards Spain, and the favouritism
she displayed to Pimentel, and told Chanut that he was
at any rate a man of intelligence and of agreeable conversation, and that she enjoyed listening to him, for he gave
her information on many matters connected with the
courts of Madrid and Brussels ; but he would never persuade her, she added, to form an alliance with Spain to
the disadvantage of France, or one that interfered with
commerce. She, however, was silent as regards the real

cause of her friendship, her conversion to Catholicism, which was at that time being very zealously forwarded. This is the interpretation of Pimentel's words that in two months' time after his departure it would be known what he had accomplished in Sweden, though at the time it was believed that he referred to his efforts on behalf of the house of Austria.

He was suddenly dismissed (June, 1653), an act on Christina's part which some ascribed to prudence, in order not to give her allies greater cause for suspicion. Others thought he was merely sent away temporarily to obtain information for his Court on Sweden's relations abroad. The latter supposition is confirmed by his own words and various circumstances. At any rate, his absence caused universal rejoicing, and everybody hoped that now he and Bourdelot had both been got rid of, the better conditions of Christina's earlier reign would be revived. His actual departure, however, was deferred from day to day, and he was continually in secret conference with the Queen. At his desire, she expressed a wish that Count Tott should undertake a campaign with the Spaniards in Flanders, which, however, did not take place. At his persuasion she sent the King of Spain her portrait, asking for one of his in return. He had, moreover, continually dissuaded her from pursuing her literary studies.

When at last he started, laden with gifts, the people assembling in a perfect tumult of rejoicing in front of his house—the Chancellor of the Empire, however, entertaining him royally at his country place—he was very nearly driven back again by a storm which arose when his ship had sailed but a little way beyond Gothenburg. Meanwhile, a counter-order had been issued by his court, commanding him to remain in Sweden ; and so his enemies had the sorrow of seeing him once more the inseparable companion of their Queen.

It was thought by some that this was a preconcerted plan between them ; but in refutation of this idea is the fact that he had applied to Mazarin for a passport to carry him through France. There was a great deal of talk about this time of his endeavouring to influence Christina to enter into a war with Holland and Denmark, and Count Magnus was more embittered than ever against the favourite.

It was not till another nine months had passed that Pimentel was again unexpectedly dismissed. Christina showed him more marked attention than usual, and for several days was a prey to melancholy. He was driven to his farewell audience with her in a carriage drawn by six horses, although he was actually residing in the royal palace and the main entrance was only a few steps off, so that the horses were already standing before it while the coach was waiting for him at his own door. He appeared to be very much upset and distraught during the audience; this, however, was thought to be an intentional display of feeling. On the eve of his departure the Queen had a ballet, in which she appeared in two parts. Pimentel, who having had his farewell audience could not appear in public, looked on from behind the stage. Christina, at the end of the first part, in which she had taken the character of a Moorish lady, retired to the back of the scenes to change her mask, which was fastened with a superb diamond ring (worth, it was said, 15,000 thalers). This she handed to Pimentel, telling him to take care of it as she was sure to lose it ; and when later he was going to return the ring, she said : " I asked you to take care of it for me ; do not forget the Moorish lady."

He remained talking with her the whole night till within an hour of starting on his journey. After he had left, she received a letter from him by every post. He was afterwards present at Innsbruck, at the ceremony admitting her into the Catholic Church, and accompanied her on her journeys.[1]

As regards her other favourites, it was Count Magnus de la Gardie who is generally supposed to have prevented the Queen from marrying her cousin Charles Gustavus. He held up Elizabeth of England to Christina as an example to be followed.

The following tale, given by Chanut, gives weight to this assertion :—

" Shortly before the Queen's abdication (1654) Count Magnus had fallen entirely out of her favour, but he found an ally in Charles Gustavus. Christina sent the latter word by Baron Fleming that he was lavishing his kindness and pity on an unworthy object, for that the Count had at one time done him bad service ; it was the Count's fault, she told Charles Gustavus, that she had not chosen him for her husband ; she had cherished the idea of marrying him, and the marriage would certainly have taken place if she had not been dissuaded from it by Count Magnus, who went so far as to speak evil of the actual person of the Prince. She assured Charles Gustavus, that in other ways also his brother-in-law had purposely missed opportunities of doing him a good turn, of which things she could give him positive evidence."

These statements are corroborated by other authorities, who, however, may only have borrowed from Chanut. Count Magnus undoubtedly stood at that time in high esteem with Christina. She made him a Privy Councillor,

[1] Cf. Grauert, W. H., *Christina u. ihr Hof*, Bonn, 1837, vol. i, pp. 556–63.

and gave him rooms in her palace as Chief Steward of the Household; he was the only one through whom the Queen's favour could be won, and he thereby aroused a considerable amount of envy. The marriage, therefore, with Charles Gustavus was not looked upon favourably by the Count; the influence of a husband might have lessened his own position of favourite at Court.

It is, however, interesting to notice that there exists a note in Christina's own handwriting to the following effect. It being stated, as she knew, that the Count was her favourite and had influenced her, she writes :—

"Nothing in the world could be more untrue; it is all a devised fable; the Queen never had a favourite. What lies! Count Magnus has never spent more than two years altogether at the Court, counting his various visits, during her whole reign, and never influenced her either as regards her likes or dislikes. She is not the person to conform to other people's opinions, and here she has met with great injustice." [1]

Modern research, indeed, has been concentrated on the endeavour to prove that the scandalous charges brought against Christina are entirely groundless.

The Count de la Gardie received many favours at her hands, and was raised to a high position at Court, but Christina never cared for him as a lover. The letters written by her to the great Condé, at the time when she was being accused of her overpowering affection for de la Gardie, show that she was harbouring warm feelings for quite another object. The noble young commander was now at the zenith of his fame, and had been known to declare that he owed his warlike successes in great measure to the example of Gustavus Adolphus. It was natural,

[1] Cf. Grauert, W. H., *Christina u. ihr Hof*, Bonn, 1837, vol. i, p. 318.

therefore, that the Swedish King's daughter should be attracted by Condé, and in fact they entered into a lively correspondence, in which each lavished much flattery and wit upon the other. Christina was fascinated by the gallant Condé, and he was unquestionably the only man who could have overcome her obstinate dislike to marriage. Unfortunately Condé was not free, for he had as quite a young man taken Cardinal Richelieu's niece to wife. Christina always preserved a warm interest in his affairs, and during the wars of the Fronde frequently exercised her influence in his favour.

As for her objection to marriage, it is chiefly attributed to the overwhelming number of offers with which she had been plagued from the time she was hardly more than a child. It was, it need hardly be said, her position rather than her person, which was the attraction, but Christina being a born Princess, found nothing insulting in this, and weighed the various alliances proposed by the potentates of Europe with political coolness. Among her suitors were the Great Elector, the King of Spain, the King of Poland, two Princes of Denmark, and several Margraves. She refused them all, only intimating to her cousin, Charles Gustavus, that she might perhaps, some future day, be willing to marry him, and if not, would at least secure the succession of the throne to him.

This last-named wooer would really seem to have cared more for her than for her throne, for he continued to solicit her hand with remarkable perseverance, and assured her he cared nothing for a crown unless he could have her with it, and indeed would be content with a crust of bread if she would consent to be his.

Christina could not fail to have been touched by his fidelity, and always displayed a distinct preference for him,

T

although she could not make up her mind to marry him.

"Christina," writes the learned Grauert, "had little of the woman about her either in mind or character, her natural disposition and the unfeminine training she had received conduced to a masculine turn of thought and taste. The rough, almost indecent customs of the country and the unpolished style of speech at that time, must be taken into consideration when passing verdict upon her, as also the unrestrained study of the ancient classics, for her reading of Martial and Petronius, feeding as they did her natural inclination to satire, could not fail to have exercised considerable influence upon her. Her love of manly sports, of riding and hunting, and her distaste for all ordinary feminine employments, her intercourse with unpolished soldiers, and with scholars, who are often equally free spoken, her interest in natural history and medicine, and she was present sometimes in the dissecting room—everything combined to add to the roughness and unwomanliness of her appearance. Then, again, there were her masculine style of dress, her rollicking manners, and her habit of swearing and of expressing herself in unconventional language, such as men use when among themselves, and on subjects generally avoided in society; as, for instance, when she remarked that she could not bear men to treat her as the peasant the field. If we further consider her passionate violence of temper, her love of satire, and her youthful thoughtlessness, which respected neither place nor person, we have a general behaviour so entirely at variance with royal dignity and womanly decency, although undetrimental to morals, that it is easily understood how her character suffered at the hands of foreign onlookers, although a juster insight might have been aware of a heart still intact behind all her loose words and imprudent conduct. Her intimacy with Pimentel was naturally, therefore, interpreted from the worst point of view, and gave rise to many distorted and fabulated rumours, to which there was no check, seeing that since Christina's abdication the reverence generally accorded to those who wear a crown had disappeared." [1]

---

[1] Cf. Grauert, loc. cit., p. 567.

Thus, sooner than submit to the wish of her country and marry, the Queen decided to abdicate. She preferred the independent state of celibacy and the life of an adventuress to a crown and a husband. Soon after her abdication she left Sweden, thenceforth to lead the life of a royal adventuress, admired and fêted by the European world.

Her journey across Europe was a genuine triumphal progress. After being solemnly and publicly admitted into the Catholic Church, at Innsbruck, she continued her travels through France and Italy, gazed upon everywhere with eyes of wonder and admiration, and fêted as a monarch of the universe. Acclamations and rejoicings had, however, no sooner subsided, than the poisonous fumes of slander arose to blacken her beyond recognition. There was no limit to the accusations brought against her ; the handsome Duc de Guise, who was commissioned to meet her at the frontier and to welcome her in the name of France, had been rewarded for his trouble by tender returns on her part, and all the young noblemen in her train were her lovers.

All these malicious tales are repeated by Bayle in his historical dictionary, but it is in the French memoirs of that time that we find the refutation of their truth. Madame de Motteville, of unassailable morality, who was no adorer of Christina, and has few good words to say of her, speaks nevertheless of her " feminine virtue but highly unfeminine behaviour."

Christina gave every occasion for slander by her unconventional manners ; she loved to sit with her feet up on the velvet couch, and continually wore a man's overcoat. Her jokes were not always quite seemly, although given in Latin. Moreover, she made a friend of the notorious

Ninon de Lenclos, on whom she lavished her flatteries, and she further allowed herself to appear in public on horseback clad in gorgeous apparel, in order to awaken the admiration of the younger nobles.   These details have come down to us through Madame de Motteville, who, with all the other ladies of the Court, was envious of the youthful ex-Queen, and yet found nothing really blame-worthy to say of her.

The disastrous affair of Monaldeschi took place on the occasion of Christina's second visit to the French Court, presumably to be present at a carnival ballet in which Louis XIV was to be one of the dancers, but actually for political purposes.   She was carrying on secret nego-tiations with Cardinal Mazarin concerning the situation of affairs in England and Spain.   Since she had voluntarily laid down her own crown she was fond of meddling with those of other countries, and exerted her-self especially in the endeavour to restore the one which had been lost by the Stuarts.   So we find her in 1655 again at Fontainebleau, where she had resided during her first visit to France.

Among others of her retinue was the Marquis de Monal-deschi, who belonged to one of the first families in Italy and filled the office of Chief Equerry to her Majesty, in whose service he had been only since she left Rome.

The details of Monaldeschi's execution are told by the Père Lebel, Prior of the Convent des Mathurins at Fontainebleau, and were published for the first time in 1660.[1]

" On the 6th November, 1657," writes the Prior, " at nine o'clock of the morning, Christina, Queen of Sweden, who was at

---

[1] Cf. Arckenholtz, loc. cit., vol. ii, pp. 5–9.

Fontainebleau, lodged at the Conciergerie of the Castle, sent one of her pages to fetch me. He had orders, he said, to take me to her, that is, if I was the Superior of the Convent. I replied that I was, and that I would accompany him in order to ascertain her Majesty's pleasure; and so, without calling for any of my attendants, being anxious not to keep the Queen waiting, I followed the page to the ante-chamber, whence, after an interval of a few minutes, I was conducted into the Queen's own room. I found her alone, and having proffered my humble respects to her, I requested to know what she desired of me. In order that we might converse more freely, she led me into the Galerie des Cerfs, and then asked me if I had ever spoken to her before. I told her that I had had the honour of doing homage to her, and of assuring her of my loyal service, for which she had graciously thanked me, but that was all. She then went on to say that I wore the garb which she knew made it safe for her to confide in me, and she begged me under the seal of confession to remain the faithful guardian of the secret she was about to reveal. In reply I told her Majesty that as regarded all secret communications I was naturally blind and mute, and that this being the case with ordinary persons, I should have even greater reason for silence in any matter regarding one like her, and I added that it was written in Scripture, *Sacramentum regis abscondere bonum est.* Thereupon, she handed me a bundle of papers, sealed in three places, but without any name or particulars upon it, and charged me to deliver it back to her in person in the presence of whomsoever might be with her when she asked for it, the which thing I promised to her Majesty. She then bid me observe carefully the time of day and the place in which she had given me the papers, after which I withdrew, leaving the Queen in the gallery.

" On Saturday, the tenth of this same month, at one o'clock mid-day, the Queen again sent for me by one of her pages, and I immediately went to my study to fetch the papers, thinking that she probably intended to ask me for them back. I followed him as before, and he led me through the dungeon door into the aforesaid gallery ; we had no sooner stepped inside than he shut the door with a haste that surprised me. The Queen was standing half way down the gallery, talking to one of her suite, whom I afterwards ascertained was the Marquis de Monaldeschi. I bowed low and advanced, and the Queen then requested me in a somewhat loud voice, in the presence of the Marquis and three other gentlemen present, to return her the packet of papers which she had confided to me. I handed it to her, and after a pause of a few minutes, during which she stood considering, she opened it, and, showing the papers to the Marquis, asked him in a hard and peremptory manner if he recognized them. The Marquis denied any knowledge of them, but he turned pale as he spoke. ' You do not know that writing ? ' she continued. The papers she was showing him were in fact only copies that she had made herself. The Queen, leaving the Marquis to ponder awhile over the documents in his hand, suddenly put out her own and drew the originals away from under them ; then holding these out to him, she called him a traitor, and forced him to acknowledge his handwriting and seal. She now began cross-questioning him, he answering as well as he could, and trying to throw the blame on others ; finally he threw himself at her feet, and implored her pardon ; but at the same moment the three other men present drew their swords, nor did they sheathe them again till they had done their work of execution on the Marquis. He rose, dragging the Queen first to one corner of the gallery and then another, supplicating with her all the while for his life. She, meanwhile, answered him nothing, but listened to him with the greatest patience, betraying no sign of haste or anger. Then as the Marquis continued to entreat her to listen to him, ' My father,' she said, turning to me, ' you are witness that I am taking no action against the Marquis '—(he was leaning on a small ebony stick with a round top)—' but that I am allowing this perfidious man all the time he wishes, and more than he might expect from the person he has injured, to make his excuses.'

" Being pressed by the Queen, the Marquis at last gave her some papers and two or three small keys tied together, that he took from his pocket, from which also fell a few pieces of silver. They conferred together for another hour, but the Marquis failed to satisfy the Queen with his answers, and at the end of that time she again addressed me, saying, ' I will now leave this man with you, father, prepare him for death and have a care of his soul.' I could not have felt more alarmed if the sentence had been pronounced against myself; I threw myself at her feet, together with the Marquis, with renewed prayers for pardon; but the Queen replied that pardon was impossible, and that the traitor was even a greater criminal than those condemned to die upon the wheel; that he was aware how she had confided to him, as to a faithful subject, affairs of the utmost secrecy and importance, not to speak of the benefits which she had conferred on him, as upon a brother, and that indeed she had always looked upon him as such, and his own conscience could not fail to be his accuser.' With these words she left us in company with the three men who stood prepared with drawn swords to fulfil the death sentence. Then the Marquis, still on his knees, begged me to go and plead for him with the Queen; the others stood, their swords turned towards him, but without touching him, and I, with tears in my eyes, exhorted him to make his peace with God. The chief of the three now went to find the Queen and beg for mercy for the Marquis, but came back greatly cast down, the Queen having only responded to his petition by telling him to make haste and dispatch the Marquis.

"'Turn your thoughts to God, Marquis,' he said, weeping, 'think of your soul, for you must die.' At these words the Marquis grew beside himself, and again threw himself at my feet, urging me to go again to her Majesty and endeavour to soften her heart. This I did, and finding the Queen alone in her room, looking composed and cheerful, I approached her, and falling before her, with tears in my eyes and anguish at my heart, besought her, by Christ's sufferings, to have pity on the Marquis. She expressed herself as grieved at being unable to accede to my prayers, since the treachery and cruelty of the unhappy man had been aimed at her very person, after which he could not hope for grace. Many, she added, had been condemned to the wheel for lesser crimes.

" Seeing that I was powerless to touch the heart of the Queen, I took the liberty of reminding her that she was under the roof of the King of France, and asked her if she was assured of his approval of the deed she was about to execute. Whereupon she replied that she had the right to dispense justice, and she took the Lord God to witness that she had no personal animosity towards the Marquis, but only wished to punish his treason, of which there had been known no parallel, and that it was a matter in which everybody was concerned. Moreover, she added, she was not living in the King's house as an escaped prisoner, but was her own mistress to do as she considered right and just as regarded her subjects, in all places and at all times; that it was to God alone she had to answer for her deeds, and that what she now did had been done by others before her. I answered that there was a difference, for if other Kings had done likewise, they had done so in their own realms and not in any one's else's country. But these words were no sooner out of my mouth than I repented of them, fearing I might have overstepped the mark and urged my suit too insistently. Rising to go, I said once more, ' Madame, for the honour and esteem that you have won for yourself in France, and for the hope the French place in your negotiations, I again humbly beg your Majesty to reconsider your action, which, although in your position as sovereign may rightly be an act of justice, is likely to be looked upon as one of inconsiderate violence ; let me beseech you rather to do an act of clemency and generosity to the Marquis, or at least, to deliver him up to the King's judges, and allow him a fair trial. You would have full satisfaction, and at the same time would retain the title for goodness which you now enjoy among all people.'

" ' What ! ' she exclaimed, ' I, the representative of absolute and supreme justice over my people, stoop to make my appeal against a treacherous servant, of whose guilt I have proofs in my possession, signed and sealed with his own hand ! '

" ' That is true, Madame,' I rejoined, ' but your Majesty is an interested party.'

" The Queen interrupted me, crying out, ' No, no, my father, I will explain the whole matter to the King ; return to him and prepare his soul for death ; I cannot grant your request,' and with these words she dismissed me. Nevertheless I was sure by the change of tone in her voice that had it been possible to draw back, or to change her present resolution, she would undoubtedly have been glad, but it was now too late to alter her resolution without running the risk of the Marquis escaping, or of putting her own life in danger.

"In this extremity, I knew not what to do; my exit was barred, nor could I think of leaving the Marquis, whom in charity and conscience I was bound to succour in his last moments. I returned, therefore, to the gallery, and embracing the weeping Marquis, I exhorted him to the best of my power to face death with courage, as there was no further hope of life for him, reminding him that in suffering thus at the hand of justice, he must place his trust in God for eternity, where he would find consolation. Hearing this, he uttered two or three loud cries, and then, kneeling in front of me, began his confession; in the course of it he rose once or twice, calling out as he did so; he finished his confession in Latin, French and Italian, according as, in his confused state, he felt he could best express himself at the moment. The Queen's almoner came in as I was questioning him, and, without waiting for absolution, he rose and went to him, hoping for a reprieve. They withdrew to a corner and spoke together for some time in low voices, holding each other by the hand. Their conversation being ended, the almoner went out, taking the chief of the three others with him; shortly after the latter returned, and said to the Marquis, 'Ask pardon of God, for you must immediately die; have you confessed?' And so speaking, he thrust him against the wall at the end of the gallery where hangs the picture of Saint Germain, and I could not turn away sufficiently quickly to prevent my seeing him give the Marquis a blow on the right side with his sword. The Marquis, in his endeavour to parry, caught hold of the weapon with his right hand and his assailant, as he drew it back, cut off three of his fingers. Then the man called out to one of the others that the Marquis had on a coat of mail which had turned the edge of his sword; this man then came up and thrust him his sword in the face. On this the Marquis called out, 'Father! father!' I went to him, the others drawing back a little, and he kneeling on one knee asked pardon of God, and told me something else for which I gave him absolution, bidding him in penance bear his death with patience, and pardon those who had to kill him. Being absolved, he threw himself on the floor, and as he fell one of the

men brought his sword down on his head, and there lying on his
face, he made a sign to his executioners to strike him in the neck,
as his coat of mail protected the remainder of his body. I continued my exhortations, still beseeching him to have patience.
The chief of the three then approached me and asked if he should
finish him. I pushed him roughly away, telling him that I had
no advice to give him on the matter ; that it was the life of the
Marquis, not his death, that I asked for. He then begged my
pardon and confessed that he was wrong to ask me such a question.
Just then the Marquis, who lay expecting the death blow, heard the
door open. Taking courage, he lifted his head, and seeing the
almoner re-appear, he dragged himself along as well as he could,
leaning against the wainscotting, and asked to speak to him.
The almoner being to the left, and I to the right of the Marquis,
the latter turned to the almoner, and putting his hands together,
said something to him which sounded like a confession, whereupon
the almoner said to him, ' Ask pardon of God,' and having first
asked my permission he gave him absolution.

" He then withdrew, telling me to remain with the Marquis,
as he was going to the Queen. At that moment, the man who had
before struck him, pierced his throat with a long thin sword,
and the Marquis fell to the ground on his right side. He spoke
no more, but continued to breathe for another quarter of an
hour, during which time I did not cease my exhortations and
prayers, until his loss of blood being great he expired at three-
quarters after three in the afternoon. I said the *De Profundis*,
and the chief of the three executioners unbuttoned his dress
and felt in his pocket, but found nothing except a small book
of hours and a little knife. They then all three departed, and
I followed to know the Queen's orders.

" The latter professed sorrow at having been forced to execute
judgment on the person of the Marquis, but it was only justice,
she said, in view of his crime, and she prayed God to pardon him.
She commanded his body to be removed and buried, and told me
that she wished several masses to be said for his soul. I ordered a
coffin, and on account of its weight and of the darkness and badness
of the road I had it put in a *tombereau*, and conveyed by my
curate and chaplain and three men to the Church, with directions

to inter the Marquis near the cemetery, which was accordingly done at three-quarters after five of Monday, the 12th of November. The Queen sent a hundred pounds to the convent by one of her pages, to pay for the repose of the Marquis's soul, and on Wednesday the 14th the memorial service took place in the parish church of Avon, where the Marquis lies buried, and masses continued to be said for the departed, according to the Queen's orders."

The death of Monaldeschi and Christina's behaviour greatly annoyed the Court of Versailles, and although Mazarin still treated her with courtesy and offered her his own apartments in the Louvre during her sojourn in France, the evident coolness of the French Court compelled her to leave the country soon after the " murder of Monaldeschi." Christina passed the last years of her life in Rome, where she died in 1689 at the age of sixty-three.

CHAPTER XIV

Louis XIV and Madame de Maintenon

LOUIS XIV was old, sad, weary, disillusioned and ill; he had come to feel the immense void of satiety. Of all passions pride alone remained to him. Fortune, who has no love for the senile, had abandoned him, death had reaped a harvest around him, sparing scarcely one child to carry on his race; Bossuet himself was no more, and would not be there to deliver one of his immortal orations over the great king.

Occupied with State questions, Louis XIV would sit in a big armchair in the middle of a large room, not his own. Facing him would sit in a species of red damask confessional a woman older than himself, dressed in a gown of the colour of dead leaves, and with a tall head-dress. Her figure was plump and lacking the contours of youth; her eyes big and expressive, still sparkling with intelligence; her mouth small and fine; her chin slightly rounded. While the King worked with his Ministers, she would silently read or do tapestry work; if questioned she would reply seriously and discreetly. When Louis XIV appeared overcome with fatigue and weariness she would send for musicians and artists to play, and to recite or act scenes from Molière, would arrange dinners and concerts, and endeavour by

LOUIS XIV.
After an engraving by R. Nanteuil.

To face page 284.

every possible means to amuse a king past amusement. This woman was Madame de Maintenon, the room her private sitting-room.

Of all the world-renowned lovers, King Louis XIV and the widow Scarron, Madame de Maintenon, are perhaps the most remarkable. A man in the full vigour of life, accustomed to the enjoyment of every kind of pleasure, surrounded with beauty and youth, becomes enamoured of a woman past her prime, and lavishes on her a pure and noble love. We have here one of the insoluble riddles of the human heart.

He was a perfect king of romance as regards the high fortune and brilliancy of his lot. Born of his parents after five and twenty years of married life, this marvellous child became at five years of age the inheritor of the proudest and foremost throne of Europe. Through the two sovereign ladies, Marie de Medicis and Anne of Austria, the best culture of Italy and Spain was imported into France, and there brought forth abundant fruit. Women and poets assembled in the Hôtel Rambouillet in order to found a kind of school of culture, which suggested to Richelieu the idea of an Academy of Science in Paris, the practical result of which was the institution of the Sorbonne. At the head of the ladies of the Hôtel Rambouillet was the Duchesse de Longueville ; their influence resided in their magical power of conversation, which can be compared only to intellectual fireworks which sent their sparks flying in all directions. Not only literature, but politics also, were subject to its irresistible power. The stormy hostilities of the Fronde, which nearly overthrew the young King's Government, and obliged the Queen-mother and Mazarin to carry off the heir, received incentive from the keen and witty sayings of the Hôtel Rambouillet.

Louis XIV, however, took the reins of government into his own hands at an early age, and succeeded in raising his kingdom to the highest pitch of power and glory. His renowned exclamation, " L'état, c'est moi ! " meant that he and the State must be one. The *roi soleil* became an object of worship. In his own person he combined all that the earth can offer of outward and personal distinction. In appearance he was highly attractive, with his dark hair, regular features, tall, powerful figure, and noble bearing, and his manners were no less fascinating. An additional allurement to women lay in the easy inflammability of his heart.

In very early years he had shown a liking for Mazarin's niece, Maria Mancini, whom he wished to marry ; but Louis was not allowed to gratify his desire. Mazarin, who subordinated his family pride to his political duties, firmly opposed the marriage, and urged the King to marry a Spanish Princess, and Louis had to make up his mind to this before he was two-and-twenty. Maria Theresa, the Infanta, had no charms and no intellectual gifts to boast of, but Louis always treated her with courtly respect. As regards his fidelity to her, that was not part of the matrimonial programme.

During the first years of his marriage he fell a victim to the charms of Louise de la Baume-Leblanc, the lady-in-waiting to his sister-in-law, Henrietta of England, the Duchesse d'Orléans. She adored the King. " Sire, je vous aurais aimé sans couronne," she once said to him, but for a long time she refused to listen to his solicitations, and indeed tried to escape from him into a convent. But the King would brook no denial, and as the Duchesse de Lavallière, she lived his mistress for ten years and bore him four children, her happiness and health both suffering from the pangs of a remorseful conscience in conflict with her love. Then came the King's unfaithfulness, which caused her the bitterest moments of her life, he having replaced her in his fickle heart by Madame de Montespan. Lavallière, thus forsaken, could now retire without opposition into a life of seclusion. She entered a Carmelite convent, became a nun, wrote pious meditations, and became the heroine of several novels.

The Marquise de Montespan replaced Lavallière in the King's affections. Her health and wit and brilliant beauty were a contrast to Lavallière's tender charms and delicacy of constitution. The former was named the noon-sun; Lavallière the morning-sun; the one who was to follow them was known later as the evening sun. Under a show of friendship with the unsuspecting Lavallière, the Marquise de Montespan contrived to win away her lover. Some years passed while this secret conflict was going on; in the end Madame de Montespan remained victor. She was openly acknowledged as the reigning mistress, and was installed in sumptuous apartments in the Tuileries and at Versailles, besides receiving several estates, among them that of Clagny, as a gift from the King. At first the Marquise de Montespan kept the children she bore the King in concealment, but after a time they were openly acknowledged, given ducal titles, legitimized, and even declared possible heirs of the throne.

Meanwhile it was necessary to place the children under some safe tutelage. The Marquise had become acquainted with the widow of the poet and satirist Scarron in the house of the wife of Marshal d'Albret, and had succeeded in securing the yearly payment to her of a sum which had been formerly granted to her by the Queen-mother, but which Louis had refused to continue to pay. It was not much, but sufficed for the modest requirements of the widow Scarron. She hired rooms in a convent and lived in retirement, occasionally visiting the wife of Marshal d'Albret, the Marquise de Sévigné, and her benefactress, the Marquise de Montespan, wishing to thank her repeatedly for her kindness. Her grave, gentle and reserved manner took the fancy of Madame de Montespan, and one day the latter made her the offer of undertaking the education of the King's natural children.

Widow Scarron's maiden name was Françoise Francisca d'Aubigné. Her grandfather, Théodore Agrippa d'Aubigné, had been a general, and a zealous supporter of Protestantism. Her mother was a Mademoiselle de Cadillac, whose husband spent his fortune and was finally imprisoned after leading a wild life. His young wife shared his imprisonment and bore him several children, the eldest being Françoise, who was born on November 27, 1635, within the walls of the fortress of Niort, in Poitou.

Constant d'Aubigné came out of prison, persisted in his refusal to abjure, and took refuge in Martinique. During the voyage Françoise fell ill and was about to be thrown into the sea as dead, when Madame d'Aubigné discovered suddenly that she was still living. Shortly after she was nearly devoured by a snake. "One is not saved from such risks for nothing," said the Bishop of Metz, who was present in after years when she was relating these events to the King.

D'Aubigné was ruined and died, and his wife returned

to France for her children's education. She made Françoise read Plutarch's *Lives*, and although she herself was a Catholic frequently spoke to her of her grandfather. Mademoiselle d'Aubigné was placed under the care of Madame de Villette ; as she refused to renounce the Protestant religion she was put to the most menial occupations to compel her to yield. " I commanded in the poultry yard," she would say, " and my reign began there." She ultimately abjured, and shortly after her mother's death Madame de Neuillant, mother of the Duchesse de Navailles, took charge of her, but she was miserly, and the young girl was stinted in every way. When fifteen years of age she was brought by this aunt to Paris, and underwent a good deal of privation, supposed to be due to her aunt's miserliness, but probably owing to the latter's poverty. The only house which she occasionally visited, and where she had her only chance of society, was that of the poet Scarron, who was a favourite in Paris on account of his liveliness and keenness of wit, and renowned for his satirical poems. He was in correspondence with many crowned heads, among them Christina of Sweden, whom he asks in one letter to tell him if her high position is not a burden to her. He begs her to forgive " an unhappy little one " for the liberty he takes—so he describes himself, for he was, in fact, a cripple, only his hands and head being whole and sound. His writings brought him in a good income, and the Queen-mother added a yearly sum to it on account of his crippled condition. He signed himself in joke : " Scarron, Queen's patient, by the Grace of God."

He kept open house, free of expense, for he entertained his guests with intellectual food alone, and among these were some of the most famous men of the day. Women

U

also, we may add, for Marion Delorme and Ninon de Lenclos were assuredly among their number.

The youthful Françoise and her pious aunt were received with open arms by this set of worldly people. They styled the former " the Indian girl," on account of her having been born in the West Indies, and were pleased with her foreign appearance. She ran considerable risk in the Parisian capital from the attentions she received; but even as a young girl her virtue was armour-proof, and it was soon understood that she was of a firm and unemotional disposition. The helplessness of her position awakened pity in the heart of the bold satirist Scarron, and one day he said to her, " Dear child, I see no way of securing an existence for you except by your entering a convent or marrying me—choose which you will do." To escape the convent the girl consented to marry the crippled poet. " It was a union," she wrote afterwards, " in which the heart counted for little and the body for nothing." But she did not hesitate long, nor seem to have repented of her speedy decision. On the contrary, she always spoke of her husband and his kindness of heart with the highest esteem and gratitude. Of her Scarron remarked : " She makes no use of her intellect except to entertain others and to win their affection."

When the marriage contract between this ill-assorted pair was being drawn up the notary asked about the dowry.

" She has only twenty crowns in money," answered Scarron, not thinking of what he was saying, " but two fascinating eyes, two small exquisite hands, beauty of body and splendid intellect."

" And what are you going to give her ? " continued the notary.

"Nothing but my name, and with it immortality," exclaimed Scarron proudly.

During the short interval of his marriage, however, he gave her a great deal more. He taught her many things, and prepared her by his kindly instruction for the position she was afterwards to fill.

Thrown among the mad youths of the Fronde, Madame Scarron needed rare and precocious tact to make herself respected without offending any one. She succeeded, not without difficulty, and accustomed herself to a discretion and prudence which became the pride and profession of her life. "All through Lent she sat at the end of the table and ate a herring," says Madame de Caylus, "and then withdrew to her room, because she realized that if she pursued a less austere line of conduct at her age the licence of that young society would know no bounds, and would become prejudicial to her reputation." "I was not happy enough," she says herself, "to act for God alone, but I wished to be respected, the ambition to make a name for myself was my passion."

Scarron consulted her, and at her request omitted several passages in his works. At his death he bid his wife a burlesque farewell, and "bequeathed her the power to re-marry." Nevertheless, at the moment of expiring he spoke with tenderness. "I beg of you," he said, "to remember me sometimes; I leave you without fortune. Virtue does not provide one, nevertheless be always virtuous." His death took place on October 14, 1660.

Scarron left her almost in as great need as she was before she was married. She was advised to ask the Queen-mother to continue Scarron's pension, and this modest fortune was allowed her. With it she paid for her maintenance in a convent, which did not prevent her mixing with the world and receiving her more distinguished female friends. A contemporary has given the following description of her at this time :—

" She was about five-and-twenty years of age, tall, of an imposing figure, and with well-rounded outlines. The hair was of a light brown, bright in colour and glossy, the nose was well-shaped, the mouth finely moulded. She had a noble carriage, her expression was gentle, playful and modest, and her beauty was greatly enhanced by her exceedingly beautiful eyes. These were dark and brilliant, gentle, passionate and full of intelligence. They had a quite unfathomable expression in them ; sometimes there was a gentle melancholy in them with all its accompanying charms, sometimes a playfulness with all the attraction which joy inspires."

But the bloom of her beauty faded without winning an admirer. For more than ten years the young widow spent her solitary life within the cloister walls. In after years, when at the summit of her fortune she ruled the Court of one of the mightiest kings, she was often heard to say that these ten years of younger life were the happiest she had known.

Upon the death of the Queen-mother, however, Madame Scarron lost her pension, and fell once more into poverty. She was advised to accept the old Duke de Villars. " Madame de Montespan and Madame de Richelieu," she said, " want me to contract a marriage, which shall not, however, take place. The Duke is ill-bred and poor as a church mouse. He would be a source of anxiety and unhappiness; it would be very imprudent to risk it. My position brings me enough unpleasantness without adopting a state which is the cause of misery to three-fourths of mankind."

The Abbé Testu vainly addressed a number of petitions to the King in Madame Scarron's name. " Oh, if I were in favour," she writes in 1666, " how differently I would behave to the unfortunate. How vain it is to count upon men ! when I had all I desired I could have obtained a palace, now that I lack everything, everything is refused to me." Determined to exile herself, she begged Madame de Montespan to approach the King once again in her name.

" What ! " cried Louis XIV, " Scarron's everlasting bothering widow again ! "

" Sire," replied Madame de Montespan, " you might have ceased to hear of her a long time since. It is amazing that your Majesty will not listen to a woman whose ancestors ruined themselves for you."

Louis XIV granted the pension. In 1669 Madame de Montespan confided to her care the children she had had by the King. " If these are the King's children," replied Madame Scarron, before accepting, " I am willing, but I should have some scruple in taking charge of those of Madame de Montespan. Therefore my orders must come from the King. This is my last word."

The King complied, and Madame Scarron became governess to Louis XIV's bastards. In those days it was a position of distinction, and although it may have been a delicate matter for a woman dreaming only of virtuous esteem, her acceptance of the post must not be charged as a crime against Madame Scarron. As to the distinction she wished to establish, it was subtle and more calculated to give an appearance of dignity than to be really dignified. From that time, whenever a child was born to Louis XIV, Madame Scarron, disguised by a mask, went secretly to fetch it. She wrapped it in her shawl and carried it to a large isolated house in Vaugirard, trembling lest the child should cry on the way. Here she brought up the King's children, supervised their education, and lavished on them the care of a good mother. At night she went into society for fear of arousing suspicion. Recognizing her good services, Louis XIV raised her pension from 2,000 francs to 2,000 crowns. When the children grew up she threw aside all restraint and followed them to Court.

The eldest, a boy, afterwards Duc de Maine, was his father's darling. Widow Scarron was politic enough to lavish especial attention upon him, and as he was delicate this was in any case necessary. She had her reward in the tender affection shown her by the boy, to which was later added the grateful acknowledgment of the King. The latter had not at first been pleased with the arrangement, and Madame de Montespan had had a good many obstacles to overcome before she could instal the widow as governess. By degrees she became aware that she had introduced a formidable rival to herself in the King's and his children's affection in this gentle, well-behaved widow. She soon began to make efforts towards the dismissal of the latter, but failed utterly in her attempts. Finding an old Duc d'Estissac ready to do his share of the business, she further endeavoured to free herself from the widow Scarron by means of a good match. But the King no sooner heard of this plan than he flew into a violent passion, and it was generally thought that the widow had appealed to him herself in the matter. In return for all the care she had taken of the royal children, the King ordered his minister Colbert to give her in his name two hundred thousand francs and also to prepare a suite of rooms for her near those occupied by the Marquise de Montespan.

The widow Scarron prudently invested her money in the purchase of the Maintenon estate, a beautiful castle and grounds near Versailles. This occasioned a good deal of gossip, but when the King was informed about the purchase, " I think," he said, " that Madame de Maintenon has acted very wisely." These words were equivalent to raising her to the rank of the nobility, and the widow Scarron was ever after known by this title.

The King's favour for Madame de Maintenon now began to be more openly expressed. Suitably but modestly dressed in a style older than her years, she depended for conquest on her charm of character and intelligence. She could read the King's mind, and worked upon his remorse, a most efficacious proceeding with persons wearied with but not exempt from the sins of youth. Convinced that God had placed in her hands the salvation of Louis XIV, she urged him to abandon sinful loves. " There comes a time, sire," she said, " when a brief passion is followed by lasting regret ; look at the Carmelites and see how some punish themselves for this." On the subject of one of Madame de Maintenon's journeys, Madame de Sévigné writes on June 4, 1676 :—

" I am going to show you a card trick which will surprise you, it is that the beautiful friendship of Madame de Montespan and her friend, Madame de Maintenon, who is travelling, is changed into real hatred for two years past. All is bitterness and anti-pathy ; when one sees white, the other sees black. Whence comes this, you will say ? The reason is that the friend is of a pride which means revolt against Madame de Montespan's orders. It does not please her to obey ; she is willing to serve the father, but not the mother ; she has consented to travel for his sake and by no means for love of her; she answers to the one, but not to the other."

As may be seen, Madame de Montespan's reign was drawing to a close. Louis XIV flitted from Mademoiselle de Ludre to Mademoiselle de Fontanges and became more and more attached to Madame de Maintenon.

"I am told," writes Madame de Sévigné, always versed in Court matters, "that his Majesty's conferences with Madame de Maintenon are becoming more frequent, and that they last from six in the morning until ten at night. They are to be found each in an arm-chair. No friend could show greater respect and consideration than the King does to her; she makes known to him an entirely unexplored country, I mean the commerce of friendship and conversation without pettiness or restraint."

Her influence over the King was now patent to every one; she exercised it in endeavouring to make him think seriously over his sinful life. Probably owing to her admonition, the King's behaviour to Madame de Montespan underwent a change. He began to think seriously of coming to a reconciliation with the Queen and of sending away the Marquise. The latter did actually leave the Court for a while, but she soon returned, and the King was so far as yet from forsaking his life of pleasure that two other ladies were associated with her in his favours, the vain and beautiful Duchesse de Fontanges and the Comtesse de Ludre.

Madame de Maintenon, however, still continued to act as his friend and adviser, though distressed at his continuing in his evil courses. She also remained in friendly relations with the Marquise de Montespan, and often invited her to Maintenon. It was there that Montespan exclaimed angrily one day to her hostess:

" The King has now three mistresses ; I am only one in name, Fontanges is one in fact, and you are dearest to him of all." The former widow Scarron must have experienced a secret triumph at these words, which she knew to be true. The King visited her regularly, and each time seemed more fascinated by her conversation. The children were always present at these interviews, and he must have experienced the pleasures of family life in a way hitherto unknown to him. Her letters to him, however, are the most charming feature of their acquaintance ; they were written while away with the children, or when the King was himself absent with his army.

In 1680 the king appointed Madame de Maintenon to be second lady-in-waiting to the Dauphine. The latter had a mass of hair which no woman but Madame de Maintenon could comb without hurting her. " You do not know," said Madame de Maintenon later, " how the talent of combing hair contributed to my elevation." Madame de Montespan vainly endeavoured to form a conspiracy against the woman who was known as her rival. She accused her of wishing to become the King's mistress.

The King's feelings for Madame de Maintenon gradually developed into a passion which was the more likely to be lasting seeing that it was no sudden fancy. He began to treat Mademoiselle de Fontanges with indifference, although he lavished such gifts upon her that she was nicknamed Danae. She, however, was not satisfied with less than the King's love, and when this failed her she almost grieved to death. Madame de Sévigné describes how she was driven off in a carriage drawn by eight horses, followed by three others drawn by six horses, "but all this pomp was nothing to her, she looked as pale as death, for the King's heart is what she desires, and that she has lost." The disloyalty of the King was the more cruel, as she was expecting a child. It was born dead, and then the mother died, too, being hardly twenty years old. Her death was a great shock to the King and he sought consolation from Madame de Maintenon; she did not spare him the truth, but endeavoured with merciless severity to awaken him to repentance. He only seemed to cling to her the more, and he visited her often against her express wish. Her position was a difficult one, especially with regard to Madame de Montespan, her former benefactress, against whom she never uttered a word. The King was struck with her magnanimity, and showed her every possible mark of respect. The Court followed his example, the Queen herself treating her with affectionate consideration. Madame de Sévigné remarks on the King's attitude towards her, and speaks of his delight in her intellectual conversation, " she leads him into a new and better world, into the realm of friendship, to which he has hitherto been a stranger."

The Queen had especial cause for gratitude towards Madame de Maintenon, for she had given the King back to her and to the Church, and had undermined the influence of the ambitious Montespan, whom the Queen had been forced to receive and to treat with a semblance of respect.

Madame de Montespan had shown not only ill-feeling, but imprudence by not concealing from the King her joy at Madame de Fontanges's death. The King had flown into a passion, and from that date took a violent dislike to his former mistress.

Madame de Maintenon knew how to make good use

of the King's temper, and as he was ready to follow her least advice Madame de Montespan was now only treated with an outward show of regard, the King never seeing her alone. The latter naturally endeavoured by calumny to revenge herself on her former dependant, but Madame de Maintenon was above scandal.

Madame de Maintenon now began to be consulted by the Ministers on matters of State, and ere long a higher honour than any she had previously enjoyed was offered her, that of becoming *dame d'atour* to the Dauphine, a Bavarian princess. But Madame de Maintenon was not yet at the full height of her power. A greater honour was still in store for her. On July 30, 1683, the Queen Marie-Thérèse, a queen with all the prerogatives of power, and suffering all possible anguish of soul, died in Madame de Maintenon's arms. None in France doubted who would fill the deceased Queen's place.

Madame de Montespan saw the danger, and endeavoured by writing to the King to recall his former affections. He handed her letters to Madame de Maintenon, telling her to answer them for him !

Madame de Maintenon was careful to maintain a strict etiquette in her intercourse with the King ; all she did only drew him more closely to her. Louis XIV was no longer satisfied with being gracious to Madame de Maintenon, he became pressing and tender. Madame de Maintenon " knows that at her age, if one can no longer please, at least virtue belongs to all ages, and the King, she says, gives her the greatest hope ; she sends him away always grieved, but never despairing." These words unveil a whole plot, a skilful and persevering manœuvre. The Abbé Gobelin, her director, assured her that God had made her the chief instrument of the King's salvation, and she ended by believing that the abbé was right, and that she ought to sacrifice herself and obey God's will.

A few months after the Queen's death an event occurred which necessitated the ignoring of etiquette, and brought about a closer intimacy between the King and his friend. Louis was thrown from his horse while out hunting, and broke his arm. At his express wish Madame de Maintenon was installed as nurse, and remained with him day and night.

Madame de Maintenon realized at last her long-desired aim; she was married to Louis XIV about 1685. The nuptial blessing was given by Archbishop de Harlay in presence of Père la Chaise, the King's confessor, in the King's study. The Minister Louvois and the Chamberlain de Montchevreuil were present as witnesses. The bride was thickly veiled, and amid tears and prayers the two were united. The precise date of the marriage is unknown, but many incidents occurred during the year 1685, which point to the fact that the marriage had taken place about this time. Madame de Maintenon was seen walking alone with the King at Marly. She occupied a room on the same floor as the King's, who called her Madame, showed her great respect, and spent a part of his days in her room. She rose for a moment when Monseigneur or Monsieur entered, " but did not disturb herself for princes and princesses of royal blood," who had to ask an audience before being received. She addressed the Duchesse de Bourgogne as *ma mignonne*, and the Duchesse called her aunt. She was initiated into State secrets and admitted to assemblies of Ministers. " What does your stable reason think ? What does wisdom think ? " Louis XIV would ask. Serious,

MADAME DE MAINTENON.
After an engraving by P. Giffart.

To face page 300.

discreet, and of sound judgment, incapable of being carried away, full of tact, penetration and gentleness, she would answer briefly and modestly. Knowing that Louis XIV had a horror of being guided, she induced him to accept her advice, while he appeared to be following his own. The Duc d'Orléans having surprised the King with her before his toilet was completed, " My brother," said Louis, " finding me in this way before Madame, you may well guess what she is to me." In public she took no rank, but remained a simple court lady.

Louis was forty-eight when he married Madame de Maintenon, as his morganatic wife, she being over fifty. She was still good-looking, and her figure never lost a certain grace and dignity. She was honoured at court as a queen, but she did not care for this outward display. In a kind of biography which she compiled for the girls of Saint Cyr, she writes :—

" My wish was never to be especially loved by any one, but to be loved by all. I desired that my name should always be spoken with respect and admiration, and that I might play a beautiful part in the world, and above all, that I might be commended by all good men. I laboured for honour, which was my ideal of happiness."

Madame de Maintenon founded Saint-Cyr, and was appointed permanent Superior of the institution; she drew up its rules, and had a private apartment reserved for her. She was often to be found there, and did not disdain to enter into the meanest details of the house. Saint-Cyr was intended for the education of poor young girls of noble birth. " To enter there," says Madame de Caylus, " it was necessary to bring proof of nobility and poverty."

The King's genealogists supplied the proofs of nobility, the comptroller of the province gave a certificate of poverty. Two hundred and fifty young girls were received. The sight of this ruined nobility, old soldiers asking for a bed at the Invalides for themselves and a place at Saint-Cyr for their daughters, must have inspired pity. Whatever has been said against the education given to the pupils at Saint-Cyr, it must be admitted that it was a noble mind which founded this refuge, founded as it was by one whose youth had been embittered by destitution and poverty.

Madame de Maintenon's political influence over Louis XIV has been greatly exaggerated. Beyond a few family interests to be satisfied, perhaps some debts of ill-will to pay, Madame de Maintenon's political influence was almost nil. Louis XIV had strong views from which none could turn him ; in religion, as in all else, he wished for unity, and had no need to be driven by any one. Madame de Maintenon's services to the private man were very real. She rescued him from the whirlwind of passion so dishonourable to old age ; she recalled him to his duties as a Christian ; and endeavoured to modify his taste for building and for war. She made every effort to dispel his depression and distract his mind. Unfortunately her devotion to the King was shown in small rather than in big things ; she made small sacrifices, but rarely big ones. Like Louis himself, she was fond of order, conventionality and appearance. Like him she had a well-balanced mind, but like him also she had not allowed her mind to expand before age came to her, keeping her intelligence within its narrow bounds. She was not the cause of the numerous faults of the King's declining years, but she did not prevent them.

Madame de Maintenon paid a high price for her power and dignity. From morn till even, without repose or truce, she was burdened by a King who was a burden to himself. Compelled to bend to vexatious habits of the master, she occasionally lets fall a cry of weariness and sorrow which would move any one to pity, who had not followed her career from infancy. " I cannot bear it ! I would I were dead," she writes to her brother. " Have you sworn to espouse the Eternal Father ? " replied the joyous d'Aubigné, with pitiless good sense. " I would I could convince you of the weariness which devours the great," she wrote to Madame de Maisonfort ; " do you not see that I am dying of sorrow in the midst of a luxury that it is difficult to imagine, and that it is only through God's help that I do not succumb ? " And again : " In truth," she said on one occasion, " I sometimes nearly lose my head, and if my body is opened after death I believe that my heart will be found dry and twisted, like that of M. de Louvois." One day seeing some carp languishing in a marble basin, " They are like me," she said to Madame de Caylus, " they regret their mud." One feels compassion for Madame de Maintenon, sighing for solitude, asking for a cottage and regretting her mud.

Yet her sufferings were practically voluntary. Madame de Maintenon had in cold blood sacrificed her happiness to her pride. She restrained all the emotions of the soul, all the dreams of the imagination, all consoling and legitimate phantasies of the mind, she put dry and inexorable reason in her heart's place. She never loved with true love, she never shed true tears.

But she was soon to be relieved of her duties. Louis XIV was dying, and that we may be better able to judge Madame de Maintenon let us watch near the death-bed of the great king. Louis had also borne his cross of expiation, an expiation a vast deal more bitter than that of Madame de Maintenon. He had seen his armies vanquished and his generals in flight; death had knocked at the palace gates; the Dauphin, Monsieur, the Duc and Duchesse de Bourgogne, Marie Louise of Savoy, had all gone down to the grave. Broken-hearted, but passive, Louis XIV had stood by the body of the Duc de Berry, and with his failing hand sprinkled holy water on his coffin. It was at this hour, when the whole of Europe was threatening him, that he really showed himself to be a great king, and swore to bury himself under the ruins of the monarchy. Pamphlets were even circulated insulting a king who had been so flattered, almost deified in the days of his power. Louis XIV, with all that was true in France, torn and wounded as she was, had faced the storm and obtained peace, but now death was awaiting him. In vain he decked himself in sumptuous garments and multiplied reviews, rejoicings and festivals. His legs could no longer support him, and he was wheeled slowly in a chair down the alleys of Versailles. In spite of all precautions death drew closer. The King received the Viaticum and extreme unction, blessed the Dauphin, and breathed his last on September 1, 1715, in his seventy-seventh year. The doors of the vast apartments of the palace were suddenly thrown open, and a child of five, wearing a blue ribbon over his violet coat, advanced, led in by Madame de Ventadour, and the assembly of courtiers and gentlemen bowing low cried, " Long live King Louis XV."

And what was Madame de Maintenon doing all this

time ? Before the King's death she had retired to
Saint-Cyr ; during his illness she had attended him
assiduously but coldly. She had offered lengthy prayers
by his bedside, but without a tear, without a heartfelt
word. " I regret you alone," said Louis, " I have not
made you happy, but every feeling of esteem and friendship that you deserve I have shown you. My one regret
is to leave you, but I hope to meet you soon again in
eternity." She made no answer.

When Louis XIV lost consciousness Louvois and
Madame de Maintenon's confessor begged her to retire.
Her reason told her that she could be of no further use
to the King ; and she withdrew. She did not close the
eyes of him who regretted her alone, she did not receive
his last breath. She accepted the advice of Louvois
and her confessor, for Madame de Maintenon never
asked counsel of her heart. She was afterwards reproached with indifference and ingratitude towards the
King at the supreme moment.

Madame de Maintenon lived two years in retirement at Saint-Cyr in the equivocal position of
dowager-queen. Here she was in her real sphere,
giving advice, reproving, instructing, listening to the
pupils reading history, interfering in the minutest
details, demanding prompt and absolute obedience. She
rose early and retired early, as was her habit at Court.
She passed much time in prayer, heard mass and received
Communion twice weekly. Her meals were short and
dainty ; she gave abundant alms to the poor. Being a
good letter-writer, it pleased her to hold an active correspondence with the superiors of various French com-
munities. A few special friends only were admitted to
her solitude, the Maréchal de Villeroi, Cardinal de Rohan,

and above all her favourite pupil, the Duc de Maine, who had free access to her at all hours. Peter the Great desired to be presented to her before leaving France.

All her life Madame de Maintenon had sighed for dignity, and all her life, strange irony of fate, she was compelled to build up dignity by means which are the least dignified. Friend of Ninon, widow of a poet whose buffoonery is proverbial, petitioner of Louis XIV and his mistress, governess of the children of Madame de Montespan, suffering the haughtiness of the favourite and combating and vanquishing it in her own fashion, and finally secretly marrying and living by expedients in a false and equivocal position in the midst of mystery. There is about her something of the superior of a convent, of a woman of ambition, of a schoolmistress, of an adventuress, but also something of the courtesan.

Her death, which occasioned no stir, occurred on Saturday, April 15, 1719, the eve of Quasimodo Sunday. The trial of the Duc de Maine before the tribunal of the Tuileries gave her the first death-blow, and when she saw him arrested she succumbed. She was seized with fever, and died at the age of eighty-three years, in possession of all her faculties.

Bibliography

Aissé, Ch. E., *Lettres de Mlle. Aissé à Mme. Calandrini*, Paris, 1846.

Alexis, Prince de G., *Catherine II de Russie et ses favoris*, Paris, 1880.

Altmeyer, J. J., *Isabelle d'Autriche et Christiern II*, Bruxelles, 1842.

Araquy, E. d', *Les Etoiles du monde*, Paris, 1858.

Arckenholtz, J., *Mémoires concernant Christine reine de Suède*, Amsterdam, 1751–60.

Assé, E., *Anecdotes sur le M$^{al.}$ de Richelieu*, Paris, 1890.

——, *Lettres du XVII et du XVIII Siècles*, Paris, 1873.

Aubigné, Th. A., *Madame de Maintenon d'après sa correspondance*, Paris, 1887.

Aubigné, Th. A., *Mémoires*, Paris, 1854.

——, *Confession de M. de Sancy*, Cologne, 1660.

Bain, F. W., *Christina, Queen of Sweden*, London, 1890.

Bain, R. N., *The Daughter of Peter the Great*, London, 1899.

Baireuth, *Margravine Frédérique Sophie Wilhelmine, Mémoires*, Leipzig, 1896.

Barrière, F., *Tableaux de genre et d'histoire*, Paris, 1828.

Barine, Arvěde, *Portraits de femmes*, Paris, 1887.

——, *Princesses et grandes dames*, Paris, 1890.

Bascle de Lagrèze, Q., *Henri IV, sa vie privée*, Paris, 1885.

——, *Le château de Pau*, Paris, 1854.

——, *La reine Caroline Mathilde et le Comte Struensée*, Paris, 1887.

Bethune, *Duke de Sully, Memoirs*, London, 1856.

Bildt, B$^{on.}$ de, *Christine de Suède et le Cardinal Azzolino*, Paris, 1899.

Bouchot, H., *Les femmes de Brantôme*, Paris, 1890.

Brantôme, Pierre de Bourdeille, *Oeuvres Complètes*, 11 vols., Paris, 1864–82.

——, *Vie des dames galantes*, 3 vols., Paris, 1879.

Brown, John, *The Northern Courts, Memoirs of the Sovereigns of Sweden and Denmark*, London, 1904.

Buelow, W. v., *Das Weiberregiment am Hofe der Königin Christine von Schweden*, 1900.

Campan, J. L. H., *Mémoires sur la vie privée de Marie Antoinette*, Paris, 1849.
Campbell, *Life and Times of Frederick the Great*, London, 1842.
Capefigue, J. B. H. R., *La favorite d'un roi de Prusse*, Paris, 1867.
——, *La grande Catherine*, Paris, 1862.
——, *Les Cardinaux Ministres*, Paris, 1861.
Castelnau, A., *Les Médicis*, Paris, 1879.
Catherine II, *Mémoires de l'Impératrice*, London, 1859.
——, *Histoire secrète des amours, par un Ambassadeur*, Paris, 1873.
——, *La Cour de*, Paris, 1899.
Catteau-Callville, J. P. G., *Histoire de Christine, reine de Suède*, Paris, 1815.
Caylus, Mme. de, *Madame de Maintenon, Louis XIV, Souvenirs de*, Paris, 1887.
Cerenville, *Vie du Prince Potemkin*, Paris, 1808.
Chanut, Pierre, *Mémoires de ce qui s'est passé en Suède*, Cologne, 1677.
Chasles, Philaèrte, *Etudes sur l'antiquité*, Paris, 1847.
Christine de Suède, Mémoires de, Paris, 1830.
Coellin, G. F. W. von., *Lettres confidentielles, etc.*, Paris, 1808.
Cramer, F., *Biographische Nachrichten, etc.*, Quedlinburg, 1833.
——. *Denkwürdigkeiten der Gräfin Maria Aurora Koenigsmark*, 2 vols., Leipzig, 1836.

Dampmartin, *Quelques traits de la vie privée de Frédéric Guillaume*, Paris, 1811.
Danilevsky, G., *La Princesse Tarakanoff*, Paris, 1885.
Desclozeaux, *Gabrielle d'Estrées*, Paris, 1889.
Desprez, A., *Richelieu et Mazarin*, Paris, 1883.
Druon, H., *Philippe d'Orléans, Ac. Nancy, Mémoires*, Série 5, Tom. 12, 1895.

Eylert, R. F., *Charakterzüge und historische Fragmente aus dem Leben Friedrich Wilhelm III*, Magdeburg, 1843–46.

Fontaine de Rambouillet, *La Régence et le Cardinal Dubois*, Paris, 1886.

Francisci, E., *Der hohe Trauersaal*, 1669–81.

Gejer, E. G., *Histoire de Suède*, Paris, 1845.
Grauert, W. H., *Christina Königin von Schweden u. ihr Hof*, Bonn, 1837.

Haggard, A. C. P., *The Regent of the Roués*, London, 1905.
Hauch, K., *Wilhelm Zabern*, Leipzig, 1836.
Helbig, G. H. W. von, *Russische Günstlinge*, 1883.
Henry IV, *Lettres inédites du Roi*, Paris, 1883.
——, *Les amours de*, Paris, 1695.
Histoire des Amours du grand Alcandre, Paris, 1660.
Hohenhausen, Fr. v., *Berühmte Liebespaare*, 1870.
Houssaye, A., *La Régence*, Paris, 1890.
——, *Galérie du XVIII siècle*.
Houssaye, H., *Aspasie, Clopâtre, Théodora*, Paris, 1899.

Imbert de St. Armand, *Portraits de femmes*, Paris, 1869.
Istoritshesky Vyestnik, 1898.

Kohut, A., *Friedrich der Grosse*, Minden, 1886.
Kostomarov, *Rousskaya Istorya*, St. Petersburg, 1888.

Lacombe, J., *Histoire de Christine*, etc., 1767.
La Ferrière Percy, H. de., *Henri IV*, Paris, 1890.
Lerne, E. de., *Reines légitimes et d'aventure*, Paris, 1867.
Lescure, M. F. A. de, *Les Maîtresses du Régent*, Paris, 1861.
——, *Les amours de Henri IV*, Paris, 1864.
L'Estoille, Journal de, Paris, 1862.
Lichtenau, Mémoires de la Comtesse de, 1869.
Lombard, J. G., *Gallerie Preussischer Charactere*, Berlin, 1808.

Marais, M., *Journal et Mémoires*, Paris, 1863–68.
Margaret de Valois, *Memoirs*, London, 1895.
Masson, A. F. Ph., *Mémoires secrets sur la Russie*, Paris, 1859.
Melnikov, P., *Knyaginya Tarakanova*, 1868.
Michelet, J., *History of France*, London, 1844–47.
——, *Henri IV*, Paris, 1881.
Mirabeau, Riquetti, H. G., *Histoire secrète de la cour de Berlin*, Paris, 1789.

Muench, E. J. H., *Biographisch-historische Studien*, 1836.

Poellnitz, B^{on.} de, *La Saxe galante*, Amsterdam, 1734.
Potemkin, Prince G. A., *Memoirs*, 1812.

Rabutin, Comte de Bussy, *Amours des dames Illustres*, Paris, 1856–75.
Rappoport, A. S., *The Curse of the Romanovs*, London, 17.
Raumer, Fr. v., *Geschichte Europas*, Leipzig, 1835.
Revue des Deux Mondes, tome LXXXVII, Paris, 1870.
Rouvroy, Duc de St. Simon, *Mémoires,* Paris, 1904.

Saint Jean, *Lebensbeschreibung des Fürsten Gregor Potemkin*, Karlsruhe, 1888.
Sainte-Beuve, *Causeries de Lundi*, Paris, 1882–85.
——, *Portraits de Femmes*, Paris, 1886.
Shoumigorsky, E. S., *Imperator Pavel I*, St. Petersburg, 1907.
——, *Yekaterina Ivanovna Nelidova*, St. Petersburg, 1902.

Tallemant des Réaux, *Les Historiettes*, Paris, 1862.

Vandal, A., *Louis XV et Élisabeth de Russie*, Paris, 1882.
Vasilchikov, A. A., *Les Razoumovsky*, ed. A. Brueckner, 1893–94.
Vehse, E., *Memoirs of the Court of Prussia*, 1854.

Waliszewski, K., *La dernière des Romanovs*, Paris, 1902.
——, *Autour d'un trône*, Paris, 1894.
——, *Le Roman d'une Impératrice*, Paris, 1893.
Wiegand, W., *Friedrich der Grosse*, 1888.
Wilsdorf, O., *Gräfin Cosel*, 1902.

Zastrow, C., *Aus dem Leben der nordischen Semiramis*, 1896.

Index

MADE AND PRINTED IN GREAT BRITAIN. RICHARD CLAY & SONS, LTD., PRINTERS, BUNGAY, SUFFOLK.

www.ingramcontent.com/pod-product-compliance
Lightning Source LLC
Chambersburg PA
CBHW032142010726
47494CB00002B/320